WE DON'T KNOW OURSELVES UNTIL WE LEAVE

WE DON'T KNOW OURSELVES UNTIL WE LEAVE

Do you know what I mean?

BRIAN GODDARD

CONTENTS

A friend and I were boarding an airplane in Paris, France in 1997. We talked about the randomness of seating arrangements on airplanes. Fate intertwines the lives of people that would normally never cross paths. We laughed about some of our most unpleasant flying experiences. Both of us were curious to get on the plane to see who we would be spending the next 9 hours with. We each hoped for a long and pleasurable conversation with an interesting soul.

On that flight from Paris to Dallas, I was the fortunate one. When I got to my seat, there was an older lady seated by the window. She smiled back and greeted me as I sat down in the aisle seat. Immediately, we struck up a conversation. We were each blessed to be world travelers. Our occupations had facilitated experiences of immersion in different cultures around the world. We both had jobs that we loved.

Although we had visited some of the same places, most of her travels were more to well-established and safe tourist destinations. Much of mine had been to off the beaten path places, too dangerous and harsh for the typical tourist.

We shared our different perceptions of various cultures. We laughed at how our experiences effectuated our own views of the world.

An hour or two into the flight, the lady made a statement and asked me a question.

"We don't really know ourselves until we leave where we come from. Do you know what I mean?" she asked.

The old lady had a special spark in her eyes that radiated a comforting warmth that I'd only seen in a handful of people. I found the question to be both painful and encouraging at the same time. I paused as I thought about her question and looked into her eyes. The painful thoughts were images of my own desires which tend to often steer me in the direction of being a selfish, greedy, arrogant and revenge seeking individual. The encouragement was that I was and still am aspiring to be a better human being. I realized that I didn't really know who I was whereas she had found something that gave her a peace and wisdom that I didn't have. I was still seeking and still am.

I, like most people, was viewing the world from my perspective, through my own eyes, and based on my own experiences and beliefs. I viewed myself as being mostly good and anyone against my own desires to be predominately evil. The old lady on that airplane helped me look at myself from a different view. You could say that I was partially blind, and she helped me see a little better.

Years later, I had a similar conversation with a friend that grew up in a small town in Wisconsin. He had once thought that everyone on the other side of his hometown were evil. His side of town had all the nice normal people. Both sides of town hated each other equally. Each group thought they were the good people. Years later, he revisited the town where he grew up. He discovered that everyone in the town were pretty much the same with only minor differences. He had become a foreigner. The people in his hometown were very much different from most other towns and countries he had visited. We made the analogy that it was a lot like living in a freshwater aquarium with a bunch of goldfish and then swimming out into the ocean. The ocean had changed both of us.

These conversations helped inspire this book. I chose to write it to capture and share my own perceptions of how growing up in a typical town in the USA in the 1960s and 70s shaped myself and others cultivated in the same generation.

This is a story about a boy growing up in an average town. The town is like all towns in that it has its good and its bad. It is a predominately white town, and the boy's best friend happens to be black.

The boy is a mathematical genius. He is gifted with an ability of math, logic, and memorization, but he chooses to hide his gift from others to be accepted and liked. He loves to run and play sports and has an ambition to excel at athletics.

His family is a good Christian family. They reside on the south side of the railroad tracks that is perceived to be the low-income part of town. The book was written from the viewpoint of a small child as he grows up to become an adult. It addresses his views of racism, homophobia, authority figures and religion during a period when America's view of itself changed almost overnight. It focuses primarily on the greatest struggle that all people have within themselves to do either good or evil.

The boy's name is Henry. He, like all people, has evil desires and struggles with his own conscience to discern what is right and wrong in the tumultuous sixties and seventies. He makes good and bad decisions that impact himself and those around him. Likewise, the people that surround him make decisions that affect him and everyone else in the community.

It is the hope of the author that the reader will reflect on their own sub-conscious thoughts and perceptions of the world around them and work towards having a more pleasant experience on Earth for their self and all people. Both in the present and for future generations.

I'd like to thank God for giving me the opportunity to travel and the privilege of getting to know many friends and acquaintances that have helped me along the way. But just as importantly I'd like to thank and dedicate this book to my wonderful parents, siblings and my own wife and children. I've been blessed to have all of them in my life.

We don't really know ourselves until we leave where we come from. Do you know what I mean?

CHAPTER 1

The Easter Bunny

"The Easter Bunny... you mean a rabbit?" asked Henry.

His mother's gleeful smile was ousted with a look of bewilderment. She lightly bit her lower lip and scrutinized Henry's eyes to try and decipher what he was thinking. Just moments before she had handed an Easter basket full of green plastic grass to Henry's older five-year-old sister Margaret. She had happily watched as Margaret hid her basket in eager anticipation of the Easter Bunny. Henry was different.

"Yes, a rabbit," responded Marsha.

Henry was struggling to imagine how and why a rabbit would come inside his house and leave a bunch of chocolate and other goodies in a basket. It wasn't making any sense to him. And not just any rabbit. His mother had said an Easter Bunny.

"*A baby rabbit,*" thought Henry, "*that's crazy.*"

"How big is he?" he asked.

Marsha hesitated. She bit her lip a little harder and tried to visualize just how tall the Easter Bunny was supposed to be. Her hand wavered up and down indecisively before settling at a position that suggested the Easter Bunny was a little shorter than her but much taller than Henry.

Henry had seen a lot of rabbits. The only rabbit that could be roughly the size of his mother was Bugs Bunny. Bugs Bunny was a grown-up rabbit and a cartoon. Henry had already concluded that he wasn't real after lengthy discussions with his father. He knew that cartoons were just exaggerated and unrealistic animated drawings from someone's imagination. Bugs Bunny was fake. He was confident that there weren't any real rabbits that were anywhere near the size of his mother.

Santa Claus was still fresh in his memory from the previous Christmas. Henry hadn't believed Marsha when she told him that some fat guy in a red suit would come down the fireplace and leave him a bunch of toys either. He couldn't figure out how someone could travel around the whole world and leave toys at every house in only one night. Flying reindeer? Maybe reindeer could fly, but Santa Claus seemed too bizarre to be true. He hadn't ever seen a reindeer, but he'd seen a lot of different people posing as Santa Claus.

Henry asked one more investigative question just to make extra sure the Easter Bunny wasn't real. He trusted his judgment, but his over-confidence didn't stop him from verifying what he thought he already knew.

"Does he only come to our house or to everyone's?" he asked.

Marsha's face transformed from a confused look back to a big smile. She misinterpreted his question as an indication that he was buying into the rabbit story.

"Oh yes, the Easter Bunny goes to every house where there are children!" she responded.

Henry reached out his hand to take the basket. He smiled back at Marsha. He was cognizant that it was in his best interest to play along. He concealed the basket in a corner behind a chair.

"Do you think the Easter Bunny will be able to find it or should I put it somewhere where it will be less difficult to find?" asked Henry.

"That is a good spot. The Easter Bunny will surely find it!" replied Marsha.

Henry didn't pose the question because he needed an answer. He found it comical when he interrogated adults with silly questions. The sillier the question the more nonsensical the response. As far as he was concerned, his mother was the Easter Bunny. She watched him hide it. How could she not find it? He considered finding a more concealed hiding spot when she wasn't looking, but he decided that might not have a satisfying ending with a basket full of goodies. He left the basket alone because he liked chocolate.

Henry reflected on how hard Marsha had tried to convince him to believe in Santa Claus. A few days before Christmas, she had alerted him that Santa Claus was outside peeking in the windows of their home. She picked him up, so he could see Santa Claus peering in the kitchen window. Santa Claus took off running. Marsha ran from room to room with Henry as they caught more glimpses of Santa at different windows. It didn't take long for Henry to squirm free of Marsha's grasp and head for the front door. If Santa Claus was outside, then Henry was going outside to find him. Looking for something outside from the inside was a futile endeavor. Henry didn't like wasting time.

Once outside, he saw Santa take off running down the street. Off he went in hot pursuit. He didn't have to run far. Santa Claus was headed for a light blue 1963 Volkswagen Beetle parked just three houses down. Before Santa got to his car, his beard and hat had already fallen off. Henry immediately recognized Santa as being the teller at a local bank. He definitely wasn't from the North Pole. The fact that Santa Claus was completely winded and worn out after only visiting his house helped reinforce Henry's thoughts about how impossible it would be for one man to visit everyone's house in a single night.

Henry walked back home. Marsha was anxiously waiting for him at the door.

"Did you see him? That was Santa Claus!" she shouted.

"I saw him," said Henry with a perfect fake smile, not in the mood to disagree with his mother. It was a lot easier to play along than disputing the obvious. When he agreed with people, they were ordinarily happy. When he didn't consent, they usually became either angry or depressed. Henry felt better when the people around him were happy, but he had a hard time comprehending what made them happy other than just doing everything that was asked of him and believing every absurd thing he was told.

On Christmas Eve, Henry snuck back downstairs after he was supposed to be sleeping. He wanted to get a final confirmation that Santa Claus didn't exist and see if he could find out what really happened the night before Christmas. As he tiptoed down the steps, he could hear his parents quietly talking and laughing. He peeked around the corner. He saw Harold eating the cookies and drinking the milk that he and Margaret had been mandated to put out for Santa. He had asked Marsha why Santa would want cookies and milk, but she had insisted on putting them out.

"If he has to deliver presents to every house in the whole world, do you really think he will have time to stop for cookies and milk?" Henry had asked.

"Cookies and milk will make Santa happy," she'd replied.

His parents were meticulously stacking the presents under the tree. Henry speculated that maybe his mom insisted on the cookies and milk because she knew his dad liked cookies. His parents were enjoying Christmas Eve. Henry relished the moment. He enjoyed seeing his parents smiling and laughing.

He tiptoed back upstairs to spend the rest of the night lying in bed impatiently waiting for the morning. He pretended to be excited when he again saw the presents that his parents had put under the tree. He even managed a smile when Marsha read a note from Santa, thanking him and Margaret for the cookies and milk.

"Yeah, right! Delivering presents, eating cookies, and writing letters at every house in the whole world," thought Henry.

Easter morning wasn't going to be any different. Henry knew he'd be happy to find the Easter basket full of goodies.

"Who doesn't like to get presents and candy?" he thought. If he had to pretend there was an Easter Bunny and a Santa Claus, then that is exactly what he would do. There were a lot of things he didn't understand. He had a hard time trying to figure out why adults could do whatever they wanted, and kids weren't allowed to do much of anything. Something was wrong, and it didn't seem quite fair to Henry.

On Easter Sunday, Henry went to church with his family. He liked going to church. There were lots of old people that were always delighted to see him, and he savored every moment playing games and listening to stories with the other children.

On the way to church, Henry couldn't stop thinking about the story he had heard in vacation Bible school. People brought children to see Jesus and the disciples tried to turn them away. Jesus told the disciples to let the children come to him. Jesus loved children. Henry liked that story where someone took up for the children and let the adults know that kids were people too. He wondered why adults seemed to be a lot more like the disciples and less like the Jesus he heard about in Sunday school. Fortunately, nobody talked about the Easter Bunny in church.

On Monday, Henry went to preschool. His class had been learning the alphabet and he really wanted to be able to read like his sister Margaret.

Margaret liked to read to him sometimes, but she never finished the story. It seemed to Henry that she was more interested in letting him know that he couldn't read like her. Every time she read to him; she would stop before ending the story.

"I can read, and you can't," Margaret would say, just after reading enough that Henry would become interested in the story.

"Not yet," Henry would respond. "But I will be able to read when I'm your age."

Then Margaret would stick her tongue out and stop reading.

Henry would tell her that she shouldn't stick her tongue out at people because it wasn't nice. He knew if he stuck his tongue out at his sister then she'd be running off to one of their parents.

"I'm telling," she'd say.

Then he'd get in trouble. Henry didn't like it when his sister told on him, so he didn't tell on her. What he did do was correct her himself. That seemed to work out okay. His older sister listened to him most of the time. When Margaret stuck her tongue out at other children, they would either stick their tongue out, cry or go tell on her. Henry was different.

"Good morning class," said Henry's preschool teacher.

"Good morning Mrs. Elliot!" the class responded in unison.

Henry was all ears to see what fun things there would be to learn. He already knew the alphabet. Maybe the teacher would show them how to read today. That is what he really wanted to be taught. He wanted to be able to read like his sister Margaret.

"Okay, I want everyone to stand up and tell the class what the Easter Bunny brought you for Easter," said the teacher.

Henry's smile promptly dissipated into a frown.

"Jimmy, go ahead and stand up. You will be first," said Mrs. Elliot.

"The Easter Bunny brought me a chocolate rabbit and lots of candy!" exclaimed Jimmy with a smile.

Henry watched and listened as each preschooler stood up and told the class what the Easter Bunny had given them.

Everyone was happy except for Henry and a few other children. At first, Henry wasn't sure why some other kids looked so disheartened. He quickly realized it was because they hadn't received anything for Easter.

They told the class that the Easter Bunny brought them something, but they looked heartbroken. They lied to try and fit in. It was evident to Henry that all his classmates really believed in the Easter Bunny. Most of them thought the Easter Bunny brought them something and Henry felt sorry for the kids that didn't get anything. He didn't like it when he was excluded from something. He could imagine how the kids that didn't get anything felt. He was apparently the only one in his class that didn't believe in the Easter Bunny.

Henry was angry. This wasn't fair.

"*Why do adults lie to us and punish us when we tell lies, get angry or are disrespectful? Don't they understand that we are human beings just like them? Why do they do things that we aren't allowed to do? And why can't my teacher see that some of the kids didn't get anything for Easter? Doesn't she care about their feelings?*" thought Henry. He continued listening to each of his classmates as his ire raged.

Suddenly, it was Henry's turn. Everyone was looking at him. So, he stood up and told them what he regarded to be the truth.

"The Easter Bunny didn't bring me anything and he didn't bring anyone else anything either. The Easter Bunny is a big lie that some of our parents want us to believe. Our parents are the ones that put stuff in our Easter baskets," announced Henry.

He felt relieved to let his classmates know the truth, but he hadn't imagined what would happen next. He thought the other kids would be happy to know the truth but several of them started crying.

"There is no Easter Bunny," they sobbed.

It wasn't what he expected. He didn't mean to hurt anyone's feelings. He looked to the front of the room at the teacher. Surely, she would fix everything by letting everyone know the truth about the Easter Bunny. But she was angrier than any of the kids. Her rage was directed at Henry. Her face was beet red. She silently glared at him before instantaneously transforming back to her typical calm demeanor as she focused her energy on the rest of the class. She walked around consoling all the sobbing preschoolers.

"It is okay. There is an Easter Bunny. The Easter Bunny is real," said Mrs. Elliot.

The children that didn't get anything for Easter looked even more dejected. The thought that their parents didn't love them enough to give them anything was even worse than the Easter Bunny not showing up.

Henry's best friend in class looked at him.

"Your stupid!" exclaimed Mike.

Henry had never been called stupid. How could it be that he was the stupid one when everyone else believed in the Easter Bunny and all the adults were lying to the kids? A few of the other kids joined in to let Henry know that he was stupid, and the teacher didn't stop them.

The rest of the day seemed like an eternity to Henry. He was happy when it was finally time to leave. He started for the door with all the other kids, but the teacher stopped him just as he stood up from his desk.

"Not you Henry! You sit down and wait for me to come back!" snarled Mrs. Elliot.

She left with the other kids as Henry remained impatiently in his seat. She came back into the room with Henry's mother several minutes later. They went to her desk at the front of the room and Mrs. Elliot told Marsha almost exactly what had happened. Henry watched his mother out of the corner of his left eye as they both listened to what Mrs. Elliot had to say.

"All of the kids were still very excited about Easter. Everyone was laughing and talking about what the Easter Bunny brought for them," said Mrs. Elliot. "Henry decided to stand up and announce to everyone in the class that the Easter Bunny isn't real."

"He did?" asked Marsha.

"Oh yes, he did!" responded Mrs. Elliot. "You can imagine what happened next. Everyone started crying. It was a nightmare! I spent the entire morning trying to console them and now a lot of the kids aren't sure if they believe in the Easter Bunny anymore. Henry ruined everything!"

"*At least she told the truth minus the details she left out*," thought Henry. "*She didn't say anything about the other kids calling me stupid or the kids that were disappointed that their parents didn't bring them anything.*"

Marsha nodded in agreement as if she understood why the other kids cried and acknowledged that Henry had done something wrong. Mrs. Elliot turned her gaze to Henry.

"Don't you feel guilty that you made the other kids cry?" she asked.

"No, I don't feel guilty," he responded in his best composed mature voice. He was learning that it was easier to express his feelings and opinions to adults if he controlled his emotions. If he spoke in a respectful manner, adults were less likely to interrupt or disagree with him. He knew that if he showed his anger or dissatisfaction then his voice would not be heard. When he showed more maturity than adults, he was learning how to gain the upper hand.

Henry paused for a few seconds and looked directly into Mrs. Elliot's eyes. Mrs. Elliot stared back at him anxiously waiting to hear his response.

"I don't like it that their feelings were hurt, but I feel angry at you," he said calmly. "I told the truth and you lied. I don't understand why I'm getting in trouble when all I did was tell the truth. It isn't right to lie to kids. It is more your fault than mine."

The teacher's face went from ghost white confusion to enraged red as her blood began to boil again. She glared at Henry but had nothing to say.

Marsha broke the silence.

"You don't have to lie. Just think that whenever you say Easter Bunny you are referring to your parents. That way you won't hurt any of the other kid's feelings," she said.

Marsha was used to inventing solutions like this, and the teacher seemed to like her idea a lot. Letting Henry in on their adult Easter Bunny scheme would help her continue keeping the wool pulled over the other preschoolers' eyes.

"I'll give you another chance tomorrow, Henry. I'll ask you what the Easter Bunny brought you again. You can stand up and tell the class what you got for Easter. Then everyone will be happy!" said Mrs. Elliot.

"Okay?" she said.

"Okay!?" she said a second time.

"Yes Ma'am," said Henry. Only because he didn't see any better options than being obedient. It was hard to not comply with adults because the consequences always just kept getting worse. Peer pressure was one thing, but adult authority pressure was the real challenge for Henry.

On the way home, Henry was dispirited.

"Why do adults make up stories and lie to kids?" asked Henry. "It isn't right to lie."

"It is just something to help kids have imaginations Henry," replied Marsha. "It is a tradition, so it isn't really lying."

His mom's explanation didn't explain anything to Henry.

"I don't think kids have a problem with imagining things. Jimmy even has an imaginary friend. Aren't there enough real things to figure out rather than trying to fabricate things that aren't real?" he asked.

"Just think that you know an adult secret. You can be the only one in your preschool class that knows, and all of the kids will be happy," said Marsha.

"Okay," said Henry. He felt a little bit better. Being treated like an adult was exactly what he desired. He wasn't buying into how lying just because everyone else lied made it acceptable.

"Can I go to Albert's house?" asked Henry as they pulled into their driveway. He thought about how Mrs. Elliot always corrected kids to use the word 'may' instead of 'can'. They weren't allowed to get a drink of water or go to the toilet if they didn't use the magic word 'may'. His parents didn't care if he used 'can'. They said 'can' on a regular basis. At preschool he said 'may' but anywhere else he preferred to use 'can' just like everyone else.

"Yes, just make sure you are home for dinner at five o-clock," responded Marsha.

Albert lived just four houses away from Henry. They played together almost every day. Although they were the same age and neighbors, they went to different preschools. Albert went to preschool in their neighborhood while Henry's preschool was on the other side of town.

"Do you believe in the Easter Bunny?" Henry asked his best friend Albert.

Albert looked at Henry with concern that his best friend might be delusional.

"No, do you?" he responded.

Henry told Albert how he got in trouble for telling his preschool class that the Easter Bunny wasn't real. They both agreed that Albert's preschool teacher did a better job with the Easter story.

Albert's older brother Tyrone smiled at the boys as he looked up from reading the newspaper.

"You did the right thing Henry," said Tyrone. "Your heart was in the right place but sometimes it is best to keep your mouth shut. Most people don't want to know the truth."

"Why do adults tell lies when it isn't right to lie?" asked Henry.

"It is called a white lie Henry. People think that it is okay to lie when they do it to try and avoid hurting people's feelings," said Tyrone. "That is what I mean by people not wanting to know the truth. If a fat girl asks you if she looks fat, then she probably doesn't want you to tell her the truth. People tend to feel better when they hear what they want to hear."

The following morning, Henry went to his preschool class. He waited patiently for his teacher to give him another opportunity to answer her question.

"Henry, what did the Easter Bunny bring you for Easter?" asked Mrs. Elliot.

Henry stood up as all the class looked towards him in anticipation. He looked around the classroom at their faces and then glanced at Mrs. Elliot. Everyone was waiting. Henry re-considered whether he wanted to lie or tell the truth.

"The Easter Bunny brought me a great big chocolate Easter Bunny," announced Henry to the class.

Most of the kids cheered and smiled. The teacher had the most colossal smile of everyone. Henry sat back down. He smiled because they were happy. Everyone wasn't mad at him anymore. He was perplexed on the inside. His conscience was consuming him from the inside out. The children that hadn't received anything for Easter were just as sad as they had been the previous day.

"If lying is wrong, then how can it be right? What will God think of me?" he thought.

That night, before he went to bed, he felt compelled to pray but he didn't really know how to pray. He put his knees on the floor, bowed his head, and closed his eyes. He said the only prayer that he knew, the Lord's Prayer. After saying it, he cried. He asked God to forgive him for deceiving his classmates and he'd forgive the teacher and his mother for persuading him to lie.

Henry felt better after he prayed and some how he felt that God forgave him. He was just a kid. How was he supposed to not lie when everyone was lying? Especially when he was being coerced by adults to lie. Surely, God would understand.

"Maybe lying is okay if I don't mean to hurt anyone? Maybe white lies are okay," thought Henry.

Life's rules weren't straightforward.

CHAPTER 2

A Near Perfect Home

Henry didn't know it, but his family was one of the wealthiest families on the south side of the railroad tracks that ran through the town of Milton. If they would have lived on the north side of the tracks, they would have been average. If they lived in the suburbs, then they would have been one of the poorest families.

He was born in the middle of the 1960s which would be one of the most tumultuous and divisive decades in recent world history. There would be political assassinations, men landing on the moon for the first time, and dramatic progress made for the civil rights of all people. Populations would take sides to either maintain a rigid structure from the past or break free of the social constraints of the 1950s with an extreme deviation of what had been the post-World War II norm. Many people would remember the Sixties as the decade of sex, drugs and rock and roll.

It was a revolution that some denounced as a decade of irresponsible excess, flamboyance, and the decay of social order. Others identified with it as a period where taboos were relaxed, and barriers were broken down with the civil rights movement. Color TVs were replacing black and white ones and the Vietnam War would become the first truly televised war with millions of Americans watching. The decade would start with most Americans being pro-war and end with most of the people being anti-war. The majority would turn against the expectations that soldiers should go off to fight in what they viewed as meaningless wars.

The tensions between the world powers, the United States and the Soviet Union increased and then cooled. Both countries vied for influence in the developing world by funding revolutions, proxy wars, and installing their own puppet governments.

The economic trend was one of prosperity and the expansion of the middle class. Most working-class people could for the first time afford televisions, refrigerators, and cars. Henry's neighborhood in Milton was full of happy working-class people. They all shared a common economic situation where the parents felt blessed to have more excesses than their parents had when they were children.

Hippies across the country were making efforts to create Utopian communities that they called communes to escape from the materialistic contemporary society. The residents in Henry's neighborhood in Milton couldn't understand why anyone would want anything differently than what they already had. In their minds, they lived in a utopia.

Henry hadn't yet recognized that his brain worked differently than most other people. He was blessed with an ability of logical reasoning, mathematical computations and memorizing things more quickly than others. Henry wasn't born smart. He was just born with extreme curiosity. He paid attention to the details to absorb knowledge like a sponge. Most people only noticed the details that they perceived to be relevant and ignored those that they considered unimportant. Everything was relevant to Henry.

He was in constant awe of his surroundings and approached the world with a sense of discovery. His gift was the result of having an unlimited imagination that crossed the boundaries of what most people considered knowledge. Henry's brain was in constant training to remember to learn more. His curiosity drove him to be inquisitive to ask the questions; 'Why?', 'How?' and 'Why not?'. The more he learned, the more he remembered. The more he remembered, the more he improved his ability to remember. The world was full of known unknowns and unknown unknowns. Henry was obsessed to making unknowns known. He was an information addict.

Henry's parents didn't drink alcohol or smoke cigarettes. They didn't swear other than occasionally Marsha would say *shit* or *dammit* as he and Margaret negotiated parental boundaries. By almost anyone's standards, his parents were model adults. They set good examples for their children and were hard-working contributors to society. Harold had been working at a local plant for more than 5 years and Marsha had just started a new job at a local bank after Henry was old enough to go to preschool.

When they prayed before family dinners, they called it 'giving thanks' and that is what they did. They thanked and expressed their gratefulness to God for everything they had. By all accounts, they were a family that perceived their lives as being a cup half full as opposed to concentrating on what they didn't have in their lives.

Harold and Marsha worked hard to teach their children to take responsibility for their actions, to be honest and truthful, and to always treat others with kindness, compassion, and respect.

They were active in church and always keen to help neighbors or friends. They often delivered food to elderly and disabled people. Henry enjoyed joining Marsha to deliver food because the people always seemed grateful that someone cared enough to bring it to them. He liked being around grateful and happy people. Gratefulness and happiness were contagious. Henry was a happy kid.

The town they lived in was both a beautiful and pleasant town. It had a main street that had dogwood trees running down the middle of the main road through town. The trees provided shade in the summer, and they had white flowers that bloomed in the spring. They had ice cream socials, parades and lots of sports and other activities like most USA towns in the 1960s. It was all Henry knew. He and Margaret were blessed to live in such a nice town with the model parents that they had. They were a happy family.

They didn't have very many relatives that lived nearby. But once or twice every month they would make the one-hour drive to a rural area where most of their relatives lived. Twice a year, they had family reunions with each set of grandparents. They enjoyed the food and socializing with relatives.

Despite not having many relatives around, their neighbors all provided a community that treated each other like family. The same compassion and gratefulness they had in their own family seemed to be infectious amongst the neighbors. When there was a snowstorm, the younger neighbors checked on the older neighbors to make sure they had groceries and were okay. New neighbors were greeted with gifts of food and flowers. If anyone died or were injured or sick everybody would stop by to console each other and give any assistance they could.

Weddings, birthdays, and holidays brought everyone together to celebrate. The entire community took pleasure in watching their neighbors find success in the pursuit of happiness. It was a community that wasn't infected with the envious poison called jealousy. Instead of neighbors living their lives wanting what other people had, they competed against each other with gratefulness, adoration and joy.

The neighborhood didn't have a keeping up with the Jones family mentality. Instead of living the rat race of greed, they created a Utopian community of joy. They had learned the secret to be content with the blessings they already had. Hate tends to beget hate and love tends to beget love. Henry's neighborhood was a loving one.

Life was good.

CHAPTER 3

Shot Dead in Chicago

Henry's ancestors were Scotch-Irish. They had migrated to America more than 200 years before he was born. They came to escape religious conflicts, the lack of political autonomy and dire economic conditions in Europe. They were drawn to a new land by the promise of land ownership and religious freedom. They found new soil for their plows and for the first time they were able to think, speak and worship as they desired without persecution and potential death for refusing to conform. The Old World was gone, and the new reality was a New World where the founding fathers would strive to provide the freedom that allowed the people to live, speak and act according to their own beliefs peacefully and publicly. The Constitution would be designed to benefit people of all religions as well as agnostics and atheists to be free to practice their faith or lack thereof without fear of punishment from the government.

They fought the British for their own independence and freedom during the Revolutionary War. During the Civil War, they returned to the battlefield to fight for the Union to retain the democratic society envisioned by the founding fathers through union instead of division. After the Civil War, most people within the region were making their livings through subsistence farming or the small-scale harvesting of timber.

Shortly after the Civil War the steel and coal industries grew with astonishing speed. Hundreds of thousands of people came to the region. They came from Europe and all over the United States. The economy was on fire, Henry's great-great grandfather was a coal miner. His best friend Albert's great-great grandfather, on his mother's side, was also a coal miner. He came to the region in search of opportunity, improved education for his children, and to escape from the Deep South during the rise of Jim Crow laws that legalized 'separate and non-equal' racial segregation. His ancestors had come to the New World aboard slave ships from West Africa. Both men helped fuel America's industrial rise by crawling underground 'together but unequal' in society but 'together and equal' in their own minds.

The coal companies played a self-serving role to ensure labor was cheap and profits were maximized. Miners of all races and creeds were housed at the pleasure of the company while coal company executives fattened their pockets. The coal companies enforced their own Jim Crow policies which placed black miners in the oldest and least-maintained dwellings within the coal camps. They gave them the hardest and most dangerous jobs with the lowest pay.

The United Coal Miners of America (UCMA) was a contrast to organized labor by the coal companies and the labor unions in the South that were plagued with internal controversy that excluded blacks from union participation. Black miners were welcomed by the UCMA and even given leadership positions. The over inflated pockets of the coal executives helped persuade the politicians to fiercely resist the unionization of their mines. The unions organized to fight for the liberties and equality of the workers whereas the coal executives self-serving greed desired to oppress the workers and further fatten their own bank accounts. The coal companies fought back by establishing no-tolerance policies towards the unions. They hired their own private mercenaries to do their own detective work and deal with the perceived 'troublemakers'.

Throughout the country, black soldiers returning from World War I had gained a much different worldly view. They had crossed the Atlantic to fight against the world's madness. They returned to a country where they were expected to feel ashamed of the color of their skin. The black veteran's outspoken voices against oppression contributed to the birth of postwar tensions. They had gained the courage to call a spade a spade. The federal government and much of the white population feared that socialist or communist influence would gain a foothold in a black civil rights movement. The country was in an economic slump and competition for jobs and housing was fierce. Many disgruntled whites burned black churches and rioted against blacks in big cities across the country. Hundreds of people were killed, and thousands of others had their properties destroyed or were displaced. Blacks in Chicago and Washington DC fought back, but blacks in many other places lacked the organization and numbers to fight the opposition. They were out-numbered and outgunned.

The newspapers would call the postwar violence the Red Summer of 1919. The UCMA's inclusion of miners of all races in Rockwell County helped spare the region from nationwide violence from anti-black white supremacist terrorist groups in 1919. The black and white coal miners established their own 'no-tolerance' policies against inequality and oppression to fight back against the coal companies and their mercenaries. They became undivided as 'We the People'. Their camaraderie, loyalty and courage saved the community from the lynching's and property destruction that were prevalent across the country. Despite the lack of violence directed through mob lynching of blacks, there was an ever-increasing bloodshed between the miners and the coal company mercenaries. It peaked in 1920 with the battle on Fable Mountain. Henry and Albert's grandfathers fought side by side against the army of deputies and private mercenaries purchased by the coal companies. Much like the shared military experience in decades that proceeded and followed, Henry and Albert's grandfathers judged others by their character. They treated each other as equals fighting for their common desire for liberty, freedom, and the pursuit of happiness. Together, they fought against oppression, inequality and hate along with hundreds of others that shared their beliefs and desires. Eventually the union succeeded in winning the war against the coal company.

Despite better working conditions after unionization, the Great Depression in the 1930s brought disaster to the industry. When coal production declined, a majority of the first miners to be laid off were black miners. Numerous white miners also lost their jobs. Many of the black miners headed to Chicago or Washington DC where blacks had established their own segregated communities that consisted of churches, community centers, and businesses. They desired to survive, sustain themselves and determine their own fate.

Albert's grandfather stayed and raised his six children through the Great Depression. After World War II, new technologies and mechanization transformed the coal industry. Coal production doubled and manpower was vastly cut. The coal executives were reluctant to train and use black workers to operate the new machinery which resulted in many of the job cuts to again be the ones held by the black coal miners. The loss of job opportunities caused another mass exodus of black miners and their families. Albert's mother took a bus to Chicago to live with relatives when she was 17 years old. Most of her relatives worked for the Melga Starch Company that had leveraged the low wages of black workers to build a profitable and thriving business. It wasn't long before she met Duane Thurman.

Duane was a few years older than Ruth. Ruth was drawn to Duane's charismatic personality and ambitious zeal for changing the world. He was studying pre-law which gave him the knowledge to use the legal system as a defense against unfair treatment from the police. He had organized a youth group of more than 1000 members that practiced nonviolent activism with the goal of achieving positive social change. They worked with local restaurants and businesses to set up free breakfasts for undernourished children and used Duane's knowledge of the law to get more equal treatment for the minority communities in Chicago. Their activism efforts improved the educational resources to help educate the young children and get better parks and recreational facilities within their community.

Ruth gave birth to Tyrone shortly after her and Duane were married. Duane continued his efforts for non-violent activism and sharpening his communication and leadership skills. He was just as comfortable talking to single mothers on welfare or college students as he was with youth gangs or white politicians. His uncanny ability to pull people together enabled the organization of community groups that patrolled the neighborhood to watch out for police brutality. He educated others on the legal system so they could use the law to protect their community from the unlawful acts of the police. The community started policing the police with what they called community supervision. In addition to police brutality, gangs within the black community were fighting each other. Duane recognized that divisions and criminal activity did nothing but keep the community entrenched in poverty. He knew that changing others started with the individual. He helped broker peace between ethnic gangs that extended to groups outside of the black community.

It wasn't long before Duane was on the radar of both the Chicago Police Department and the FBI. His efforts had extended to a multi-racial group that was growing and becoming increasingly more undivided. Community violence in Chicago started decreasing. The people became motivated and optimistic that positive changes could happen. The Chicago PD and the FBI perceived Duane as a threat. They started covertly smearing Duane and his organization under the guise of protecting national security. The FBI had become experts at planting fake news. They knew that perception becomes the new reality for the population. Their fake news would be believed by the masses. They were competent with their work. They forged documents, planted false reports in the media and harassed Duane and others in Chicago that were involved in the non-violent movement for human rights. Duane was arrested twice during peaceful demonstrations. He was charged with promoting mob violence. Despite the fake news and harassment, he maintained his determination to continue his efforts.

When Ruth was pregnant with Albert, Tyrone was 11 years old. A car bomb had killed their other two children two years before. The media presented the bombing as a black-on-black crime, but Ruth was confident that the government had been responsible. Despite losing two children, Duane didn't stop. Neither did the Chicago Police Department or the FBI. The FBI now perceived Duane as a national threat. They wanted to use all necessary means to eradicate the programs that he had initiated. They used criminals to infiltrate the coalition as paid confidential informants, tapped phones and continued psychological warfare to pass false news to denigrate the group as a terrorist organization.

Despite the FBI's efforts, Duane continued to grow his coalition into a nation-wide effort seeking to improve equality and conditions for all people. Two months before Albert was born, the police and FBI stormed into their apartment in the middle of the night. A confidential informant that had his felony charges dismissed and received a monthly paycheck from the FBI had slipped some barbiturates into Duane's drink the previous night. The informant had duped Duane into trusting him by pretending that he was on the look-out for an informant amongst their coalition. Duane was adamantly against drugs and wasn't a drug user. He had dosed off on the couch. He didn't even wake up when the first gunshots came blasting through the front door.

A young teenage Tyrone stood at his bedroom door in Superman pajamas in shock. He heard his pregnant mother screaming. A policeman pushed her against the wall as she tried to get to her husband. Duane was soaked in blood from multiple gunshots to his chest and torso. His eyes were open, and his mouth was moving slowly. No words escaped his gasps.

"Is he dead?" asked a policeman entering the room.

"He is just barely alive," responded one of the policemen that was among the first to arrive in the apartment.

Tyrone heard three more-gun shots as he watched a policeman holding his pistol at point blank range at his father's head. Ruth gave a loud scream and then crumpled to the floor sobbing. Duane's body lay motionless on the couch.

"He's dead now," said the same policeman that had fired the shots after asking whether he was dead.

The police forcefully removed Tyrone and his mother from the apartment along with two other men that had been sleeping in another bedroom. The two men were both indicted by a grand jury for armed violence and several other weapons charges. The confidential informant would be paid a healthy reward for sitting up the assassination. In the trial, the charges were dropped after the police departments claims that they had not fired the first shots were disproved by a citizen civil rights group. The police had fired 128 shots with no evidence of anyone in the apartment ever firing a single shot.

Several years later, evidence would be found in FBI headquarters that shed light on an illegal counter-intelligence program that included a plot to kill Duane while concealing the role of the Chicago Police Department, FBI, and deputy attorney general.

Justice didn't come. Ruth decided to leave Chicago with Tyrone and her new baby Albert. They moved to be close to her parents and other relatives which just happened to be four houses down from the Reynolds family in Milton. Harold and Marsha were the first neighbors that knocked on their door to welcome them to the community.

"Mom, it's a white family," said Tyrone suspiciously, as he peeked through the front window curtain. "They have flowers and a baby?"

Ruth looked through the window as she held Albert tightly to her chest. She slightly cracked open the front door in fear that the white family were there to do them harm.

"Hi! Welcome to the neighborhood!" said Marsha with a welcoming smile. "We brought you some flowers."

Ruth opened the door just a little bit wider as she observed the Reynolds.

"They have a baby too!" said Margaret.

"I ... I am sorry. Where are my manners?" said Ruth after a long pause. "Please come in."

The Reynolds family walked in the house and spent the next two hours talking and laughing with Ruth and Tyrone. Henry and Albert met each other for the first time as small babies lying on a blanket on the floor while Tyrone played with Margaret.

Tyrone would go to a fully integrated school with black and white children all standing side by side as they said the 'Pledge of Allegiance' together. The state school superintendent left integration in the hands of each of the state's county boards of education. Rockwell county was one of the first counties to integrate the schools. In some counties, black children were threatened as they made their way past crudely painted signs 'No Negros Wanted in Our Schools' with angry mobs of people shouting racial slurs at them. Rockwell county had people that objected to integration, but for the most part; the community managed to talk and act like responsible adults. It didn't take long to have black and white kids sitting side by side in class. It was Tyrone's first time to study, laugh and play with white children.

Positive change was good.

CHAPTER 4

New Congregation

Henry embraced the privilege of sitting in the sanctuary with grown-ups. He felt like a big boy. He enjoyed being with the other children, but he relished every opportunity granted to him to explore and learn. Most children his age desired to stay in their comfort zone, but Henry was enticed to continually push his boundaries. He was obsessive to growing stronger, wiser, and more confident.

It was only the second time that he was permitted to join his parents in the adult sanctuary. He had enjoyed the singing the first time, but the sermon had been excruciatingly depressing. As he listened to each word, he started feeling worthless and ashamed of himself for not being perfect. He looked around and saw that everyone looked sad and ashamed as the pastor informed them of how their sins were against the scripture in the Bible.

Henry started regretting that he had asked his parents to join them. The grownups service wasn't anything like what he was accustomed to during the children's service. It was always upbeat and fun. The children learned about a God that loved them unconditionally as opposed to a God that was going to punish them for eternity. He felt uncomfortable and struggled to not fidget.

For the next several weeks, Henry went to the children's service, but he couldn't stop thinking about what he had heard in the adult sanctuary. He didn't like listening and being around depressed and fearful people, but his curiosity continued tugging at him. He was inclined to learn more about what was being preached in the adult sanctuary. He yearned to understand why the children and adult services were completely different.

Marsha gave him a pencil and some paper, so he could draw pictures instead of fidgeting. They were sitting near the front with lots of other people they knew all around them. Henry could overhear several different conversations. He was attentively listening to what everyone had to say but being careful to not let anyone know that he was absorbing every word. Adults said a lot of things to other adults that Henry found interesting. He knew that they didn't like to have adult discussions when they were aware that he was listening. It was funny to Henry why adults didn't seem to recognize that kids had ears. It perplexed him why they were angry at him if they found out he was digesting what they said. He learned to listen quietly and find an appropriate time to ask more questions.

"*The adults are the ones talking,*" he would think. "*If they don't want me to hear something then they shouldn't be saying it in front of me.*"

Suddenly complete silence fell over the sanctuary. At first, Henry thought maybe the service was getting ready to start, but he didn't see anyone in the front of the church or hear the organ. He saw that a few people were hastily getting out of their seats to leave. His friend Mike's dad was sitting with his wife just in front of Henry. He watched as Mike's dad leaned over close to Mrs. Rodgers.

"There's a *nigger* in the church," whispered Mr. Rodgers.

Henry looked at Mr. Rodger's red face and could see that he was angry. He was the chief of police. If he was agitated because a *nigger* was in the church, then something atrocious had to be happening. Mrs. Rodgers looked frightened to death as if God was going to send lightning bolts to destroy their church.

"*I wonder what a nigger is?*" thought Henry.

He turned around to see what Mike's father and everyone else were looking at. All he saw was an old man and woman walking up the center aisle of the church. The man was smiling. He walked confidently and slowly. He bent over and extended his right hand at each pew.

"Good morning, Sir. Good morning, Ma'am. God bless you," said the man as he smiled at each person.

Most of the people that he was greeting were looking at him with disgust. Only a couple people shook his hand of which he offered to everyone. The rest just glared at him as if they hated everything about him.

The man's wife had a pretty hat with flowers and a veil covering half of her face. She wasn't smiling. She looked scared to death just like Mrs. Rodgers as if she was also expecting lightning bolts from God at any moment.

Henry thought that if he were walking into the church that he would probably be scared too. He couldn't help but admire the courage of the old man who looked like he wasn't afraid of anything. It was evident that pretty much everyone hated the old man, but he faced every one of them with kindness and a smile. To Henry, the old man looked like the perfect example of a Christian. He couldn't figure out why hardly anybody seemed to want him in the church.

"*Whatever a nigger is it must be something terrible,*" he thought.

Just after the old man and woman sat down in an empty pew near the front of the church, the organist started playing a hymn. Henry enjoyed the harmonious sound of the organ. He was amazed at how the demeanor of the entire congregation seemed to change from fury to calmness with the euphonious music.

The pastor entered the sanctuary and walked up to the pulpit. He said a prayer and made some announcements of which Henry found disappointingly uninteresting.

Henry thought about the Bible story of Jesus being crucified. The people made fun of him with insults and wanted to kill him even though he did nothing wrong. The old man reminded him of Jesus. He wondered if the congregation would have crucified the old man if they weren't in a church.

Henry snuck a few peeks at the man during the service. His admiration grew with every look.

What Henry didn't know was that just a little more than two years before, a man named Martin Luther King Jr., was shot, and killed after preaching about nonviolent resistance to oppression.

The old man and woman had been inspired by this movement. They knew that the only way to free themselves from injustice was to become free of hate themselves; even though they had a good excuse to hate. Many of the people in the church hated them to the core because of the color of their skin. They came to the church in hope and faith that they could have the strength to love their enemy and change their enemy's heart. They were non-violently being disobedient to oppression by white Americans.

After church, Henry couldn't wait to get into the car with his family.

"What is a *nigger*?" he asked Harold as soon as the car doors closed.

Harold's brief pause allowed Marsha to answer first.

"It is what some people call colored people, and it isn't nice to say," said Marsha.

The answer surprised Henry, he had expected that a *nigger* was going to be something bad.

"Surely it can't just be because of the color of someone's skin," thought Henry.

Since Marsha had told him that *nigger* wasn't nice to say, he wanted to find out if *nigger* was like *fuck, dammit,* and *shit.* He knew that he wasn't ever allowed to say *fuck, dammit,* or *shit.* Or maybe it was like *hell* or *ass.* He could get away with saying *hell* or *ass* when used in the right context. Like, if he was referring to the opposite of Heaven or a donkey.

Henry had learned that some words were inappropriate to say. He didn't understand why some people could say them, but he couldn't. He also didn't comprehend how people could be offended by a word. The concept of inappropriate words didn't register very well in Henry's mind. The first inappropriate word that he had learned was *fuck.* He had carefully digested how it was used by some older boys. He had been mesmerized of how a single word could be used in so many ways.

Marsha always seemed to be impressed with Henry speaking new words and making sentences. So, he had made a little poem especially for her. He hoped that her reaction might help him understand what *fuck* meant.

"*Fuck* the duck. *Fuck* the truck. *Fucking* ducks and *fucking* trucks. Ducks and trucks are *fucked*," recited Henry.

"Henry! You don't say that word! Where did you learn it?!" exclaimed Marsha. Horrified at the words that were coming out of young Henry's mouth.

Henry tried to ask some questions to figure out why it wasn't nice to say or what it meant, but he decided that he would just have to remember it as another rule.

"*Kids are not allowed to use the word fuck. Adults can say fuck, but it isn't nice to say. Nobody should ever say fuck,*" Henry had committed to memory.

Shit had an easier explanation. He knew *shit* was just another word for poop. He didn't understand why people used it in other ways that didn't seem like it was always interchangeable with poop. He came up with a nice poem about *shit,* but never did get to recite it out loud because he had learned it was inappropriate to say before he could ever use it.

"*Fucking shit. I shit my pants. My pants are fucked from the fucking shit,*" thought Henry.

"So," Henry asked. "Does that mean that Flip Wilson and Albert are *niggers*?" The *Flip Wilson Show* was a new funny show on television that he and his family liked to watch. Henry's favorite part of the show was when Flip Wilson dressed up like a woman named Geraldine.

"No, they are not *niggers,* and don't you call them or anyone else *niggers*!" shouted Marsha.

Henry filed *nigger* away with *fuck, dammit,* and *shit* as four words that adults could say but he couldn't. But he was still confused. Surely *nigger* must mean something more than being black.

"Why do people call black people *that word* then?" he asked.

This time Harold answered before Marsha could speak.

"Black people used to be slaves to white people and some white people think that they should still be slaves and not be allowed to intermix with white people. It wasn't too long ago that they weren't even allowed to go to school, eat at restaurants or use the same restrooms as white people," said Harold.

"So, why were black people slaves?" asked Henry.

"I don't know," said Harold. "People have been enslaving other people since antiquity."

"Then why do white people hate them?" asked Henry.

"Most white people don't hate them. They are just fearful that the black people will take their jobs. Some people are afraid that maybe they will become slaves to the black people. Others think they are better than black people just because they are white," answered Harold. "Other white people have common sense."

Henry respected the answers he got from his father. Harold almost always tried to be honest with him and his answers generally made a lot of sense. He told Henry what he thought. If he didn't know something, he never tried to make up answers to questions when he was unsure of the answer. Harold recognized the difference between what he knew and what he didn't know.

Just a couple of weeks before, Henry had been helping Harold take out the trash.

"Dad how can the sky just keep going on and on forever without an end, and if it ends then what is on the other side and the other side of that?" he'd asked.

"I don't know Henry. There are some things that we just can't understand, and only God knows," Harold had responded. They both stood for several minutes looking at the stars. Henry and Harold both felt overwhelmed with a good feeling of what God had created.

Henry asked his teachers and other adults the same question. Most of them tried to answer the question, but their answers didn't made any sense to Henry.

Henry contemplated about Harold's response to why some white people didn't like black people. If he was a slave, then he'd be infuriated at whoever enslaved him too. He could imagine how someone could be afraid of someone that they had made a slave but was now free. That was exactly how most people were. They did things to retaliate and had a hard time getting over anything that offended them. He often wanted to fight back or get even himself. His parents didn't allow him to retaliate.

"Two wrongs never make a right," they'd say.

His father's answer had made sense. He was glad that he had been provided with a reason. Otherwise, he would have found it hard to forgive and not hate a lot of the people in his church. It was easy to hate but Henry didn't like the way he felt when he was angry. He had grown accustomed to finding ways to not hate others because he enjoyed being happy. He was happiest when he wasn't angry. Living with unforgiveness wasn't desirable to Henry so he chose to find a way to forgive others most of the time.

The old man and woman came into the church to change their enemy's hearts. There was a part of Henry's heart that wanted to hate the people that didn't like black people. If there were people that didn't like Albert and Flip Wilson, then he wasn't sure if he would be able to love them. He liked most of the people in the church and couldn't imagine them hating anyone on purpose.

"I feel better when I get over being angry," thought Henry. *"Angry people waste their energy creating their own pain and nobody would do that to them self intentionally. It is better to forgive them but not forget."*

He also liked Albert and Flip Wilson. He couldn't envision them ever wanting to do anything bad to him. Mostly, he thought about the old man that was brave enough to walk into an all-white church. Henry wasn't afraid of black people, but he could imagine how the angry people in church were fearful of the man. There were lots of cowards that lived in almost constant fear. What he couldn't understand was why some of them thought they were better just because they were white. That came across as surreal to Henry.

"Well, some people do act like they are better than everyone else sometimes," he thought. *"Especially when they have a nice new car or outfit. Some people are weird."*

"Can I go to Albert's house when we get home?" Henry asked Marsha.

"After you change out of your church clothes and eat your dinner," said Marsha. "Albert won't be home for a couple of hours anyway. His church lasts longer than ours. Don't you repeat *that word* you learned today Henry."

"I won't Mom," said Henry. "Do you think Albert gets called *that word* at his church?"

"No Henry," smiled Marsha. "Albert goes to an all-black church. That man that came to our church today use to be the Pastor of Albert's church. He is retired now."

"You mean they integrated the schools but haven't done the same thing for churches?" asked Henry.

"I guess that is what is happening now," said Marsha. "Your dad and I have been to Albert's church before. There are a few white people that occasionally go to their church, but it is mostly a black congregation."

"Did they call you any names when you went to Albert's church?" asked Henry.

"No," laughed Marsha. "They were happy to see us coming to worship with them."

"Was it just like our church?"

"It looks the same, but they sing and dance a lot more than the people in our church," replied Marsha.

Henry waited patiently for Albert to get home so he could ask him more questions about his church. He was sitting on Albert's front porch when Mrs. Thurman pulled into their driveway with Albert and Tyrone.

"Hi Henry," said Mrs. Thurman with a big smile. "How was church today?"

"Good," said Henry. "The man that used to be the pastor at your church came to my church today with his wife. Do you know his name?"

"That would be Reverend Walter Bailey and his wife is Helen," said Mrs. Thurman. "I will fix you boys some lemonade."

"At my church, Jesus is white," said Henry. "Is he black at your church?"

"He's white with blue eyes and blonde hair," responded Albert. "All of his disciples eating the Last Supper are white too, so is Mary and Joseph."

"Do you have pictures of angels in your church?" asked Henry.

"Yep, they all white too," said Albert. "Maybe all the black angels weren't there for the picture."

"They were all probably in the kitchen preparing the dinner for the others," laughed Tyrone.

"Do you think Jesus was white?" asked Henry.

"No," said Tyrone. "He was probably brown. He was somewhere in between being black and white."

"Then why is he white in all of the pictures?" asked Henry.

"He's white because all the people that made the paintings were white," said Tyrone. "Nobody knows what he looked like for real."

"Why doesn't someone just make new paintings and make him brown?" asked Henry.

"What color is Tarzan?" asked Tyrone.

"Tarzan is white," responded Albert and Henry in unison.

"Exactly, does that make any sense that the king of the jungle in Africa is white?" asked Tyrone. "Tarzan is the only white man in the jungle. He is the only one capable of talking to animals, and he just so happens to find a pretty half naked white woman named Jane to protect from all the black Africans. The real Africans are the bad guys and Tarzan single handedly beats them all up with the help of all the wild animals."

"There has been systemic racism going on for hundreds of years," said Tyrone. "The President of the United States lives in a white house.

Black cats are considered bad luck. In movies, the cowboys are always the good guys. The red *Indians* that were in this country first are the bad guys and treated like savages. When white cowboys fight other white cowboys, the good guy always has a white hat while the bad guy has a black one. Lots of cowboys were actually black but they aren't in any of the movies. Angel food cake is white and devil's food cake is chocolate."

"Devil's food cake is a lot better than angel food cake," smiled Henry.

"Yeah," said Albert. "I like chocolate."

"Why is everything so messed up?" asked Henry.

"I don't know, but things are getting better," replied Tyrone. "The two of you are like brothers. When I was your age, there wasn't a white kid alive that wanted to be my friend. I can't say I really wanted to have a friend that was white myself. Maybe your generation will figure out how to change people's hearts. You have to change one heart at a time. It is hard to change people's ignorance."

"Let's get some brown paint so we can paint Jesus brown," said Henry.

"Yeah," smiled Albert. "We can make him brown in both churches."

Tyrone laughed.

"The world isn't ready for that yet," he said. "Don't go painting in the church. There are too many people that would hate you for it. That would be called vandalism and you would get in trouble. The Bible says to not be overcome by evil but overcome evil with good. As long as it depends on you, you have to try and live peacefully with everyone else. The greatest struggle that every man has is the struggle he has with himself. It is hard to be a real man. Everybody is their own worst enemy and they don't even know it. You have to carry your own cross and be better than everyone else instead of expecting everyone else to change their own evil behavior. There are only two sides – Good and Evil. The challenge is that you can't take the evil out of the people. If you could then everyone would be acting right all the time."

The next Sunday, Henry decided to go back to the kids Sunday school.

"Did you know there are *niggers* coming to our church?" Henry's friend Mike asked.

"You should call them black people. It isn't nice to say *that word*," responded Henry.

"I hate *niggers*," said Mike.

Henry remembered seeing Mike's dad in the church the previous week. He had been the one that introduced Henry to the word *nigger*. Harold had told him that the people in the church didn't really hate them.

"*They are either afraid or think they are better than them,*" thought Henry.

He guessed that Mike and his father had a different conversation than what he had with his own father. Tyrone had told him that he had to change one heart at a time.

So, he decided to try and change Mike's own ignorance.

"Do you hate Flip Wilson?" asked Henry.

"No, he's funny. I like when he dresses up like a woman – Geraldine – and blames everything he does wrong on the Devil!" laughed Mike.

"Well, then you don't hate black people and you'd probably like the black people that are coming to our church too," replied Henry. "The man used to be a pastor at my friend Albert's church."

"My dad said we aren't coming to this church anymore if the black people stay," said Mike.

"Well, I hope you stay," said Henry.

"*How can the chief of police be afraid of black people or think that he is better just because he is white,*" thought Henry. "*That's scary. The man charged with protecting the community is either a chicken, an idiot or maybe a combination of both. He is a stupid coward?*"

Henry's congregation grew by 2 people but lost about 10 times that amount. Henry wasn't happy to see his friend Mike leave but most of the other people that left weren't much of a loss as far as he was concerned. The ones that left were either the ones that thought they were better than everyone else or the ones that were most afraid that the end of the world was coming soon. Henry had a hard time enjoying being around arrogant or depressed and ungrateful people anyway. Everyone that did leave went to an all-white church on the north side of town.

Life was strange.

CHAPTER 5

The Pyramid Scheme

Harold pressed the gas pedal to the floor. He quickly shifted his 1967 Plymouth Belvedere into second gear. Henry was sitting in the back seat with his sister Margaret. He liked the rumble of the 383 V8 engine and the way his whole body pressed against the back seat when Harold accelerated. Margaret was playing with two barbie dolls that seemed to be having a conversation. Henry watched her for a while wondering why she enjoyed having conversations with plastic dolls. He had a GI Joe, but he never really figured out what he was supposed to do with a doll. So, he just left it in his closet.

His parents were in the front seat talking about something called a pyramid scheme. Marsha was excited and asking lots of questions. From what Henry understood, the pyramid scheme had something to do with a way to make money for doing nothing. Marsha was trying to convince Harold to drive by the community building to see who all would be participating in the pyramid scheme.

Harold reluctantly agreed to drive by with the condition that he wasn't stopping. It was already dark and a little bit chilly outside. The car seat felt cold as Henry pressed his hands against the seat to see out the window as they got close to the community building. He could see lots of cars. The parking lot was completely full of people and the parked cars filled up the road between the community building and baseball fields where Henry played baseball.

"*Whatever this pyramid scheme is; it must be a lot more important than a baseball game because it looks like half of the town are here,*" thought Henry. His interest peaked even further.

"Oh my, the mayor is here, and is that Mr. Thompson? ... It is, and look even the Martins, the Rowlings, the Rembrandts ..." sighed Marsha in disbelief.

Harold shook his head like he did when he was disappointed with something. Marsha continued announcing everyone she saw as if she was in shock that so many people were in attendance.

Henry saw his friend Mike's dad, but he wasn't in his police uniform. He saw a bunch of other people that he knew from around town. It seemed to Henry that just about anybody that thought they were somebody were there.

As they drove away, Henry couldn't remain silent anymore. He needed to understand more about what the pyramid scheme was all about.

"Why aren't we stopping to join the pyramid scheme like everyone else?" asked Henry.

Harold looked at him through the rear-view mirror. He looked even more disappointed knowing his son had overheard another adult conversation.

"Because it isn't right. Nobody wins. A few people will get a bunch of money and everyone else will lose out," said Harold.

"How does it work?" asked Henry.

Harold explained the pyramid scheme.

"One guy has two people pay him money and then those two people find two more people to pay them. Then those people find more people, so everyone doubles their money," explained Harold.

"After a while, there are so many people looking for other people to get in the scheme that they run out of people," continued Harold. "The people that start the scheme get richer and most other people just lose their money. The people that started it go to another town and repeat the process."

"If it takes advantage of people and most of them lose their money, then why are so many people doing it?" asked Henry.

"I don't know," responded Harold. He turned up the radio.

When Harold turned the radio up, Henry knew that meant he was done answering questions.

A Buffalo Springfield song started playing. It drowned out all other sound except the rumble of the Plymouth. The words seemed to be about the pyramid scheme. The singer sang an ominous warning to children to take a good look around. A battle was going to be fought and people were picking sides. Everybody thought they were in the right, but the reality was that everyone was wrong.

Henry listened to the lyrics.

"Everyone in town sure do seem to be in the wrong," thought Henry. *"Maybe this song is a warning to kids like me?"*

The song continued with how paranoia would creep into everyone that was afraid. People would start protesting. They would all stand up in defiance for their side. The man would then come and lock everyone up for stepping out of line.

Henry started feeling a little afraid himself. It was almost as depressing as listening to the pastor preaching to the adults in his church. He thought that the song was a good warning to be careful to not get on the wrong side. He hadn't seen anyone carrying signs and taking up sides, but he could imagine the two sides that would come out of the pyramid scheme. One side would be the ones who doubled their money, and the other side would be the ones that lost all of theirs.

"That won't end well," thought Henry.

He wondered if the song was about the pyramid scheme or maybe it had something to do with the people called hippies and the people that didn't like them. Henry liked most of the hippies he had met because they always seemed so friendly.

"Maybe it's the hippies that might get taken away for stepping out of line," he thought.

Henry liked giving them the peace sign. They always smiled and joked with him, but he knew that some people didn't want them around.

What he didn't like about the hippies was that many of them looked like they were from a different planet. They were dazed and confused and sometimes had a hard time walking. Tyrone had told him it was because they used drugs. He couldn't understand why people would take drugs if it made them look stupid. But there was a lot of things that people did that he couldn't understand.

"Drugs make people feel good. People get hooked and they can't quit. Then it is too late, and they are stuck," Tyrone had told him and Albert. "The best thing to do is just never do drugs. If you start doing drugs, then you'll end up just like those hippies. Consider drugs to be like donuts. If something tastes too sweet, then it probably will end up having negative consequences. It is best to stay away from donuts but even more important to stay away from drugs. Donuts will make you fat, but drugs will destroy your life."

The people that didn't like the hippies were generally the same people that didn't like black people. They were the people that Henry had the hardest time liking himself. Sometimes, they talked about communists which seemed to be anyone that opposed them. Henry struggled to figure out exactly what communists were because he hadn't been able to find anyone that claimed to be a communist. He questioned hundreds of people and not a single person had ever admitted that they were a communist. Even Tyrone didn't know anyone that was a real communist. Communists were imaginary adult boogeymen that weren't present in Milton.

Harold told him that communists were people that thought everybody should have the same things and nobody would be rich or poor. The concept sounded pretty good at first but as he asked more questions it progressively seemed worse. He kind of liked the thought that if you wanted something then you could go work hard to obtain what you desired.

"If everyone got the same thing then what would be the point of working hard? If I wouldn't get anything special for working, I'd rather just have fun playing than going to work," thought Henry.

What Henry found strange was that most people that worked hard weren't really concerned about the communists. The people complaining about the communists were mostly the lazier ones. They seemed to think they were entitled to something for nothing. Their perceived problem in the world was all the communists of which didn't seem to be around. That confused Henry even more.

"Why are the people that would benefit the most from communism be the most upset with the concept?" he wondered.

Henry looked up at his parents in the front seat of the Plymouth. His dad had grown long sideburns and a mustache. His mom had a hairstyle that she called a beehive. Henry smiled at how Marsha's beehive looked just like the hornet's nest that he knocked down with a basketball at a family reunion. He had gotten stung more than anyone else. Everyone but his grandma had been mad at him. His grandma had taken him into the kitchen and put onions on all twenty-three of his sting marks. Henry had been impressed at how the onions seemed to really help. He apologized to his angry relatives, and they soon forgave him. Inside he felt good about successfully knocking down the hornet's nest on his first try. His mission had been accomplished.

Henry thought that both of his parents looked kind of funny. Most of his friend's parents had similar hair styles. They weren't hippies and they weren't against hippies. They were somewhere in between. Henry's parents were inbetweeners. They weren't free loving hippies, and they weren't part of the establishment or anti-communists.

As far as Henry was concerned, his parents weren't really on either side. They were the best of both worlds. They were into peace and love and for being hard working and responsible. He was glad that his parents weren't greedy or stupid enough to be participating in the pyramid scheme. He didn't feel afraid anymore. Everything was going to be alright. He smiled.

Life was good.

CHAPTER 6

First Kiss

The pain was agonizing. Henry hit the ground hard.

He felt a writhing pain in his arm like he had never felt before. He felt like crying, but he wasn't going to cry in front of Lisa. Lisa had just pushed him off the side of their babysitter's back porch. Moments before, they had been sitting on the porch talking. Henry had been mesmerized at how Lisa's blond hair fell over her face. The sun glittered off her face and sparkles of light effused from her blue eyes. Lisa had been playing with a barbie doll. Henry was overcome by a feeling that compelled him to kiss Lisa. He couldn't stop himself. It was a lot like looking at freshly baked chocolate chip cookies that just came out of the oven. He had a hard time looking at cookies without having a strong desire to eat them. Lisa obviously wasn't a cookie but there was something about her that just made Henry feel like kissing her. He could resist cookies but the temptation to kiss Lisa was too intense to resist.

He acted without giving it much thought. Lisa was the same age as Henry, and he really liked her. He bent towards her to give her a kiss. As soon as his lips touched her cheek, she gave him a swift push that knocked him off the side of the porch.

"Maybe she just doesn't want to be kissed," thought Henry. *"I feel the same when adults try to kiss me. She probably just doesn't feel the same way I feel towards her. I should have asked first."*

He had never had a broken bone before, but he was confident that it must be broken. The pain was the most excruciating physical pain that he had ever experienced. He felt rejected but wasn't mad at Lisa.

Henry opened the back door and walked inside to the kitchen where the babysitter was making dinner for her family.

"I broke my arm," said Henry to the babysitter.

"Go sit down and watch television Henry. Your mother will be here shortly to pick you up," said the babysitter. She gave him a familiar look that meant she didn't believe him. Henry knew better than to disagree with the babysitter. He could try to explain but it was pointless. She wasn't very good at understanding reality.

He laid down on the floor and started watching the *Flintstones*. It was hard to find any position where his arm didn't hurt.

When Marsha arrived after picking Margaret up from kindergarten, he heard the babysitter and his mother talking in the kitchen.

"How was Henry today?" asked Marsha.

The babysitter laughed.

"He was good until he decided to start making up stories again. He said his arm is broken!" said the babysitter.

The babysitter and Marsha seemed to get a kick out of the comment. They started laughing about the imaginations of kids. Henry wondered why adults didn't believe him when he pretty much always told the truth.

"They have a bizarre sense of humor," thought Henry.

Marsha walked into the family room where Henry was watching television.

"Hi Mom, my arm is broken," said Henry. He hoped that Marsha would believe him over the babysitter. But he knew the odds were that his mother would believe the babysitter. After all, she was the adult. He was just a little kid.

"Your arm isn't broken. Let's go. Margaret is waiting for us in the car," responded Marsha. Henry knew better than to argue, so he got up and went to the car with Marsha.

After they got home, the pain in his arm continued hurting more and more. He managed to make it through dinner, but bedtime was more challenging. He couldn't sleep with the pain.

"My arm is broken, and I need to go the hospital," he said politely to Marsha.

After several attempts. Henry resorted to using the magic word.

"Please take me to the hospital. My arm is broken," he said, as he respectfully asked Marsha again.

"Go back to bed. Your arm is not broken," said Marsha. She continued washing the dishes and was undaunted by the magic yielded by the word please.

Finally, two hours after bedtime, Henry gave up on being a respectful tough guy or magician with the appropriate word selection. He resorted to expressing his anger and frustration by crying and screaming.

"I can't take it anymore!" he sobbed. "This isn't fair! My arm really hurts, and you won't help me! You have to take me to the hospital!"

The crying and screaming tactic worked.

Marsha called a neighbor to watch Margaret, so she could take Henry to the hospital. When they got to the hospital, Marsha held Henry's good arm as she dragged him to the front door. She lifted him off the ground by his arm and leaned over close to Henry's ear.

"If your arm isn't broken then I'm going to break it for you," said Marsha.

When she said that, Henry started losing his confidence in his ability to determine if his arm was broken or not.

"*Maybe it isn't broken yet,*" he thought.

After he had the X-Ray, time started moving exceptionally slow. He impatiently waited to hear if his arm was broken or not. He could tell that Marsha was tired, and she still didn't think that it could be conceivably possible that his arm was broken.

Finally, the doctor came in and put the X-Ray up against a light.

"Well, it looks like Henry is right. His arm is broken. He has a fracture on his humerus bone right there," said the doctor as he pointed at the X-Ray.

Henry smiled with a sigh of relief. He hadn't ever heard of the humerus bone, but he didn't find it humorous when he broke it. He looked at Marsha to see her jaw drop. Guilt and remorse overwhelmed her heart.

When they got home, Marsha gave Henry a glass of milk and a cookie.

"It is after midnight. You can stay up until your dad gets home," said Marsha.

Harold was working afternoons and didn't get home until well after midnight. Henry had never been allowed to stay up until after 12 o'clock in the night. He relished every second of Marsha's affection after she learned that his arm was really broken.

When Harold got home, Henry just told him that he fell off the porch. He didn't want to mention that he had tried to kiss Lisa. During the previous day, he had already figured out that it wasn't a good idea to try and kiss a girl without first asking. He didn't want to hear his father tell him the same thing he had already learned. Lisa had taught him a good lesson.

A couple of days later, Lisa's mother brought her to their house with a wrapped present. Henry opened it and was delighted to get a fire truck.

"Wow, thanks," said Henry, as he thought about how blessings always seemed to follow pain. He didn't find very much enjoyment in playing with toys, but he appreciated that someone thought enough of him to give him a gift.

"You're welcome," said Lisa.

Henry smiled. "*There is that feeling again. I sure wish I could kiss you,*" thought Henry.

Marsha and Harold gave Henry his first used bicycle and it wasn't even his birthday or Christmas. Henry asked Harold if he could use his tools to remove the training wheels after a few minutes of riding the bike. Marsha was worried that Henry might break his other arm, but Harold helped him remove the training wheels anyway. Henry had already been thinking about how he needed to stay balanced. He pushed the bike with his good arm to build up some speed and then leaped on and started pedaling. Off he went down the sidewalk. When he ran out of sidewalk, he jumped off the bike.

After a couple trips back and forth down the sidewalk, Henry mastered making a one-armed turn, coming to a stop, and starting from a complete stop.

"Can I ride in the street?" Henry asked Harold.

"Okay, but you have to stay on the side and stop at the curb if a car is coming. You can't ride near 9th Avenue because it has too much traffic and don't go further than the Helder's house," replied Harold.

Henry followed the rules and felt happy to have new boundaries. His bubble just got a little bit bigger.

Life was good.

CHAPTER 7

Library or Bathroom?

"This isn't a bathroom. It is a library. You need to be quiet and go somewhere else," whispered Margaret.

She put her finger in front of her mouth like any good librarian would. Margaret and Tammy stood defiantly in the middle of the only bathroom in the house.

Henry looked around at the books stacked all over the bathroom. Margaret and Tammy had put forth a lot of effort relocating all the books they found elsewhere. He shifted his gaze back to Margaret and Tammy.

"It almost looks like a little library," thought Henry. *"But I need to pee."*

"This is not a library. It is a bathroom. Please leave so I can pee because this is the only bathroom we have," requested Henry. "You can play after I finish."

"Shh! You have to be quiet in the library!" shouted Tammy.

Henry stood motionless. He looked at Margaret and Tammy as he wondered what was wrong with them. Playing pretend games wasn't of interest to Henry. It confused him that other kids seemingly enjoyed an alternative world outside of reality.

"Go outside like you normally do!" Margaret shouted, no longer whispering.

Henry briefly thought that maybe he should just go outside like he ordinarily did do. It was more fun peeing outside instead of trying to not make a mess on the toilet seat.

He was also contemplating the option of resorting to his sister's tactics by going to snitch to his mother. He decided instead to take control of the situation himself. He gleefully pulled down his pants and commenced peeing all over the books stacked on the toilet, the bathroom floor and purposely peed just a little bit on Margaret and Tammy. It felt good to teach the girls a lesson.

"I'm telling on you!" screamed Margaret and Tammy simultaneously. They ran from the bathroom and headed down the steps to find Marsha.

Henry patiently waited in the bathroom as he formulated a plan of how to use the pretend game to make a new reality. Marsha followed Margaret and Tammy as they ran back up the stairs to the bathroom. They smiled and stuck their tongues out at Henry, in happy anticipation of watching Marsha get the revenge they sought.

"*Watching Henry get a good spanking will be perfect,*" they thought.

As soon as Marsha entered the bathroom, Henry initiated his own pretending game.

"I'm sorry Mom, I couldn't hold it anymore. They told me it was a library and wouldn't let me pee. I couldn't hold it anymore ...," he said sniffling like he was going to cry, and he was the victim.

His pretend act worked. Marsha turned her attention to the girls.

"This is a bathroom. Clean up the mess and go find somewhere else to play librarian," said Marsha. She gave the girls a stern look.

"What? That isn't fair! He peed all over everything on purpose!" exclaimed Margaret. "He even peed on us! Look Mom! My shirt is soaking wet!"

Margaret's argument was a reasonable one since it was exactly what happened. But it didn't work.

"Don't you raise your voice at me Miss Missy," said Marsha. "You get this mess cleaned up right now or *else*." *Else* meant a lot of different things. None of them were ever consequences that Henry or Margaret enjoyed. So, Margaret and Tammy reluctantly started cleaning up the mess and preparing to find somewhere else to play.

Henry felt bad that he got his sister in trouble, but he thought that it might teach her a lesson to not make the bathroom a playroom. More importantly, he hoped that she might learn to not mess with her little brother. He didn't like people messing with him. Margaret and Tammy both stuck their tongues out at him again when Marsha turned around to leave. He felt like he probably deserved what they intended to achieve with their tongues but stuck out tongues didn't have much effect on Henry.

Henry speculated that he got the better of Margaret this time, but his conscience was playing tug of war in his brain. One part telling him great job getting away with something and fooling his mother, and another part telling him that he was in the wrong. Henry tried to discern what his conscience was saying.

"Is it right to fake emotions to get my way? Is it right to twist a story to manipulate my mom to teach Margaret a lesson?" he wondered.

His conscience couldn't tell him yes or no.

Life was confusing sometimes.

CHAPTER 8

Door to Door Salesman

Margaret and Tammy blissfully painted rocks with colorful flowers and peace and love signs. They displayed the rocks on a table by the street in front of their house.

"What are you doing?" Henry asked. "I like your rocks. They look nice."

"We are painting rocks and are going to sell them," said Margaret.

Henry was eager to make amends after the library bathroom incident. Margaret was still angry at him for peeing on her and ruining her playtime with Tammy. He decided to offer her some help.

"How will anyone know that you are selling them?" asked Henry.

"Oh, they will know because they will see us," replied Margaret.

Henry provided what he thought was good advice.

"Why don't you put up a big sign that says rocks for sale? Then people might stop to buy some," said Henry. "If you don't have a sign nobody will know the rocks are for sale."

Margaret was exasperated with her little brother always telling her what to do. The painted rock stand was her and Tammy's business. They didn't want Henry involved.

"Give you a quarter if you leave," said Margaret. She had started using money to bribe Henry when she wanted to get rid of him. Henry had just wanted to help, but if his sister wanted to give him a quarter then he would accept it. He'd have taken a nickel or just left if she asked him politely. A quarter was a lot of money to Henry.

He put the quarter in his pocket, picked up some rocks from the driveway, and headed off.

"Where are you going with those rocks?" Margaret asked.

"I'm going to sell them," said Henry.

"Ha ha ha," laughed Tammy. "They aren't even painted! Nobody will buy rocks that aren't painted. You're stupid!"

Henry was determined to show the girls that he wasn't the idiot they thought he was. He walked off to prove that he could sell rocks better than the girls. Next time, maybe they would listen to his advice when he tried to help them out.

He headed down the street. He decided to start with the older people that might have the most interest.

"Hi Henry, what are you up to today?" asked Mr. Thompson, as Henry walked up to the front porch. Mr. Thompson was sitting on a swinging chair. He was a World War II veteran and worked at a local plant. He enjoyed Henry's company and sometimes liked to play the guitar and sing.

"Hi Mr. Thompson. I'm selling rocks. Would you like to buy some?"

"How much are they?" asked Mr. Thompson.

Henry didn't have any idea of how much to ask for the rocks. They were free to anyone that wanted to collect them. The thought of selling them seemed absurd to Henry, but he had learned that what seemed nonsensical to him often made perfect since to others. If people would buy painted rocks from his sister, then they would probably be stupid enough to buy ordinary rocks. If they wanted to paint them, they could do it themselves. At the end of the day, they were rocks.

"Depends on how much you would like to pay for them," responded Henry.

Mr. Thompson had a look at the rocks and offered 10 cents for a rock. Henry didn't want to take too much of Mr. Thompson's money for ordinary rocks. So, he offered to give him 3 rocks for 25 cents. It seemed like a good idea to accumulate money faster.

"One dollar every four houses will be a lot better than 40 cents," thought Henry. *"And the rocks will be cheaper. Instead of 10 cents they will only cost 8 point 3, 3, ... forever ending 3's.... cents."*

"Helen! Henry's selling rocks. Bring me a quarter so we can buy some!" Mr. Thompson called to his wife. Henry waited patiently as he thought about how it was impossible to divide 25 cents into 3 exact pieces.

"Good thing I don't have to share the money with other people," he thought.

Mrs. Thompson came outside with some cookies and a quarter. She knew Henry liked cookies. Henry smiled and thanked Mrs. Thompson. He ate a cookie and asked Mr. Thompson some questions. Mr. Thompson liked to talk. Henry liked to listen and ask questions. As a result, they got along well. After spending some time with the Thompsons, Mr. Thompson started getting excited and then overly agitated about the communists. Henry decided to say goodbye. He headed off to the next house and then the next and the next. He skipped Albert's house because he didn't want to look foolish in front of Albert or Tyrone. He knew they would think he was crazy. He would have thought they were insane if they tried to sell him ordinary rocks. After a few houses, he gathered some more rocks to sell and continued knocking on doors. He soon ran out of houses where he knew the occupants, but Henry had gained a lot of confidence as a door-to-door salesman. Thus, he moved onward into uncharted territory.

"Get out of here kid! I'm not buying rocks from you. Where are your parents? You're too little to be out by yourself!" shouted an angry man.

"My dad is at work and my mom is at home. Have a nice day Sir," Henry responded. He made a mental note of what the man looked like and where he lived so he'd know not to visit again. Henry didn't enjoy talking to people that were always angry. He went to the next house wondering why some people seemed to like getting angry and being mean. Henry preferred to be happy. At the next house a lady answered the door holding a baby.

"Hi, my name is Henry," he said. He smiled at the baby.

"I can't tell if it is a boy or a girl, but it looks just like a little lizard," thought Henry. He knew that smiling at the reptilian looking baby would get a smile out of her mother. Henry liked it when people were happy and smiling. He knew better than telling people what he really thought.

"I'm selling rocks. Want to buy some?" he asked.

The lady smiled. She called to her husband to come to the front door to buy some ordinary rocks. Some people purchased rocks and others didn't. Henry advanced through Milton going door to door selling his merchandise. He liked meeting people. Selling rocks gave him a good excuse to get to know people in other neighborhoods. He met a few people that he didn't like and a lot of others that he did like.

After a while, Henry was getting tired. He struggled to keep his pants up with the weight of all the quarters in his pockets. He decided that the next house would be his last. An old lady answered the door. She was surprised to have a visitor. When Henry told her he was selling rocks, she asked him if he would like to come inside so she could get a better look at them. Henry was thinking that he could use another cookie. So, he followed her through the front door. He knew he wasn't supposed to be going into the homes of strangers. He wasn't even allowed to be talking to them.

"What is the harm if my parents aren't around to stop me. I can talk to whoever I want to talk to and there won't be any consequences if my parents don't know what I'm doing," thought Henry.

When he walked inside it was dreadfully dark. The house had an unfamiliar appalling odor that smelled nothing like cookies. Whatever it was, Henry didn't like the strange smell.

He saw a wedding picture on the mantel of the fireplace.

"Is that your husband?" Henry asked.

The old lady was despondent as she told him that her husband Edwin passed away 12 years before from a heart attack. She had a look on her face that convinced Henry that she must have really loved her husband. It was evident that she missed him a lot.

Henry started asking questions. It didn't take long before the old lady brought out a view-master. She showed Henry pictures from past vacations that she had taken with her husband. Henry had never seen a view-master before. He was astonished when he looked at the first picture. When he looked through the eye pieces, he felt like he was peering into the past. He appreciated getting to see all the pictures and learning more about all the places that he'd never been too or even heard about before. The old lady told him about Old Faithful in Yellowstone National Park and other places that were interesting. Peering into the view-master felt virtually like being on vacation with the old woman. Henry felt like he was traveling back in time. The old lady was traveling with him to a time when she had been much happier.

He saw children in the pictures with the old lady and her husband.

"Who are those children? Are they your children?" asked Henry.

"Yes, they are my children," said the old lady with a frown.

"Where are they now?" asked Henry, eager to learn more about them.

The old lady didn't want to talk much about her children. He asked a couple more questions and learned that they didn't come to visit her anymore. When he noticed she was heartbroken, he changed the subject. He resumed talking about her husband and all the other things in the pictures like strange animals and scenery. She was overjoyed talking about anything other than her children.

After a while, Henry started thinking that his mother might be getting worried about him. She didn't like him disappearing for very long. If the old lady was sad because her children never visited her, his own mother would probably be getting worried that he hadn't been home for most of the day. He knew he had broken two of his parent's rules. He went further away from the house than he was allowed, and he was talking to strangers.

"It was nice to meet you. I better leave now. My mom will be expecting me to be home," said Henry.

"Oh, okay. You better go. She will be worried about you. It is getting late. My name is Mrs. Washington. What is your name?" she asked.

"I'm Henry," he replied. He turned and headed for the front door.

On the way home, he realized that he had forgotten to sell any rocks to Mrs. Washington. He tossed the remaining rocks by the street amongst other rocks and held up his quarter filled pants with both hands. It was getting dark. Henry didn't have a watch and he wasn't very good with time. It seemed that time went too fast when he was having fun and lasted forever when he wanted it to go fast. As he got close to his house, he looked to see if his sister Margaret was still selling rocks. He knew that she had probably given up a long time ago. He had wanted to show Margaret how successful he had been in selling rocks. He wanted to share the money he made with Margaret and Tammy. If it hadn't been for them, he wouldn't have ever thought about selling rocks.

He saw Mrs. Thompson waving her arms at him from up the street.

"Henry, where have you been? Your mother has been worried sick about you! She is looking for you!" shouted Mrs. Thompson. "You know better than running off!"

Henry saw Marsha frantically coming off another neighbor's porch. He could tell that she had been actively searching for him for a while. Fortunately, Marsha was happier to see him back home and safe than she was angry that he had been gone for several hours and broken her rules. Margaret's friend Tammy had gone home. Henry didn't get to show Margaret and Tammy all the money he made. Marsha heated up some leftovers for Henry and Margaret was already in bed sleeping.

Henry slept well that night. He was a happy kid. Life was exciting, and every day was a new adventure.

Life was good.

CHAPTER 9

Another Kind of Salesman

While Henry was sleeping, another salesman drove into Milton. He parked his car in the shadow of a local gas station. Hank Wilson didn't sell 'ordinary' or 'painted' rocks. He sold drugs without a doctor's prescription. The thought of using the drugs he sold would have been a ridiculous concept to Hank. He knew firsthand what the drugs did to people, and he didn't have any inkling to use them himself. He took advantage of the gullible people that were too blind to see their future after drugs. He had become the best friend of addicts. They understood the consequences of their drugs of choice but lacked a time machine to escape their deadly grasp. The addicts in Milton were his best customers, and Hank was always on the lookout for future clients.

The US Treasury Department had created the Federal Bureau of Narcotics (FBN) in 1930 to combat drugs in the population. For over thirty years, the FBN had increasingly criminalized drug use with penalties that included eliminating suspended sentences or probation and even the death penalty for selling drugs to minors. As they increased the number of laws and severity of punishment, they ended up creating a larger number of criminals. Every new law resulted in more law breakers. The drug dealers won the war against the FBN's fear tactics. Greed won the war with the drug dealers. Ignorance won the war with the addicts. The consequences intended to frighten people from using drugs achieved practically nothing. The only way to fix the problem was to fix the ignorance. Fixing human stupidity wasn't an easy task.

Henry's parent's generation were told that illegal drugs caused acne, blindness, and sterility. Marijuana usage was blamed for bizarre cases of murder, insanity, and sex crimes. They grew up listening to the FBN propaganda of myths and horror stories about drugs. Rather than educating people with the truth about drug abuse, the FBN fabricated far-fetched stories that resulted in most people not believing the government's warnings about drugs. They fooled the stupidest people, but their scare tactics failed to stop illegal drug use. Most people became observant enough to notice differences between out of the ordinary warnings and facts. Unfortunately, many of the smarter ones couldn't discern which parental warnings were factual or myths. The bliss they found from falling for drugs was temporary. It was better to be ignorant enough to believe all the scare tactics than it was to regard all of them as lies.

The 1960s had given birth to a rebellious movement that popularized drugs. Marijuana became fashionable on college campuses. Hippies sought to expand their minds by taking trips outside of reality with LSD and other hallucinogens. Ivy league professors urged the world to try LSD and expand their minds to a higher level of consciousness. Thousands and thousands of people eagerly followed their instructions in hopes of finding an advanced level of spirituality. Milton had hippies as well as soldiers that had returned from the Vietnam War with marijuana and heroin habits. It was a good time to be a drug salesman. The demand for drugs was skyrocketing.

President Lyndon B. Johnson and his administration recognized the sharp rise in drug abuse. They passed a Narcotics Addict Rehabilitation Act in 1966 in hopes of helping the addicts overcome their addictions. Although drug use was still considered a crime, the Act identified being an addict as a form of mental illness. Similarly, they called homosexuality a mental illness that needed to be treated with drugs and counseling. Anybody that didn't conform to the established view of how people should behave needed to be treated to obey the law with an appropriate behavior as deemed necessary by the State. The attempt to rehabilitate addicts lacked the funding to make a dent in the ever-increasing demand for drugs. Many of the drug salesmen got rich. Hank Wilson wasn't an exception. Hank had the most successful business in Milton.

The drug epidemic became severe enough that President Richard Nixon took it a step further. He declared a war on drugs. The Nixon administration recognized that if there is a demand, somebody would always be willing to take the risks to meet the demand. Dealing drugs was a lucrative business. Desperate people were eager to chase fast money. Instead of fighting the war to shut off the supply at the source, they understood that the only way to really fight the war was to change the masses desire to want the drugs in the first place. They knew they had to convince the masses that doing drugs had severe consequences for the individual. If the desire dissipated, then there wouldn't be a demand. The drug dealers would be out of business.

Soon after declaring a war on drugs, President Nixon elected to not follow the advice of intelligent experts or his own logic of fighting the populations desire to use drugs. The Drug Enforcement Agency (DEA) was created and soon after went to Mexico to stop the source. It was easier to blame the Mexicans than acknowledge that the problem was in America. The war on drugs had commenced. The US government spent hundreds of millions of dollars. A lot of people would get rich fighting the war on drugs. They managed to stop much of the marijuana from crossing the border. They also consequently halted large quantities of Mexican crops that rotted at the border. Unfortunately, people in America had weed seeds and Colombia quickly replaced Mexico as the US's preferred external supplier of marijuana. American's grew marijuana in their houses, back yards, and even national parks. The DEA would spend countless amounts of taxpayer money to find and destroy the weed fields as local growers continued finding new locations to grow it. Drugs continued to cross the border in low flying Cessna U206 airplanes. Soon after, they would be carrying cocaine which was significantly more profitable per kilo.

One hundred years before, Sigmund Freud's initial belief that cocaine was a miraculous wonder drug for depression and pain had been masked by the pretense that it wasn't addictive. Within a decade, Freud's reputation as a physician would deteriorate as cocaine addiction and overdoses began happening all around the world. Freud, like many others would learn that things weren't always as they initially seemed. The first impression of drugs like cocaine would continue deceiving others.

Hollywood would give the drug cartels and dealers free marketing with multitudes of movies that glorified criminality and drug use. Hollywood's propaganda and myths that promoted drug use would be just as far-fetched as the government's propaganda. The producers did a much better job in making their propaganda seem believable in the guise of entertainment. American citizens would finance the propaganda by flocking to theaters around the country. They would leave the theaters brainwashed into thinking that drugs would add meaning and happiness to their own boring lives.

"Maybe I was right," thought Nixon as he scratched his head. *"If you stop the supply then somebody else will just keep filling the void. We are fighting a war that we can't win. The problem is the demand for drugs."*

Fortunately, a lot of private citizens tried to fight the war against drugs by educating potential drug users. James Brown's 1972 song "King Heroin" did more for the war against drugs than 40 years of effort from the government. His logic was to just sing about the truth. He sang about how heroin was a deadly killer that would make schoolboys forget to do their homework and men to cheat on their wives. Heroin would turn young girls into a prostitutes and men into thieves just to get their next fix. Heroin didn't care about race, religion, or sex. It made people feel good and then destroyed their lives.

Hank Wilson didn't listen to James Brown. He had never even heard of the song titled "King Heroin". He grew up in the South being passed back and forth between his divorced parents. Hank's mother finally found the strength to get away from Joe Wilson's regular beatings. Hank either lived with his mother in Huntsville, Alabama or with his biological father in a small town in Southern Louisiana. In Southern Louisiana he developed an ear for the same swamp billy music that his father listened too. As a teenager, he became infatuated with any music from the Southern Rebel Records that specialized in music for Cajun white people that identified themselves as segregationists. Some of his favorites were "Kajun Ku Klux Klan", "Some *Niggers* Never Die (They Just Smell That Way)" and "*Coon*town". Hank was a racist in training from a young age.

In Alabama, Hank had been in the 6th grade when his elementary school became the first integrated school in Alabama. Young Hank had been confident that Governor George Wallace would be able to stop the federal efforts to integrate schools. Despite Governor Wallace's vain attempts of personally standing in front of Livingston Auditorium trying to block black students from entering the University of Alabama, he would ultimately lose his power struggle with the federal government. Governor Wallace's and Hank's hopes of a segregated society were slowly vanishing despite the 'Lost Cause' seeds planted with post-Civil War efforts of the daughters of the south and other non-profit organizations that attempted to justify the southern war efforts. A small portion of black Americans shared Hank's desire for a segregated society. They also wanted to retain a divided country where blacks could have their own society side by side with a white one. Neither view fit the founding fathers' vision of *'E Pluribus Unum'* (out of many one) mentality. Both groups had set their minds on a view that out of many would be two divided groups. They didn't understand the consequences of living in a divided nation. A divided nation by definition was a country of unequals in constant conflict.

Gloria Jones walked into Hank's classroom as the first black student to be integrated into an elementary school in Alabama. She held her head high in defiance and did her best to nod respectfully to her new white classmates. Some of them gave welcoming nods in return while many of the others looked at her in disgust.

"It won't be long before Alabama is run by Martin Luther King and a bunch of other commies," whispered one of Hank's classmates.

"Not in my lifetime," said Hank in disgust. "The two things that I hate most are commies and *fucking niggers*. We should just kill all of them."

Martin Luther King's approach of overcoming evil with good had been working. The non-violent protests of black students at segregated lunch counters in North Carolina morphed into a national movement that spread throughout college towns across the country. People of all shades and colors launched more peaceful demonstrations on interstate buses throughout the South. They called it the Freedom Rides and non-violently pushed back against segregation in waiting rooms, bus stations and bathrooms.

The white southerners that identified as being segregationists used the opposite approach of Martin Luther King and others pro-integration believers. Several local police departments colluded with the KKK to fight what they viewed as evil with all the evil they could muster. They fire-bombed the Freedom Bus. They beat and tortured the protesters. People across the nation and world watched in shock as Birmingham police used fire hoses and dogs on peaceful marchers. Their brutal treatment made the front pages of newspapers across the US as they violently arrested more than 1000 peaceful protesters.

The police and KKK brutality airing on national television helped the Civil Rights Movement gain momentum as more and more citizens sided against the segregationists. Non-violence was a more powerful sword than violence when swaying the support of the people. The Interstate Commerce Commission issued nationwide regulations that prohibited segregation on buses and train stations in 1961. The violence in the south even shocked the federal government. It gave birth to the 1964 Civil Rights Act which outlawed discrimination on the grounds of race and gender. Most civilized people didn't understand why an Act was required for what they deemed to be human decency. Ignorant and uncivilized people would protest that the Act infringed on their own personal liberties. Their argument was that discrimination was their God given right. Soon after, voting rights were changed to allow blacks and women to vote, and the Supreme Court legalized mixed-race marriages.

Despite the significant strides made in the 1960s, many civil rights activists weren't satisfied with the progress. By the time Hank was graduating from high school, many restless black Americans had started becoming more militant as their successes in advancements for civil rights gave them a scent of victory. Martin Luther King's peaceful and non-violent demonstrations were too much of a struggle and slow paced for their taste. They lacked the virtue of patience. They wanted an immediate rapid change and were upset about all the money the government was spending on the war in Vietnam instead of for the poor and disadvantaged. The sentiment was spreading throughout black communities in cities across the country. The assassination of Martin Luther King elevated their anger. The increased tensions escalated to rioting across the country which further amplified the friction between both sides. The former Attorney General and Democratic Presidential Candidate, Robert F. Kennedy was assassinated in Los Angeles, California as opposition to the Vietnam War continued to spread across the country's college campuses. Tension and division regained its ugly foothold within the masses.

After high school, Hank immediately joined the Marine Corps. He wanted nothing more in life other than to go to Vietnam to fight. He had a sense of obligation to do his part to stop the communist expansion. Despite his hatred for people of other races, Hank felt privileged and fortunate to live in a country with the freedoms he enjoyed. He was grateful to be an American. He was patriotic and considered himself to be a patriot. His country was calling for men like him. He felt the same calling to serve as did his ancestors. His father had served in Korea, his grand-father had died heroically in World War I, and his great-great grandfather had fought for the Confederacy in the Civil War and lost. Hank still wanted to win the war his great-great grandfather had lost. He was a lost cause.

Hank was a staunch supporter for George Wallace in his run for president in 1968. George Wallace had retained an inkling of hope that the southern states could win the power struggle with the federal government to retain a segregated society. Hank shared that hope for division. In the 1968 presidential election, George Wallace promised voters generous increases in Social Security and Medicare. He wouldn't win the presidential candidacy, but he would win five states in the Deep South. His tactics of manipulating racial and social issues to appeal to millions of alienated white voters would be the instruction playbook for many future presidential candidates that would be elected as presidents. Richard Nixon became the new president after winning the tumultuous 1968 election. He had promised to restore law and order in the nation's cities and to be the leader that the country needed to end the Vietnam War. The words that came out of his mouth persuaded the masses to vote for him. He told them what they wanted to hear.

Hank was unpleasantly disappointed when he started his basic training at Camp Lejeune, North Carolina. Most of the other Marines lacked his motivation and vigor to serve their country in Vietnam. Not everyone wanted to stop the red invasion of communism and somehow obtain world peace by killing for it. Hank had chosen the infantry as his military occupational specialty (MOS) code. The infantry appealed to Hank as the most honorable and courageous occupation in the military. He loved his country enough to die for it. Many of his fellow infantry Marines had either been drafted or were poor and uneducated. They chose the Marines because they didn't have very many options. Numerous other Americans had gone to Canada or became professional students to avoid being drafted. Others signed up so they could select more desirable non-combat MOS's. Hank wanted to be on the front lines. Right or wrong, he was ready to die for his country.

For the first time in his life, Hank Wilson was in a small minority group. He was a white Marine that wanted to be a Marine. Americans were becoming increasingly non-supportive of the Vietnam War and racial tensions had escalated significantly. Many of the black Marines were on edge and it didn't take much to set them off. Most of them had looked up to Martin Luther King. He had given them hope. His assassination by a white man had caused them to lose hope in the civil rights movement. As far as they were concerned, Martin Luther King had been killed by a white racist society. It was the same institutionalized racism they found in the Marines. Their white counterparts were no happier than they were and many of them exacerbated the tensions. When some white Marines learned about the assassination of Martin Luther King, they made Klan uniforms and paraded around with a Confederate flag. Others couldn't resist to express that they were overly joyous with the news.

On July 20th, 1969, Hank went to the Camp Lejeune theatre to watch the Apollo 11 landing on the moon. He and his friends stood watching silently as an intense physical thrill penetrated their bodies. Some of them had tears of joy and excitement after Neil Armstrong's famous lunar landing statement. The giant leap had seemed so surreal that it was almost unbelievable. As they walked back to the barracks, they were all laughing and felt proud to be United States Marines. Somehow, they thought the moon landing would make the world a better place. The USA had beat the communists to the moon.

As Hank and his friends strolled around the last corner heading towards their barracks, a group of black Marines approached them from the opposite direction. Months before, racial tensions had escalated into an explosion of racial violence with black Marines rioting on the base. The rioting left one white Marine dead and multiple others were seriously injured. After the violence, additional lighting had been added in large and secluded areas. All the lights were kept on throughout the night. The lighting hadn't eased the tensions and even seasoned combat veterans were fearful of walking around at night. They were more afraid of each other than they were of the Vietcong.

The black Marines glared angrily at Hank and his friends as they passed. One of them brushed shoulders with Hank's friend Walt.

"What's your problem *splib*?!" shouted Walt.

"We have just as much right to this space as you do!" said the black Marine. He stepped towards Walt and gave him a shove.

Walt immediately retaliated with a punch to the face. A black marine tackled Walt to the ground and pummeled him with a flurry of punches to the face. Hank picked up a brick without hesitation. He smashed it against the back of the black Marine's head. The Marine fell limp on top of Walt.

"Hey! Stop what you are doing! Get on the ground now!" a voice shouted from the distance.

Hank looked up to see a racially mixed patrol group running towards them. The patrol groups had been initiated to help ease tensions and prevent more trouble. The Marine that was hit in the head didn't die but it killed Hank's career as a Marine. Hank Wilson received a dishonorable discharge. Not getting to go to Vietnam to fight for his country wasn't the only consequence. Hank wouldn't be able to vote or obtain a bank loan, and he knew that finding a civilian job would be a long and arduous task. A dishonorable discharge was universally regarded as just as shameful as a prison sentence. Hank knew that he would have a permanent record that would follow him the rest of his life. He was too stubborn and ashamed to return home defeated.

After Hank's court martial, he wanted to get as far away from Camp Lejeune as he could. He caught a bus to Charlotte, North Carolina and stepped into a bar to try and drown his misery. He sat at a bar stool staring at his third beer. He felt useless and depressed with the last remnants of hope of a future being sucked out of him.

"Hi, so what brings you here today?" asked a stranger that sat down on the bar stool next to him.

Hank glanced at the man and then redirected his eyes back to his beer. He swirled his beer as the aroma of sadness perpetuated the darkness of the bar. The stranger continued to sit next to Hank. He was apathetic to the silence that would make most people feel uncomfortable.

"It's okay to be depressed," said the stranger. "Whatever it is that has got you down isn't the end of the world."

Hank flashed him a look of uncertainty. He stared straight ahead for a minute before taking a deep breath.

"I ... I was just kicked out of the Marines," said Hank holding back tears. "All I wanted to do was go fight for my country. I don't have a job.

I'm out of money and I can't go home because I am a disgrace to my family. I hate my life and just want to disappear."

"I'm sorry to hear that," said the stranger. "You seem like a good man."

The stranger was a good listener. Hank needed someone that was attentive enough to acknowledge him as a fellow human being. The stranger didn't care about Hank's predicament. He had come to the bar to find someone that felt down on their luck, overlooked, and unimportant. He was moving up the ranks of drug dealing. He needed recruits that would be willing to risk everything they had to sell drugs. Hank was a perfect candidate, and the stranger couldn't have been any happier.

It wasn't long before Hank found a passion. Selling drugs was easy. He made far more money than he did when he was a Marine. He knew that if he ever got caught, the consequences would be hundreds of times worse than a dishonorable discharge. But the stranger taught him well. The stranger was just as good at finding desperate crooked policemen as he was at finding down and out anguished civilians to sell his drugs.

The stranger was from New York City, he had learned how to draw police officers into corrupting relationships where they turned a blind eye to the offenders they had pledged to control. He traveled through small to medium sized towns across multiple states. He frequented the bars and donut shops looking for policemen to befriend. He had learned that no police department in the country was completely free of misconduct. Every human had the capacity for evil and good and all of them were selfish and greedy to an extent. People were people regardless of what uniform they wore. Every police department had to either fight or accept the bad behavior of their personnel. All of them were essentially independent entities without governance. Nobody policed the police.

The stranger was a good actor. He used his charisma to win the trust of sheriffs or chiefs of police with relatively small police departments. The promise of quadrupling their salary for doing very little was too hard to resist for many of them. After they received cash in their pocket, lawmen were experts at keeping it a secret. Most of them didn't even tell their wives or closest friends. They even had a name for it. They called it the blue code of silence.

Chief of Police Fred Rodgers first met the stranger at the Milton Fire Departments annual ice cream social. The stranger had befriended two of his officers. It took him several months before he found the right time to make his sales pitch to Fred Rodgers. He had learned that Fred hated blacks almost as much as he did. He was struggling to feed his four children and finance his wife's addiction to Tupperware and Avon makeup parties. He also desperately wanted a fishing boat.

"What if I told you that you could make thousands of dollars a month and have a good reason to lock up half of the *niggers* in town?" asked the stranger.

"Ha, making money for locking up *niggers*," laughed Fred. "If it sounds too good to be true then it ain't true."

"Your wife could buy everything Tupperware and Avon have to sell and you could buy that fishin' boat that you deserve," responded the stranger.

"Yeah, right? For doing what?" asked Fred.

"I already told you," said the stranger. "You would just be locking up *niggers*."

"Who would pay me to lock up *niggers* and what would be the reason to lock them up in the first place?" asked Fred.

"I would pay you and give you a reason," said the stranger.

"What would be the reason?" asked Fred.

"Drugs," said the stranger. "I'll pay you and tell you who has drugs. All you have to do is arrest them."

A couple of weeks later, Hank Wilson had a free ticket to sell drugs in Milton. The Milton police department turned a blind eye. Fred Rodgers got a new boat. His wife was happier than ever with her increasing collection of Tupperware and Avon products. She was elated to be the envy of all her friends. Her friend's jealousy convinced them to overspend their husbands' paychecks which resulted in arguments and conflicts behind closed doors. Fred would end up arresting one of the husbands for domestic abuse. He had slapped his wife a couple of times for not being able to understand that money didn't grow on trees. Hank would tip off the police with who was buying drugs from him and they made arrests of their choosing. After a year, the police would make even more money by making drug busts and selling the drugs back to Hank directly from the department's vault.

Nobody would ever know the stranger's real name. He kept himself far away from the front lines. Fred Rodgers and his officers would regret their decision, but they would go to their graves with their secret.

Most often, the worst transgressions occur behind closed doors that are out of sight and mind of the people.

CHAPTER 10

Igloos and Flower Bouquets

"Let's build an igloo!" shouted Fred.

"What's an igloo?" asked Henry.

Fred was two years older than Henry and Albert. They had been crawling around making tunnels through the several feet of snow amassed on the ground. It was the biggest snowstorm the boys had ever seen. Albert and Henry listened intently as Fred explained how people called Eskimos cut out big chunks of ice to make houses that they called igloos.

"The snow is too soft to cut into ice," said Albert.

"We can make ice," said Henry. "Let's get some 5-gallon buckets from the garage."

Henry showed them how to put snow in 5-gallon buckets, compact it and add a little water to make it hard ice. Fred was the only one that knew what an igloo was supposed to look like. He supervised the positioning of the ice blocks to build the igloo walls. They used some wood and metal stakes to support the snow and ice on the igloo roof.

They had a single entrance and a small window that doubled as an emergency escape route. They packed fresh snow on the exterior and smoothed it out to make it look exactly how Fred thought an igloo should look. Inside the igloo, the boys felt cozy and warm. They were all proud of their achievement. Fred's mother even came outside and took some photos of them with their igloo with her Polaroid camera. After the pictures, it was starting to get dark, so Albert had to go home. Albert wasn't allowed to play outside after it got dark.

Henry and Fred decided that it would be fun to spend the night in the igloo. They found some old blankets that they put inside. In the comforts of the igloo, they discussed a strategy to convince their parents that it would be safe to sleep in it overnight.

"They will tell us that it might collapse on us," said Henry. "We can tell them it won't fall down because it will get colder tonight. Then they will say we will freeze to death."

"We can tell them we will start a fire to keep warm," said Fred. "The Eskimos make fires inside that make the igloos harder ice and more structurally sound."

"Good idea but your parents aren't Eskimos or engineers," said Henry. "They won't believe that. They will think that fire will melt the ice and make it fall on us. We can tell them that we will get more blankets and come inside if it starts getting too cold."

"Good idea," said Fred.

"Hey, what are you idiots doing in there?!" another boy shouted from the outside of the igloo. Henry and Fred crawled out of the igloo to find Greg. He lived next door to Fred and was with his cousin Billy. Greg was the same age as Fred and liked picking on other kids Henry's age or anyone else that was much smaller than himself.

"It's an igloo. We are going to spend the night in it," said Henry.

"No, you are not. We are going to knock your stupid igloo down!" shouted Greg.

Billy started kicking the igloo. Henry grabbed him by his winter coat and flung him to the ground. Greg tackled Henry and they started fighting. The much bigger Greg got the best of Henry.

"I'm telling!" shouted Fred, as he ran for the house. Greg gave a final punch with his right elbow to Henry's face before he took off running with Billy.

Fred's parents quickly came to the door just as Henry was throwing another snowball at the retreating boys. Fred's mother had Henry come inside. She wiped the blood off his face and put some cotton in his nose to stop the bleeding.

"You are bigger than both of those boys Fred. You need to learn to stand up for yourself!" said Fred's father. He looked at Fred disappointingly.

Henry hadn't heard that one before. Most parents were telling their kids not to fight. They instructed them to do exactly what Fred had done.

"*Which one is it?*" thought Henry. "*Do we go get a parent or fight back?*"

Henry tended to agree with Fred's father. Snitching was for sissies. He preferred to fight back. Fighting back was the manly thing to do. Other kids normally had more respect for kids that didn't always go running to find someone else to protect them. Henry preferred to try and solve problems himself. He didn't like using adults as a crutch.

"We are going to spend the night in the igloo," said Henry. He decided to tell Fred's parents what they were going to do instead of asking. The tactic often worked well with his own parents and other adults. He also hoped that they might feel sorry for them after wiping the blood off his face instead of being overly concerned about spending the night in an igloo.

"Oh no, you're not sleeping outside in an igloo. You will freeze to death," said Fred's mom.

"We could get more blankets and we will come inside if it gets too cold," said Fred on cue.

"No. You boys aren't going to sleep outside in an igloo," affirmed Fred's dad.

Henry headed home. He was happy that at least they managed to keep Greg and Billy from knocking their igloo down. He smiled with the thought that it would still be there the next day. His smile vanished as he remembered how depressed his mother had been for the last couple of days. Her younger brother Frank's helicopter had been shot down in Vietnam. Frank had been killed. Henry had been sad when he first heard the news, but he didn't like feeling depressed. He concentrated on remembering everything that he liked about his uncle Frank. He would miss him, but he decided that he was just going to be grateful for having the opportunity to have had his uncle Frank in his life. He had a lot of good memories of spending time with him. He would remember them for the rest of his life.

"I loved Uncle Frank, but I don't think he would want us to be sad for long," thought Henry. *"If he is watching us now, I bet he would tell us to stop crying. He'd say that crying is alright for a little while but sooner or later you must get over it. Sooner is better than later."*

Henry tried to think of something he could do to cheer up Marsha when he got home.

"I definitely won't tell her that I got beat up by Greg," he thought. *"That would just make her even sadder."*

"That's it, flowers," thought Henry.

Henry had been trying his best to cheer Marsha up. No matter what he did, he wasn't able to give her any comfort. He'd smile and say nice things, but nothing he did helped. She liked flowers. He knew just how to prepare a nice bouquet of flowers even though it was the dead of winter.

He snuck into the house quietly to clean the rest of the blood from his face in the bathroom. After his face looked like he hadn't been beat up, he opened the door below the sink and pulled out the mysterious box full of plastic tubes inside of plastic wrappers. He read the letters on the box to himself T-A-M-P-O-N-S. When he pulled on a string, a mass of absorbent material came out of the plastic tube. When he put it in water it grew to triple the size. He had experimented with several of them. As far as he was concerned, they looked just like a flower after he put them in water. It interested him to see how they rapidly expanded when he put them in a sink filled with water.

He found a basket and started making flowers until it was full. All they needed was some color. He took the tampon flower bouquet into the kitchen and found the food coloring that Marsha used for coloring icing when she made cakes. A few squirts of red, yellow, green, and blue and the tampon flower bouquet came alive.

"*They are beautiful. Mom will love them,*" thought Henry.

He walked into the living room with a colossal smile and extended the colorful bouquet of tampon flowers out to Marsha. The television was showing demonstrators protesting the Vietnam war, but his parents weren't watching. Marsha was sitting on the couch with Harold. Harold had been doing his best to console and cheer her up. Henry smiled even more thinking that he had a solution that even Harold hadn't thought of.

"*Dad will be happy to see Mom smile again too,*" thought Henry.

When Marsha saw the flowers, her eyes grew big in trepidation. Henry waited patiently for her to smile and thank him for the flowers, but she just looked horrified. She put her head into her hands and started crying and sobbing uncontrollably.

Henry wasn't sure what to do. So, he just stood there with the flowers until Harold motioned for him to go away. He went back to the bathroom and started trying to put the flowers back in the plastic tubes. He had already made things worse. He didn't want to get into more trouble for getting something out and not putting them away.

Just after he started trying to put the flowers back into the plastic tubes, Harold walked into the bathroom.

"I thought Mom liked flowers. I thought they would make her happy," said Henry.

Harold looked sorrowfully at Henry.

"It's alright Henry," said Harold. "She likes flowers and you had good intentions."

Harold helped Henry clean up the mess. He threw the colored tampons into the trash can.

"Why did the flowers make her sad Dad?" asked Henry.

"Well Henry, she just isn't happy right now. She really loved Frank and it is hard for her to let him go. It isn't your fault. We just have to give her time to grieve."

"Is it the flowers? Are they something she doesn't like?" asked Henry.

"Well, they are something women use that you shouldn't play with," replied Harold.

"What do they use them for?" asked Henry.

Harold showed him the tampon instructions diagram on the paper from the box. The diagram showed a woman lying on her back while inserting the tampons in what looked to Henry as her butt.

"They put them in their butt? Why would they want to do that?" asked Henry.

"It's just something that woman have to do," responded Harold. He patted Henry on the head. A few days later, Tyrone would educate Henry on why women really used tampons.

Henry felt dejected. All he had wanted to do was to cheer up his mother. He had put forth a lot of effort to make her happy. Now, he was disappointed in himself for making things worse instead of better. His heart was in the right place. He felt guilty for not being able to help her be happy. He felt even worse because he wasn't still sad about his Uncle Frank dying.

"*Why does everything have to be so complicated?*" he thought.

He had heard adults say so many times that he should treat others like he wanted to be treated. Henry went out of his way to help others and make them feel better when they were down. It felt good when he managed to make someone smile but sometimes it didn't go the way he expected. Then he felt the pain.

"*Why is it when I try to help someone the most it always seems to be myself that hurts the most,*" thought Henry.

"Dad, I don't like seeing Mom cry," said Henry.

"It isn't your fault, Henry. Just be patient and don't let her sadness make you sad. It has nothing to do with you. She'll get over it. She just needs some more time," replied Harold.

Marsha did get over it and it wasn't long before she was back to her normal happy self. Happy most of the time and sometimes a real pain in Henry's butt.

Life is full of challenges.

CHAPTER 11

The Wooden Spoon

In 1960s Milton, there wasn't any debate about whether spanking children was an effective tool for behavior modification. All adults agreed that corporal punishment was a necessary means to teach their children right from wrong.

World renown psychologists had invented new behavior modification theories that assumed kids were just like rats. Good parenting was the essential ingredient to produce well behaved children. Bad behavior from a child was assumed to be the consequence of bad parenting. People tended to believe theories from anyone that had a name preceded or followed by capital letters. The threat of getting spanked was all that Margaret needed to obey Marsha and Harold's rules. Henry was different. He didn't have the cooperation skill set of a caged rat. If the rules didn't make sense to Henry, he rebelled.

Marsha struggled with finding appropriate consequences for Henry. Regardless of how hard she tried, nothing seemed to work to modify Henry's behavior to match Margaret's. Margaret was keen to please through obedience whereas Henry questioned rules. Marsha struggled to find answers that met Henry's expectations. Her exasperation, impulse and anger attributed to using a wooden spoon on Henry. It was her favorite spoon for stirring soups and anything else cooked in a pot. It was eighteen inches long with a thick handle and a large flat end that had cracked from years of use. She felt guilty striking Henry with it the first time, but she finally found a stick that seemed to work. Explanations, raised voices, time outs, and her hardest open hand spanking had minimal effect in modifying Henry's behavior. Marsha had found the perfect weapon.

Henry wanted to do what he wanted to do. He was annoyed that Marsha had her heart set on him doing what she perceived as best. She ruined a lot of his fun. He ruined a lot of her good intentions. Things that made him happy didn't always satisfy Marsha's view of what a well-behaved child should be doing. It seemed to Henry that just about everything fun had consequences. He didn't like consequences. So, he was constantly trying to find ways to avoid them. The more consequences he managed to avoid brought about even harsher consequences. Basically, he occasionally had a power struggle with his mother. He'd make a mess.

"Clean up your mess Henry," Marsha would say.

"I'm busy," Henry would politely respond.

"Clean it up or you won't be allowed to go to play with Albert today," Marsha would say.

"Why can you say you're busy when I ask you to do something, but I can't say it to you?" Henry would ask.

"Because I am the parent and you are the child," Marsha would respond.

"I'll do it later," he'd respond. "I am going to Albert's house now."

"Clean up the mess or *else*!"

When he refused, Marsha would get out her favorite wooden spoon. Spoon in hand, she would give him another chance to clean up his mess. If Henry disagreed, then he preferred the spoon. Harold had taught him to not be afraid to always stand up for what is right. Henry valued being courageous and resilient but his view of what was right rarely corresponded to the view of everyone else. His dad taught him to think for himself and be a man while his mom tried to get him to conform to societal rules to fit in and not get in trouble. Their tactics and world views were different, but he was blessed to have both as his parents.

He didn't let fear hold him back from exploring new opportunities, and he had the grit to stick with something until he succeeded. Fortunately for Henry, Marsha was just as determined to not let Henry win the parent child power struggle despite being driven to her limits.

The first time he was spanked with the wooden spoon it had hurt. The cracked spoon had a special pinching effect. It produced a large red swollen area with a bruised welt from the crack on the spoon. Henry was a fast learner. He started to scream and holler and watch Marsha out of the corner of his eye. When she brought the spoon back, he would move backward with her arm and then he'd move his body forward to make sure his speed was about the same speed as the spoon. It was just like catching a baseball to Henry. He didn't swat at the ball. He moved his mitt with the ball.

The secret trick was to make it look like it hurt more than it did. That way, he didn't feel anything while Marsha thought she was overdoing it. He had seen how guilty she had felt when she had produced bruises the first time. The more guilty he made her feel, the less harsh the punishment. It was almost like not even getting a spanking. The punishment hurt Marsha the most. Henry was becoming a good actor.

Marsha learned after the first couple of spankings that she needed to hold Henry by one of his arms when she spanked him. If she didn't have a good grasp, he moved fast enough to not get spanked. Henry perfected using his arm like a pendulum to achieve a near perfect painless spanking.

Catching Henry became increasingly more difficult as he grew older. Sometimes, he would take off running to temporarily avoid the consequences. Marsha had a tendency of not chasing him all around the neighborhood. It was embarrassing in front of the neighbors to be chasing a small rebellious child that she couldn't catch. He stopped that tactic after a while because the consequences always grew in proportion to the time it took Marsha to catch him. Eventually he would get hungry. When he went home to eat, he'd get caught. The spoon always stood in between himself and food.

What Henry disliked the most was that he still had to follow orders even when he took a beating. If he didn't comply with his mother's instructions after a spooning, then he would just get spanked again. It was a pointless battle that he eventually concluded couldn't be won. So, Henry learned Marsha's rules and it didn't take long for him to pretty much avoid the wooden spoon altogether.

Harold had another approach for discipline. When Harold disciplined Henry, it was almost always the result of Margaret telling on him. Margaret would get mad at Henry and start irritating him to the point that he felt he had to protect himself. She stretched out a wire hanger and started swatting Henry with it. He was afraid she was going to put out one of his eyes after the sharp end of the hanger stuck in his shoulder and drew blood. In what he viewed as self-defense, he grabbed Margaret by both arms and pushed her against her bedroom wall right between two studs. It put a Margaret sized impression in the dry wall.

"I'm telling Dad," said Margaret with a smile.

Sometimes Henry wondered if she meant to tempt him just to watch him get in trouble.

When Margaret came running back into her room, Henry was still standing by the hole in the wall. Patiently waiting for Harold of whom was coming up the steps. Harold's look of disappointment was all the punishment Henry needed.

"What happened Henry?" asked Harold.

Henry didn't bother explaining the details to his father. He knew better than arguing with Harold. It didn't matter what atrocity Margaret did, he wasn't allowed to push or hit girls. No excuses were allowed. The only option that he had with Harold was to man up and take responsibility for whatever he did that was wrong.

"I pushed Margaret into the wall and made that hole," responded Henry.

"Go to the couch Henry," said Harold.

Henry went downstairs. He sat down on the couch all by himself with nothing else to do but think about what he could have done differently to not get in trouble. After a while, Harold would show up and ask him the same question he always asked when Henry got in trouble. Every time that Henry finished thinking about what he could have done differently, he would think about what answer he was going to give his father when he would be asked the question. Sometimes, he thought maybe he might say no, but he never did.

After about 10 minutes, Harold entered the living room. He stood in front of the couch where Henry was sitting. Henry looked up to hear the all too familiar question that was asked after every timeout.

"Do you think you deserve a whoopin'?" asked Harold.

"Yes Sir," said Henry. He stood up from the couch and turned away from Harold to get spanked.

Harold's whoopin' was with a bare hand and it never really hurt. But every whoopin' made Henry just a little wiser about how to not get into trouble.

Henry learned the rules of his parents, but he rarely liked them. He didn't understand why Marsha was able to do things but when he did the same things he would get in trouble. He also didn't comprehend why Harold could make decisions for everyone in the family, but he couldn't make decisions for anyone including himself. Margaret could do things to him, but if he did something to her then he would get in trouble. He even got in trouble after she almost put his eye out with a wire hanger. Margaret was rewarded with a full-sized Michael Jackson poster to cover the hole in her wall.

Henry continued questioning Marsha.

"Why do I have to wash my glass when you just put your glass in the sink, and you didn't wash yours?" he asked.

"Because I said so," said Marsha. That answer didn't make any sense at all to Henry.

Henry was seven years old when he received his last spanking with the wooden spoon. He was playing with his friend Albert and a couple other neighborhood boys. One of them saw a piece of dog poop in the yard.

"Oo that is poop, let's get out of here!" he shouted.

Even Albert looked scared. Henry wanted to show Albert that it wasn't anything to be afraid of. It was just a dried-up piece of dog poop. If it was mushy or a fresh piece of poop, then Henry wouldn't have picked it up. An old hard piece of poop that didn't even smell much like poop anymore was nothing to be concerned about.

Henry picked the poop up to show Albert and the other boys that it was nothing to be afraid of. They all took off running. Henry took off after them with the dog poop, eager to convince them too not be afraid.

"What is going on?" asked Marsha, as Henry ran into the back yard following his friends.

"Henry is chasing us with dog poop," said one of the boys. He started crying uncontrollably. Henry knew immediately what his consequence would be.

"It is a hard-dried up piece of poop Mom," said Henry. "I was just trying to show them that it isn't anything to be afraid of."

He held up the dog poop to show her as evidence.

"You don't pick up poop," responded Marsha. "And you don't chase people with poop!"

That was the last time Henry got a spanking with the wooden spoon. He didn't scream and holler or even sway his body with the motion of the spoon. Picking up dried up dog poop was another rule that he hadn't learned yet. Failure to understand all his parent's rules hurt Henry much more than the spanking.

Henry woke up the next morning eager to see what new things he was going to learn and experience. As far as he was concerned, if he pressed all the right buttons then he had a lot of control over how well his day was going to go. His goals were to learn as much as he could, have fun doing it, and not getting into any trouble that resulted in undesirable consequences.

He was a confident 7-year-old, but he had a hard time figuring out other people. He liked life best when everyone around him were happy. Henry tried hard to make sense of the world. He was a rational person in a world where most people operated primarily on their own feelings and emotions.

He had a hard time backing down when he knew or thought he was right, and this resulted in conflict. He was learning that most people associate feelings to facts and situations. When he gave them rationality it frightened or hurt them without Henry understanding why. Being too rational was irrational in an irrational world. Especially when the rationality came from a child.

Life was hard to figure out.

CHAPTER 12

New School

"I don't want to go to a new school with Margaret," said Henry. "I like my school, and I want to go to school with Albert. I am not going if Albert doesn't come with me."

"You don't have a choice," said Marsha. "Margaret is going into the fourth grade and has to go to Peale Elementary. I need both of you in the same school because I can't pick you up at the same time from different schools."

"I can walk home with Albert," said Henry.

"Albert will join you next year when both of you are fourth graders," responded Marsha. "Your school only goes thru the third grade. I am not giving you a choice. Deal with it."

Peale Elementary was a much bigger school and right across the street from the savings and loan bank where Marsha worked. Henry knew lots of the kids from playing baseball and church. He was sad that he wouldn't see his best friend as much, but he dealt with it by making the choice to look forward to going to a new larger school.

"There is no point of practicing anger when I can practice optimism," he thought.

In the first and second grade all of Henry's classmates had gotten along with each other and their teachers. Henry liked school and had lots of fun learning and playing. His first impression of his new school wasn't what he expected. Right after walking into Peale Elementary, he saw some boys laughing and teasing another boy who was wearing glasses. Bullying hadn't been tolerated at his old school.

"Four eyes!" shouted the bullies.

They laughed and pointed at a red-haired kid wearing glasses. The boy started crying.

Henry had just gotten glasses a few days before school started. He was grateful to have them because he could see a lot better with glasses. It felt good to see things more clearly.

One of the boys pointed at Henry.

"Ha ha, you are a four-eyes too!" he laughed.

"I wish I had four-eyes. Two in the back of my head just like my front ones. That'd be nice," said Henry.

The other boys looked at him with open mouths as they thought what to say next.

"I like your glasses," said Henry. The boy with glasses stopped crying. He smiled and thanked him.

"I'd rather be dead than red on the head! Look at his head, he is red on the head!" laughed one of the boys, as he pointed at the red-haired boy wearing glasses.

"I'd rather have red hair or even purple hair than to be dead," responded Henry.

"Everyone get in line to see who your teacher will be this year," said a teacher.

"*The kids in this school are stupid*," thought Henry. "*Maybe the teachers aren't very good teachers.*"

A teacher told Henry that he was going to be in Mrs. Black's class. She pointed Henry in the direction of his classroom down the long corridor. The classroom looked much nicer and more modern than his last school. It had lots of maps and posters on the wall. Mrs. Black welcomed him to her class, and he was happy to see his friend Mike. He hadn't seen Mike very much since his family started going to another church.

Henry's desk was right in front of Mike and there was a big kid sitting next to him. The big kid looked at him like he was angry about something.

"Hi, I'm Henry. What is your name?" asked Henry.

The big kid looked back at him and growled like a dog. Henry considered asking the question again, but the teacher started the class.

"Okay, everyone be quiet. Welcome back to school. My name is Mrs. Black, and I will be your teacher," she said.

"Good morning Mrs. Black," said the class in unison.

They stood to say the "Pledge of Allegiance" and sat back down to begin class. At first it didn't seem much different than the second grade. At Henry's old school, his teachers had encouraged cooperation. The students were taught teamwork and the importance of helping each other to learn and succeed in class.

"You learn best when everyone works together," they'd say. "If anyone doesn't learn then everyone fails."

Every student was required to help each other until everyone understood each lesson. Henry enjoyed helping his classmates. Everyone appreciated being helped when they needed assistance. If anyone misbehaved the entire class suffered the consequence. Nobody wanted to let down their classmates, so everyone was normally at their very best behavior. They had fun helping each other learn.

"You are competing against each other," said Mrs. Black. "I will be tracking your grades and you get star stickers based on good behavior and answering questions. Everyone needs to work hard to be first in the class."

Henry liked competition. So, he raised his hand every time she asked a question. That way, he had a chance to get picked and get more star stickers by his name. Mrs. Black smiled when the kids answered her questions and played along with her games.

"Very good," she would say. "Good job!"

Henry had an exceptional knack for remembering things. He only needed to hear something once. He'd commit it to memory to regurgitate the same information later. His challenge was to listen to what was being said as he was easily distracted to start thinking about something else when he wasn't hearing anything of interest.

The competition aspect helped encourage Henry to listen more often. He remembered all the answers so that he could get more stickers by his name. He didn't recognize that his ability to remember things wasn't something that most other kids or people in general shared. It was an unfair advantage in school. Most people needed to hear things several times and still had difficulty remembering everything.

Recess was Henry's favorite subject in the first and second grade. He was excited to hear the teacher tell the class that it was time for recess after a whistle blew. Henry got in line to follow the teacher outside with his friend Mike and the rest of his classmates. As soon as they got outside, one of the kids he was with looked at the biggest kid in their class.

"Your fat," said the boy.

Then recess started. The biggest kid in the class chased Henry and the other boys, while they constantly reminded him that he was fat. Henry knew from roll call that the big kids name was Ralph, but everybody called him *fatso* or *fatty*. Ralph caught one of them. He gave him a good squeeze and growled like a dog. The other kids with Henry ganged up on Ralph until he let their classmate out of his suffocating grasp.

Henry grew tired of the game within a couple of minutes. He decided that he would rather do something else. He looked around and saw there were three other groups of kids. A bunch of girls were casually talking and gently swinging on a swing set. A separate group of boys were doing the same thing as the girls on a separate swing set. Quietly standing around didn't appeal to Henry very much. So, he headed in the direction of some other kids that were standing in a field of grass with a ball. The kids were finishing picking teams and just getting ready to start playing a game they called kickball. To Henry it was a lot like baseball but easier. All he had to do was kick the ball anywhere there wasn't someone who looked like they could catch it.

When recess finished, the teacher blew a whistle. Everyone ran to get in line to go back into the class. Henry got in line right in front of the big kid that growled like a dog.

Ralph kept poking him in the back. Henry turned around and politely asked him to stop. Ralph started poking him even harder. Henry wasn't sure how to get him to stop so he decided to ignore him. The poking stopped once they were safely back in their classroom. Henry made a mental note that he wouldn't get in line next to Ralph again.

On the second day of school, Marsha told Henry and Margaret that they would be taking the bus to school. Henry was the only third grader at the bus stop. All the other third graders still went to the small school in his neighborhood. The bus stop had fourth through sixth graders as well as some other older kids that took different buses to the junior and senior high schools. Henry was excited to be riding a bus, but he didn't care much for most of the kids at the bus stop or on the bus. He had hoped that his friend Fred would ride the bus, but his parents didn't allow him to take the bus. They dropped him off at school to avoid his neighbor Greg from bullying him. Greg and a few of the older boys liked picking on the smaller kids. They were always trying to get them to do stupid things. Fred's parents thought they were protecting their son. They were unknowingly weakening him further by depriving him of the opportunity to learn and grow by experiencing the harsh reality of the environment.

The bullies convinced a couple of the fourth graders to eat worms that they picked up in the street after a rainy day. At first the fourth graders were afraid to eat the worms, but they eventually succumbed to the peer pressure. They couldn't take being called a chicken anymore. Nobody liked being called a chicken. The offer of being paid a nickel for every worm they ate helped egg them on to become official worm eaters.

Henry wasn't very receptive to the peer pressure or bribes. He didn't comprehend the point of eating worms when he wasn't even hungry. The older kids weren't eating worms and he wasn't going to eat them either.

"Maybe they ate worms when they were fourth graders," thought Henry.

After a few days of watching the worm eating, the rain stopped and there weren't any more worms to eat. The older kids found a new game to pass the time while waiting for the bus. They tried to convince the 4th graders to fight each other. They weren't very successful for several minutes. Most of them were friends that didn't like the idea of physically harming each other. One of the junior high school kids started whispering to the kid that ate the most worms.

"Henry said that only *queers* eat worms. If I were you, I wouldn't let him call me a *queer*," whispered the older boy.

"Henry didn't say that?" said the fourth grader. He looked towards Henry as the older kid continued his pressure.

"What? You are afraid of a third grader? You are a little *queer*, aren't you?" asked the older boy.

Queer was a word that Henry had never heard before. He figured that it must have something to do with being weak and afraid or a coward. Nothing was worse than being a coward.

Greg walked over to Henry and told him that the worm eater wanted to fight him.

"I don't start fights with people and I don't have any reason to fight him," replied Henry.

Greg started saying similar things to Henry just like the other boy was telling the worm eater.

Henry thought about asking what a *queer* was, but he didn't want to look stupid. He would ask Tyrone later. He didn't say anything. He just listened to both conversations and made sure he could see the worm eater with his peripheral vision. He had been in a lot of fights in the last few years with other boys. He had lost just about every fight because all of them had been with bigger and older kids. Nobody seemed to start a fight with anyone bigger than them. Henry's strategy was to never back down from a fight, never cry, and never give up.

He had seen the movie "Cool Hand Luke" and had admired the way that Luke fought the much bigger and stronger man named Dragline.

Although Luke was severely outmatched by his opponent, he just kept getting up only to be knocked down over and over again. Eventually, it was Dragline that refused to continue the fight. Luke's tenacity earned the respect of everyone else including Dragline himself. His fearlessness resulted in being given the nickname 'Cool Hand Luke' after he won a game of poker on a bluff.

'Cool Hand Luke' was just the kind of person that Henry aspired to be like. Fearless, smart, and loved by everyone that mattered.

Henry watched the worm eater. The worm eater was smaller than most of the other kids he had been in fights with. He was only a few inches taller than Henry. It was clear that he was getting angry. Henry knew it wasn't going to be long before he was going to succumb to the peer pressure and want to fight him.

He saw the worm eater ball up his fists. His facial expression showed that he had reached his limit. It was his time to show all the older kids that he wasn't afraid of a third grader. He was going to prove his manliness. The worm eater ran full speed towards Henry.

Henry watched him running at him out of the corner of his eye but pretended that he didn't see him. He dropped down with perfect timing and grabbed the worm eater's right arm just as he was flying over him. A well-timed raising of his body back to a standing position left Henry standing over the worm eater who hit the ground squarely on his back.

Henry picked up his left foot and knocked the wind out of him. He stomped it directly in the worm eater's stomach.

"I don't want to fight you. Don't ever do that again," Henry sternly said, as the other fourth graders and older kids all looked on. The embarrassed worm eater remained on the ground grimacing with the pain of having the wind knocked out of him.

Henry's action impressed the older boys. They laughed and seemingly enjoyed the quick fight. Henry was careful to not take part in any celebration or even make eye contact with anyone. He had mixed emotions. He felt good that he had won the fight without any scrapes. He felt sorry for the fourth grader and was agitated at Greg and the older kids. He didn't have any hard feelings for the worm eater. His mistake was eating the worms when all he had wanted to do was fit in with the other kids. It was the older kids that started everything, and Henry wasn't going to participate in their childish games.

"When I am older there won't be any worm eating or fighting at the bus stop," thought Henry.

A few weeks into the school year, Marsha took him to the mall. Henry preferred the stores downtown. They had more personalized services. The salespeople liked to talk and could tell him about the differences between all the items. Marsha liked the new super-sized indoor mall. It was one-stop shopping where she could efficiently find everything that she needed without wasting anytime. Harold was disappointed that all the local stores downtown were going out of business and that Marsha started buying things they didn't need.

As they were walking, he saw his classmate Ralph coming towards them. As they got closer, Henry looked up as Ralph scowled at him. Ralph's face turned red as he made fists.

"Grr!" growled Ralph.

"Hi, *fatso*," said Henry with a smile. He wanted to aggravate Ralph and get back at him for poking him at school. Henry knew that Ralph would not chase him if he was with an adult authority figure. It felt good getting revenge from being poked at school.

He wasn't surprised when Marsha jerked him by the arm and scolded him. He knew he wasn't allowed to call other kids names. Name calling wasn't appropriate.

"But it's the truth. He's fat," Henry said to Marsha, feeling good about how he stood up to the bully. Marsha scolded him some more.

Several minutes later, Henry and Marsha went the opposite direction on the way to their car. He saw Ralph walking towards them again. He looked at Henry with an even angrier look than he had the previous time. He postured as if he was going to take a swing at Henry.

"Hi Slim," said Henry with a smile.

Marsha jerked his arm even harder.

"But I was just trying to be nice, Mom," said Henry. He smiled with the sweetness of revenge streaming through his bloodstream. It was worth the consequence of only getting his arm jerked.

"Don't be a smart aleck Henry," said Marsha.

Life seemed good.

CHAPTER 13

The Kid that Walked Differently

There was a boy in Henry's class that walked differently than everyone else. He waddled from side to side as if his knees were permanently stuck together. The other kids called him *cripple*. When the kids called him *cripple*, it didn't seem like he had a problem with the name like Ralph did when he was called *fatso*.

One day, just before school started, Henry saw the boy that walked differently in the hallway on his way to their classroom.

"Hi *cripple*," said a boy from Henry's class, as he walked by them.

"Hi Jeff, how are you doing today?" replied the boy that walked differently.

"Ha ha. *Cripple!*" laughed Jeff.

"Hi, how come everyone calls you *cripple*?" asked Henry.

"Because I'm *crippled*," said the boy that walked differently. He looked down at his legs.

"Ah, I didn't know what *crippled* was," said Henry. "Do you like it when other kids call you *cripple*?"

"No, I don't really like it, but it is better than being called *retard*. Some people call me *retard*. My name is Owen," he responded.

"Nice to meet you, Owen. I won't call you *cripple*. I will call you Owen," said Henry.

"If you don't like being called *cripple* then why don't you let the other kids know? You could tell the teacher?" asked Henry.

"I tried that last year, but it just makes it worse. They know where I live. When I tell on them, they beat me up at recess or after school," responded Owen.

"Ah, that makes sense. I don't like being a snitch either," said Henry.

The other kids seemed to take pleasure in calling Owen a *cripple* and laughing at him. Henry couldn't understand why they would want to hurt Owen's feelings. He admired how Owen handled the situation. He could have asked them to stop, told them they hurt his feelings or even started crying. Alternatively, he could have been a snitch just like about everyone else.

Owen was learning how to take the wind out of an *asshole's* sails. He had learned to not give a *shit* or at least act like he didn't give a *shit* about what other people said to him. As much as the other kids tried to demean, disrespect and ridicule Owen; he didn't fall into their trap. Most kids their age, and even a lot of adults were so thin-skinned that they took offense to things even when they weren't personal.

Henry thought that Owen was one of the nicest and coolest kids in his class.

They both smiled at each other. They started talking about LEGOs and Lincoln logs and other things that they both liked.

"Hi Henry. Hi *Cripple*," interrupted Mike.

"His name is Owen. He doesn't like being called *cripple*. You can call him Owen," said Henry.

"I know his name but he's a *cripple*," said Mike, as he rolled his eyes.

Later that day, the teacher took the class to the gymnasium to play another new game called dodge ball. Henry liked games. He was excited to get started. He was on the same team as Owen, Ralph, and Mike. Most of the other boys were on the other team. The teacher blew her whistle. All the girls ran to get as far away as they could from the other team. They all lined up against the farthest walls on opposite ends of the court. The boys on the other side concentrated all their efforts on Owen who was waddling around in between the girls and boys. Owen was the first one on Henry's team to exit the game after being bombarded with several balls.

Henry, Mike, and Ralph managed to take out a couple of the boys on the other team while they were focused on Owen.

The remaining boys on the other team all started concentrating on Ralph who was the next to go. Ralph moved well for a big kid. He survived long enough for Henry and Mike to knock out all but one of the boys on the other team.

Henry, Mike, and the other boy all picked up a ball. The other boy was trying to watch both Henry and Mike. He started getting nervous. Mike and the other boy simulated throwing the ball but were afraid to take the first move. They were both waiting for a good shot and didn't want to be without a ball.

Henry slowly moved off to the side as the other boy concentrated solely on Mike. He waited for an opportunity. Both Mike and the other boy threw their balls at each other. Henry threw his ball at the other boy with perfect timing to hit him just as he was catching the ball that Mike threw.

Only Henry and the girls remained. Henry let the girls battle each other until there was just one girl on the other side. He teasingly pretended that he was going to throw the ball. The other girls on his team pelted her with multiple balls and won the game.

Henry felt proud of himself for being the last boy to survive the dodge ball game and that his team won. But nobody congratulated him for winning other than the remaining girls on his team. He could see that all the boys in his class acted like they were angry with him for winning.

When they got back in class, the teacher called Henry to the front of the room along with two other kids. She pointed to the poster where she tracked everyone's performance and announced that Henry was the number one student in the class. Sally and Kyle were second and third placed respectively.

Henry felt good to be identified as the best student . He looked at Sally and Kyle to congratulate them for being second and third. All three kids had beaming smiles on their face. Henry noticed that Sally and Kyle looked at him with envy as if they wanted to be the ones that were the best student. He smiled at the rest of the class. All he saw was angry faces. Nobody was happy for them except the teacher. It didn't feel very good to have everyone except the teacher being angry at him.

At lunch time, one of the boys in his class asked if anyone wanted his cookie. Henry looked up to see if anyone else wanted it. He already felt bad that everyone hated him. He didn't want to take the cookie if someone else wanted it. He was the champion kick ball and dodge ball player and the smartest kid in the class. He didn't want to add being the only kid that got two cookies to the list.

Nobody said anything. He noticed a few other kids were snickering like it was some kind of joke. Even Mike had a smile on his face.

"Give it to Henry," said one of the boys. "He's a nerd."

"I'll take it if nobody else wants it. I like cookies," said Henry. Nerd or not, Henry liked cookies.

As the other boy handed the cookie to him, Henry noticed that he was holding the cookie very carefully. He only touched the sides and didn't put his fingers on the top or the bottom. He looked like he was up to something while the other kids were still snickering.

Henry was careful to take the cookie by only holding the sides. He didn't touch the bottom or top just like the boy handing it to him. He carefully looked at the top of the cookie and then turned it over to look at the bottom. The bottom was covered with a thick nasty mass of snot.

"No thanks. I like cookies but I don't care much for eating snot. You can keep it but thanks for offering it to me," Henry politely responded. He placed the cookie back on the side of the other boy's plate with the snot facing down on top of his mashed potatoes.

Henry felt really bad. He ruminated on the time he had told his class that the Easter Bunny wasn't real and how everyone had been angry at him. This time all he did was try to do well in school, to learn as much as he could and win at every contest.

"*Isn't that what I'm supposed to do?*" he thought.

His new school wasn't anything like his previous school. Henry missed Albert and all the other kids and teachers from his small neighborhood school. He felt all alone. Hardly anybody at Peale Elementary seemed to like him except for the teacher and Owen.

He had no friends on the school bus and once he got to school just about everyone hated him.

Life wasn't very good.

CHAPTER 14

Why is Everyone so Stupid?

"Grandpa why is everyone so stupid?" asked Henry. He had been rummaging through his grandpa's workshop looking at old tools and the leather saddles and harnesses his grandpa had used with his horses. Grandpa George always had good answers for the most difficult questions. Henry saved his most important questions to ask his grandfather. He had lived through two World Wars and the Great Depression. Grandpa George was a parent of parents and not just any body's parents. He was the father of Henry's mother Marsha.

Grandpa George provided logical explanations of why people did what they did. Henry had a hard time understanding other people's behavior, but his grandfather had over 70 years of experience in figuring out empathy. Henry found his advice useful to better understand how other people ticked. Sometimes his answers surprised Henry, but they always made sense. Henry would be annoyed at his parents because they didn't let him do what he wanted to do. Grandpa George would explain that it was because they loved him. Love seemed to come up a lot. They loved him and didn't want to see him get hurt or suffer dire consequences. They loved him and wanted him to behave appropriately so he could grow up to be a successful adult. They even bossed him around because they loved him.

Grandpa George also taught him how to do a lot of useful things like how to use a saw and a hammer. Henry tended to try too hard sometimes. His grandfather taught him how to get things done faster without working so hard.

"Let the saw do the work Henry," he'd say.

Then he would show him how to lightly push the saw back and forth as it effortlessly cut through the wood without wasting unrequired energy. Henry had been amazed at how he learned to accomplish more with less energy.

"It isn't how hard you work. It's how smart you work," said Grandpa George.

They were standing at the top of a long dirt driveway. Grandpa George was smoking his pipe as he listened to Henry. Henry had been talking for a prolonged period. He was asking lots of questions without giving his grandpa an opportunity to speak.

He told him all about his new school. He started with the kid that tried to give him a cookie with snot on it. Then how the other kids made fun of Owen and Ralph and picked on younger kids at the bus stop. He explained how only a few kids ever answered the teacher's questions and a lot of the other kids made fun of the kids that answered questions.

"Why do the kids call the other kids that answer the questions nerds?" asked Henry.

"Why doesn't everyone just answer the questions?" He moved on to tell him about playing kick ball and dodge ball and how other kids got mad whenever they lost.

"Why are they so angry for losing?"

"Why don't they just try harder?"

Henry paused. His grandfather was listening and nodding like he understood. So, he started telling him how the whole town of Milton was completely messed up. He had been forced to lie to his entire preschool class that the Easter Bunny was real and some people in his church hated black people. They didn't even think they should be allowed to mix with white people.

"Why do they hate black people? And why do they hate communists?" he asked. "I haven't even seen a communist."

Henry explained the pyramid scheme that had come to town and how just about everyone was involved to either take people's money or lose their own.

On and on Henry went as he told Grandpa George about everything that was on his mind.

Occasionally Grandpa George would give a slow exhale of smoke and nod his head as he listened intently. Henry eventually recognized that he'd been talking for a long time. He hadn't heard his grandpa say anything. After a good 20 minutes of talking, he stopped and looked at his grandpa. Grandpa George was staring back at him with his pipe in his mouth. That is when he asked the main question on his mind.

"Grandpa why is everyone so stupid?"

Grandpa George looked at him for a few seconds without saying anything. He took another drag from his pipe and then slowly exhaled the smoke before he removed it from his mouth.

"God must really like stupid people. Coz' he made a lot of 'em. Watch'em Henry and you might jus' learn somethin'," he responded. Then he turned around and started walking back up the hill to the house.

Henry wanted to shout at him to come back so he could ask him more questions, but he knew that his grandpa was done talking when he was done talking. So, he just sat down to digest Grandpa George's response.

"Why would God like stupid people?" he thought. *"If I can learn from stupid people then how stupid does that make me?"*

From Henry's perspective Grandpa George was the wisest and smartest person that he knew. He had just told him that he could learn something from all the stupid people that God apparently loved.

Henry had a big ego. His grandpa had just advised him to lose it and stop thinking that he was smarter than everyone else. He didn't know what an ego was, but he knew what his ego was telling him. Henry liked to think he was smarter than everyone else and he didn't like the idea of letting go of his ego. It felt good to think he was smarter and better than everyone else. But if Grandpa George advised him to watch the stupid people to learn something then that is what he would do. Nothing else seemed to be working.

On the long drive home, Henry didn't say much. He was thinking about all the times that he had done something stupid only to learn later how stupid he had been. His grandpa's advice was starting to make sense.

"God loves stupid people because everyone is stupid. Only God is truly wise, and he loves all of us stupid people. God must love racist people, bullies, liars and thieves just like he loves everyone else," thought Henry.

A song came on the radio by a singer named Kris Kristofferson called "To Beat the Devil". The song started out with talking about being hungry and out of money and then making the choice to step inside of a bar. An old man in the bar borrowed the singer's guitar and sang a song. The old man sang about how it was a waste of time to try to instruct people of how they could change themselves and the world around them. In his opinion, he thought it was pointless to help other people because nobody cared. He even made a reference to another singer that had been crucified for trying to help people. Henry thought that he might have been referring to Jesus.

"Why would the truth be that no one wants to know?" he thought.

He remembered another conversation that he had with his Grandpa George.

"Why do people get mad when I tell them the truth?" Henry had asked.

"People are jus' fraid of the temporary pain of knowing the truth that they want to live with the longer-term consequences of lyin' to themselves." Grandpa George had said. "For most people it's temporarily easier to live outside of reality. Reality is jus' too painful for them."

Henry had wanted his grandpa to agree with him that everyone else was the problem. It was easier to blame other people than himself. Grandpa George had brought him back to reality by not agreeing with him. At first it hurt, but it was starting to make sense. Henry had been complaining about everyone else. Grandpa George was telling him that he needed to stop complaining and change his own behavior.

Then Kris Kristofferson started talking again. He had evidently already heard the song the old man sang. He had some advice of how to beat the Devil instead of joining him. The song seemed to imply that the man in the bar was the Devil. Kris Kristofferson drank his beer for free. He also stole the Devil's song and changed the words.

The thought of drinking the Devil's beer for free and then stealing his song got a smile out of Henry. He knew stealing was wrong but taking something away from the Devil had to be okay. Then he listened to a different rendition of the song.

Henry liked the latter version of the song that Kris Kristofferson sang. There were people that wanted to hear the truth. He didn't want to join the Devil. Henry wanted to be someone that would tell people what they needed to hear. At first, he hadn't liked his grandpa's answer, but he liked it more now after hearing the song. Henry was someone that wanted to hear the truth. Even if it hurt. Henry did care, and Grandpa George was hoping that he'd listen to his important advice. Henry had listened.

He thought about how sometimes he heard things on the radio or out of someone's mouth which was exactly what he needed to hear.

"Is it just a coincidence or is it God trying to tell me something?" he thought.

He could relate to the song. It reinforced what his grandpa had told him. The world might be deaf and blind, but Henry wasn't going to give up trying to help others and himself find some peace and satisfaction with life. He was going to take his grandpa's advice to talk less and listen, watch, and learn.

Life was good.

CHAPTER 15

Watching Other Stupid People

On Henry's first day back to school after visiting his grandfather, he was eager to put Grandpa George's advice into practice. He couldn't wait to start watching all the kids and teachers at school to see what he could learn from them.

In class, Mrs. Black reviewed the capitals of all 50 states with her students. Henry looked around at his classmates. He noticed all the kids were listening to try and memorize all the state capitals. Henry had all the state capitals cemented in his brain from the first time the teacher wrote all of them on the blackboard. He observed many of the kids silently mouthing the names of each capital. Some were writing the state capitals in their notebooks while other befuddled students sat with blank stares.

"They act like they are hearing the state capitals for the first time," thought Henry.

Mrs. Black had already taught them the capitals of each state.

"Nobody told us to write them down," wondered Henry. *"Why are they writing?"*

Normally, he just watched the teacher and focused on remembering what she was saying. It was his first time to closely observe his classmates.

"Maybe they can't remember things like I can," he thought.

After the teacher reviewed all the state capitals, she started giving the class the name of a state to see if they could tell her what the capital was. Henry decided to just watch and observe instead of participating in answering the questions. Kyle and Sally had memorized most of the capitals. Most of the rest of the class raised their hands in eager anticipation whenever they did know the answer. A few of the kids weren't raising their hands at all. They were the same kids that liked to make fun of the other kids by calling them nerds and four-eyes when they did well.

After a while, Henry noticed that the teacher was occasionally looking at him as if to encourage his participation. He saw Sally turn around to look at him with a prideful smile after she answered another question.

"Why is she looking at me like that," thought Henry. *"Doesn't she know that I already know the answers?"*

He saw that some kids looked frustrated when they didn't know the answers. A few of them looked resentfully at Sally and Kyle when they correctly identified more capitals. Henry sensed that the boys in the class had a growing hatred of Kyle. Kyle focused solely on pleasing the teacher and ignored everyone else in the class. His only goal was to be the number one student in their class.

"Everybody wants others to do well as long as they don't do better than them," he thought. *"Sally and Kyle are happy because they are beating me. Everyone hates me just because I am the smartest kid in the class."*

Henry felt a competitive urge to start raising his hand to make sure he retained his position as the smartest kid in the class. But he decided that learning everything without letting anyone know that he was smart might be a better way to be liked and accepted by the other children. The only thing he got for being number one was more stickers and gratitude from the teacher. Stickers weren't going to help him succeed in life. The more he learned the more he would know. Learning was more important than trying to impress the teacher and the other kids.

Mrs. Black finished her state capitals lesson. Henry watched her turn around to start writing on the blackboard as she began a new subject.

"*Oh no, here we go again*," thought Henry. Every time Mrs. Black turned her back to the class a few of the kids that hardly ever answered any questions started acting out. They would start pulling the hair of the girl in front of them, making faces at someone else or flicking wadded up paper balls at each other. The victims were normally the kids that answered the most questions and had their feelings easily hurt. Kyle had become the number one target.

Kyle or one of the other victims would tell on them. The teacher would turn around to spend the next few minutes disciplining whoever she identified as responsible. More often than not, everyone in the class knew she punished the wrong person.

"*Why doesn't she occasionally turn around. She's so stupid*," thought Henry.

Henry was wondering what he was supposed to learn from the teacher mindlessly talking to a blackboard with half of the class not even listening. He thought how amusing it would be to flip the rubber band he had on his pencils at her. Without intending to go through with it, he put the rubber band around the end of his right thumb and pulled it back with his left hand as he aimed at the back of her neck.

Mike saw Henry aiming the rubber band at the teacher and pushed Henry in the back.

"Don't do that you idiot," whispered Mike.

The push was all that was needed for Henry's left hand to lose grip on the taut rubber band. It launched across the classroom with a perfect strike on the back of the teacher's neck. The teacher immediately stopped writing. She grimaced and put her hand on the back of her neck. Then, she spun around towards the class. She glanced at the rubber band laying on the floor and then looked back up at the class.

"Who shot a rubber band at me?!" Mrs. Black angrily asked the class.

"I did," said Henry without hesitation. "I was trying to get it off my pencils and it slipped." Normally, the guilty student remained silent and waited for someone else to tell on them. Henry knew that it was always best to admit to any wrong doings promptly. He also knew that twisting the story slightly often helped to reduce the consequences.

"Don't let it happen again," said the teacher. She turned back around to talk to the blackboard.

Henry looked around at the other kids who had seen what happened and wondered if anyone was going to tell the teacher what really happened. But they were just smiling at Henry. The kids that typically were the ones getting in trouble thought it was funny and the other kids deliberated that Henry had probably just made an honest mistake. They assumed he was telling the truth.

The teacher resumed writing on the blackboard, but she started peeking over her shoulder occasionally.

"*I guess she's learning,*" thought Henry.

Henry became bored when the teacher again started repeating herself. He looked at the clock.

"*Thirty minutes until recess,*" he thought. He glanced towards Ralph.

Ralph was attentively listening to Mrs. Black and taking notes.

Henry started wondering what he could learn from the other kids calling him *fatso* and then running around as Ralph chased after them.

"*What is there to learn about that pointless exercise?*" he wondered.

By the time the bell for recess rang, Henry had a plan. As soon as the first boy opened his mouth to remind Ralph that he was fat, Henry interrupted with a question.

"Want to play kick ball?" asked Henry. He made eye contact with Ralph.

"Yeah. Sure," replied Ralph with a confused look on his face.

"Good," said Henry. "Let's go."

He turned around and asked the other boys if they were coming. They all took off running after him and Ralph.

When Henry got to the kick ball field, he picked up the ball and announced that he would be one of the captains. One of the kids that normally spent recess being chased by Ralph decided to be the other captain and they started picking their teams.

"I'll take Slim," said Henry.

Ralph walked towards Henry with a smile. Next, Henry picked Mike and then he picked one other kid that he knew was fast.

"Us four will play everyone else and Owen will be full time catcher," said Henry without continuing to pick more players.

Most of the other kids laughed as they thought how they would be the sure winners against just four kids.

"They don't stand a chance!" shouted the other captain. "They only have four people."

Henry put Ralph at first, Mike as short stop, Jordan in center field, and he was the pitcher. The other team scored a couple of runs but Henry's team didn't have any problem getting the kids that couldn't kick very well or run fast out. Then it was their turn to kick. They continued scoring for the rest of the recess just as Henry had planned. All four of Henry's team could kick the ball wherever they wanted and were fast enough to never get out. In Henry's mind, it was more important to not have the weak links than having all the best players. Quality was better than quantity. The score was 21 to 2 when the whistle blew. All the kids ran to line up to return to class.

Henry got in line right behind Ralph.

"If the other boys call you fat, don't chase them. Just act like you don't care and sooner or later they will stop. They are just stupid," said Henry to Ralph.

"Okay," said Ralph, as he nodded back at his new friend.

A couple of days later, it was raining, so Henry's class got to play dodge ball again. Henry delegated himself as captain. He picked his *crippled* friend Owen first. Several of the other kids snickered. Next, he picked Mike because he didn't want to disappoint him more after seeing his face when he picked Owen first.

"I'll take Slim," said Henry. He pointed at Ralph for his third choice.

"That isn't nice Henry!" said the teacher. "You don't call people names, or you won't be allowed to play!"

"My name is Slim," said Ralph, to the surprised teacher who had rarely heard Ralph speak.

The other students were just as surprised as the teacher. From that moment onwards, Ralph was called Slim. There wasn't any more calling him fat. Henry and the other captain continued picking their teams until there wasn't anyone left.

Henry pulled Owen, Mike and Slim together to give them the game plan. "Owen, you be a decoy and we will protect you," said Henry. Everyone nodded and then the game commenced just like it normally went.

The other team all targeted Owen as they worked to avoid the balls thrown by Henry, Mike and Slim. The game was a complete massacre. Henry's team casually picked off the other team one by one and intercepted all the balls thrown at Owen. When there was only one boy left on the other team, Henry started faking like he was going to throw the ball. He watched Owen pick up a ball out of the corner of his eye. Owen didn't have any problem with his arms. He threw a perfect high speed and unseen throw to get the other kid out.

The look on Owen's face was priceless. Henry, Slim and Mike all high fived Owen as they congratulated him for winning the game.

Just one week before, Henry had been at a low point with hardly anyone liking him. He learned two important things. The first was to be the smartest kid in the class without anyone else knowing it. The second was to help others win instead of always winning for himself. Winning was only fun when there were others to participate in the celebration.

Life was good.

CHAPTER 16

Learning from Other Stupid People

"Have a good day Henry," said Harold. He picked up his lunch box and headed out the door for work.

"You too Dad," replied Henry. "See you later."

Henry finished eating his Frosted Mini-Wheats. Saturday was Henry's favorite day of the week. He had the whole day to do whatever he felt like doing. Nothing was better than waking up with the realization that he didn't have anything he had to do or anywhere he had to be. He always got up early to make sure he had the full day to enjoy the freedom. Marsha and Margaret were still sleeping. He was eager to get outside to practice what his grandpa had taught him. He had learned a lot in the previous wcck at school.

It was late November and getting chilly. He could still smell the fall foliage. Red and golden leaves were scattered on the ground. As he rode his bike down the street, he couldn't help but smile at the morning peacefulness with the fresh crisp aroma of fall. It was a calm and quiet that he didn't have on any other days of the week.

"I wonder why everyone doesn't get up early to enjoy Saturday mornings?" thought Henry. *"Most people just want to sleep."*

Knowing that his mother was still sleeping widened his smile. He could ride just a little further than normal because she wouldn't be awake to stop him.

He saw Mr. and Mrs. Thompson working in their portion of the community garden. Most of the neighbors paid the man who owned the land to use a small part of it as their very own garden. Henry liked going with his parents to work in the garden. Growing their own food made everyone feel happier and more optimistic. The fresh air and sunshine provided therapeutic relief that reduced stress. He enjoyed the way all the neighbors came out and socialized as they worked in their respective gardens. It fostered interaction of people of all ages that strengthened the cohesiveness of the neighbors. Growing food was a healthy hobby that raised everyone's spirits and helped feed the neighborhood. Everyone grew more food than they needed so they could share with anyone that didn't have their own garden.

Mr. and Mrs. Thompson's section of the garden was the best one according to all the other neighbors. They didn't have hardly any weeds. Mr. Thompson liked using stakes, strings, and old car tires to keep all his plants straight and looking nice.

Henry wondered why they were working in their garden in November. There was nothing left to pick. They wouldn't need to plant anything until the following spring.

"*That's stupid*," he thought.

He thought about what his grandfather had told him.

"*God must really like stupid people because he made a lot of them, but you just watch them and maybe you will learn something,*" he thought.

Henry stopped his bicycle next to the garden. The Thompson's were pulling up old plants and hoeing the ground.

"Good morning, Henry," the Thompson's said in unison. They looked up and smiled at Henry.

"Good morning," said Henry.

He bit his lip to avoid asking the question that was on the tip of his tongue. He wanted to ask them why they were working in their garden in November, but he was just supposed to watch them. Grandpa George had said to watch them. So, he watched. It only took Henry a couple of seconds to look at the Thompson's Garden compared to the other ones. All the other gardens had a bunch of dried-up weeds and plants, but half of the Thompson's Garden was fresh soil with compost that looked like it was ready to plant another garden.

Henry thought about how everyone else would show up next spring to remove all the rotten plants from the year before. The Thompson's would be one step ahead of everyone else. Henry smiled at how smart the Thompsons were when it came to gardening. He looked forward to watching them next spring.

The next person he saw was Mr. Parvis pulling into his driveway. Mr. Parvis was unloading groceries to take inside of his home.

"*That's stupid,*" thought Henry. "*Who goes to the grocery store early on Saturday morning? Most people don't even leave their house.*"

"Hi Mr. Parvis!" Henry shouted.

"Hey, good morning, Henry. How are you doing?" he responded.

"I'm doing good, you been grocery shopping?" asked Henry.

"Yep, always do my grocery shopping on Saturday morning to avoid the crowds," smiled Mr. Parvis.

Henry thought about going to the grocery store with his mother. Marsha normally went to the grocery store right after work and school when it was full of people with lines that seemed to last forever. The grocery store was a boring place to Henry. Marsha didn't let him do much of anything when shopping after he dropped a bottle of A-1 Sauce that he was playing catch with.

He also got in trouble roaming the aisles collecting the price tags of everything. The store manager had given Marsha an earful.

"You need to keep control of your son! How are we supposed to know what the prices are for everything?!" shouted the store manager. "Your son has removed the prices from half of the items in the store!"

"I am so sorry, Mr. Taylor. It won't happen again. He knows that he isn't allowed to remove the prices now," said Marsha.

"I can help him put the prices back if you want," said Henry.

"They have to go in the right places. That is the problem," said Marsha.

"I know where they go," said Henry.

"Stop fibbing Henry."

"*116 dollars and 36 cents in total. Peanut butter 1.26, jelly 1.04, bread 0.84 ....,*" thought Henry, as he remembered all of the prices for each price tag he had picked up.

Henry thought about trying to explain to Marsha that he really did remember all the prices, but he didn't want to help the man after the way he had talked to his mother. If the manager of the store didn't know the prices, then that was his problem and not Henrys.

Walking behind Marsha doing an imitation of his *crippled* friend Owen hadn't been much more successful. He had found it interesting how people looked at him until Marsha turned around and saw what he was doing. The other people in the store had been giving him different looks. The looks ranged from pity that he had to suffer with being *crippled* to ones of disgust as if he shouldn't be allowed to be in the grocery store with the so-called normal people. He wondered how Owen would feel when he went to the grocery store.

"*He'd probably wish that everyone would just look at him like the normal human being he is,*" thought Henry.

Marsha turned around after noticing the looks of disgust from people moving in the other direction. She wanted to see what was so detestable. What she found was Henry doing a near perfect imitation of Owen. When Marsha reprimanded Henry, he watched the faces of disgust look away in horror as they imagined what evil had inspired Henry to walk like he was *crippled*. They looked at him like he was the Devil himself.

"*Smart, Mr. Parvis,*" Henry thought. "*I think I will do the same thing when I grow up and have to go the grocery store.*"

He continued riding his bicycle as he thought about how nice it would be to shop for groceries early in the morning. Both of his parents would be happy with the parking situation. Marsha liked to drive around looking for the closest spot, but Harold always parked far away where there weren't any other cars around. Marsha thought Harold was stupid and his father probably thought his mother was stupid.

Henry thought that Harold's grocery store parking philosophy was more practical than Marsha's. It was always faster to park, easier to get out, and nobody ever dinged the door of their car. Marsha's technique took 10 minutes of driving around or waiting. It saved a few seconds walking but backing out when you were close to the grocery store entrance could take forever. Most other people were driving around trying to get what they perceived to be the best spot just like Marsha did.

Henry continued riding his bicycle through Milton. He saw Gina walking with a bag of groceries. Gina was one of Albert's cousins. She was 6 years older than Henry and Albert.

"Gina is smart too," thought Henry. *"She already did her shopping just like Mr. Parvis."*

She had a light caramel colored skin, green eyes, and her hair wasn't as curly as most of Albert's other cousins. Henry had asked Marsha why Gina looked almost kind of white.

"Well, she is probably part white," responded Marsha.

"Gina's parents are both black. How could she be part white?" asked Henry.

Marsha explained how a lot of slave owners had children with their slaves. The slave code had allowed for and even encouraged slave owners to abuse black women. There weren't many laws to protect slaves from abuse. The treatment of slaves relied solely on the morality of their owners. No matter how brutal the sexual or physical abuse was, the slaves had no legal right to defy the wishes of their master. The slaves were considered property. There weren't any rules to prevent rape and other forms of abuse. The plantation system dismantled any perception of consent. Slaves were by definition; deprived of their own free will. They had no choice but to consent or be punished at the mercy of their owner. Slave owners viewed it as the duty of their slaves to fulfill their desires even when they were evil. Children of slave owners and black women weren't legitimate or illegitimate. They were slaves without any privilege.

"Weren't the slave owners married to white women?" asked Henry. "What did their wives think of them raping black women and having children with them?"

"I imagine they didn't like it," replied Marsha. "They would have felt like their husbands desecrated on their marriage vows and wondered why they preferred someone else over them."

"Do you think they would have felt sorry for the black women that were raped?" asked Henry.

"I doubt it," said Marsha. "They probably hated them even more and blamed them for their husband's bad behavior. They would have been jealous and probably abused the slaves even more than their husbands."

"How about black men having children with white women," Henry asked. "Did the men slaves impregnate their owners too?"

"That would have been against the law," Marsha informed Henry. "Even if it was consensual. It was only recently that mixed-race mar-riages have been allowed in our state. It used to be that a white woman who had a mixed-race child was fined or even put in jail. If they weren't punished by the law, then the community would have treated them as outcasts of society. Many people still think that it shouldn't be allowed."

"Hi Gina. How are you doing?" said Henry, as he rode up behind her.

Gina was startled. She turned around quickly and almost dropped her bag of groceries.

"Hi Henry. You scared me! How are you doing?" said Gina.

"Sorry, I didn't mean to scare you. You want a ride?"

"Sure," said Gina. She climbed on to the handlebars of Henry's bike as she carefully balanced her grocery bag.

Just before they got to Gina's house, a car slowed down as it passed. Henry looked at the man driving. He didn't recognize him as someone that he knew. Hank Wilson had long curly dark hair and was wearing dark sunglasses. His window was down despite the chill in the air. He looked at Gina in an odd way. Gina didn't make eye contact with him. She started shaking. Henry struggled to keep his bicycle stable.

"Do you know that man?" asked Henry.

"Yes. He isn't nice," whispered Gina. "He scares me."

Gina was still shaking. Henry decided to not ask her any more questions. He could see that Gina was afraid of the man. He would remember him if he ever saw him again. He dropped Gina off at her house.

"Thanks Henry," said Gina. "I'm glad you gave me a ride."

"I will look for you next Saturday," said Henry. "I don't have anything else that I have to do on Saturday mornings."

After riding around for a while, Henry stopped at Albert's house. He had been thinking about Albert's brother, Tyrone. Albert's mother had mentioned that Tyrone had tried to protect Gina from someone.

"Maybe the man with the curly hair that gave her an odd look was him," he thought. *"That would explain why she acted like she was afraid of him."*

Tyrone was 12 years older than Henry and Albert. They both looked up to him as a role model. Most young men didn't have much time for kids Henry's age, but Tyrone had always given the boys his undivided attention. He'd spent endless hours showing Albert and Tyrone how to swing a baseball bat, dribble a basketball or just to give them good sound advice.

Once he had caught Albert and Henry trying to smoke Mrs. Thurman's cigarettes. Albert and Henry had seen lots of adults smoking cigarettes. They thought it looked cool. Most adults would have told them that cigarettes were not for kids and that only adults were permitted to smoke them. Tyrone told them that smoking cigarettes was stupid.

"How about the Marlboro man on TV? He doesn't look stupid," asked Henry.

"Don't believe everything you see on television, Henry," replied Tyrone. "That's just marketing to try to get people to spend money so someone else can get rich off everyone else's misery. If you want to not be able to run past 3rd base and play a full 40 minutes of basketball, then smoke cigarettes. Cigarettes kill your lungs. They make you slow, and you'll die too young."

That is all Albert and Henry needed to know. They wouldn't ever smoke cigarettes because they didn't want to be slow, stupid, or dead.

Sometimes, Henry wished that he had a big brother like Tyrone, but he was happy that Tyrone had treated him like a second little brother to Albert. He felt sorry for Albert and Tyrone because their father Duane had been killed in Chicago. He knew that he had been murdered just before Albert was born. Ruth had moved them to be close to his grandparents which just happened to be right down the street from Henry.

"If Mr. Thurman wouldn't have died, then I'd never have gotten to know Albert or Tyrone," thought Henry. *"It's funny how bad things sometimes lead to something good and sometimes good things end up bad."*

Just a couple of months before, the police had taken Tyrone to prison. Henry was at Albert's house when they came to take him away. Just before the police showed up, Albert and Tyrone had just finished eating. They didn't have much. Tyrone always took less than anyone else even though he was the biggest.

He was one of the most selfless people that Henry knew. Everyone that knew him loved him. Tyrone wasn't surprised when the police came to take him away. His mother had cried.

"Please, don't take my son away," Ruth had sobbed.

The Police didn't care what Albert's mother said or thought. They pushed Tyrone to the ground and shouted at him as they put him in hand cuffs.

"Stop resisting!" they shouted. Tyrone did everything he could do to respectively comply with their instructions.

Both Henry and Albert thought Tyrone should have fought back. Tyrone was the toughest guy they knew, and he could have gotten away if he tried.

Henry wondered why the policemen in Milton seemed to have a lot in common with several neighborhood bullies. They were easily agitated, had thin skin, and didn't seem to understand the common rules of society such as treating others with respect.

A few weeks later, after Ruth wasn't crying as much, Henry had asked her why the police took Tyrone to jail.

"He was just trying to protect Gina," she had replied.

"Protecting her from what?"

"From a man that was doing bad things to her Henry," said Mrs. Thurman.

"Hey Henry," said Albert as he opened the front door.

"Want to pass baseball?" said Henry.

"Sure," said Albert. He picked up his glove first and then Tyrone's glove with a frown. "You can use Tyrone's mitt."

Henry and Albert liked to catch and pass fast. Both had their right hands on the ball as soon as it hit their mitts exactly like Tyrone had taught them.

"Put your right hand on the ball right after you catch it," he'd told them. "You will never drop a ball and you can make the throw faster to get the runner out almost every time."

"Do that and remember that speed and accuracy are everything," he'd told them.

"I saw Gina earlier. Do you know who Tyrone was trying to protect her from?" asked Henry.

"I haven't ever seen him, but he drives a Cadillac and has long curly dark hair," said Albert.

"A white Cadillac?" asked Henry.

"Yep," replied Albert.

"I just saw him. What did he do to Gina?"

"He was raping her. Tyrone told him to stop but he didn't listen. He beat the man with a 2 by 4 and broke his leg," said Albert.

"How come he didn't go to jail for raping Gina?" asked Henry.

"The police didn't care about him raping Gina. They arrested Tyrone for beating him up and they said he was selling drugs. He is going to be in prison for 10 years," said Albert.

"Tyrone was selling drugs?" asked Henry.

"No, Tyrone said that the man that was raping Gina is a drug dealer, and the police don't care," said Albert. "Tyrone didn't sell drugs, but they said he did."

Henry was the first to make a bad pass. It sailed over Albert's leaping outstretched left hand. Albert started to run after the ball but stopped as if he was afraid to go get it.

"It went into the other yard," gasp Albert as he turned towards Henry.

"So, go get it," said Henry, as he wondered why Albert was acting stupid and afraid to go into the neighbor's yard.

Albert walked slowly between the high shrubbery between his and his neighbor's yard.

"Get out of my yard, you little *nigger*! I have rock salt in my shotgun. I will pepper your hide!" exclaimed the neighbor.

Albert didn't waste any time getting back through the shrubbery.

After hearing about the shotgun, Henry wasn't sure he wanted to get the ball either. He thought about Grandpa George's advice again.

"*Another stupid racist*," thought Henry. "*Go look. Maybe I will learn something.*"

Henry cautiously walked through the shrubbery. He saw an old lady standing on her back porch with a shotgun.

"Hi Mrs. Washington!" shouted Henry. He recognized her as the old lady that had a funny smelling house that he had first met when he was selling rocks. Sometimes, he liked to visit with her to look at her view master pictures and talk about all the places she had visited. He hadn't ever noticed that her house was directly behind Alberts.

"I'm sorry that I threw a baseball in your yard. Can I come and get it?" he asked.

Mrs. Washington lowered her shot gun and squinted. "Henry is that you?" she asked.

"Yes Ma'am," said Henry. "I'm passing baseball with my friend Albert, and I made a bad pass. It was my fault."

Henry turned around and waved to Albert to come out from inside the shrubbery. Albert didn't budge except to shake his head from side to side.

"Oh, sure Henry. You can get your baseball," Mrs. Washington said. She calmed down and started smiling. Henry motioned for Albert to come out from behind the shrubbery again. He gave him his don't be a chicken look. Albert pushed through the shrubbery even more cautiously than he had the first time.

"This is my friend Albert. He's black," announced Henry.

Both Henry and Albert flinched to take off running when the shotgun in Mrs. Washington's arms raised a few inches. They relaxed when it went back down. Mrs. Washington stood silently on her porch looking at them. The boys waited to see what she was going to do.

"Heh. Hi … Al … Albert," said Mrs. Washington.

Henry looked at Albert and gave him a nod to say something.

"Good morning Mrs. Washington," said Albert. He bowed respectively as if he was in church or perhaps a Samurai warrior.

Henry walked to get the baseball with Albert walking slowly behind him. After he picked up the ball, they both continued walking up to Mrs. Washington's back porch.

"What kind of shotgun do you have? Was that Mr. Washington's shot gun?" asked Henry.

Henry couldn't figure out if Mrs. Washington was confused, embarrassed or both. She told him that it was just a 4-10 shotgun, and she didn't really have rock salt in it. They all laughed as Henry and Albert wished her a good day and went back to Albert's yard.

As they continued passing baseball, Henry thought about how he'd imagined Albert had been stupid to be afraid to go into Mrs. Washington's yard. Albert had been the only smart one. He could have gotten Albert killed. It was stupid for him to go in Mrs. Washington's yard. Mrs. Washington was stupid, but her stupidity was just because she was as much afraid of Albert as he was of her. Henry hoped that she wouldn't be as ignorant in the future. He'd have bet money that her shotgun did have rock salt in it or maybe even loaded with real shotgun shells.

When Henry got on his bicycle to go home, it was getting much colder. Snowflakes started falling. Henry smiled as he thought about sleigh riding and throwing snowballs after the first winter snow.

On Sunday after church, there was a big snowstorm. Henry called Mike to see if he could come by to have a snowball fight. Mike's mother dropped Mike off with several other kids from his neighborhood. They went to get Albert and a few other kids from Henry's neighborhood.

After having a prolonged snowball battle, the boys started getting bored with throwing snowballs at each other. They decided to start throwing them at cars. The first car that came along was Mr. Thompson. He was caught by surprise when his car was bombarded with snowballs. He rolled down his window and shook his finger at the boys. He had a good laugh with them.

Mrs. Washington seemed to really enjoy getting her car hammered with snowballs. She laughed even harder than Mr. Thompson.

Mr. Parvis returned fire when the boys started throwing snowballs at him while he was shoveling his driveway. It was evident that he had a lot of practice in throwing snowballs. Everybody in the whole neighborhood was enjoying the first snow of the season.

"Who is that coming up the street?" asked one of the boys as they looked at an unfamiliar car coming towards them. Nobody in the group knew who it was. It only took one of them to throw a snowball to trigger an onslaught of multiple snowballs fired in rapid succession at the oncoming car. The car stopped. A man jumped out of the driver seat with a tire iron.

"You little *fucking* hoodlums! I'll kick every one of your *asses*!" shouted the man.

"It's always fun until someone gets their feelings hurt," thought Henry. He and the other boys ran behind a house and down the alley.

The boys all regrouped and started walking back down the alley towards the street. They laughed off the incident and tried to imagine why the man was so upset about snowballs in the first place.

"Look, a police car!" shouted Mike. He picked up some snow and formed it into a snowball. "Let's get him!"

"No! Don't do it!" shouted Henry and Albert simultaneously. They already knew better than throwing snowballs at the police. The police had their own rules. They didn't tolerate any kind of fun.

It was too late. Mike's snowball hit the roof of the police car with a thud. A police car siren immediately pierced the winter air with the familiar unnerving sound with flashing red and blue lights. The boys took off running. Henry turned to look back to see if the policeman was going to chase them on foot. Albert and Henry were accustomed to being chased by the police and the police were familiar with chasing them.

"Stop," Henry told the other boys. "He's turning around, let's see where he goes."

When Henry and Albert had been younger, they were too afraid to run from the police. The police always seemed to show up whenever they were doing anything fun. At first, they were just kids trying to figure out what they could do and what they weren't allowed to do. After a while they figured out that the police just seemed to enjoy harassing them. There were two different sets of law in their town. On the north side of town, people could do just about anything. On the south side where they lived just being outside was apparently a crime.

They weren't allowed to ride skateboards in the street, on the sidewalks or in most parking lots. They weren't allowed to ride their bikes in empty lots, construction sites or most other properties. They weren't allowed to throw apples, snowballs, or rocks. They weren't allowed to play baseball or football in the street. They weren't allowed to climb on the caboose or airplane in the park or most other things. They weren't allowed to fish off the bridge. Basically, they weren't allowed to do anything that they liked to do when the police were around. Even just standing with their hands in their pockets was a reason to be questioned of what evil they were up too.

When the police caught them doing something, they always spoke to them in a threatening manner and often escorted them home. They would give their mothers an earful of how they didn't have control of their children and how they were going to end up in a juvenile detention center and probably destined for prison.

Henry and Albert had learned to always keep an eye out for the police, so they could stop whatever they were doing and get away to escape having to listen to their threats. They had become experts of seeing the police before they were seen and quickly slipping away to avoid any confrontation. In a way, it became a game to them. Every time they managed to avoid the police; they found some pleasure in not getting in trouble for doing nothing but trying to enjoy themselves. It felt good to outsmart the police.

"He's going to my house," said Albert, with a sigh of frustration. He started walking towards his house.

"Let's go with him," said Henry to Mike. "You can tell him that you were the one that threw the snowball."

"I'm not going," said Mike. "My dad will kill me! Albert better not snitch on me!"

"Albert isn't a snitch and you're a chicken. It's your fault and you aren't man enough to stand up for what you did!" shouted Henry as he walked after Albert. "They aren't going to arrest the chief of police's son for throwing snowballs. Coward!"

He wasn't going to let Albert take the wrath of the police without being by his side. He knew Albert would do the same if it were him.

"Albert is next. He is going to end up just like Tyrone!" shouted the policeman at Ruth, as Albert and Henry arrived at the front door.

"You little pieces of *shit*! You should know better by now. I ought to take both of you to juvenile detention right now!" exclaimed the policeman when he saw Albert and Henry.

"It wasn't us," said Henry. "It was another kid and we told him not to do it."

"Don't lie to me boy! I saw it happen and you and I both know it was one of you two. If it was someone else, then who was it? Where are they?!" said the policeman.

"Just what I thought," he said after a second pause. "It was one of you."

Henry and Albert didn't snitch on others. Henry imagined that if the policeman were a kid, he'd probably have been a snitch or maybe a kid that would allow other kids to get in trouble for something he did just like Mike had just done.

The policeman started walking back to his police car.

"He's next! Albert is next!" he shouted, as he swung back towards Ruth.

"I'm sorry Mrs. Thurman," said Henry. "It wasn't us that threw the snowball, it was another kid, and he wouldn't come with us."

Henry could hear Ruth shouting at Albert as he walked away.

"Albert! How many times do I have to tell you?! Your grounded!" shouted Ruth.

"*This is bull crap,*" thought Henry as he walked home. "*I hate cops. They don't do anything but stop everything we do that is fun. Now Albert isn't even going to be allowed outside. What kind of world is this that the police are the enemy? They are supposed to be the ones protecting us, not harassing us.*"

Tyrone had been trying to protect Gina from a drug dealing rapist. The police accused him of selling drugs and the real drug dealer was free to rape and do whatever he wanted. Henry's blood was boiling. Tyrone was the most selfless person he had ever known. It didn't make any sense that he was imprisoned for seeking justice. The police lied and covered up the truth. Life didn't seem fair.

"*How can they lock up Tyrone and let a rapist and drug dealer be free?*" thought Henry.

The previous summer he had been swinging on a grapevine far back in the woods with a bunch of other kids.

"Look out!" Albert had shouted.

Henry was holding onto the grapevine and swinging in the opposite direction he was looking.

Immediately after Albert's warning, Henry collided with an unseen tree with a hard thud. The back of his head made the initial impact.

It didn't hurt much. The worst part was that he couldn't see. It was a sunny day, but everything became pitch dark. Albert and the other kids were bent over him asking if he was okay. He could hear them and knew they were there, but he couldn't see them.

"I can't see," said Henry. Albert immediately took off running through the woods to get help. His sister Margaret and another older girl stayed with Henry. Henry was afraid that he would be blind for the rest of his life. He felt like he needed to go to sleep. The older girl kept telling him that he had to stay awake.

"Stay awake Henry," she said. "If you go to sleep you will never wake up again. You have to stay awake."

Henry forced himself to stay awake. He didn't want to die. He could hear the unconcerned voices of the other older kids who were still swinging on the grape vine. He could smell the cigarette smoke from some of them smoking.

Tyrone was the help that arrived. "I got you Henry. You're going to be okay," he said. He easily slung Henry over his shoulder and took off gently running back through the woods that he had come through.

As they exited the woods at the top of Henry's street, Marsha was just frantically pulling up in her car with Albert in the passenger seat.

Tyrone put Henry in the front seat after Albert stepped out. Marsha took him to the hospital to find out that he had a concussion. The doctor told him that he had hit the tree with his occipital lobe which is the back part of the brain involved with vision.

"Don't worry," said the doctor. "You will be able to see again soon."

"*I hate the policemen in this town*," thought Henry. "*They need to pay for locking up Tyrone and they better not mess with Albert.*"

Life isn't fair sometimes.

CHAPTER 17

The Predator

"Do you want a ride?" asked Hank Wilson.

Gina looked through the open window of the white Cadillac. It was common in the neighborhood that people often stopped to give her a ride. She was normally ecstatic to oblige a ride, but she immediately distrusted Hank Wilson. Hank wore dark sunglasses and didn't have the typical friendly demeanor like most people in Milton.

"No thank you Sir," responded Gina. "I don't have far to go and it's a nice day to walk."

"Get in the car *bitch*," said Hank. He pointed his 357 Smith and Wesson at her.

Gina froze. Hank pushed the passenger door open before she had a chance to think of anything other than complying. She entered the car drenched in fear.

"Please don't hurt me," she whispered.

Hank smiled to himself at the thought of how much control he had over a poor defenseless teenager. He drove to the other side of town and pulled all the way into the driveway of his best friend, Officer Carl Lucas. He opened the car door for Gina as if he was being a gentleman on a first date. Gina remained glued to her seat, frozen in fear.

"Get out of the car," he said. Gina impulsively got out of the car. He flicked his head towards the back door of the house. "Inside the house."

"Ooh, what do you have here?" said Carl. He smiled as he aggressively clutched Gina's rear end with his right hand. Gina trembled but said nothing.

Carl and Hank started undressing Gina. Her muscles tensed as if she were a marble statue. She closed her eyes with her mouth agape and silently screamed to God for help.

"Please stop," she whispered.

Hank grabbed the back of her neck and shoved her face forcefully onto Carl's couch. She smelled the cigarettes and spilled beer and then felt Hank's penis as it entered her from behind. It went from slow and careful to violent. At first Gina felt as if her soul had left her body. She felt intense pain as Hank squeezed her neck and groaned with each thrust. She started bleeding. Tears silently poured from her eyes. Deep inside she felt an anguish and coldness that exceeded the physical pain as she lost her innocence. Then she didn't feel anything. It was as if she wasn't a person anymore. Her soul was slowly drifting off into space.

After Hank finished, Carl took his turn without Gina knowing they had switched positions. She eventually opened her eyes to find herself looking face to face with Officer Carl Lucas. He had the barrel of his pistol firmly pressed into Gina's mouth with his finger on the trigger. His eyes were bulging as he screamed in delight as his penis went in and out of Gina's bleeding vagina. She could taste the gunpowder.

The cognizance of having a pistol in her mouth at first furthered deepened Gina's shock. She started praying that Carl would pull the trigger to end her misery. Death seemed a better ending than the torture she was enduring.

She lay motionless and was wondering if she was in the middle of a nightmare. She awakened to find herself still naked with her knees on the floor and face on the odor wretched couch.

Hank and Carl were sitting in the kitchen drinking beer as a trembling Gina picked her head up off the couch and looked their way.

"Want some more *bitch*?" laughed Carl.

"You ever tell anyone about this, I will kill you and everyone in your family," said Hank Wilson. He smiled to himself at the power he had over his victim.

Gina slowly picked her clothes off the floor and painstakingly dressed herself with trembling hands. She slowly walked towards the kitchen door as she stared at Hank and Carl to see if they were going to stop her.

Carl stood up from the table and placed himself directly between Gina and the door. He grabbed her tightly and kissed her passionately with his tongue entering her mouth.

"Please let me go," she whispered.

"You can go but don't be a stranger," said Hank. "And remember that if you ever tell anyone you're going to be a dead *bitch nigger*."

Gina rushed out the door. She ran down the driveway and turned left on the street.

"What's wrong with you?" said Tyrone through his passenger window as he caught up with his cousin Gina running down the street.

Gina stopped running, opened the passenger door, and sat down sobbing in Tyrone's car. She buried her face in her trembling hands.

Tyrone put his hand on Gina's shoulder. Hatred filled his heart. Gina couldn't find the strength to talk but it wouldn't take him long to figure out what had happened. He felt his cousins' pain and he wasn't going to tolerate it. Revenge would be sweet, and he would get it.

Tyrone would end up being buried in a jail cell for 10 long years. On the way to prison he would remember something his father Duane had told him as a small child.

"If you seek revenge then you might as well dig two graves," his father had said.

Life wasn't always fair.

CHAPTER 18

Ambush

On Monday morning, Henry had mixed emotions. He listened to the radio to hear that every school in Rockwell County was closed. Normally, a snow day was good news. It meant that he could go outside to sleigh ride and play with his friends. Albert wouldn't be allowed outside after they had gotten in trouble with the police. Henry would just as well go to school if Albert was grounded. He was angry at Mike for not having the courage to be accountable for throwing a snowball at the police.

He continued lying in bed with his eyes wide open. Anger steadily built up inside of him. His blood pulsated through his veins more rapidly. He felt an internal pressure that made him wonder if his cranium was going to explode. His rage was directed at the police. They always seemed to interfere with everything fun. They had put Tyrone behind bars. Gina had been raped without getting justice. The real perpetrator was a free man that could do as he liked. A blizzard raged outside. He listened to the wind beating against his bedroom window. The blizzard was insignificant as compared to the rage in Henry's head. Suddenly, he knew exactly what he was going to do. His rage convinced him to act.

He got out of bed, brushed his teeth, and got dressed. He normally ate breakfast every morning, but food wasn't on his mind. It was cold outside. He put on long underwear under his pants and dressed in multiple layers. He found an old nylon thin black pull over that Harold didn't wear anymore. Just about every other man in Milton had one just like it. He put it over his winter clothes. The pullover went almost to his knees. It concealed his own winter jacket. He put his black toboggan hat on that covered his entire face except his eyes and mouth.

"*Perfect*," he thought. "*Nobody will recognize me.*"

It was before five o'clock in the morning. He knew there wouldn't be many people out even if there wasn't a blizzard outside. He went out the back door to avoid making any tracks at the front of his house. He found a vantage point from the carport at the side of his house where he could see up and down the street. He made sure that none of the neighbors were outside or peering out their windows. He jumped from the carport to the sidewalk of their neighbor's house and carefully made his way to the street.

A snowplow had plowed the roads during the night. Huge piles of snow lined the roads, covered cars, and blocked driveways. The wind was blowing hard enough that it was difficult to walk. Henry smiled. It was a perfect day to do what he was going to do. The wind helped to quickly conceal any tracks that he made on the icy streets. Nobody in their right mind would be out in this weather unless it was an emergency. The only way to avoid consequences was to not get caught and to ensure there weren't any witnesses.

It was a 15-minute walk to Mike's neighborhood. Henry continued tweaking his plan as he proceeded through the blizzard. As soon as he arrived in Mike's neighborhood, he went into action. There weren't any tracks in the snow. The whole neighborhood was still sleeping in the comfort of their warm homes.

Henry picked a good spot in the alley behind Mike's house along 18th Avenue of which was the main road through the neighborhood. Mike's back yard was three houses away from 18th Avenue on 39th Street. Henry ran up the alley and took a left into Mike's back yard. He carefully walked backwards from the alley all the way to Mike's front porch. He spent the next 20 or 30 minutes running in circles around houses and back and forth making tracks in every direction. He ran through every front yard of each house on the street multiple times.

The last house he made tracks to was to Mike's front door. He made a special effort to make sure the tracks looked perfectly how he wanted them to look. He returned to his spot in the alley behind Mike's house using the same tracks he had already made through Mike's backyard. He made two snowballs. He compressed them with his hands until they were hard balls of ice. He left the snowballs on top of a trash can 1 house down from Mike's house. He made two more non-compacted snowballs and sat down to wait at the ideal spot.

From his spot, he could see in both directions on 18th Avenue. It was behind a garage that had some protection from the wind. The trash cans and shrubbery provided good concealment to remain hidden.

After several minutes, a Ford pickup truck with a snowplow drove by Henry. His fingers and toes were starting to get cold. He balled his fingers into a fist inside of his gloves to try and warm his fingers as he watched the truck pass.

Time moved slowly. Henry patiently waited. The cold was becoming almost unbearable. He heard a car start a couple streets away. He knew that if he didn't have an opportunity soon, he would have to abort his mission and head back to his house. It wouldn't be long before potential witnesses would be up and about.

He stood up and started doing jumping jacks to get himself warm. The sound of a car interrupted his quest to get warm. He peeked through a crack between a trash can and the garage. A police car slowly edged up 18th Avenue. Henry picked up the two snowballs. He took a deep breath and said a prayer as he leaned against the garage.

He listened to the sound of the police car and waited until it was just nearing the alley to make his move. He leaped into the alley and stepped onto 18th Avenue where he unleashed both snowballs in rapid succession directly at the front windshield of the police car. He watched the confused and fearful expression of Officer Carl Lucas. Henry smiled. Both snowballs hit the driver side windshield with thuds. Officer Lucas struggled to get the car in park and exit the car. Henry slowly ran back into the alley in hopes that Officer Lucas would think that he might be able to catch him.

He grabbed the two hard compressed ice balls that he had left on top of a trash can. The police car door slammed shut. Henry had recognized the policeman as being one of the ones of whom had arrested Tyrone and took him away to prison. Officer Carl Lucas had been the roughest of all the policemen. He had told Tyrone to stop resisting as he kneed and pressed his arm to the back of Tyrone's neck. He stood waiting for the policeman to turn the corner into the alley with both arms to his side and the ice balls concealed in his gloves. He was eager to payback Officer Lucas for what he had done to Tyrone.

"Come here you little *shit*!" said Officer Lucas. He slowed to a walk and continued moving towards Henry. Henry stood motionless and said nothing. The policeman confidently walked towards him thinking that he had him caught.

He waited until Officer Lucas was about 20 feet from him and then he reared his right arm back. He stepped forward with his left leg and threw the ice ball with all his might directly at the policeman's head. It was a direct hit in the left eye. Carl stumbled. He put his left hand over his eye. Henry threw the second ice ball and hit him in the neck just as Carl pulled his gun out of his holster with his right hand.

Henry didn't waste any time to turn around and run up the alley as fast as he could in a zig zag pattern like a rabbit. Once he made the turn into Mike's yard, he sprinted in a straight line.

"I wonder if he would really shoot at a kid for throwing snowballs," thought Henry.

After he reached the front of Mike's house, he slowed down and meticulously followed his previous footprints to make it look like he went into Mike's house. He jumped off the porch and perfectly landed into another set of tracks. He continued sprinting up the street past two more houses where he turned right and headed back towards the alley. He stopped at the rear of the house to make sure the policeman wasn't still in the alley or back yard. He saw Officer Lucas half running and walking as he labored to the back of Mike's house.

"Thank God, he's a smoker and frequents the donut shop," thought Henry.

Henry waited until the policeman disappeared behind Mike's house. He continued his sprint to the alley. He took a left to head for the woods.

Once Henry got into the woods, he slowed to a walk and cautiously moved towards the top of Mike's dead-end street.

He crawled along the ground and found a good spot where he could peer down the street from under a fallen tree. Officer Lucas was standing on Mike's front porch. Henry pushed snow in front of him to fill the gap between the tree and the ground to make sure he was concealed.

Mike's mother was at their front door talking to Officer Lucas. She opened the door a little wider and the policeman's gaze shifted away from Mike's Mother to someone smaller standing next to her.

"He's probably looking at Mike still in his pajamas," thought Henry.

He tried to imagine what Officer Lucas was saying and how embarrassed he would be talking to the chief of police's wife and son about getting hit with a snowball.

"I just got hit with a snowball in the face by a little kid. Have you seen him?" thought Henry.

He imagined what Mike and Mrs. Rodgers would be thinking. They would think it was as funny as he thought it was. A grown man looking for a little kid that hit him with a snowball.

"Oh, how terrible. I hope you catch him," he imagined Mrs. Rodgers saying to the policeman.

Officer Lucas stepped off Mike's front porch onto the sidewalk. Mrs. Rodgers closed the front door. He walked towards the street looking at the tracks in the snow. He started trying to follow the tracks. He stopped and looked back and forth at all of Henry's tracks. They were everywhere and must have looked like the tracks of a hundred kids.

"That would be funny if 100 kids came out and all started throwing snowballs at him," thought Henry.

Officer Lucas started to scratch is head only to recognize that he was still holding his 45-caliber pistol in his right hand. He looked at the gun as if he was confused of why he even had it in the first place. He put it back into his holster.

Henry sunk down as low to the ground as he could. He remained completely motionless. Officer Lucas stared up the street at the woods where he was hiding. His heart was still beating fast. He wondered if it was from running or from the fear of being shot or caught.

"*Probably a combination of both,*" thought Henry.

As he watched Officer Lucas walking back toward Mike's house, he felt several different emotions. He felt happy to have gotten back at the police and not getting caught, fear that maybe he was going to get caught and guilt that he was victimizing a defenseless cop. At first, the sweetness of the sugar of revenge exceeded any emotion of fear or guilt.

The policemen that Henry knew were generally the aggressors that victimized others and could seek their own vengeance. Henry had victimized a policeman. He started feeling sorry for the cop who looked like a defenseless kid. As soon as the policeman turned the corner around Mike's house, Henry counted to 50 to make sure the policeman wasn't going to have second thoughts and come back to take another peek up the street into the woods. He jumped up and ran as fast through the snow as he could to deep in the woods. He removed Harold's black nylon jacket and toboggan and put them inside his winter jacket. Seconds later, he looked like a different person wearing a Pittsburgh Steelers toboggan and a bright green winter parka.

He jogged through the woods toward his own neighborhood. He came out several blocks away from his house where he could take the street. He wanted to make sure if anyone did have the energy to find and follow his tracks through the woods that they'd have a hard time to track them all the way to his house.

He walked down the street. Mr. Parvis was already shoveling his driveway. The wind wasn't blowing as hard as it had been, and the morning sun was shining brightly.

As soon as he got home, he hid the black jacket and toboggan. He changed his pants and put on his boots. He got the snow shovel out of the shed and started shoveling the sidewalk and driveway at his house.

After he finished, he started knocking on doors and shoveling snow for his neighbors. He didn't waste any time shoveling. The more snow he shoveled the less likely the police could track him down.

Officer Lucas would figure out that another policeman's car was hit with a snowball the previous day. They already mistakenly suspected that Albert and Henry were the guilty party. Henry had thought about the risk of being a suspect earlier in the morning. It was one of the reasons that he had made the ambush in another neighborhood.

Officer Lucas slowly turned onto Henry's Street. Henry was shoveling snow at his 5th house. He watched out of the corner of his eyes as he pushed the shovel under another big heap of snow. Officer Lucas looked in his direction. Henry could barely see that the left side of his face was swollen and already turning blue, but he was careful not to make eye contact or look directly at him. He wasn't going to do anything that would make him look suspicious.

Officer Lucas continued driving slowly up his street. Henry smiled. He knew that he wasn't going to get caught. He felt an urge to let Albert know but he knew that was an urge he had to resist. He trusted Albert more than anyone, but secrets were best kept if he was the only one that had to resist the temptation of being truthful.

"Nobody will ever know it was me except for God and myself," thought Henry. *"The policeman isn't going to tell anyone, but Mike's dad will find out from his wife and then all the other policemen are going to find out. The policeman will be the laughingstock of all of them."*

He prayed that maybe the ambush would humble Officer Carl Lucas and make him think twice before harassing kids anymore. Maybe it would change his perception about the kids in Milton. The kids on the south side of town were out shoveling snow to make money while kids on the north side were out throwing snowballs at the police.

When Henry got home, it was just a little after 11 am. He thought about the successful ambush and the $37 he made from shoveling snow. Shoveling snow was even a better business than selling rocks.

"I'll be shoveling more snow, but I think this was my last snowball ambush. It is easy to fool someone once but hard to fool them twice," thought Henry.

By lunch time, the sweetness of revenge had already worn off. Henry's conscious was biting at him. He knew that what he had done was wrong. Guilt started eating away at his heart. He remembered Tyrone telling him that he was supposed to not be overcome with evil. He'd read the same words in Romans 12. The only way to really overcome evil was with good. Throwing snowballs at policemen was wrong.

Life has consequences even when we don't get caught.

CHAPTER 19

The People of the Forest

"Go to the bleachers and everyone be quiet. Nobody says a word!" shouted the teacher.

Henry, Albert and Slim disappointingly walked towards the bleachers. During the first two weeks of the fourth grade, they had been allowed to play basketball while they waited for their school bus after school. All the kids except for Kyle were socializing or playing games. Kyle was the only one already seated studiously in the bleachers. He used every minute of his free time to study and was becoming more of a recluse. Kyle preferred to ignore the other kids and just focus on his schoolwork.

Henry, Albert and Slim's bus was the last one. It picked them up 45 minutes after school was out and it took another 30 minutes to get to Henry and Albert's bus stop. Henry enjoyed riding the bus now that Albert had transferred to his school. They had been having lots of fun playing basketball with Slim and several other boys.

"Why do we have to sit in the bleachers, and why aren't we allowed to talk?" asked Henry as he walked off the basketball court.

"Because I said so!" exclaimed Mr. Daniels.

"If we can't talk then what are we supposed to do?"

"Everyone is going to do their homework," replied Mr. Daniels. "Then you will already have it done when you get home. I'm doing you and everyone else a favor Henry."

"I don't have any homework," said Henry. "Can I play basketball?"

"No, you can sit down like everyone else."

All the kids except for Henry opened their books. They either did their homework or at least pretended to do so. Henry always left his books in his desk at school. If he had any assignments, he made sure he finished them in class. He didn't see any need to take books home to study things that he learned at school. Henry's goal was to make the third best grades in class. Kyle and Sally put forth a lot of effort in doing homework and special projects. Henry didn't have any difficulties regurgitating information on tests, and he didn't see any reason to devote his free time to doing schoolwork. It was already hard enough to not make better marks than Kyle and Sally. Being first in class did nothing other than make him a target to be bullied and detested by everyone else. Kyle and Sally both worked diligently competing against each other to be first in the class. At least Sally tried to socialize and have friends. She had good success in befriending other girls. Kyle had abandoned all efforts in trying to get the other kids to like him. Being a smart girl was socially accepted but smart boys were prime targets of victimization. Nobody liked smart boys.

"Henry! I told you to do your homework!" shouted Mr. Daniels.

"Sir, I already told you that I don't have any homework to do," said Henry. "If I don't have any homework to do then I don't understand why I can't play basketball. School is over and most other kids are already outside playing or doing something other than schoolwork. It isn't fair that we have to continue classes just because our bus comes last. I don't understand why you want to punish us."

"You better open your book or get up here to meet Mr. Hickory," responded Mr. Daniels. He slowly and sensually caressed Mr. Hickory.

Henry immediately stood up and walked out onto the basketball court to receive his punishment. He knew better than trying to explain to Mr. Daniels that he couldn't open a book if he didn't have one to open. It would just lead to getting in trouble for not having a book to open. He had heard about Mr. Hickory. Everyone in his school knew that Mr. Daniels called his paddle Mr. Hickory. Most of them were terrified of the thought of getting their butt beat by Mr. Daniels. Henry and his friends thought Mr. Daniels' relationship with a paddle made of hickory wood seemed bizarre. He treated Mr. Hickory as if he were his best friend.

"Sir, I told you I don't have any homework. I don't have any books to open up and look at," said Henry. He turned and bent forward with his hands on his knees to find out if Mr. Hickory hurt as much as everyone thought. Mr. Hickory wasn't anywhere near as terrible as Henry had anticipated.

"You better bring your books tomorrow. If you don't, Mr. Hickory isn't going to be happy," said Mr. Daniels.

"*I'm walking home tomorrow,*" thought Henry. He didn't mind getting spanked, but he couldn't stand sitting doing nothing for 45 minutes. Albert handed Henry one of his books so he could open it and pretend like he was reading.

Once on the bus, Albert and Slim decided that they would prefer to walk home from school with Henry. They all agreed they would try to convince their parents to allow them to walk instead of waiting for the school bus.

"Oh no! You aren't going to walk home from school. It is more than three miles," replied Marsha.

"Mom, you know that I can't sit down for 45 minutes doing nothing. All the old people are always telling us kids that we have it too easy these days getting to ride a bus. If they had to walk home for miles through the snow and rain then I should be allowed to do the same thing," said Henry. "Please. You know I can't just sit in the bleachers for 45 minutes doing nothing. Albert and Slim are going to walk with me, and I will get home before the bus does."

"Alright Henry," said Marsha. "But you have to come straight home and be careful."

"Thanks Mom," said Henry. "I will."

Albert and Slim weren't as successful in convincing their parents to grant them permission to walk. It would take then another week of practicing persistence before they could walk with Henry.

Eventually, all three boys were allowed to walk home from school.

Every day they modified their route slightly to try and find the fastest way to get home. "I wonder where that path through the woods goes," said Albert as the boys looked at a small trail going into a forested area that surrounded a stream that ran through town.

"That's Lincoln Creek," said Slim. "It comes out just by my house."

"Let's try it out," said Henry.

The sun dimly came through the trees as the boys entered the darkness of the forest. They quickly found lots of distractions. There were trees and rocks to climb and a tire on a rope that swung out over Lincoln Creek.

The following day, the boys had a hard time waiting for the clock to strike 3 p.m. They ran all the way to the forest and climbed high into a tree they had found with a long trunk at 45 degrees.

"I see somebody coming," said Albert as he peered through the tree branches.

Three older boys rode their bicycles through the forest.

"Look! There's a *nigger* in that tree!" shouted one of the boys.

Albert had climbed the furthest up into the tree and Henry was right behind him. Slim was struggling to keep up with them. He stood at the base of the tree looking at the older boys. They all stopped their bicycles to laugh at him.

"What is your problem fat *fuck*!? Trying to catch a *nigger*?" said one of the boys to Slim. They laid their bicycles down and started throwing rocks at the boys as they continued shouting racial slurs and obscenities.

"Stop throwing rocks!" shouted Henry. "We aren't trying to catch anyone. We are just climbing this tree." Henry's explanation didn't help. The onslaught of rocks and insults continued.

Henry and Albert slid and jumped down from the tree as they avoided the flurry of rocks. Slim and Albert used their book bags as shields to block the rocks. Henry found a big stick that he used as a bat to try and hit the rocks like a baseball.

"Nice block Albert!" said Slim as Albert effectively blocked a rock directed at his crotch.

"Yeah, thanks," laughed Albert.

Henry managed to get a good swing with his stick. The rock almost hit one of the older boys. He barely got his leg out of the way of getting hit with the same rock that he had thrown.

The rock throwing continued for another minute or two without any words being said. The victimizers at first enjoyed shouting insults and hurling rocks. It became less amusing when they noticed that their victims all enjoyed the rock throwing more than they did. They got back on their bicycles and slowly continued riding through the dark forest.

Albert picked up a rock. He motioned like he was going to throw it at the retreating older boys and then dropped it on the ground with a smile.

"Let's go climb that big rock cliff that we found," said Slim. They all ran towards the rocks.

The boys soon made their own smaller secret trail through the forest where they could covertly make their way through the dense trees. Occasionally they would stop to listen for other people in the forest. When they heard someone, they would conceal themselves to observe them without being noticed. They often saw the same group of boys that had bombarded them with insults and rocks either smoking cigarettes, riding their bikes, or throwing rocks at birds, squirrels, or rabbits.

Moving stealthily without being seen was just as much fun as climbing rocks and trees. The trek through the dark forest was something they looked forward to and they saw something completely unexpected almost every day.

"Shh, I hear someone screaming," said Albert. He put his finger to his lips.

"Sounds more like moaning," whispered Slim. "Let's go see what is going on."

They climbed on top of a rock outcropping and worked their way down the hill to a good vantage point. They all slid on their bellies side by side inside of a rhododendron bush. The boys saw a big white hairy butt moving up and down. Two long slender legs stuck straight up in the air on each side of the big hairy butt.

"They are having sex," said Albert with a smile.

"Why would they be having sex in the woods?" asked Slim with a look of confusion.

"I don't know, but it sounds like they are enjoying themselves," said Henry. "Look at that squirrel in the tree. He is eating nuts just above them."

All the boys had a hard time not laughing out loud when the squirrel dropped an acorn that landed in the crack of the man's butt.

"I think he did that on purpose," quietly laughed Albert.

After the couple finished fornicating, they pulled their clothes back on.

"I don't think he knows about the acorn in his butt," snickered Albert. "I never saw it fall out."

The boys smiled. The man lit up a pipe that he shared with his girlfriend. The boys immediately recognized the smell as marijuana. They often saw small groups of hippies in the woods and had immediately noticed that the smell was much different and more pungent than cigarettes. They slid themselves out of the rhododendron bush backwards on their bellies and crept back up through the rocks to continue their way.

"In school we learn math, science and English," said Henry. "In the woods we get to learn about the birds and the bees."

"Bees? I haven't seen any bees," said Slim.

"The 'birds and the bees' is a euphemism," said Albert. "It is when adults try and explain sex to us kids. We got to see it with our own eyes."

The next day, they heard another commotion coming from the same place.

"Sounds like the birds and bees are out again," said Slim.

They stopped and listened.

"That sounds like a kid screaming," said Henry. "Let's go."

They quickly followed their secret trail and squeezed themselves into the rhododendron bush.

"That's one of those kids that threw rocks at us," said Albert.

An older man was holding him against a tree with a knife to his throat. The boy's bicycle was lying nearby in the path.

"We've got to stop this," whispered Henry. He quickly reversed himself out of the rhododendron bush.

They each picked up 3 or 4 baseball sized rocks by the rock cliff and went into action. All three of them unleashed their first rock. Albert's rock hit the man in the leg.

"Leave him alone now!" shouted Henry. "We already sent someone for the police!"

The man confusingly let go of the boy. He looked up to see where the voice and rocks had come from and then took off running through the woods.

The boy jumped on his bike and took off in the opposite direction. He turned his head towards the boys, made eye contact, and nodded his head in gratitude.

"I wonder what he was going to do to him," said Slim. "I don't think he has much to be robbed other than maybe cigarettes."

"Maybe he was going to rape him," replied Albert.

"He's a boy. Why would he rape a boy?" asked Slim.

"Some people apparently do that," said Henry shaking his head in disbelief.

"At least we saved him," said Albert proudly. "I bet he doesn't throw rocks at us again or call us names."

"Yeah," said Henry. "Hopefully, we just made another friend."

The boys called everyone they saw in the forest the 'people of the forest'. In town, they saw people walking their pets and babies. They were almost always courteous and respectful members of the community. The 'people of the forest' were breaking laws or generally up to no good. It was a nice contrast to normality. The boys liked being in the forest.

The spot where they learned about the 'birds and bees' and stopped the boy from getting raped ended up being the preferred sex spot for the 'people of the forest'.

"That's Kyle's sister," said Henry. He watched her pulling her pants back up. The sexual encounter had been different than the normal sex in the forest. Most of the time, both parties seemed to enjoy themselves but the man having sex with Sheila had been aggressive. Sheila was void of any emotion. Her face was expressionless, and she didn't make a sound. The man had held her arms tightly behind her back. The sex almost looked as if he was assaulting Sheila.

"She's a drug addict," said Albert. The man took out his wallet and handed Sheila some money. She stuffed it in her pocket without a word. "Why is he giving her money?"

"He must be paying her for sex," said Slim.

Kyle's sister slowly staggered down the path by Lincoln Creek. The man lit up a cigarette and casually walked the other way.

"Did you see how sad she looked?" asked Henry.

"Why would anyone want to be a drug addict?" asked Slim.

"Nobody wants to be an addict," responded Albert. "I think she has had a hard life and she found drugs to escape it. Now the drugs own her, and she will do anything to get more drugs."

"I saw her mom shouting at her at the swimming pool once," said Henry. "She was screaming at her and asking why she couldn't be more like her brother Kyle. Kyle was sitting in the car with his head down like he didn't know what to do. I feel sorry for the whole family."

"I don't know why Kyle always seems angry," said Slim. "Whenever I speak to him, he just looks at me like he is mad at me for something."

"Yeah, I've almost given up trying to talk to him," said Henry. "But I feel sorry for him and his sister. I don't know how to get him to talk. It is like he doesn't want to have friends. He just wants to do good in school."

"His sister is going to kill herself," said Albert. "She is on a dead-end road without much hope but there isn't anything wrong with doing good in school. Good grades just open up more doors to succeed."

Some people's circumstances are hard to escape.

CHAPTER 20

Church Camp

Every summer, Henry's family went to church camp with other Baptist families from across the state. From a young age, Henry and Margaret also went to a separate church camp just for kids. Both camps were at the same rural location with cabins in the wilderness and the rumbling of a nearby white-water river. It had a peaceful ambiance in nature.

Henry enjoyed going to church camp with his family. It was a perfect utopia. They met lots of nice people that were all practicing their best behavior. Everyone smiled more than usual. They sharpened their niceness skills as they competed to outdo everyone else in being the most loving. Church camp was good training to know how to apply the Golden Rule.

It was hard for Henry not to smile and be on his best behavior when everyone else was so nice. He wondered why everyone couldn't do the same thing in the real world. As soon as church camp would end, things went back to normal. The same people would stop being so kind all the time. It wasn't that they weren't nice people, but there was an obvious kindness reduction in the real world.

"Dad why isn't everyone so kind in the real world?" asked Henry.

"It's easy to be kind when you are surrounded by it," replied Harold. "Kindness is contagious just like everything else. The problem in the real world is that most people are struggling to find kindness. Life is hard. When people are drowning in despair and wickedness all around them, they don't have the strength to be kind. Not many people are strong enough to be kind in adversity. It's easy to repay kindness with kindness but hard to be kind to someone punching you in the face."

Church camp gave Henry an opportunity to ask questions to lots of people from other churches and towns. When he had a question, he rarely only asked the question to a single person. He liked asking the same questions to a wide variety of people to see what different answers he would get. For some questions, he'd get the same response from almost everyone. For others, he got a wide variety of answers. He tried to rationalize what answer made the most sense. He liked asking the difficult questions where he got the most varying responses and opinions the most. Church camp gave him a bigger polling audience.

One of the questions that he asked a lot was, "What do you think heaven is like?" After getting responses that ranged from mansions with streets paved in gold to a state of eternal bliss in the presence of lost loved ones, he'd ask his follow up questions.

Will people all be the same age, the age they die or a different age? Do dog's go to heaven? Will people be married in heaven? What if their husband or wife died and then they get remarried? Do you think there will be black people and communists in Heaven? What happens if a rapist becomes born again? Will he be in heaven with whoever he raped and her parents? What would eternal bliss feel like? Wouldn't you get tired of being constantly happy and at peace? What would you do in eternal bliss? What about my Uncle Jim? He doesn't go to church but is one of the nicest people I know. Will he get to go to heaven?

Henry didn't care much about material things. He preferred a dirt path through the woods to walking on streets made of gold. He was happy almost all the time. He had the impression that most people were searching for happiness externally. They were always in want and never satisfied. Henry didn't need much to find contentment. Bliss was always there whenever he needed it. Heaven was hard to understand.

Most of the time, after two or three follow up questions the person being asked the questions would start getting confused themselves. Their sadness would progressively increase with each question. Henry knew to stop asking questions when they started creating pain and distress. He would change the subject by thinking of something else to say to try and cheer up the people he interrogated. He found heaven depressing himself but continued asking the questions. He hoped someone could give him a good answer that made it not seem so depressing. He had his best discussions with Albert and Slim. They could discuss anything without worrying about hurting anyone's feelings. They valued honesty over their personal emotions.

"What do you think heaven is like?" Henry asked.

"I don't know," replied Albert. "I hope I get to meet my dad and that there isn't any racism in heaven."

"I would like to meet him too. I would also like to meet my dad's dad," said Henry. "They both died before we were born. But I feel like I already know them. That is why I'd like to meet them. If I didn't know what I know about them then I wouldn't want to meet them. Since I already feel like I know them, I don't really need to meet them in person."

"I think people in heaven would be kinder and there wouldn't be anyone disabled or sick," said Slim. "Nobody would make fun of Owen for being crippled because he would be able to walk like everyone else."

"Why would anyone want to make fun of someone that is crippled in heaven?" asked Henry. "Wouldn't everyone not care about stuff like that? I'd think people would look past appearances and see people's true character. Everyone would find it easy to love Owen just like we do."

"I guess you are right," said Slim. "Everybody would be perfect people full of compassion and love."

"That would mean we wouldn't see the bad traits of anyone," said Albert. "Everybody has flaws. I don't think love and compassion can exist if everybody is perfect. If there is no pain, then there isn't anyone that needs love. If I get to meet my dad, I'd like to meet the real him. Just as he was."

"Would we still want to get revenge, be angry and hate other people?" asked Henry. "What would it be like to not desire anything but good? I can't imagine not struggling with my conscience to do what is right. It would feel like a prison to me. Not doing the evil I want to do is what makes life satisfying. I feel best when I don't do what I think I want to do."

"I can't imagine being 100% selfless," responded Albert. "It seems too much like slavery to me. We would be slaves to everyone else."

"Yeah," said Slim. "But everyone else would-be slaves to us as well. Everybody would be trying to help everyone else all the time. It would be a kindness competition."

"Sounds suffocating to me," said Henry. "I prefer being free to have a choice. I don't want to be a slave or a master. I like life as it is. I agree with Albert. If people have no pain and suffering, then there isn't anyone that needs loved. Life is already a kindness competition."

"Why does everyone want to get in the pearly gates if there isn't any heaven?" asked Slim.

"Who said there isn't a heaven?" asked Henry.

"You did," said Albert. "You seem to think we are in heaven on Earth."

"No. I think there has to be something after death," said Henry. "I just can't imagine it being mansions with streets paved with gold or a family reunion for eternity. If there isn't any reward for living a good life, then everything is permitted. There must be some kind of heaven. I just can't imagine what it would be like."

"Everything isn't permitted. We have laws," said Slim. "You get punished when you break them."

"Laws only punish actions within narrow limits put in place by people. They kind of justify immoral actions outside of their limits," said Albert. "The law and morality are two different things. Good people don't need laws and evil people always find a way around the law."

"Some people break the law and don't get caught," said Henry.

"Some laws are stupid," said Slim. "Robin Hood broke the law. When laws become too oppressive and stupid maybe they need to be broken."

"Harriet Tubman and other abolitionists broke the law too," said Albert. "I agree some laws are stupid. Like us black people having to ride on the back of a bus."

"I don't know what heaven is going to be like but I'm sure God will know what to do with us when we die," said Henry. "Call me crazy, but I have faith that God knows best. All we can do is to try our best to make the right choices. I am grateful to have the freedom to choose to do good or evil. I can't imagine not having that freedom. The better the choices we make, the better our lives will be even if heaven didn't exist."

"I think faith is more important than belief," said Albert. "Beliefs don't carry much weight if you have doubt. Faith is the opposite of doubt. If you have faith, then you are confident in the outcome. Faith is when you know God knows best. Beliefs are in our brains, but faith is in our hearts."

"I like that," said Slim. "Everyone's mind plays tricks on them, but we have to have faith in our hearts."

"I don't think anyone is good enough for heaven or bad enough to go to hell," said Henry. "It would be nice if there weren't so many greedy, envious, ungrateful, and angry people but I can't imagine a world completely void of evil and sin. Who would we help and what would we do? Life would be boring."

"I guess we need reminders to feel blessed," said Albert. "If we didn't get to fall down, we wouldn't feel good when we get back up."

"Exactly," said Henry. "How can anyone be happy that doesn't ever get to experience unhappiness? Everything is relative. One man's garbage is another person's treasure."

"Maybe temptations and trials in life are just the consequence of freedom," said Slim. "I don't think I would like the oppression of a prison without temptations void of my own freewill either. I have faith and trust that God knows best. God is great. Thank God we have the freedom to make choices."

After several days of church camp, Henry started missing the real world. As much as he liked being immersed in a kind utopian world, he found the real world more exciting. He missed his friends and even the 'people of the forest'. As family camp was nearing an end, Henry had a conversation with an older boy about streaking. It was 1974. Streaking had become a popular past time.

Henry liked going to dirt track car races just to see who would decide to take their clothes off and run around the middle of the track. The car races were exciting, but the streakers were more entertaining. The nude runners were almost always hippies. They had the courage to entertain the masses without fear of the consequences. They would be completely naked except for their shoes, socks and sometimes a hat if it was cold enough. The funniest part was watching the police trying to catch them. Henry was amazed with how much pleasure everyone in the stands had from watching the streakers. Someone would run around naked as the police worked diligently trying to catch them. After they caught them, they seemed to find detaining a naked person even more challenging than catching them. Nobody wanted to aggressively tackle and wrestle with a naked hippie. All the people watching would cheer and laugh. The streakers always got a standing ovation.

There was even a funny song that had just came out by Ray Stevens called "The Streak". In the song, the singer's wife, Ethyl, couldn't resist stripping and joining another streaker to the embarrassment of her husband.

"Why don't you go streaking?" asked the older boy. "You like watching streakers. Why not do it yourself?"

Henry laughed at the thought.

"I can't do that," said Henry. "My mom will beat me senseless."

"Think how cool you would be," said the older boy. "You said it yourself. Everyone loves to watch a streaker. Why not give everyone something to be happy about?"

Henry knew that streakers always seemed to get caught. If he went streaking it wasn't like nobody would know it was him. There wasn't much he could do to disguise himself if he was buck naked but there weren't any policemen at church camp. He doubted anyone would call the police because a 9-year-old was running around naked.

"You're afraid, aren't you?" asked the older boy.

"I'm not afraid," said Henry. "It just isn't appropriate to run around naked at church camp."

"Chicken," said the older boy. "Adam and Eve were naked in the Garden of Eden."

Henry found some privacy behind their cabin. He took off his clothes and started running. Everyone in the church camp started pointing and laughing. It was just like the car races. Christians or not, streakers created happiness and laughter. Henry enjoyed the moment. His ego was exploding in being the first ever streaker at church camp. He felt so elated and free. Adrenaline surged through his brain. Everyone loved it and they loved Henry. Nobody could stop him.

The only person that wasn't laughing was Marsha. She yelled at Henry to stop. Henry just kept running with a special smile reserved only for naked runners. An embarrassed Marsha tried unsuccessfully to catch him. After a while the people stopped laughing. The adrenaline wore off. Henry headed behind the cabin to recover his clothes.

"Henry, you get out here right now!" shouted Marsha.

"I can't, I'm naked," said Henry, knowing it was a lame excuse after just going for a streak.

"You get out here right now! Everyone has already seen your nakedness!" exclaimed Marsha.

"Is nothing sacred anymore?!" screamed another lady.

Henry thought for a moment. He decided that his mother was right. He'd go out and take his whipping bare butt and all. He walked towards Marsha and all the other people that had come out to watch his streaking show. The only person still laughing was the older boy that had convinced him to do it. Several of the women were shaking their heads like Henry was Satan himself. It was discipline time. Streaking evidently wasn't something a good Christian boy would do. Marsha gave him a good whipping. Henry was grateful she hadn't brought her wooden spoon to church camp. It was easy to avoid any pain from Marsha's open handed spanking.

Several of the adults made disparaging comments to Henry. Perhaps it was their guilty conscience after enjoying the sinful moment that compelled them to remind Henry that he was the guilty party.

"*You were just laughing and enjoying the show*," thought Henry. "*Discipline yourself.*"

It didn't take long for Henry to forget about the punishment. He suddenly became the most popular kid in the camp. All the other kids looked up to him for being brave enough to run around naked. The older kids were impressed with his courage. It felt good to be noticed by the pretty hippie girls without any jealousy from their boyfriends.

If Henry had a time machine, he'd have went streaking again. Whippings didn't bother him much, but he really liked all the attention he got. It was Henry's MO to take any consequences that came along and then never look back. It didn't make any sense to trip over what was already behind him. In most cases, the thrill of whatever he did wrong was worth the consequences. It wasn't like Henry didn't know what the consequences would be before he did something.

Henry was proud of himself. He was feeding his own desires and embracing the deadliest sin of all. The worldly attention he got helped to egg him on to be a disobedient prideful child. Henry did whatever he wanted to do.

A few years later, Henry was back at the kids only church camp without his parents. The kid's camp didn't have the same perfect utopia feeling as the family camp did. It was more like an extension of public schooling. Adult counselors policed all the children and demanded good behavior. Henry enjoyed playing sports with the other kids and singing Kumbaya songs around the campfire. He didn't care much for all the rules and structure involved. There wasn't very much free time. Whenever he tried to sneak off to have some fun with other rebellious kids there was always another counselor redirecting them back to another organized event.

The worst part of each day was nap time. Henry was 12 years old. He thought naps were for babies. Sitting in his bunk for one complete hour felt like an extended time out. Sixty antagonizing minutes was an eternity to a hyperactive teenager.

To make the best of nap time, Henry wrote letters to his parents, relatives, and friends. He didn't like writing letters, but it gave him something to do. Most of the other kids and adults all seemingly enjoyed a nap. Henry heard someone groaning. He peered over the side of his top bunk to see where the noise was coming from. A counselor across the room had his pillow against his crotch. He was rhythmically thrusting the pillow. He moaned and groaned in pleasure. Henry watched his butt move away from the pillow and then thrust back into it repeatedly. He was confident from his experiences of watching the 'people of the forest' that the counselor was having sex with his pillow. A couple of the other boys that didn't take naps also noticed. They all smiled in bewilderment from their bunk beds as they watched.

After nap time, one of the boys told Henry that the counselor humped his pillow because he was a homosexual.

"We'd better be careful around him," he advised Henry.

"How do you know if he thinks his pillow is a man or a woman?" asked Henry. "Maybe he just likes pillows."

"It's the way he is humping it," the boy responded.

Henry wasn't sure if the counselor was a homosexual, but he knew it would be best to ensure he wasn't ever alone with the pillow humping counselor. He wasn't someone Henry was going to trust.

Henry and a few other boys finally managed to sneak away without being seen by the counselors. They all sat down under a big tree. One of the boys pulled out a can of snuff. Henry hadn't ever tried snuff before, but he had seen the marketing commercials. A star athlete had convinced Henry with his southern draw that snuff was cool. If he used smokeless tobacco, then it couldn't be that bad. Henry wondered what Tyrone would have to say about smokeless tobacco. Tyrone would have told him that he shouldn't listen to commercials.

All the boys including Henry took a pinch of the snuff. They all immediately laid down on their backs as everything began to spin. It didn't feel relaxing like the commercial promised, but it sure did feel good. After Henry spit out the tobacco and stood up, he still felt euphoric with everything spinning and going in slow motion. He heard a counselor shouting at them. He looked up to see one of the older counselors coming down the road towards them.

The boys all walked towards the counselor to see what punishment was in store for them. They all wondered if he would figure out that they had been dipping snuff. The counselor was one of the ones that Henry and the other boys identified as being too religious. Too religious to the boys was the fire and brimstone type of counselors. Their tactic was to try and instill fear into the children. Evidently, they felt compelled to ensure all the kids were scared so much that they would be afraid to do anything they themselves viewed as being immoral.

"What are you boys doing?!" asked the counselor.

They all lied by omission and said they were just hanging out. The counselor then started a fishermen of men sermon. It started with a long reprimand and a good description of what hell fire would be like. The conclusion was that there was only one way to avoid hell fire. The boys needed to become believers that agreed to devote their lives to be fishermen of men. It was mandatory that they believed that Jesus died for their sins, was beget by God himself and was resurrected after 3 days. The fishing trip wouldn't end until everyone in the world became a believer.

Henry listened intently to try and make sense of the speech. He had read in the Bible about fishermen of men. Jesus had told Simon Peter and Andrew to follow him, and they would become fishers of men. In Henry's mind, being a fisherman of men had something to do with helping other people. Maybe it was helping them to avoid dark temptations like escaping reality with smokeless tobacco, disobedience to authority figures, having sex with pillows, or streaking to keep them out of trouble and find more satisfaction with a life of less sin. Alternatively, maybe it did mean that everyone needed to believe what the counselor was telling them. As Henry watched and listened, he couldn't help but wonder why the counselor seemed so angry.

There were a lot of verses in the Bible that warned people not to become angry. The counselor seemed to be more focused on saving them from eternal damnation than on controlling his own anger. He promised that they could all have eternal salvation. Everyone just needed to believe him.

"*Whoever is slow to anger has great understanding, but he who has a hasty temper exalts folly,*" thought Henry. "*He might be more believable if he wasn't so angry.*"

Henry had read the Bible several times. He knew from talking about the Bible with other people that most people hadn't ever read it. A lot of people that had read the Bible didn't remember most of what it said. Most people got hung up on the meaning of a specific verse or two. Not many people desired to discuss the rest of the Bible.

The counselor continued with his speech. Spit came out of his mouth proportionally with the magnitude of his shouting. He stopped screaming for a brief second and positioned himself directly in front of one of the boys. He put his hand firmly on the boy's head.

"Do you believe?!" he shouted.

"Yes, I believe!" the first boy shouted back.

The man moved down the line. He repeated the sequence with each boy. Each exclaimed that they did indeed believe.

Henry was surprised. All the boy's demeanor had changed in the presence of the counselor. Just a few minutes before they had all been trying to act like they were their own bosses. They were rebels sneaking off to use smokeless tobacco and not doing what they were told. They had all lied to the counselor by omission. Even the boy that had brought a few cans of snuff to church camp became a believer.

"*Do they really believe? Or are they just afraid of the counselor,*" thought Henry.

Henry looked at the counselor's face. He felt his hand pressing hard against his forehead. He squinted his eyes and tightly closed his mouth to try and not get spit in them.

"Do you believe?!" he shouted at Henry.

"I'm not sure if I believe or not," responded Henry in the calmest voice that he could. He didn't want to enrage the counselor further.

The counselor's eyes grew to the size of Henry's fist. His shouting increased as he attempted to put the fear of God into Henry.

"You are doomed for eternal damnation if you do not believe! Do you believe?! Do you believe?!" he shouted. "You must believe!"

"I'm sorry Sir, but I'm not sure I believe what you believe. I don't understand why you are getting so angry," responded Henry.

The counselor took the conversion to a level that Henry had never experienced. He became even more angry. He raised his voice several notches. Saliva spewed from his mouth.

"How am I supposed to just believe without really knowing?" Henry asked the man.

"You are being a doubting Thomas! You must believe!" the counselor shouted.

Henry had been called a doubting Thomas before when he asked too many questions. He didn't understand how being a doubting Thomas was bad. Thomas had been a disciple of Jesus. He had known Jesus personally. He would have probably seen him change water to wine, raise Lazarus from the dead and even walk on water. He thought about the passage in the Bible where Satan tried to tempt Jesus by telling him that if he worshiped him then everything could be his. Jesus hadn't accepted the offer.

If someone told Henry that he could have everything, he knew he would refuse the offer too. Who in their right mind would want to have the responsibility for everything? A lot of people might think they would want everything but once they had everything then what would they do? Maybe look at everything and be happy for a few seconds, minutes, or days. Then they would probably just wonder what to do next with nothing more to gain. If people aren't happy with what they have then they aren't going to be happy with more of the same stuff.

Maybe they would try to rid the world of evil only to find out that every human being had the evil in them. Being the ruler of the world wouldn't be an easy job.

"You can't ever make everyone happy," thought Henry. *"Having everything would be a lot like trying to be in God's shoes. Thank God that God has that job and not a human being."*

The counselor continued shouting to make sure Henry knew that he was doomed for eternal damnation if he didn't agree with him.

"What would Jesus say if he was in this situation?" thought Henry. *"Would he accept the invitation to have eternal life by agreeing with the counselor? Would Jesus be afraid and state something that he isn't sure of?"*

Henry had similar conversations with several adults before. He got a variety of feedback when he expressed his own beliefs or thoughts. He had a hard time believing anything if he couldn't verify that it was true. Some adults told him to just keep praying and seeking God. Others were convinced that he must believe or else he was doomed for eternity. Some of them were genuinely concerned about Henry's future after death. Most others seemed more concerned about their own personal future after death.

Henry felt bad having the conversation with people that seemed to be genuinely concerned about him. He had determined that the best solution was to avoid having the conversation by not letting them know everything that he believed or didn't believe. He didn't want them to feel more sorrow or pain. He chose to be dishonest to avoid hurting them. Likewise, he felt sorry for the people that became worried about their own future after death. He tried to avoid those conversations as well. In this case, he wasn't given a chance to avoid the conversation. The counselor was demanding an answer. Henry didn't feel comfortable to lie about such an important question. His conscious forced him to be honest.

"Sorry Sir. I see that you really want me to believe. Thank you so much for caring enough about me to try to help me have eternal life but all I know is that I'm going to try and be the best Christian that I can be. I love Jesus and I love God but I'm not confident enough to say that I share your beliefs," said Henry. "I have faith that God will know best for what to do with me when I die."

The counselor calmed down a little bit. Henry wasn't sure if it was by choice or just because he had worn himself out shouting and spitting. He couldn't help but feel sympathy for the man. He had a feeling that the man hated life so much that he needed to know that there was something better waiting for him when he died. It was tempting to agree with him just to try and make him happier, but Henry wasn't very good at agreeing with what he didn't agree with. Especially when it dealt with the Creator of the Universe.

As a last resort, the counselor tried to use CS Lewis's approach where Henry was forced to make a choice between Jesus being God, the Devil, or a lunatic. Henry already knew what CS Lewis had written in 'Mere Christianity'.

In Henry's opinion, he thought CS Lewis missed out on a couple of alternatives. He didn't think that CS Lewis could possibly know the true intentions of Jesus. If the Bible was the infallible and inerrant word of God, then maybe Jesus had said that he was God but that didn't necessarily make him crazy. To Henry, it only confirmed that he was human. Everyone was crazy. If the Bible was written by people, then maybe some people thought Jesus was God but that didn't mean Jesus was God. It only meant that some people believed that Jesus was 100% man and 100% God.

What Henry did know was that most of the teachings in the Bible attributed to Jesus elevated him to being far greater than a great moral teacher. The Jesus in the Bible taught people how to live blessed lives. He encouraged people to repent and walk the talk in their own lives. He cared about other people regardless of how much they sinned. He taught people to not follow everyone else just because they were told to do something. He wanted his followers to exceed the righteousness of the Pharisees and the teachers of the law. Henry's interpretation was that the Jesus in the Bible was an example of whom to aspire to be like as opposed to waiting for a time when everyone else would act more like what Jesus taught. Without a doubt, Jesus was the perfect example of what God incarnated on earth as a human would be like.

Life was confusing and so was religion.

CHAPTER 21

Making a Choice

Albert cast his fishing line into Lincoln Creek.

"How was church camp Henry?" asked Albert.

"It was alright," responded Henry. "I'm thinking about getting baptized."

"I already got baptized," said Slim. "I did it three months ago."

"You got baptized and didn't tell us?" asked Albert. "How did it feel?"

"It didn't really feel like anything," replied Slim. "Just a cold dab of water on my forehead."

"That isn't being baptized," said Henry. "Baptism is being fully immersed in water. What do you mean a dab of water?"

"A finger with holy water placed on my forehead in the name of the Father, the Son and the Holy Spirit," said Slim. "That is how people get baptized at my church."

"That isn't baptism," rebutted Albert. "You have to be fully immersed just like the way John the Baptist baptized Jesus in the Jordan River."

"Then all of us are already baptized," said Slim. "We've all been fully immersed in Lincoln Creek."

"You have to do it publicly at church," replied Albert. "Lincoln Creek doesn't count."

"Am I baptized if I stand in water up to my waist in church?" asked Slim.

"Nope."

"Am I baptized if I stand in water up to my eyebrows?"

"Nope."

"Am I baptized if the water goes over my head?"

"Yes!" responded Albert. "Exactly, now you got it. I'm thinking about getting baptized too. You can come to my church and get the real deal Slim."

"Maybe it doesn't matter how it is done," said Henry. "If that is the way Slim's church does it then I'd call it a baptism."

"The best part for me was the classes I had to go through before being baptized," said Slim. "I learned a lot about what it means to be a Christian and how to live like one."

"We have discipleship classes at my church too," said Henry. "I'm going to get baptized. How about you Albert?"

"Yes," said Albert. "Let's do it. What did you learn about how to live like a Christian Slim?"

"You know," replied Slim. "Love God with all your heart soul and mind and love your neighbors even when you want to hate them. That kind of stuff."

"At my church, we don't have very many Christians that live like that," said Henry. "My church is full of a lot of depressed, angry, envious and ungrateful people. Most of them could care less about their neighbors. Especially if they don't go to church. A lot of them are living in hopes of a better life after death. Others think they are God's chosen people and better than everyone else. The ones that aren't depressed and ungrateful are mostly arrogant hypocrites."

"Same thing in my church," said Albert. "Most people are selfish whether they go to church or don't."

"Yep," agreed Slim. "Same thing at my church. I know some people that don't go to church that act more like Christians than a lot of the people in church."

"Yeah, like Mr. Parvis and Mr. Kuhn," said Henry. "Neither one of them go to church but they act like perfect Christians. They are like the good Samaritan."

"What religion are Samaritans anyway?" asked Albert. "Are they gentiles?"

"Nope," said Henry. "Samaritans were Jewish. They weren't taken into captivity in Babylon. They were Babylonians that were forcibly settled in the land of Israel by Assyrian Kings. They evidently thought they were practicing the original religion of the ancient Israelites. In their minds, they were the real chosen ones. They weren't very different than other Jewish people except that they worshiped at Mount Gerizim instead of in Jerusalem. They had a slightly different belief system and Torah than the Pharisees, Sadducees, Scribes and Essenes. Kind of like today where all our own churches are different. People keep coming up with new religions or have different beliefs within their religion. I think that is why Christians are all different, it isn't any different now than it was 2000 years ago. Everyone thinks they are right and wants to think they are special. Every time there is a debate, people segregate and divide themselves instead of looking for common ground."

"Yeah," said Albert. "People tend to embrace our differences instead of our likenesses. I think it is human nature to want to feel more special than others. We all want to feel good about ourselves."

"So, what kind of Jew do you think Jesus was?" asked Slim.

"I don't know," said Henry. "To me, he was a devout Jew that believed in the laws of Moses but not with all the laws created by man. He was at odds with the Jewish people that created their own laws. Especially when they were contradictory with the laws of Moses. They expected everyone to follow their rules to their benefit but didn't practice what they preached."

"It isn't any different today," said Albert. "Everybody thinks they are right even when everyone else knows they're wrong. Everyone wants others to abide by their rules regardless of how silly they are. People like making rules for others but they don't like following rules from other people."

"My Grandpa always says the smartest people are the ones that know what they know and know what they don't know," said Henry. "The older I get the more I realize that I don't know as much as I think I know. Sometimes rules that don't make sense start making more sense."

The boys decided to categorize everyone they knew into Biblical categories. The Pharisees were modern Christians that believed that they would be resurrected after death. They had a long list of rules and practices that they tried to follow, and they hated anyone that didn't follow their rules. Most of them were living to die and hoped for a better life after death. They were mostly depressed, angry, envious, and ungrateful. The vast majority of all the adults in Milton fell into the Pharisee category.

"They want a free ticket to heaven," said Slim.

"Yeah, just like the song. People get ready. There's a train a-coming," sang Albert. "You don't need no ticket. You just get on board. All you need is faith. To hear the diesels humming. Don't need no ticket. You just thank the Lord."

"They live in a bubble," said Henry. "I feel sorry for them. Most of them have good reasons to be so depressed. Life isn't always easy."

They identified the Sadducees as a smaller group of modern Christians that didn't believe in a resurrection. They were more focused on improving their own behavior than the Pharisees and were more satisfied with their lives on Earth. They seemingly lived relatively happy and blessed lives, but they were arrogantly proud of themselves. They thought they were more special than everyone else.

"They are free ticket Christians too," said Henry. "Most of them have good jobs and think that they are better than the Pharisees. They think they are the new chosen people and would probably buy tickets to be in the VIP section of the train to heaven with the Pharisees sitting in the back."

"How about all of the doomsayer people that read "The Late, Great Planet Earth" and think the end of the world is coming on December 31st 1988? What do we call them?" asked Slim.

"Let's call them the Essenes," replied Henry. "They should have their own sect."

"I don't care much about that prophecy stuff," said Slim. "Why worry about tomorrow? We have enough to worry about today and it doesn't do any good to waste time worrying about the future. It is too depressing."

"Yeah," said Albert. "If you pray to God why worry? If you worry why pray?"

"Amen," said Slim. "Who will be the scribes?"

"That would be any pastor or religious leader that thinks they know everything," said Henry. "The teachers of the law."

"Maybe we should add the politicians, police, and the judges," said Albert. "They make and enforce the laws."

"Good idea," said Henry. "They can be scribes too."

"We just renamed just about everyone," said Slim. "What do we call the Christians that don't fall into any of those categories? The ones that follow the narrow path instead of the wide road of destruction."

"Maybe Christian soldiers?" asked Henry.

"I don't like that!" said Albert. "It reminds me of that song about onward Christian soldiers marching off to go to war."

"Good point," said Henry. "Let's just call them real Christians. Any Christian that isn't a real Christian is a Pharisee, Sadducee, Essene, or Scribe. The non-Christians that seem like real Christians are good Samaritans and everyone else can be a Gentile."

The Bible was the only book that Henry had read more than once. He found it difficult to put all the pieces together, understand contradictions and come up with a simplified explanation of what it all meant. It rained for the next 4 days and nights. Henry diligently read from Genesis to Revelations in a delusional hope that he could somehow correlate the Bible into a massive jigsaw puzzle of scripture that made perfect sense.

Henry knew that he had lots of temptations that he found hard to resist. His first impulse had the tendency to get him in trouble. He desired to do things that he knew he shouldn't do. He hoped that being baptized might help him be less susceptible to the temptations of life. He wanted more holy spirit with less desires of the flesh.

"*I want to avoid sinning,*" thought Henry. "*Pride, Greed, Sloth, Ire, Lust, Envy and Gluttony. Nobody likes arrogant, greedy, lazy, angry, and envious people. Lust and too much of anything can't be good for anyone.*"

From Henry's perspective, there had to be multiple groups of Christians so that everyone could find a sense of belonging. He had overheard his friend Fred's father tell Fred that everyone was either a taker or a giver and he had to pick what he wanted to be. In the case of Fred's father, Henry figured that he probably decided early in his life that he was going to be a taker and take whatever he wanted. Fred was mostly a giver like his mother. His father probably didn't think he was aggressive enough.

"*No matter what I do, someone will be telling me to do the opposite,*" thought Henry. "*Fred is sometimes too nice and needs to be more fearless.*"

Henry knew that it was probably best to give and take and not follow the advice of Fred's father. He wanted to be more of a giver that was occasionally a taker. He could give his time to others but sometimes he needed to take some time for himself. Henry didn't think it was a good idea to do too much of either one. Everyone needed to eat.

He decided that if he was going to get baptized it would be good to lay down some rules for the type of Christian he wanted to become. He elected to not worry so much about the unknowable grace of God and concentrate solely on working towards becoming like the Christians he most admired and respected. They lived what appeared to be mostly happy, blessed and satisfying lives.

"*It seems kind of selfish,*" thought Henry. "*Shouldn't I be more worried about how happy and blessed everyone else are?*"

Henry often had a hard time with how sometimes the definitions of words didn't seem to describe reality. Selfish was identified as a bad thing and it was. In this case, it seemed that being selfish might be a good thing. The people that prioritized their own personal welfare first seemed to cheer up, tolerate, encourage, and show compassion to others the most. They were the people that he perceived to live the most blessed and happy lives. Yet, they were also the most compassionate and loving people he knew. They evidently cared enough about themselves to look out for their own personal welfare. In taking care of themselves, they were better prepared to help everyone else.

"If you don't take care of yourself then you become an empty basket with nothing left to give," he thought.

Henry thought about the opposite of selfish. He could think of a lot of people that had some selfless qualities where they put the needs and wishes of others before their own. Much of the Pharisee group tended to help others because they felt guilty if they didn't help. To them it was more of a moral obligation to be obedient. Their selflessness often made them even more depressed. They had a hard time saying no. They seemed like completely broken and tired people, worn out in trying to help everyone else. The Essenes were so depressed that they didn't bother helping anybody anymore. They were anxiously waiting for Armageddon.

The Sadducees and Scribes groups tended to enjoy helping others and sometimes selectively decided whether to help or not. They weren't selfless as they considered their own needs as well as the needs of others, but they were more judgmental of others than the Pharisees. Sometimes they took advantage of the Pharisees for their own gain. If they didn't like someone else, then they wouldn't go out of their way to help them. They often cared far more about themselves than they did for anyone else.

The real Christians weren't easily offended. They had the best behavior and an uncanny ability to help just about everyone. They were the only people that had compassion for so-called Christians and everyone else. They didn't care if someone was a Pharisee, Sadducee, Gentile or even an Infidel. Their lives seemed to be almost perfectly voided of sin. They walked the Christian talk. Other people tended to love and respect them.

Henry made a list of some rules of life that he felt were the most important ones he wanted to apply in his own life. He came up with 8 rules along with the opposite extreme which verified to himself his logic behind each of the rules.

His view of the world was more of a gray one as opposed to everything being either black or white. So, he also came up with exceptions to most of the rules where he thought a wise person should break them. In Henry's mind, rules were like records. They were made to be occasionally broken.

His 8 rules were:

Rule 1 - LOVE everyone genuinely

HATE results in being enraged with anger and focusing energy on what is wrong with others. HATE the sin and doing wrong. LOVE righteousness and doing what is right above all else. Make friends instead of enemies. Do NOT hate other sinners as that would be hypocritical.

Rule 2 - FORGIVE others

UNFORGIVENESS is continuing to live with the torture even when the tormentor is long gone. FORGIVE easily to not ever feel like a victim. Acknowledge the wrong doings of others, defend yourself/others and work towards correcting and helping others improve their own behavior. Recognize that people really don't know what they do. If they did then they wouldn't do what they do.

Rule 3 - Be GRATEFUL

UNGRATEFULNESS is a never-ending thirst for more stuff that never results in happiness. Learn to be grateful for what is most important, find contentment with less and don't be envious of others. God doesn't need to be thanked. People need to be thankful. Set goals and work hard to achieve goals as opposed to waiting for miracles. Teach others to do the same. Nobody can be happy if they aren't grateful.

Rule 4 - Be HUMBLE

ARROGANT people end up having more enemies and aren't honest with themselves. Learn to excel without showing off. Practice and strive for perfection but acknowledge your weaknesses. Never lack confidence but recognize that only God is all knowing and good.

Rule 5 - Be PATIENT

IMPATIENT people become agitated and frustrated. Learn to accept setbacks and focus energy on positive changes to learn from and overcome the setbacks. Have the courage to change situations within your power to avoid stagnant bad situations.

Rule 6 - Live in HARMONY with others

CONFLICTS are time consuming and generally the consequences result in two losers and decades of backlash. Work towards having a peaceful environment that results in HAPPY people living blessed lives on both sides of the tracks. Take actions when it is not possible to live peacefully i.e., self-defense or defending GOOD.

Rule 7 - Do GOOD

EVILDOERS gain enemies in proportion to their evil deeds and live a life of CONFLICTS and ultimately UNSATISFACTION, HATE and UNHAPPINESS. Choose to do things that will earn the respect of others. Pray and ask God for direction whenever in doubt. Recognize there are only two sides (GOOD and EVIL). Both reside in all people and it is not humanly possible to destroy either. We choose to feed the GOOD or EVIL within us. The one we feed will be the one that grows within us and our surroundings.

Rule 8 - Have FAITH always

WORRIED people dwell on an emotion that serves no useful purpose. Have the self-confidence to LOVE, TRUST and FEAR God above all else. Continuously seek to follow and accept the will of God. Never depend 100% on God's grace but know that grace is required to find God's peace. Recognize that there are consequences for all actions but be GRATEFUL to God for free will.

Henry cemented important things in his brain by coming up with a sentence using first letters of key words. For his 8 rules:

Love, Forgiveness, Grateful, Humble, Patient, Harmony, Good and Faith.

He came up with:

Let's Follow God and Help People Help God Find <blank>.

He smiled at the multiple words he could use to fill in the blank. It fit nicely with his perception of God as the only one who would really know what to put in the <blank>.

Some words that Henry thought of to put in the blank were peace, liberty, happiness, and love. One word that he didn't think of was obedience. Lying, stealing, and getting an appropriate revenge were all things that Henry thought were okay to do if the intent was for a common good. He had a hard time of leaving vengeance with God and felt compelled to occasionally not be an obedient child to all authority figures. Every action needed appropriate consequences. Discerning what was good and evil was the hard part for rules with a gray area. Only God would know what choices were best in every situation.

Henry's goal was to become someone that set the example in following his rules and to become a man like the ones he looked up to that followed similar principles. The hardest part was discernment and his own evil desires. He knew constant prayer might help but how was it possible to establish a direct link with God to be a perfect person that always did what was right?

If he could distinguish what was the right thing all the time, then life wouldn't be very interesting to him. Being a perfect person without flaws would make for a dull boring life. Perfection was something to strive for knowing that it can never be reached. As much as Henry liked order, it was the imperfections in the world that made it beautiful. He liked surprises and learning new things.

Henry couldn't imagine a world without suffering and evil. In his mind, it was necessary to experience and know suffering and evil to fully appreciate and be grateful for anything good. The world would be a better place if there was less suffering and evil. He smiled at the thought of asking God for help with all the suffering and evil in the world. God would probably just tell him that he did send help. Henry was supposed to be one of the people to provide that help. *"If you don't like it then help change it,"* thought Henry.

He decided to get baptized and take the next step to discipleship. He was committed to work towards becoming what he envisioned as a more perfect disciple. From a practical standpoint, Henry knew what kind of person he wanted to be. He wanted to die to live instead of living to one day die.

Prior to being baptized, Henry participated in a discipleship class with the pastor of his church along with several other teenagers and a couple of adults.

The discipleship class lasted for several weeks. Henry made sure that he didn't ask too many questions. He listened to what the pastor said and found the class to be much like the rules he had made for himself.

When Henry was baptized, he thought maybe he would feel different or receive a sign from God. Other than being all wet he didn't feel anything of spiritual significance.

"Did you feel anything special when you came out of the water Albert?" asked Henry.

"Nope," said Albert. "I just felt heavy from being soaking wet."

"Me too," said Henry. "I didn't feel anything special either. Slim was right. The best part was the discipleship class."

"Yup," said Albert. "He was right."

Life was good.

CHAPTER 22

Preacher Sinned

"He deserved an *ass* kicking. I would have done the same thing." Henry overheard a man say as he walked through the church corridor.

"*What is this all about?*" he thought. He continued down the hallway. People in church didn't typically talk much about getting revenge and kicking *ass*. He slowed his walk and continued down the hallway in hopes of finding out more information. He stopped to chat with a friend that was standing by several older women that appeared to be gossiping. He eavesdropped to the conversation. Women in Milton tended to say and talk more than most men did.

It didn't take long for Henry to figure out that the pastor had an affair with a married woman in the church. The pastor had just baptized him after spending several weeks with him in a discipleship class. The husband of the woman had come into the church, locked himself and the pastor in his office and then beat the living crap out of him. The pastor didn't fight back and hadn't pressed charges.

"*Not pressing charges would have been the Christian thing to do,*" thought Henry.

The women and men's conversations were different. The men were more focused on putting themselves in the man's shoes and justifying his actions whereas the women were more interested in finding out any tidbits of information related to the whole affair. They all seemingly enjoyed the gossiping.

As Henry listened, he tried to put himself in everyone's shoes starting with the pastor. Why would the pastor have an affair in the first place? He thought about the pastor's big office where he had his discipleship class. It was easy to imagine the woman coming to tell the pastor about all her problems. The pastor would have showed his compassion and encouragement through biblical practices. Maybe it started as a pat on the back or a small hug. He envisaged the pastor feeling the heat of the woman and maybe the smell of her perfume. He knew that temptation was hard to resist. He often experienced it himself.

Maybe the woman felt something similar. The pastor was a good talker. It was his job as a pastor to know how to say all the right things. She could have been more impressed with his encouragement and good words than what she had at home from her husband. After all, that was part of the pastor's job to teach others how to love. He was a love expert.

He thought about the pastor's wife. She seemed like a model Christian woman. In Henry's mind, she was much prettier than the other woman too. What would she be thinking? Why hadn't the pastor thought about her feelings when he cheated on her? Maybe, the temptation was too much and in the heat of the moment he couldn't resist. Regardless, the pastor's wife had to feel hurt. Henry felt the most compassion for her. She was the real victim.

"The person that gets hurt last always take the brunt of the pain," thought Henry.

When Henry put himself in the disgruntled husband's shoes, he thought of how he would have been angry at himself. What did I do wrong? Why is my wife having an affair? Doesn't she love me? Am I not good enough for her? I've failed to be the best husband that I could be. How did I let this happen? He also would have felt anger at his wife. They'd made a commitment for life. They chose each other as husband and wife through thick or thin. How could she do this?

He could easily visualize why the man would be angry at the pastor. That was probably the man's first thought. Get revenge. I'm mad at my wife. I'm mad at me. I can't beat my wife and I don't want to harm myself. I'll just go beat the pastor. It is all his fault. It is always easier to blame someone else for problems in your own life.

"Revenge is sweet like sugar, but sugar isn't good for anyone," he thought.

No winners thought Henry. Everyone loses. That was the temptation of sin. It always seems right at the time, but it never works out well. One sin leads to more sin. Envy and lust lead to anger, pride, and hate. Evil begets evil. Sin begets sin and love begets love. Doing right or wrong is contagious. Every wrong is a cancer that keeps spreading until someone has the strength and courage to stop it.

Henry continued down the corridor. He saw Harold talking to two other men. He had a lot of respect for all three of them. They all set an example of what he wanted to be like. He knew that they'd be talking about the future of the church. They would already be past the gossip and formulating a plan of what needed to be done to get things back in order.

The men stopped talking before Henry got close to them. They were always aware of what was going on around them. They knew how to keep their important conversations private unlike most other people.

"Good game yesterday, Henry! I read in the morning paper that you got two doubles and a triple! Way to go!" said one of the men to Henry with a smile.

"Yes Sir. Thanks", responded Henry. He recalled the previous day of baseball. Harold and several of his friends coached Henry's team. Albert and Slim both played on his team. They always won. The city recreation league had several rules. They included a 10-run rule where the game stopped after 4 innings if a team was winning by 10 or more runs and they only allowed a maximum of 9 batters for each team in every inning. Henry's team almost always only played 4 innings and even managed to get 9 runs in a couple of innings where the last batter hit a home run. Henry hadn't experienced a defeat in more than three years.

Winning had once been fun but the thrill of victory vanished. Henry knew they would win their games before they played. Winning was expected and it didn't seem fair. Most of the other coaches were just someone's dad with limited knowledge of the game. They coached the team because they couldn't find a real coach. Harold and his friends knew how to teach kids how to keep their elbows up, their eye on the ball and how to stay in front of the ball when fielding grounders. They also knew the importance of having 2 or 3 of the best pitchers. The best pitchers could throw strikes harder than most kids could hit. Henry got to practice hitting with the best pitchers which made getting hits from the other pitchers unchallenging. Winning had become standard procedure. Henry wished they could divide up the teams to be a little more equal. It was obvious that all the other teams hated him and the rest of his team because they were pretty much unbeatable. Baseball had become boring.

Since Henry was now a baptized member of the church, he decided that it would be alright to involve himself in an adult conversation that included his father.

"What is going to happen with the pastor? Will he continue to be our pastor?" asked Henry.

"No, we will be getting a new pastor," responded Harold.

"Since everyone is a sinner, and nobody is perfect, then why wouldn't we just forgive him and let him stay?" asked Henry.

"Pastors are held to a higher standard than the rest of the congregation. If he were to stay at this church, then it wouldn't be good for the church. We forgive him, but it won't be appropriate for him to stay," replied Harold.

"Will he still be allowed to be a pastor in another church?"

"That will be up to the American Baptist Convention," responded Mr. Green. "It isn't our decision."

Henry nodded and told the men to have a nice day as he moved off towards his Sunday school class. He thought about how the actions being taken seemed to make sense and followed a lot of what the Apostle Paul had written in the epistles. Harold and some of the other church elders seemed to have a similar impression of what was expected of a pastor or a saint. Having an affair wasn't something that would be an acceptable behavior to continue pastoring the flock in their church. He couldn't help but compare the situation with the pastor to King David and Bathsheba. In that case, King David not only had an affair. He also sent Bathsheba's husband to his death and the affair eventually ended up in Solomon's birth that resulted in the lineage of Jesus.

"Crazy world," thought Henry. *"Maybe the lady will have a child from the pastor that will end up doing great things."*

Henry often wondered why people spoke so often of David slaying Goliath as a young boy but very rarely discussed the evil he did.

He found the rest of Sunday school and church to be depressing. There was a dark cloud over the church. The gossiping was over. Most of the congregation were worried about the future. People were losing faith and hope in a brighter tomorrow.

Henry had confidence that everything was going to turn out alright. It reminded him of the time when the first black family had started coming to his church. All the congregation acted in a similar fashion. It wouldn't be long, and they would have a new pastor. Maybe he would bring a renewed sense of hope. The congregation would eventually become blessed people full of happiness, gratefulness in today and hope in the future. It was all a matter of time that could come sooner or later.

He prayed that both the pastor and his wife and the husband and wife from the congregation could find a way to rebuild their marriages. They could all come out stronger on the other side rather than continuing to build a wall to grow further apart. That would be up to them.

Henry never saw the pastor and his family again. The church had some fill in pastors for several weeks while looking for a new full-time pastor. He enjoyed the variety of having different variations of preaching. One of the preachers played his guitar. Henry liked the country music approach. It was kind of like listening to Johnny Cash singing "Folsom Prison Blue's", but the words changed from murdering someone in cold blood to having hope in the salvation of Jesus. Others weren't as musically inclined, but they all brought their own distinct flavor. Henry appreciated listening to all of them at least once.

It wasn't long before there was an adult only meeting at the church to discuss the church's future. 12-year-old Henry wasn't invited even though he was a tithing member. He couldn't wait for his parents to get home to see who was going to be the new pastor and what was discussed.

When Harold and Marsha came home after the meeting, Henry was careful to not look too eager and interested in finding out how the meeting went. He knew he would get more information from Marsha when she was by herself without Harold. Neither one of them would say much if he was trying to pry it out of them.

"Hi, what's for dinner?" Henry asked Marsha.

"It's 9 o'clock, you and Margaret should have already eaten," she replied.

Marsha typically either left money on the table for Henry to ride his bike to buy some food or more often than not they had food in the house. It was Margaret's job to prepare the food when Marsha wasn't home. Margaret enjoyed preparing food. She aspired to be as good of a cook as her grandmothers and her mother. She was incentivized by preparing something that Henry would express his gratitude by letting her know that she was indeed a good cook.

Henry was more of an eat to live person as opposed to living to eat. He didn't really care what he ate. If it wasn't sauerkraut, liver, or worms, he'd eat pretty much anything. He always thanked Margaret for preparing the food and told her how good it was. He appreciated her efforts. She was a good cook. She would normally even help with drying the dishes after Henry washed them. Washing the dishes was Henry's job.

Henry baited Marsha into the kitchen.

"Margaret wasn't hungry, so we didn't eat anything. I will eat some cottage cheese and a peanut butter sandwich," said Henry.

"You need something better than that. Let me see what I can find to make for you," said Marsha. She headed for the kitchen. Harold went upstairs to change his clothes.

Marsha looked in the refrigerator and started making suggestions. Henry convinced her that cottage cheese and a peanut butter sandwich would be perfect for him since it was already getting late.

"I thought you would have been back a couple hours ago, what took so long?" he asked, as he dished out some cottage cheese and opened the peanut butter.

Henry's question was all it took to get Marsha to start telling him everything that happened in the adult church meeting. He was careful to not ask any questions or let her know his opinion.

He just emulated his mother and her friends when they were sitting around the kitchen gossiping by showing interest. Occasionally egging her on with a comment like, "You've got to be kidding?"

From what Henry learned, the meeting at church had primarily been a discussion amongst the congregation of whether they should stay or leave the church. Apparently, lots of people thought that the church was cursed with evil spirits that had led them astray. The pastor's affair was the final straw and a sign from God.

Some people had started speaking in tongues. Whatever they were talking about and feeling led them to believe that the only rational decision was to leave the church. They would go to the same all white church on the north side of town where many others had gone to when the first black family started coming to the church.

Fortunately for Henry, his parents had decided that there wasn't an evil dark cloud over the church. They were going to stay to rebuild and to continue being part of the same church.

Just as Henry had heard about everything that he thought he wanted to know, he heard Harold coming down the steps. He asked the only other remaining question he had just as Harold was reaching the bottom of the steps.

"When they were speaking tongues, did you understand what they were saying?" he asked.

Hearing Marsha confirm his hopes that she didn't understand was exactly what Henry wanted to know. "Good," he said to Marsha, as Harold entered the kitchen. The conversation changed to whether Harold wanted a piece of apple pie before he went to bed.

Henry finished his cottage cheese and thought about how his church congregation was going to get smaller again. It would end up with the best of the flock and become even stronger. The ones that were leaving were mostly the 'free ticket' group of Christians. Most of them had good jobs, relatively nice houses, one or two nice cars and their kids were mostly on the right track to succeed in society. They would probably be okay somewhere else.

The congregation that remained were the ones that Henry most respected. They were the ones more tolerant of others. They were more focused on what they needed to do in their own lives to help the whole community become better as opposed to creating a utopia of isolation where all the other sinners were excluded. The people that remained saw themselves as the church. It was their responsibility to fix it.

The ones that left thought they were special and the ones that stayed knew they weren't perfect. They were making efforts to make themselves and the community better which made them even more special to Henry.

Life was good.

CHAPTER 23

Cutting Grass

"Why would anyone want to kill themselves?" asked Henry.

"I don't think anyone really wants to kill them self. They just don't like the life they are living. Life can be painful sometimes. Lots of people suffer from depression," replied Marsha. "Sometimes people have so much pain that they think death is the best alternative. The Devil is a good liar."

"*I feel sad sometimes,*" thought Henry. "*But never enough to kill myself.*"

"If you ever feel that way let us know," said Marsha. "We don't want you to end up like Jeremy and we can't help you if we don't know. Pain and depression are always temporary."

A few days earlier a neighborhood boy had put the eight-inch barrel of a 44 Ruger in his mouth and pulled the trigger. Jeremy was three years older than Henry. The 44 Ruger pistol didn't have the capability to pull its own trigger. It took Jeremy several minutes to find the false courage to assist the pistol in doing its job. The Ruger was his dad's gun. Jeremy's father had showed him how to use his dominant hand high on the grip and how to then position his left hand prior to assuming a proper shooting position. Jeremy extended his arms to fire it for the first time.

"Not too tight," said Jeremy's father. "You are squeezing the gun. Just hold it firmly. Put your tongue back in your mouth so you don't bite it off."

He struggled to hold the six pounds of heavy metal steady. Despite his dad's warnings, the recoil surprised him. The Ruger almost hit him on the forehead. It was more explosive than he had imagined. Father and Son both enjoyed their next thirty minutes together. At first, Jeremy felt nauseous with fear and anxiety. After a few shots, he gained confidence. He was overwhelmed with a feeling of intense power and control. The paper target and aluminum cans became his enemies. The 44 Ruger put his mind in overdrive. The sugar of destroying his enemies raced through neural highways to his brain. His heart raced. The serotonin rush felt good. Really good.

Jeremy's parents loved him. They wanted to see him succeed. They put a lot of parental pressure on him to do well in school and athletics. He tried hard to make them proud. In the confines of his bedroom, he cried a lot. He felt an emptiness and hopelessness that became overwhelming. His depressive warped mind played a nonstop broken record of lies.

"You will never be good enough. You are a loser for life," said the depression. "You are a burden that your parents and friends will be better off without. There is only one way to escape the pain. The gun will kill your enemy and end your misery. The 44 Ruger is your only friend."

Tears streamed down Jeremy's face. He held the 44 Ruger firmly but didn't squeeze it. He closed his eyes and lightly pressed his teeth against the barrel.

"*Will it hurt*," he thought.

"Do it," said the depression. "Don't be afraid Jeremy. Do it!"

Jeremy pressed the trigger with his right thumb. It felt good to shoot the depression that was bullying him. The bully didn't die but Jeremy did.

Jeremy was the second person that Henry knew of that had recently committed suicide. Neither were close friends of Henry, but he knew each of them well. Both were seemingly normal and relatively happy teenagers. In the 1970s, the suicide rate for young white males had increased by 50%. Firearms had replaced poisoning as the primary method for suicide. More than half of all deaths with firearms were self-inflicted. Suicide victims rarely planned their death extensively. Jeremy wasn't an exception.

Suffering from depression or any form of mental illness was considered unusual or even shameful. People didn't talk about their symptoms. The reality was that mental illnesses were so common that almost everyone developed at least one diagnosable mental disorder in their lifetime. Mental illness was the normal. The rare exceptions were the people that managed to live abnormal lives of being mentally well for an entire lifetime.

Henry was already experiencing the initial symptoms of bipolar disorder. He was generally full of adrenaline and energy. He felt an exaggerated sense of self-confidence and had a decreasing need for sleep. His mind was constantly racing with seemingly unstoppable thoughts. Henry often took risks that other people considered to be stupid without any fear of the consequences.

One out of every twenty of the human population suffered from bipolar disorder traits. The people born with homosexual or pedophile traits each also accounted for five percent of the population. Being a psychopath, narcissist or having schizophrenia each amounted to one percent of the population whereas having depression, anxiety or an unreasonable phobia accounted for a much larger percentage of the population. Just about every person had some form of mental illness or other desires that were identified as not being normal. Nobody perfectly fit the description of being normal. Normal was a societal pinnacle of perfection that didn't exist. Even though it wasn't achievable, people needed a definition of what was morally acceptable for society to function.

Mankind had tried to decipher and understand mental illnesses such as bipolar disorder for hundreds of years. The ancient Greeks and Romans came up with the term's 'mania' and 'melancholia'. Later generations called it 'manic' and 'depressive'. Eventually, someone decided to call it bipolar disorder to avoid calling the affected maniacs. Political correctness has been around for a long time.

The Greek philosopher Aristotle acknowledged mania and melancholy as a condition while citing it as the inspiration for many of the great artists of his time. For thousands of years, it was common practice to execute anyone suffering from bipolar disorder or other mental conditions. Strict religious dogma from the world's religions identified the mental illnesses as the result of people being possessed by demons. Killing the possessed was perceived to be a rational and reasonable method of dealing with the illnesses. For centuries, people killed others to rid the world of evil only to see new people to be born with the same illnesses and desires. They never learned that eradicating people doesn't rid the world of evil. It isn't people that kill people, it's the evil in the people fighting against itself.

In the 19th century, a French psychiatrist would call bipolar disorder 'la folie circulaire' which translates to 'circular insanity' in English. One day, bipolar people are on top of the world. They are full of energy with grandiose ideas and the next day they are ready to cut their own throat because everything seems so hopeless. Henry's insanity was mostly on the up pole of bipolar. His mental state befuddled him just as much as it confused the researchers and doctors that were still trying to understand it themselves. He knew that he was different but elected to keep his thoughts and feelings to himself. It was evident to Henry that what raced through his brain was different from what most people considered to be normal. All he could do was to try and take actions that helped his thoughts approach what he perceived as normal. It wasn't easy but it was necessary.

Harold and Marsha both worked. They divided up their responsibilities at home. Marsha was responsible for shopping, cooking, cleaning, and doing the laundry. Harold looked after cutting the grass, washing the cars, and fixing anything that needed fixing. Occasionally they would help each other but their routine was a clear division of work. Henry and Margaret perceived the work their parents did as either being men's work or women's work. Regardless of who did the work, it was equally important. They needed to eat, and someone had to cut the grass.

Henry gravitated to men's work. He liked acquiring the skills to fix things. He enjoyed helping Harold so he could learn how to fix the cars, repair the house, and cut the grass. Keeping himself occupied and busy helped to calm his mind down. Contributing to family chores helped Henry feel useful. Occasionally, he managed to get a good night's sleep. The harder he sweat during the day the better he slept.

He didn't care much for cleaning things after they got dirty on their own, but he had a higher standard for orderliness than the rest of his family. His philosophy was to put things away and clean up after himself as he went about his daily routines. He didn't like having a mess to deal with later. When everything was in order around him, he felt better on the inside.

His bedroom was always the cleanest and most orderly place in the house. He made his bed in the morning, kept dirty clothes in the hamper, and always knew where everything was. If everything wasn't in order, Henry wasn't able to get comfortable enough to rest. The orderliness of his room was a necessity to relax his brain. His thoughts mirrored his environment. When the outside was in order, his thoughts were at peace. When the outside was disturbed, he was disturbed.

The rest of the house was different. Household items were left in random places without any conscious decision. When the house became messy enough, Marsha would clean and reorganize everything. Occasionally, Henry made exceptions and did women's work. He would help Marsha clean the house. He especially liked organizing the kitchen. It only took a week or two before somebody would put the peanut butter with the canned food or the pasta sauce with the cake mixes. Henry didn't like the idea of looking through multiple cabinets to try and find something. It was an unnecessary waste of time. It annoyed him.

Harold cut the grass because it was a necessary chore. He rushed through it to get the job done. Henry was more of a perfectionist. He couldn't just cut the grass. He felt compelled to make sure there wasn't a single blade of grass out of place. He snipped the grass along the fence with the perfection of a hair stylist and ensured there wasn't a single weed growing out of cracks in the sidewalk.

It made Henry happy to have everything in a perfect order as he envisioned in his own mind of how things were supposed to be. It was a lot like making a painting in real life. Whenever something was out of order, he had a yearning to put it in the exact condition he imagined in his brain. What he didn't like to do was to clean up other people's messes. He devised his own boundaries where he took care of his room, his stuff, and the grass. His boundaries didn't stop his annoyance of the messes left by other people.

Whenever it was Mother's Day, Valentine's Day, or his mother's birthday he would spend a few hours cleaning the house and doing all the laundry. He worked during the night, so he could surprise Marsha in the morning. He tried to work quietly but always managed to wake Harold.

"What are you doing? It is 3 o'clock in the morning," Harold would ask.

"I'm cleaning the house to surprise Mom," Henry would say. Harold would shake his head and return to bed thinking his son was insane.

Marsha always acted like she appreciated his efforts, but he had the perception that she was more embarrassed than thankful. After cleaning the house a few times, he realized that Marsha didn't really want him to clean the house. She felt he was rubbing her nose in not cleaning the house up to his standards. It reversed the parent child role model relationship.

Harold appreciated having Henry cut the grass. It gave him more time to go fishing, relaxing, or playing ball with Henry or his own grown-up friends. He wasn't bothered from Marsha's comments that rubbed his nose in not being able to cut the grass to Henry's standard.

"The yard looks so much nicer than when you cut it," said Marsha.

"Yep," said Harold. "It looks nice."

Henry liked cutting the grass because it gave him something else to do. He liked the smell of freshly cut grass. The tediousness felt more like good therapy for his racing brain rather than actual work. The heat of the sun and strenuous work made him sweat. It also released endorphins that made him high. The endorphins were natures way of replicating morphine in a good way. Henry was getting hooked.

As soon as he mastered cutting the grass at his house, he started knocking on neighbor's doors to find more grass to cut. He took advantage of his addiction to endorphins and endless energy to make some extra cash.

Henry was a good salesman. Word spread quickly of the great job that he did. There were other kids in the neighborhood that tried to do the same thing. They left yards half-finished and didn't always show up when the grass needed cut. As a result, Henry's lawn care business flourished. It kept him busy throughout the summers. He loved cutting grass and people tend to do well at things they enjoy.

He had so many customers that he hired Albert to help. They split the money fifty-fifty. Henry retained the boss responsibility. He liked being the one to identify who was going to do what, how they would do it, and when they were finished with a job.

The boys enjoyed their time together and both were happy to make money. Albert bought himself clothes and sometimes food. Henry put all his money in a shoe box. He had a hard time figuring out what he wanted to buy. His parents already bought him pretty much everything that he needed. He couldn't think of anything he wanted to buy for himself.

Albert helped Henry less than half of the time. Henry cut grass from early in the morning until the sun went down to feed his addiction. Albert was closer to being a normal person. He desired to have an occasional break or maybe even go do something else that involved socializing with others or some other form of fun. Cutting grass gave Henry exactly what he needed to try and stay sane. He didn't need the money, but he couldn't ever get enough exercise. The more he worked, the more he enjoyed it and the better he slept at night. He enjoyed it so much that he became dependent on it. Cutting grass reduced the levels of his stress hormones. It stimulated the production of endorphins. The endorphins were natural pain killers that elevated his mood.

Both Henry and Albert played baseball together in the summer. Neither of them went to the local swimming pool much. Most of the other kids in Milton frequented the swimming pool daily. Henry and Albert found it boring. They didn't like lying around in the sun to get darker. They got more than enough sun cutting grass or just being outside. Swimming and diving were kind of fun, but they didn't like being around adults. The swimming pool was full of adults. Every adult had their own rules. Henry and Albert didn't like other people's rules.

Neither one of them understood why they had to occasionally stop swimming to let adults have the pool to themselves.

"Why do they get to swim all the time and we can't?" asked Henry.

"I don't know. I wish I was a lifeguard so I could blow my whistle at them," responded Albert. "The lifeguards let the adults do whatever they want to do. I prefer swimming in Lincoln Creek where we don't have anyone telling us what we can and cannot do."

"Me too," said Henry. "Lincoln Creek is open twenty-four hours every day. The swimming pool is just like being at school. I hear what the adults say but I see what they do. If they don't follow their own rules, then why should we?"

When they cut grass, they got paid. They didn't have lifeguards blowing whistles or adults shouting at them. Henry decided how and when he was going to cut grass. His customers treated him like an adult. He preferred socializing with them more than the entitled adults at the swimming pool. He enjoyed the freedom of being his own boss.

While Henry was cutting grass, he started singing a lot. He couldn't hear anything over the roar of his mower. When people tried to talk to him, he had to shut it off to hear what they wanted to say. He took advantage of the noisy mower to practice singing.

The Sony Walkman hadn't been invented yet. The normal people in the seventies thought walking around with headphones was anti-social, rude, and inconsiderate. They didn't like the thought that anyone would secretly listen to something other than themselves. A few years later Henry would find a new normal where he could listen to music without disturbing anyone. The normal people would change their minds. Playing music out loud would become the new rude and inconsiderate.

Henry was singing a Simon and Garfunkel song called "Cecilia". He had heard it on the radio. It had a nice rhythm to it. He wasn't a good singer. It might have been the endorphins or the noise of the mower that gave him the confidence to think differently. He belted it out at the top of his lungs. He imagined a screaming audience of thousands of people filling an arena. He smiled as he imagined himself entertaining the masses.

He stopped singing when he saw Margaret sitting on the curb across the street. She laughed uncontrollably. Her feet danced on the pavement with amusement.

"*What is wrong with her*," thought Henry. "*I don't see anything funny.*"

He realized she was looking and laughing at him. He remembered the words he had just been singing. He had been making love to Cecilia in his bedroom. Someone took his place with the love making when he decided to wash his face. Margaret had heard the whole thing.

Henry smiled and waved at his sister. If he had been her listening to himself singing about making love, he would have been laughing just as hard.

When he got home that evening, Margaret had already told their parents about his song selection. Everyone including Henry had a good laugh.

"*Thank God I wasn't really making love to Cecilia,*" thought Henry. "*That would have been embarrassing if Margaret caught me in real life.*"

The summer after the 6th Grade, Henry decided that he wanted to get a better lawn mower. Some of the people on the north side of town had a lawn mower that looked like it was a lot better made than the one he had been using. It was quieter, stronger, and more powerful than the mower he had been using. Harold's old mower was completely worn out and about ready to break in half.

Harold agreed to take Henry to the lawn mower store. He was surprised to see how much more expensive it was than their old one. It was $429. He knew they could get another one like they had before for just $89.

As Harold was talking to the lawn mower salesman, he tried to think how he could convince Harold to buy the one he wanted. The salesman did a good job of persuading Harold to spend the money. Henry didn't get a chance to give his own sales pitch.

"Henry, I'll pay $100 if you continue to cut our grass. You can pay the rest," said Harold.

Henry hadn't thought that he would be the one to pay for most of the mower. He hadn't bought their last mower, but it sounded like a good idea. Harold would pay a little more than what a regular mower would cost. He would pay the rest. He knew that he had $4,462 in his shoe box at home, and he would still be able to double his money over the summer. The new lawn mower had a 1-gallon gas tank and cut a 2-inch wider path. He could finish any yard that he cut faster and cut several yards on a single tank.

"Thanks Dad," said Henry.

The salesman gave them a strange look. He wondered what 12-year-old in their right mind would want to spend $329 of their own money on a lawn mower. Most of the people that visited the Lawn-Boy store were the ones that wanted the best mower because they could afford it. Henry wanted the mower because he knew he could make more money with it. He could now cut more grass faster. It was an investment. More grass equated to more money.

As soon as they got home, Henry tested out the lawn mower on their own yard. Then he headed down the street to show it to Albert. They decided that they would cut Albert's yard and then Mrs. Washington's grass next.

Mrs. Thurman paid each of them $2 and they headed to Mrs. Washington's house. Mrs. Washington was already coming out of her house. They met her on the front porch. Something didn't look right.

She looked really scared and was holding her chest like something was wrong. She fell to the ground at the bottom of her steps.

"Go, call an ambulance Henry!" shouted Albert. "She is having a heart attack!"

Henry ran to tell Albert's mother to call the ambulance and then ran back to Mrs. Washington's front yard. Albert was pumping on her chest and blowing in her mouth like he knew what he was doing. Mrs. Thurman showed up just as the police and ambulance arrived at the scene.

One of the paramedics took over doing exactly what Albert had been doing. The policeman told them to get back and give Mrs. Washington space. The other paramedic brought something out of a bag and eventually Mrs. Washington started breathing again after they connected a box with wires to her body.

A paramedic looked at Albert. He nodded his head with respect as they wheeled her to the ambulance.

"Good job. You saved her life," he said.

"Where did you learn to do that?" asked Henry, as he looked at Albert in admiration.

"Tyrone taught me," said Albert. Tears welled up in his eyes as he thought about his older brother. Henry looked at the tears streaming down Albert's cheeks. He had never seen Albert cry. Albert wiped away the tears and silently watched the ambulance go down the road.

"You and Tyrone both saved her life then. You did good Albert. Tyrone would be proud of you," said Henry. "I bet your dad is looking down on you right now with a big smile. You're a hero."

He patted Albert on the back. He admired his courage and heart to save someone's life that use to shout racial slurs and threaten him with a shotgun.

It rained the next day. Henry was happy to hear that Mrs. Washington was doing okay. Marsha and Albert's mom had gone to visit her in the hospital. Sometimes, Henry liked rainy days, but he felt mixed emotions. Happiness that Mrs. Washington was okay, proud of his friend

Albert for saving her life, and depressed that Tyrone was taken away. It didn't seem like things ever really changed for the better. Bad things kept happening to good people.

With nothing better to do, Henry decided to read the Bible to see if he could find something to cheer him up. He went straight to the Book of Ecclesiastes. It seemed to be the most consistent book to what he was thinking about. He read the words of King Solomon slower than he normally did when he read.

He found it really depressing to read the same thoughts he was thinking. The words escalated his depressive thoughts. Everything is in vain. Nothing will ever change. Gaining more wisdom is all useless. Cut the grass and the grass grows back again. Cut it again and one week later it just grows back. Be nice to someone that is evil and they just keep being evil. Henry started thinking about how pointless everything in life seemed to be.

"*I'd rather be dead*," he thought.

It was his first time to seriously experience the down pole of bipolar disorder. He felt suicidal. Depressive thoughts did their best to manipulate Henry with lies.

Henry remembered his mom telling him to let her know if he ever felt depressed. Harold was home from work. He needed someone to help him change his mind about whether life was worth living. Suicide seemed like the best alternative. He hoped Harold might be able to cheer him up. He recited part of the book of Ecclesiastes to Harold.

"What is the point of everything?" Henry asked. "If everything is vanity and becoming wiser just leads to vexation and more sorrow then how are we ever supposed to be happy?"

"Did you read the end of the book?" asked Harold.

"Yes, I read the whole thing," replied Henry.

"Go read the end again," said Harold.

Henry went back to his bedroom and re-read the end of the book of Ecclesiastes. It clearly stated the answer to his question. The whole duty of man is to fear God and keep his commandments. In the end, God will judge us based on how we lived our lives.

"That's it," thought Henry. *"Fear God and just keep being obedient? Honor my parents, don't steal, don't murder someone, don't want what other people have, and the other six commandments?"*

Henry still felt like killing himself. He understood how Jeremy and other kids could reach the state of taking their own lives. He also knew how much pain Jeremy's parents and friends went through after he took his life. They still hadn't recovered. Jeremy hadn't been a burden like he thought. Lots of people loved him. They were still grieving. They couldn't stop beating themselves up wondering what they could have done differently.

"I hope God forgave Jeremy," thought Henry. *"I miss Jeremy. I'm not going to kill myself because I don't want to make my family and friends sad. I can't just quit."*

It wasn't fear of God that kept Henry from killing himself. It was love that convinced him to keep living. He loved his family and friends too much to leave them. He knew they loved him and didn't want them to have to grieve his loss.

The next day, the sun came out again. Henry got back in his groove of cutting grass and his own happy normal self.

"I am glad that I didn't kill myself," he thought. *"Life is a lot of fun."*

At the end of the summer, he decided that it would be a good idea to clean up his lawn mower. He disassembled and cleaned each component. He wanted to make it look new again. Curiosity in how it was made and worked urged him on. He ended up taking everything apart. Hundreds of pieces were scattered all over the carport. Nothing was left to take apart.

Harold got home from work to find Henry standing over all the pieces imagining how best to reassemble it. He had been careful to lay out all the pieces in the order he took them off and to remember how everything looked when assembled. He had even counted how many turns to turn the screws to hold springs in the right places. It looked overwhelming with all the pieces spread out on the carport.

Harold looked at him disappointingly.

"Why did you take everything apart?" he asked. "It was a brand-new lawn mower!"

"I just wanted to clean it before winter. I'll put it back together," said Henry.

Harold shook his head in disbelief. He was sure the lawn mower wasn't ever going to be a lawn mower again. Henry was slightly concerned that his father might be right. It didn't even look like a lawn mower anymore.

"*Why do I get myself into these situations?*" thought Henry. "*It seemed like a great idea an hour ago. I'm an idiot.*"

Henry started putting everything back together just the way he remembered taking it apart. He didn't go inside for dinner because he wanted to raise his mower from it's deathbed. He didn't want to forget any important steps. Finally, the lawn mower looked exactly like it had when they first brought it home. It was clean again.

The only problem was that it didn't start. Henry fooled around with everything he normally fooled around with when trying to get a lawn mower started. Nothing worked. He gave up only after Marsha told him to come inside to eat or *else*.

He stayed awake all night angry at himself. He felt for sure that it wasn't ever going to work again. If it did, the Lawn-Boy dealership would charge an arm and leg to fix it.

The next day, Harold took Henry along with the mower to drop it off at the shop. It was still under warranty and only cost $3.68 to fix. It only needed a new float in the carburetor which Henry had apparently damaged.

"*Thank God,*" thought Henry.

Life was good.

CHAPTER 24

Kids Acting Like Their Parents

"Where did you get those shoes? Pic-Way?" asked a 9th Grader. Another boy stood beside him snickering. It was Henry's first day of junior high school.

"Yep, Pic-Way, do you like them?" said Henry.

"Ha, you got your shoes from Pic-Way! Pic-Way shoes!" exclaimed the other boy.

"Yeah, I got my shoes at Pic-Way, and I picked them out all by my-self. I really like them a lot," said Henry. He smiled back at the boys to show them that he thought as much of their childish joking as they did about his shoes from the cheapest shoe store in town.

The bully kept laughing. He restated the same thing repeatedly. His friend started feeling embarrassed. Their poking fun wasn't working. His friend looked delusional in front of their peers. Other kids started laughing at them.

"Come on let's go," said the bully's friend.

They moved off down the hallway looking for someone else to pick on. Henry thought that maybe the kids that were picking on other kids were the same ones that had been picked on the most when they were 7th graders. Being a bully was contagious. Victims often became future bullies.

He had enjoyed his last few years in elementary school. He was delusional in thinking that the kids in junior high school would be more mature versions of the kids in elementary school. What he found was a bunch of kids that reminded him of junior versions of their own parents. Some of the kids looked like they should still be in elementary school. Others were well into puberty. Girls with visible breasts had been a rare sight in elementary. Breasts were much more abundant in junior high school.

Many of the older kids that he knew from before now looked and acted much like their own parents. They weren't more mature. Their bad habits were exaggerated to an almost comical level. It was his first time to see kids showing off their clothes and shoes and walking around like they were suddenly the most important people in the world.

Older boys sauntered around the hallways with Letterman jackets. They comically swung their shoulders and arms around as if they owned the school. God forbid someone else was taking up a small space near the wall. Albert and Henry shook their heads in laughter. They pressed their bodies against the wall as a few older boys shoved their way down the hallway.

Making fun of anyone that didn't meet the junior high school abnormal standard was taken to a new level. A girl wearing her cheer leader jacket conversed with Owen as if she was interested in going on a date with him. She gave him an L sign before turning to walk away.

"Loser!" she exclaimed to Owen to ensure he knew what the L sign meant.

Owen looked at Henry.

"I don't think she is my type," he said with a smile.

"Nope, you are too much more intelligent than her," said Henry.

Owen had grown some. He had become much more mobile, but he still walked twisting his body with his knees seemingly stuck together.

Slim was cornered at his locker by three large boys. They re-initiated him with the same fat jokes he had heard in the third grade.

"You are so fat that you have to pull your pants down to get something out of your pockets," laughed one of the boys.

"You are so skinny that you need to jump around in the shower just to get wet," laughed Slim.

Kyle and some of the other kids were being ridiculed for looking like they cared about grades. They hadn't figured out that the masses didn't like anyone with intelligence. Kyle looked as if he had been stretched six inches taller, but he hadn't gained an ounce.

A 9th grader grabbed Kyle and shoved him in his empty locker. Another locked the door. They all laughed and sauntered down the hallway to look for another victim. Kyle was the perfect size to occupy a locker.

"What is your combination, Kyle?" asked Henry through the locker air vents. Fortunately for Kyle, he was smart enough to remember the combination and the manufacturer had the foresight to install vents. Before the end of the year, most of the 7th grade class would know Kyle's combination. Putting him in his locker became an everyday routine. Kyle would continue his antisocial behavior. He became more of a recluse.

Henry was happy to see friends that he hadn't seen over the summer. He enjoyed watching the 8th and 9th Graders putting on a show that seemingly made them all happy. Most of the new 7th Graders just tried to figure out how to circumvent the insanity.

Owen, Slim, Albert and the other kids he liked the most all handled the bullying well. They had learned a lot in elementary school. Kyle hadn't fared very well and neither did Mike. His older brother put on a masculinity bullying show in front of his friends to demonstrate how much control he had over his much smaller brother.

"*What a jerk,*" thought Henry. "*He acts just like the policemen in this town. He will probably end up being a cop just like his dad.*"

The best part about junior high school was switching classes every hour. It was nice to have a wider variety of teachers and to not have to be with the same classmates all day long. They didn't do much in the first few days other than boundary building. The teachers and students pushed the boundaries to see what was going to be tolerated and who would really be in control of each class.

For the most part, Henry thought that all his 7th grade teachers did a pretty good job of acting like mature people. In most cases, they even acted like he thought responsible adults should act. Their maturity allowed them to put appropriate boundaries in place and they practiced what they preached.

His music class was in a much larger room with more students than any other class. He immediately liked the teacher, but she had a lot of challenges getting control of the class. She tried to convince the kids of truths that they didn't want to believe.

"Classical music has been around for hundreds of years," she said. "All the music you listen to is just a fad that will pass away. People will continue loving Bach and Beethoven for many years to come. Classical music is beautiful!"

Several students did their best to convince the music teacher that they would be listening to a song about someone leaving a cake out in the rain for the rest of their lives. The teacher liked getting everyone in the class involved. Her good intentions backfired. Hardly anyone wanted to like Classical music. The class joined together to disagree with her. Lots of the kids just wanted to try and be funny. It would have probably been okay if the teacher understood their humor, but she didn't. After a few days, she broke down and showed her anger for the first time.

"If I had a nickel for every time one of you made a joke of something, I would be rich!! You need to stop it now! This will not be tolerated anymore!" exclaimed the music teacher.

Perhaps she failed to add *'or else'* or clearly communicate what the consequences would be. Or maybe she just waited too late to start getting control of the class at an acceptable behavior level. Her angry protest didn't work. A student threw a nickel to the front of the room. Henry sat and watched with a smile as nickels, dimes, quarters, and pennies started falling to the front of the classroom like rain.

At first Henry thought it was amusing. The teacher got what she asked for, but then he noticed that the music teacher was crying. She walked to the door to exit the classroom after she tried her best to unsuccessfully regain her composure.

Not having a teacher in the room quickly resulted in lots of laughter and talking. The class became even more unruly. Henry got up and picked up all the coins. He put them all in the teacher's purse.

"Hey, I want my quarter back!" shouted one of the boys in the back of the room.

Henry had already made the decision that he was going to make sure the teacher got the money the class had donated to her. That was going to be their punishment. She asked for it and they gave it to her.

"If I had a dollar for every time that you threw a nickel at Mrs. Dorman, I'd be a rich man," Henry said to the class.

Henry was hoping that maybe they'd be stupid enough to start throwing the rest of their lunch money at him. He thought it would be a good way to teach the class that throwing your lunch money at someone would result in not having money to eat.

"*If you give someone something then you shouldn't expect to get it back*," he thought.

The kids stopped smiling. They started thinking about how they would just like to have their lunch money back. Their unruliness stopped as they silently stewed in their stupidity.

The teacher reentered the room. Henry sat down, and she did her best to continue the class. She finished a couple of minutes early and told everyone to wait quietly in their seats for the bell to ring. Lester, the boy next to Henry, reached under his seat and pulled out his school bag in a quick motion. Lester had a problem keeping his pants pulled up. He was a primary target of other kids throwing paper into his butt crack when he bent over and cracked a butt-smile at everyone.

He didn't seem to care too much about the paper, exposing his butt crack, or much of anything else. Lester was just naturally happy. Nothing could erase the smile from his face. When he pulled his bag out from below his seat, a pistol flew out of the bag. It scooted across the floor and came to a stop a couple feet in front of the teacher.

The entire classroom went completely silent. Everyone watched to see what the teacher was going to do about the gun. Mrs. Dorman stood motionless. She stared at the pistol on the floor. After several seconds, she shifted her eyes to look at Lester. Then she looked at the gun and back to Lester. Lester was just as confused as the teacher. He too moved his smiling gaze back and forth between the gun and the teacher.

After achieving absolutely nothing with her eye movement, the teacher decided to run out the door as fast as she could. Everybody sat in silence waiting to see what would happen next.

Henry leaned towards Lester.

"That's your gun, isn't it?" he whispered.

Lester nodded an acknowledgment that it was indeed his gun.

"If that was my gun, I'd go get it and put it back in my bag," suggested Henry.

Lester got up and leaned over to pick up his pistol. He unintentionally showed the whole classroom half of his butt and then put the pistol back in his bag. Nobody made fun of him or made any of their typical comments about his butt crack.

"It's funny how people's demeanor changes when someone has a gun," thought Henry.

After Lester sat back down in his chair, all the class looked towards the doorway. The school principal peeked around the corner. Not seeing a pistol helped him gain the courage to expose his entire body to the class. He slowly stepped into the classroom. The music teacher hid behind him as if he was a bullet proof vest.

He motioned for Lester to come with him and took his bag. He opened it and immediately zipped it up when he saw the gun. The three of them exited the classroom. The bell rang for the next class.

The following day, Lester was back in music class. Henry was eager to find out what kind of punishment there was for bringing a gun to school.

"Why did you bring a gun to school?" asked Henry.

"I was going to go shoot rabbits on the way home," answered Lester.

It seemed like a good reason to Henry. Lester would have something fun to do on his way home from school. Bringing a gun to school was good planning for time management.

"What was the punishment?" asked Henry. He thought that it didn't deserve any punishment at all. If the school didn't want kids to bring guns to school, they should at least tell them about a no gun policy.

"He just told me to not bring a gun to school again. My parents will need to come pick it up if I want my gun back," responded Lester.

"That sucks," said Henry.

They shook their heads in mutual disappointment.

"So, you didn't get to shoot any rabbits yesterday?" asked Henry.

"Nope," said Lester. It was Henry's first and only time to ever see Lester frown.

Most of the classes were excessively easy for Henry, but he had learned that grades didn't matter until the 9th grade. All that really mattered was that he passed to the next grade. Colleges only looked at grades from the 9th grade through the 12th grade. He decided to do the absolute minimum required to get at least a C in each class. In some classes, it was hard for Henry to do anything other than make A's. In others, there was lots of homework. He preferred to take the tests and get zeros for anything that required any effort outside of school. Especially if it didn't provide any information that Henry deemed beneficial, like practicing what they had already learned. He didn't understand the point of trying to re-learn what he already knew.

Every Friday, his math teacher had a special lesson that she called brain teasers. She read her first brain teaser problem to the class. Henry sat in his chair looking around at the other students. Everyone else started trying to solve the problem by writing something on their papers.

The teacher noticed Henry wasn't making any effort to solve the problem.

"Aren't you going to solve the problem, Henry?" asked the teacher.

"60 miles," said Henry.

The teacher was confused with his response. She looked at her own paper.

"Very good Henry," she said surprisingly. All the other kids turned around and looked at Henry in wonder of how he figured out the answer so quickly.

After giving the class several minutes to figure out the first answer, the teacher gave them the correct answer. She spent a few minutes to show them how to solve the brain teaser.

After asking the second question, the teacher looked directly at Henry. He stared back at her.

"Henry, do you have the answer?" she asked.

"7," responded Henry. He could tell from her expression that it wasn't normal to solve the brain teasers like what he was doing.

"Wow, how do you do that?" asked a couple of the girls in the class. They turned around in awe at Henry's ability to solve the brain teasers.

Several of the boys looked at Henry with spiteful glares. They wanted to be the ones impressing the girls and didn't like competition. Junior high school boys didn't like smart boys, but they all wanted to be smart.

"Just lucky I guess," said Henry. Nobody liked the smartest kid in class. Answering brain teasers out loud wasn't something he was going to make a habit of.

He made eye contact with the teacher. She understood his hint of involving luck as opposed to just being smart. After that, she never asked him to give an answer, but she always looked at him after every question. He would give a small nod to let her know he knew the answer. Then he would just sit and think about something else or draw pictures like he did in any class where the teacher allowed it.

The following Friday, Henry noticed his math teacher asked a couple of harder questions. He figured she probably came up with them just to evaluate his own capabilities. Her gaze was more intense. She watched in awe at the child prodigy she had discovered. It didn't take Henry more than a couple of seconds to solve the hardest of the problems, but he was becoming more adept at understanding the way his classmate's brains operated. He knew they wouldn't be able to solve these problems even if they had the entire class period.

After the 2nd Friday of brainteasers, the teacher asked Henry to stay behind in class. She waited until everyone else left the classroom.

"You know you have an exceptional gift, Henry," she said.

"Yes, Ma'am. I know, but I don't want anyone else to know," responded Henry.

He gave a courtesy smile and then walked out of the classroom. He had thought about what would happen if someone discovered his mathematical ability. He knew that he could easily breeze through school at a young age, but he just wanted to enjoy being a kid. He wanted to keep his gift as a secret from everyone. His math teacher understood. She kept his secret.

It was easy to not advertise his ability to memorize spelling words or a list of information. It was harder to keep his mathematics or problem-solving ability a secret. Most teachers expected him to sit writing something on his paper to try and logically work out the solution. They watched the students to make sure everyone was putting forth the appropriate effort. Sometimes, Henry pretended to act like he was trying to solve problems he already had solved. When he didn't feel like pretending, he would act like he was uninterested and get in trouble. Either option was better than blurting out correct answers.

It didn't take long for the kids in junior high to separate themselves in cliques. There were the preppy rich kids, the jocks, the cheerleaders, the geeks, the outcasts, and everybody else. Kyle was in the only clique with one member. He didn't meet the requirements to be a geek or an outcast. The everybody else was the biggest group. Henry liked that group the best. His goals in junior high school were to be the star athlete and smartest kid in the school. He didn't want to act like he was either one.

Henry's attraction for the opposite sex hadn't relinquished any since he had tried to kiss Lisa when he was 4 years old. He decided that he'd save any girlfriend business for a much later time. He was mostly interested in the girls that looked more like women, but he was well behind them on the puberty side of things. He knew that the Bible advocated waiting for marriage before having sex. He wasn't sure if he could overcome his desires to wait until marriage, but he chose to try. It was obvious that most of the other boys had the same sexual desires that he had because they talked about lust a lot. Having a girlfriend was tempting to fit in with his peers but the Biblical view made more practical sense. Having a girlfriend was a lot like having a wife. Henry wasn't interested in the drama of a relationship. Girlfriends evoked jealousy, envy, and anger. Other boys bragged about their girlfriends, but none of them seemed to be in happy relationships. When they were happy it didn't last very long before drama would raise its ugly face. Teenage boys were socially clueless while the girls were more socially sophisticated. The girls aggressively manipulated the emotions of boys, and the socially inept boys were tricked into being physical aggressive with each other. Henry preferred to spend his spare time with Albert and Slim more than any girls that he knew.

He had some challenges with the girl that sat next to him in his science class. Every time the teacher turned around, she grabbed his penis and smiled at him.

"What am I supposed to do about this?" thought Henry. He continued to gently grab her arm and remove it to her side of the table. Eventually she stopped. Henry never did figure out what inspired penis grabbing or the best way to deal with it.

One of the teachers in the school was just as impressed with one of the more mature looking girls as were all the boys in the class. It was common knowledge that he had a replacement teacher because the girl's parents complained to the school about his sexual advances. Henry overheard some adults calling him a child molester. They thought he should be imprisoned for life or executed. The consensus of most of the boys was that at least the teacher had good taste in women. Most of them agreed that they would have done the same thing if they would have had the opportunity. The girl was attractive.

Life was good.

CHAPTER 25

Football and Faggots

Football was Henry's favorite sport. It fit well with his innermost nature and desires. It was action oriented, violent, and aggressive. He relished the opportunity to hit other kids without any repercussions. Harold liked football just as much as Henry. He started Henry in pee-wee football one year early to give him some exposure. There were more than 50 other kids on Henry's first football team. Henry was the littlest on the team. It wasn't until his 3rd year of playing, that he finally got an opportunity to play in a game.

It was the second game of the season. Henry was the 3rd string full-back. His team was losing 6 to nothing and it was late in the 3rd quarter. The game had been a defensive battle. Neither team was able to move the ball and the coaches started putting in other players trying to find a way to score.

"Henry, you are going in as fullback. 32 Dive on 1, got it?" the coach told Henry.

"Yes sir," replied Henry. He ran onto the field to let the quarterback know the play. Before he reached the quarterback, he had already come up with his own plan.

The offense huddled up and the quarterback told everyone the play was 32 Dive on 1. Everyone nodded and clapped their hands to acknowledge they understood the play.

"I am coming right behind you," Henry said to Slim.

Slim nodded in understanding as they ran to the line of scrimmage.

Henry knew what every position was supposed to do on every play. He had memorized the playbook the first time he looked through it two years before. He was the fullback and 32 Dive meant he was going to get the ball. He was supposed to go right between the center and the right guard but that wasn't where he was going to go. He was going to go right behind Slim. Slim was the right tackle. He was the only player that could consistently block any defensive lineman as well as any linebackers that got in his way. Slim almost always did whatever Henry asked him to do. Henry generally gave good advice that led to a happy ending for Slim. They trusted each other with their lives.

The quarterback handed off the ball to Henry. He took one more step towards the 2 hole and then cut to the right and followed Slim. He knew he would be blocking towards the sideline just like he was supposed to do on 32 Dive. He had helped Slim remember what he needed to do on every play. They had spent hours practicing together with Albert.

Slim efficiently displaced the opposing team's defense. Henry ran as fast as he could directly for the corner of the end zone with nothing but green grass to stop him. Nobody touched him as he ran for a 23-yard touchdown.

The whole offense ran to Henry in celebration. Henry slapped Slim on his helmet and commended him for being the one that had allowed him to score. Anyone on the team could have scored the touchdown. All they had to do was just follow Slim.

Henry wasn't surprised that the coaches called the same play again. That was the normal protocol. If something worked, they kept doing the same thing until it stopped working. This time Henry decided that he would go through the 2 hole as the play was designed. He stared at the 4 hole to bait the defense just like Harold had taught him. The defense remembered the last play and knew the coaching protocol of repeating what worked. They watched Henry's eyes and took the bait.

Henry accelerated on the snap and took the football just as the quarterback turned to hand it off. He lowered his shoulder pads and managed to get across the goal line for a 2-point conversion.

Henry's team won the game 14 to 6 and Henry scored both touchdowns. From then on, he was the first-string fullback. His team went on to win the pee-wee football championship. Henry felt good to be part of the winning. Football was fun when he wasn't on the sidelines.

The following year, Henry played with 6th and 7th Graders. He was again sidelined with new coaches. They let the bigger, faster, and stronger kids play. Henry gave 100% effort in practice to work towards the privilege and enjoyment of being allowed to participate in the games. After a few weeks, one of the coaches noticed his fearlessness. Henry wasn't afraid to go full speed tackling other players that were a good 1 foot taller than himself. Despite being acknowledged for his effort, the coaches still didn't let him play. Near the end of the season, they played a team that their defense couldn't stop.

"Hey, where is that little kid that isn't afraid to hit?" shouted the defensive coach down the sideline. Henry made eye contact. He ran towards the coach with eager anticipation of getting a shot to play. On defense, things didn't work out quite as well as Henry would have liked. He was the smallest player on the field and not the fastest. He didn't impress anyone enough to achieve a starting position, but he enjoyed the opportunity to participate.

Henry decided to play on the junior high school 7th and 8th grade team when he was in the 7th grade. Most 7th graders continued to play pee-wee football. Slim and a couple others immediately got to play with the 8th graders. Henry hadn't grown any since the 4th grade. He had been smaller than everyone else in the 4th grade. The other kids had grown several inches. He had a hard time impressing the coaches. He occasionally got to scrimmage but spent most of his time either standing or taking a knee on the sidelines watching.

Standing around watching other kids play wasn't Henry's idea of having fun. He chose to practice having patience. Eventually the coaches would have a need for someone that knew what everyone was supposed to do and was fearless. Henry was a good runner that didn't get tired as fast as the other boys. When they ran sprints, he finished near the front every time. He always gave 90% to conserve his energy for the next sprint. Several other boys could beat him once or twice, but nobody could beat him ten times in a row. They ran laps around the field after practice. Henry easily achieved a few hundred yards lead ahead of the rest of the team. The coaches routinely blew the whistle to come in for the final huddle when the 2nd runner finished the second lap. Henry was happy to burn energy running an extra lap. None of the coaches seemed to notice that Henry always ran an extra lap. By the end of the season, he was able to run three laps faster than anyone else ran two.

"*Faggot*! You're a *faggot*," said an 8th grader. The 8th grader was a take a knee on the sideline's member of the team just like Henry.

Henry had heard other kids calling each other *faggot*. He knew what the word was intended to mean, but most kids used it more as a way of saying that they were manlier than the person being called the name. It was a masculinity challenge. The 8th grader was a good bit bigger than Henry as was everyone else on the team. Henry stared back at the boy to see what he would do next.

"You are a little *faggot*!" the 8th grader said louder. He shoved Henry.

"If you're looking for a date then you need to go look somewhere else. I'm not interested," responded Henry. He spoke in a slow calm voice and stared through the 8th grader with the meanest and most confident face that he could muster.

It took a few seconds for the 8th grader to digest what exactly Henry meant by his response. His face turned red as his eyes started bulging out of his head. He realized Henry had just basically told him that he was the one that had lustful desires for other boys. Henry watched him until he thought the other boy was about ready to resort to blows.

"Ha! I know you aren't gay! I'm just messing with you," said Henry. He slapped the other boy on the shoulder pads and smiled.

The other boy's face immediately expressed his relief. He smiled with happiness that he wasn't being called a *faggot* for real.

Henry didn't know any of his classmates that claimed to be gay. It was clear that most people in Milton detested and hated homosexuals. Some people claimed that God destroyed Sodom and Gomorrah because they were homosexuals. Henry knew the Bible indicated that the people of Sodom and Gomorrah were inhospitable, cruel, proud, and sexually immoral. They weren't just homosexuals. They were much like a lot of people he knew in Milton.

"The Bible says all sexual immorality is a sin," thought Henry. *"Lust is one of the seven cardinal sins. It doesn't just apply to gay people it is a sin for everyone. The people that hate gay people are probably just as sexually immoral as the people they hate."*

Most sins were tempting. Stealing, killing, lying, fornicating, and seeking revenge were things that Henry felt tempted to do. Having sex with a boy or a man wasn't tempting. Being a homosexual was even less tempting than eating his own feces. Sins or not. Henry wasn't interested in either. His propensity for sexual immorality was associated with the opposite sex.

Most of the boys that called other people *faggots* seemed to be the ones that might have the temptation of being a homosexual. They struggled with their own masculinity. That was the situation in most hate cases that Henry observed. People generally hated others that had something they wanted. He tended to hate people that had what he wanted as well. Part of him wanted to hate all the kids that were out on the field playing football. He would rather have been out on the field playing instead of them. He envied them. It didn't do him any good to envy or hate them. So, he chose to resist being envious or hating them.

When Henry started the 8th grade, he was confident that he would get noticed and become a starter. Unfortunately, all the kids that had played pee-wee football as 7th graders showed up. They were immediately assigned starting positions in front of Henry. They all had experience. Henry just knew the plays. Halfway through the season, he finally got to play on the kickoff team in a real game. He ran onto the field ready to prove himself. The first few times on the field, the kickoff either didn't go very far on the opposite side of the field or went out of bounds. Finally, the kicker kicked the ball high and down the field on Henry's side. He ran down the field and lowered his shoulders at full speed. He collided with the boy who had caught the ball.

The other boy lowered his shoulders as well. Henry's arms weren't long enough to wrap up like he had been taught with his over sized shoulder pads. But he got the best of the much larger boy. He knocked him backwards a couple of yards and his teammates quickly tackled him to the ground.

Henry ran off the field disappointed at himself for not wrapping up. He felt better on the way home.

"Great hit! It was the only hit that I heard from the stands in the whole game," said Harold.

"Yeah, but I didn't wrap up and make the tackle," said Henry.

"If you wouldn't have stopped him then he might have scored a touchdown. Your teammates tackled him right after you hit him. Football is a team sport and you contributed to stop him. It was a good hit," responded Harold.

Henry didn't say anything, but what his father said made sense. Harold had been a high school football star. He was an all-state quarterback and free safety and even earned a college football scholarship to play quarterback in college. Harold knew football better than any of his junior high school coaches. Football was a team sport and he had knocked the runner backwards.

"I can't wait to watch the film on Monday to see my hit. Maybe the coaches will notice me," thought Henry.

When Monday came, Henry waited impatiently for school to end so he could go to football practice and watch the film. Normally, he sat towards the back since he wasn't ever in the film. He sat down Indian style just beside the coach and the projector in the middle of the dark room.

Henry watched and listened intently when they came to the kickoff play where he had assisted in a tackle. The projector buzzing overshadowed any noise from the crowd and the hit that Harold had heard from the stands. He had to squint to see his hit which was partially obscured by other players. The coach stopped the film.

"Who was that who made the first hit!" shouted the coach.

"*This is it*," thought Henry. "*I'm going to be noticed and maybe I will get to be a starter.*"

"It was me, Sir. I made that hit," said Henry. He proudly looked up at the coach.

"Reynolds! How many times do I have to tell you! Wrap up! Wrap up!" shouted the coach. He backed up the film and used Henry's hit as an example to the rest of the team of what not to do.

Henry kept his eyes on the screen as if he was watching but he didn't see or hear anything else the coach said. He had the opportunity to prove himself. He had failed. Henry was angry at himself. He knew that he wasn't going to get another chance in the 8th grade, but he wasn't going to give up. He was confident that he would prove himself to new coaches in the 9th grade.

The following year, Henry was happy when football practice started. Most of the other take a knee on the sideline kids were no longer playing on the team. They knew that they weren't going to get to play. They didn't want to waste their time going to practice every day. The school team had never lost a game. They won the county championship in both the 7th and 8th grade. There wasn't any doubt in anyone's mind that they would be the champions again.

They had a new sit of plays. Henry quickly memorized what everyone was supposed to do on each play. The coaches picked their first-string offense and defense. There weren't enough kids to have a 3rd string. He was the 2nd string middle linebacker on defense and shared 2nd string running back responsibility with another boy. They went through a lot of abuse from the 1st string defense when they ran the ball in practice.

Henry enjoyed every moment of scrimmage, but he liked playing defense the most. The coaches announced the plays from a distance. That allowed him to know the plan before the 1st string offense ran the play. Henry shifted the defensive linemen to the left or right to make it harder for the offensive linemen to block them. He easily moved around and went through gaps to make most of the tackles. The first-string offense had a hard time ever making a first down in scrimmage. Against other junior high schools, they normally scored 6 or 7 touchdowns as they freely moved the ball down the field.

The first-string offense were frustrated in scrimmage when they couldn't gain any yards. Sometimes, Henry and the 2nd string defense would continually tackle them for a loss and move them in the opposite direction.

Henry found it fun and amusing. He thought that maybe the 2nd string could beat the 1st string offense in a real game. But he knew that the real advantage they had was because he knew all the plays. Knowing the plays was the amusing part.

Despite the fun, his goal was to secure a spot on the 1st string so he could participate in winning games against other teams. Unfortunately, he remained on the sidelines except for 1 or 2 plays at the end of games when there wasn't any possibility of losing.

Near the end of the season, the first team running back was fed up with Henry tackling him every time he got the ball. Most of the tackles were for a loss just after he was handed the ball. It wasn't enjoyable getting tackled. He liked scoring touchdowns. Practice wasn't fun.

"Somebody better block Reynolds!" he shouted to the rest of the offense, as they came to the line of scrimmage for the next play. He pointed at Henry just to make extra sure everyone knew Henry's last name.

Henry smiled to himself. He knew the play. The fullback that was supposed to block him wouldn't be able to block him unless he knew what Henry was already planning to do. Nobody would block him. He was going to be in the backfield to tackle the running back just as he would receive the pitch from the quarterback.

The running back picked himself off the ground after getting tackled for another loss.

"*Damn* it! Why is nobody blocking Reynolds!" he shouted.

"*Why doesn't anyone recognize that the coaches are shouting the plays to everyone,*" thought Henry. "*If there is anyone to blame it is the coaches.*"

The next play was a pass to a wide receiver. Henry shifted a little to the left. He took off running to the sideline where the pass would be thrown. The wide receiver caught the ball. The corner back wrapped him up by both legs as Henry arrived at full speed. He lowered his shoulders and leveled him from the blind side.

Henry loved hitting people hard. It was the hardest hit he had ever made. It felt good. The wide receiver got up staggering. He looked at Henry in a non-appreciative manner.

The next play was a running play. "I'm going to get you Reynolds!" shouted the wide receiver.

He jogged to his position and pointed at Henry.

Henry gave him a nod of acknowledgment and then proceeded with making the tackle. He knew he'd get to the ball carrier before Tony would be able to get anywhere close to him. After the tackle, Henry stood up. He watched Tony out of the corner of his eye. Tony was running full speed to level him with a cheap shot after the play was over.

Henry bent down. Tony went flying over him and landed on the ground a few yards away. Henry pretended as if he was retying his shoe. He acted like it was just a coincidence with the exception that he was laughing without acknowledging Tony.

Tony became even more angry after failing to get his revenge. He re-stated his threat, "I'm going to get you Reynolds!"

On the next play, Henry and Tony ignored the play. They ran full speed at each other. They collided with the best hit either one of them could accomplish. Tony was a good bit bigger than Henry, and both stumbled after the collision. Tony got the best of Henry.

"Great hit! Keep it up!" shouted Henry. He slapped Tony on the shoulder pads and smiled at him. Tony's anger slowly dissipated. His enraged face transformed to a smile of an inflated ego.

"Thanks Henry," said Tony with a nod.

"Okay, kick off team line up! We are going to practice kick offs," shouted the head coach.

Henry lined up deep to receive the ball so the first team kicking team could practice tackling him.

The coaches all stood a few yards behind Henry. He overhead one of the coaches talking to the head coach.

"We need to find a spot for Reynolds," said Coach Leach.

"*Finally, they've noticed me and I'm going to get to play,*" thought Henry. "*They probably saw all the tackles I made today.*"

He listened and watched intently to see what would be said next. The head coach made a face like he was disgusted with something. He shook his head back and forth without saying a word.

Henry knew at that moment that his football career would end in the 9th grade. He wasn't going to have another chance. It didn't stop him from trying unsuccessfully to return the kick offs back for a touchdown against the first team kicking team. He liked trying to avoid getting tackled almost as much as making them.

Some of the bigger boys liked to pick on the smaller boys in the locker room. Especially if they were still in the early stages of puberty. Mike liked intimidating smaller kids the most. He put icy hot in several of the boy's jock straps or underwear. Everyone enjoyed watching them jump around with a burning sensation on their penis and balls. Henry was always careful to not leave his jock strap or anything else lying around. He didn't have any desire to find out what icy hot felt like on his own penis and balls.

Since his football season and career were about over, Henry decided it would be good to get Mike back. Mike took off for the shower along with the others. He took Mike's icy hot and put a bunch of it in his underwear. He put everything back like Mike had left it.

When Henry returned from his shower, Mike was just pulling up his underwear. Everybody had a good laugh. Mike was more bothered with the icy hot on his penis and balls than any of his victims.

He looked around to get revenge.

"Who put icy hot in my underwear!" he shouted.

Nobody responded. Henry moved close to Mike.

"It was Slim," Henry whispered. "Don't tell him I told you. I think he is afraid of you."

Henry knew that Slim wasn't afraid of anyone in junior high. He was 6 inches taller and a good 40 pounds heavier than Mike. He thought that if he inflated Mike's ego just a little bit, he might believe him. Slim wouldn't mind.

It worked.

Mike immediately confronted Slim.

"Henry said you put icy hot in my underwear!"

Slim looked at Henry. Henry shrugged his shoulders and shook his head without adding any additional details.

"If I did put icy hot in your underwear, then what are you going to do about it?" asked Slim. He moved a little closer to Mike's face and looked down at him.

Mike looked up at Slim. He turned around, grabbed his towel, and headed back to the showers to try and wash off the icy-hot. Everyone else smiled and laughed, especially the boys that had experienced having icy hot on their own penis and balls.

During the play offs, Henry cheered for his teammates from the sidelines. He was happy to see that they continued to play well. Deep down he had mixed feelings. Part of him wished that he was out on the field playing for the opposing team. He liked participating more than watching his team win. His team went to the championship game again. They won like they always did.

Life doesn't always turn out the way we hope for.

CHAPTER 26

Good Fortune of a Baller Dad

In junior high school, only four 7th graders made the boys basketball team. The odds of making the team increased each year since one team was made up of the 7th and 8th graders while the 9th grade team had 12 boys. After that, the odds of making the high school team decreased rapidly as four different junior high schools all went to the same high school and repeated a similar process.

Henry enjoyed playing basketball almost as much as he liked playing football. Harold and Henry had sat up a basketball hoop in their driveway just before 7th grade started.

He went to the basketball try outs as a 7th grader along with 27 others. He wasn't very disappointed when he didn't make the team. There were several other boys much better than him.

He was dismayed that Albert didn't make the team. It wasn't a secret that Albert was without doubt the best of all the 7th graders. Everyone knew he was the preeminent player in the tryouts. Mrs. Thurman didn't let him play football, but she let him participate in basketball and baseball. Albert had been practicing basketball everyday while Henry and the other boys were at football practice.

In the 8th grade, Albert made the team. Henry didn't make it even though he had been more optimistic. He ended up playing in the city recreation league instead. His team didn't have a coach, so Harold volunteered to coach the 14- to 16-year-old boys' team. Henry had just turned 14 just prior to the cutoff date so he was one of the few 8th graders in a league that consisted of mostly 9th to 11th graders.

Harold was the best basketball player that Henry had ever seen play in real life. They often played one on one, a game of horse, or competed to see who could make more foul shots. Harold always won by 1 point or 1 letter dependent on the game being played. Henry enjoyed playing against Harold, but he knew that his dad had a lot of skill for him to always win by 1 point or 1 letter. He had watched Harold play with other grown men in pickup games in the various playgrounds around Milton. Harold made grown men look like children. Everyone at the playground respected and looked up to Harold as a local basketball legend. Sometimes, it almost seemed as if they worshiped him.

Harold was a good coach too. His coaching helped his team to win almost all their games and reach the championship game. Harold always tried to be consistent and fair with everyone on the team regardless of their basketball skills. During the regular season, he let all the kids play roughly an equal amount of time. Everyone on the team felt as if they contributed to the success.

During the championship game, Henry waited patiently on the bench wondering when he would get to play. The first quarter passed and then the second quarter. At halftime, Henry hadn't been in the game.

"When will I get to play?" he asked.

"We will see," replied Harold.

After the 3rd quarter, the game continued to be close. Each team took the lead back and forth several times. The end of the game was decided at the foul line. Henry watched his team lose by 1 point from the bench. Harold did exactly the opposite of everyone else's dad. They always played their son more than everyone else regardless of how good they were.

On the drive home, Harold could tell that Henry was angry. He tried to console him.

"The championship game is the only game where you don't have to play everyone equally. The other coach played his son the entire game without putting him on the bench," said Harold.

"So, then you decided to not let me play because the other coach played his son the whole game? That doesn't make any sense," responded Henry.

From that point on, Henry didn't listen to anything Harold told him. When they got home, he grabbed his basketball and ran up the street to another basketball hoop. It was 11 feet 4 inches at the rim. The kids up the street had a father that didn't know a basketball rim is supposed to be at 10 feet. Henry's hoop was exactly 10 feet because Harold knew to put it 2 inches higher than 10 feet because it would settle 2 inches after cementing it in the ground. His hoop was the only actual 10 feet rim in the neighborhood. Most of them were a couple inches shy of 10 feet. Henry and Albert had measured every single one of them. Tyrone had taught them to make sure they didn't spend too much time practicing with rims that weren't at the correct height when they were little. Henry went up the street because he wanted to get as far away from Harold as he could.

He wasn't angry at Harold. He was angry at himself. The only reason to not get in the game when his own father was the coach was because he wasn't good enough to play. He was going to show Harold that he was good enough to make the 9th grade team. Now was the best time to start practicing. Harold walked up the street to try and talk to Henry. He regretted not putting him in the game. Henry kept shooting as tears ran down his cheeks. Not being good enough to participate was painful. He refused to acknowledge Harold.

The following summer, Henry spent more time playing basketball with Albert and Slim. They played in the evenings after he finished cutting grass and on any rainy days when he couldn't cut grass. He was a good shooter and jumper. He wasn't the best ball handler and didn't have much experience of playing 5 on 5 basketball in real games. Lots of practice helped him improve his skills.

In August, he backed Harold's boat into his basketball post. It broke at the base and fell to the ground. Henry was only 14 but he liked to drive cars. Playing basketball was always a good excuse to move his parent's cars. Sometimes he would take a spin around the block or up the street to turn around and park them in the street. Backing up with a boat attached was more challenging than he had expected.

Harold was at work and Henry decided that he'd walk to the lumber store. It was only two miles from his house. He decided to get a 16 feet long treated 4 x 4 to replace the two painted 2 x 4's that had served as the existing post. He paid the clerk with some of his lawn mowing money.

"Pull around back and give them the receipt. They will load it up for you," said the lumber store clerk.

"Okay, thanks," said Henry. He didn't want to bother trying to explain that he didn't have a car. His parents wouldn't allow him to drive by himself all the way to the lumber store since he didn't have a driver's license.

"Where is your car?" asked the two men Henry met in the back of the lumber store.

"I got it," said Henry. He positioned himself in between the two men. They stooped down to rest the 16 feet 4x4 on Henry's shoulder. They stood in disbelief, as they watched a 5 feet tall 90 pound 14-year-old take off walking with a 16 feet 4x4 on his shoulder.

It wasn't that heavy for the first few hundred yards, but Henry stopped and switched shoulders more frequently as he continued his journey. After his second stop, he managed to get the 4x4 back on his shoulder. He noticed a car slowing down beside him. At first Henry thought it was someone that wanted to stop and give him a hand.

"What the *fuck* are you doing, *shit* for brains?" said an older boy. Henry remembered him from elementary school. He was one of the same boys that had encouraged other younger kids to eat worms at his bus stop. Greg was sitting in the passenger seat laughing.

"I'm carrying a 4x4 to my house to use as a new basketball post. I backed a boat into my old one and it broke," responded Henry.

The older boys laughed amongst themselves. They shouted a few more insults at Henry. He smiled to himself as he considered going into a spin motion to see how much damage a 16 feet 4x4 could do to their windshield.

"Thanks for the encouragement. I really appreciate it," said Henry. He continued up the street. The older boys did a spin out and left tire marks all over the street.

Once home he managed to dig out the previous cement and get his new post sit up before Harold got home. Henry was small, but he was determined. Some people had the opinion that he was a little bit stupid.

After 9th grade football season finished, Henry was excited to go to basketball tryouts and prove to Harold that he was good enough to make the team. The try outs lasted a week. Every day the boys anxiously looked at the list to see if they had been cut.

The last day before the final cut, Henry was concerned that he might not make the team. There were a couple new kids that were well over 6 feet tall and pretty good basketball players. Everyone that were still in the race for the final spots were kids that Henry really liked. He wished that they could just have two teams and he could then play with his better friends. He would have taken Albert and Slim on his team along with the other kids that didn't make the 7th and 8th grade team in the previous year. The other 6 boys could have a few other boys that wouldn't make the team otherwise. Then they could maybe have a team to win the championship as well as the runner ups.

He knew that one team per school was another rule that wasn't allowed to be broken. There wasn't any point of even asking about it. Some things can change, and other things never do.

After the final cut, Henry was happy and sad. There were 3 other boys that made the 9th grade team despite not making the team in previous years and 2 boys that were the last to get cut. His friends that didn't make the team were devastated. They congratulated him and the other 3 boys for making the team. Henry could see they were heart broken. They wanted to make the team as much as he did. The coach went to his church and was a friend of his parents. That didn't make him feel any better since it might have been the deciding factor between him and one of the other kids.

"It isn't how good you are as much as who you know," he thought. *"Life isn't always fair."*

Making the basketball team was almost comparable to a girl making the cheer leader squad. His classmates smiled and congratulated him for the achievement as he walked around school the next few days. The concept that teachers and students alike created an environment where cheerleaders and athletic stars were given special privileges seemed bizarre to Henry. Making good grades only resulted in higher expectations to do more and being picked on. Kids were incentivized to be popular but not smart.

Basketball practice wasn't as enjoyable as he hoped. They spent a lot of time watching and walking through different play sets. Henry found it boring. It wasn't much different than sitting in class repetitively hearing the same things over and over again. Henry only liked to hear or see something once. Repetition was painful.

Before they played the first game, the coaches had a new board set up so they could measure the standing vertical leap of each boy. Henry had grown 3 inches since he started the 9th grade. He was the second shortest player on his team. Slim was one of the tallest at 6 feet 4 inches. Albert was 6 feet 2 inches and their best all-around player.

Everyone was surprised to see that Henry had the highest standing vertical leap of anyone on the team.

Henry wasn't surprised at all. He knew he was a pretty good jumper. He could almost dunk a volleyball despite being only 5 feet 3 inches tall. He practiced jumping a lot. Sometimes he would jump up and down for an hour or two. It was a good way to try and wear himself out, so he could sleep at night. Counting sheep didn't work. That was one of the stupidest things Henry had ever tried. He was constantly trying to jump and touch something to watch his progression as he had grown from a small child to a below average sized teenager. He remembered when he first touched the net, the ceiling at home and then the rim. The other reason he had the highest recorded vertical leap was because he cheated.

Each time one of the boys had raised their arm to measure their standing reach the assistant coach had said, "Stretch it out all the way!"

Each boy did exactly what they were told. They stretched their arm as high as they could possibly reach and then were told to jump up and touch the highest point.

When Henry stepped up to have his vertical jump measured, he reached up his arm but dropped his shoulder. The coach told him to stretch it out all the way. He relaxed his shoulder a little. His fingers moved up a couple inches just like the coach saw from the other boys. Henry watched both the coach and his fingers when he was told to stretch out. He enjoyed being able to get the coach to fall for his trickery of not actually stretching out as far as could.

"Good job Henry," said Albert. "You jumped 2 inches higher than I did."

Henry told him how he cheated.

"That's hilarious," laughed Albert. "I never thought of doing that."

Henry's team won every game of the season. All the boys got to play at least a little bit once there wasn't any chance for the other team to win. Despite not playing much, Henry enjoyed watching Albert and Slim and the other boys on his team successfully win games.

At the end of the Season, they had a special day. All the fathers of the kids that played for the junior high school teams were invited to play a friendly game at the school against the best players from all grades.

Henry didn't get to play in the game. He watched from the bench as the best four 9th graders and an 8th grader took the court. The fathers were extremely cocky and mostly overweight men that lacked any basketball skills.

The junior high school boys were smiling and laughing as they walked onto the court. They arrogantly thought that the game was going to be just as easy as playing other schools. In their minds, they were unbeatable. They were just as cocky as their fathers, and they had never lost a basketball game. Albert was the only one that had seen Harold play basketball. He warned the other boys to watch out for him. The other boys looked at Harold. To them, Harold looked just like an older version of Henry.

Henry and Albert had played 2 on 2 when they were small kids with Harold and Tyrone. Albert still remembered how effortlessly Harold had embarrassed his older brother. Tyrone was a high school basketball star. If Harold could embarrass Tyrone, then he wouldn't struggle much with a bunch of junior high school boys.

Henry watched as the point guard dribbled the ball up the court.

"Better get your dribble lower Ricky and watch out," thought Henry.

Harold slapped the ball. It bounced right through Ricky's legs. Harold went up for a dunk before Ricky realized what had happened.

All the boys and the other dads looked at each other in disbelief. The smallest dad of all was the only one that could dunk. They scratched their heads in bewilderment and wonder of how he had even stolen the ball in the first place.

Harold didn't ever smile or celebrate when he played basketball. But it was next to impossible for anyone to watch him play and not smile. He made moves and passes that seemed to defy gravity and all laws of science. He was an entertainer on the court.

The next time Ricky brought the ball up the court, he passed to Albert without getting anywhere close to Harold. Slim got the ball in the paint and Harold immediately stripped the ball. He put on a dribbling display as he maneuvered down the court and all the way to the other rim. Four boys all jumped up to try and block his shot only to realize that he didn't have the ball. Harold had dished it to another dad who had an easy open layup.

The dads destroyed the boys. Harold made more than half of all the points and assisted on most of the other baskets. He made all the dads look better. The boys looked as if it was their first time to play basketball.

"You can tell he played college ball!" said one of the mothers in the stands. Henry turned around. He looked at how all the parent's watching the game were smiling and enjoying the show that his dad was putting on.

"*Nope, he played football in college. He was even better at football than he is at basketball*," thought Henry.

"You must be really proud," said Joey, who was sitting on the bench next to Henry. "I wish my dad could play like your dad."

Henry felt somewhat embarrassed. He was proud of Harold, but his objective was to try and get his dad to be proud of him. He'd have rather been out on the court entertaining everyone else. But he was proud to watch. It wasn't Harold's basketball skills that made Henry proud, it was the way he carried himself. Henry and the boys on his team admired Harold. They valued humility over arrogance.

"Yeah, he had a really good teacher," Henry said to Joey.

"Who was his teacher?" asked Joey. "Your grandfather?"

"No. Practice, lots of practice. He says that practice is the best teacher you will ever find," said Henry. "His dad died when he was still a kid."

Henry watched the rest of the game as the dads demolished the boys. He started thinking about what sport he could play in high school. He would have to practice a lot to make the basketball team in high school.

"*Maybe I should just play baseball*," he thought. "*I've always been good at baseball.*"

Henry wasn't a superstar, but life was good.

CHAPTER 27

Math Genius

Henry started the 9th grade with the goal to make straight A's. He wanted to go to college and hoped he could get a scholarship to pay for it. Higher grades would open more doors and possibilities for his future. The 9th grade was the start of a resume.

Since Henry could memorize things easily, making straight A's wasn't a challenge. All he had to do was to focus, listen, and try a little more in class. His biggest challenge was homework. He had never studied or taken work home. School work was boring enough at school, but he was committed to do whatever it took to make straight A's.

In the 7th and 8th grade, Henry had gotten in trouble in several of his classes. He was disciplined frequently for not paying attention or drawing pictures instead of following instructions. Occasionally he said things to make the rest of the class laugh or to embarrass teachers that he didn't like. Most of the time he just tried to make school more interesting by asking questions. He was inquisitive and wanted to learn more than what was taught. Some teachers identified his questions as being facetious while others appreciated his participation. The class clown was a friend of Henry's named Hector. All the students enjoyed having Hector in their class. Laughter made boring subjects and dull teachers more tolerable. Hector pushed the boundaries of inappropriate humor. The best teachers learned that humor was an important teaching tool for children to become critical thinkers. The worst teachers took their assigned subjects too seriously. They were intolerant of any sarcasm or irony from the students. They especially didn't like students that questioned what they were teaching them. They desired to have the students to blindly and unquestionably learn illogical biased and subjective facts.

Hector quickly accumulated so much detention hall when he was a freshman that he had a free ticket to continue being funny. The effects of corporal punishment by spankings wore off for junior high school kids. Beatings had instilled fear in elementary school. Problem children in junior high school couldn't be spanked hard enough to correct their behavior. The only punishments were detention hall, suspension, or expulsion. Some teachers ended up going overboard with lengthy detention hall sentences. For most kids, it was worse than being suspended. Ignorant teachers gave longer periods of detention in hopes of stopping what they perceived as unacceptable behavior. Hector ended up with a life sentence within the first few weeks of the school year.

Hector and Henry were the only two people that seemingly knew that more detention hall was no longer a punishment for Hector. Teachers continued to dish out more punishment completely oblivious to Hector's life sentence. Henry hated detention hall. He started avoiding asking any questions or making funny statements in class.

"I like detention hall," said Hector. "I do all of my homework and study for tests. If I have any questions, then Mr. Barnes always helps me. It is like having a free tutor. He is my favorite teacher. He teaches me things that aren't in the curriculum, and he likes to listen to my own opinions. I put all my books in my locker and don't have to worry about forgetting something at home."

"You are smart Hector," said Henry. "I couldn't take another hour of sitting in class. At least you take advantage of the punishment."

All of Henry's classes were unchallenging. The social studies teacher had a review before every test. He told everyone the questions and answers the day before the test. English only required memorizing spelling words, vocabulary words and understanding a bunch of rules and exceptions for the rules.

History class had reviews of what would be on the test just like social studies. Henry's history teacher genuinely liked history. He passionately shared interesting stories from the past. It was one of the few subjects that Henry found not to be boring. Mr. McCauley liked to be asked questions even if it wasn't something they were supposed to be learning. He encouraged everyone to learn as much as they could about history.

"What I am teaching you is just the tip of an iceberg," said Mr. McCauley. "You can read and study history for the rest of your lives and you wouldn't know 1% of everything. History helps us to not repeat the same mistakes. If you understand where we've been, then it will help you with today and to build a better tomorrow."

One day in history class, Henry looked up to see Hector mouthing to him like he was talking. His mouth was moving but he wasn't saying anything. Henry started pretending as if he was talking to Hector. Albert joined in and soon the whole class were all silently running their mouths. Whenever someone started doing something out of the ordinary, it typically caught on fast. All the kids liked mindless new games that might result in a funny ending. Hector, Henry, and Albert were the only ones that were also watching Mr. McCauley. They smiled at each other as he reached for his left ear. He adjusted his hearing aide. They waited until he adjusted it a second time and then started screaming. All the other kids followed suit. Mr. McCauley jumped as if his eardrums were going to burst.

Most of the class started laughing at Mr. McCauley's abrupt pain. His stern glare quickly dissipated the laughter. Hector, Henry, and Albert all looked regretfully at each other. Sometimes good ideas ended up being bad ones. They hadn't intended to cause Mr. McCauley any pain or hardship. After class, they all stayed behind to apologize.

"I am sorry Mr. McCauley," said Hector. "I started it. It was a bad idea. It was a stupid thing to do. I didn't mean to hurt you. I thought it would be funny, but it wasn't."

"Thank you for apologizing," said Mr. McCauley. "I lost much of my hearing in Vietnam. What you did was a terrible thing to do. Learn from it and don't ever pick on anyone else. My hearing aid works well for me. I am grateful that I didn't come back in a body bag, addicted to drugs, or paralyzed like a lot of my friends."

"We are really sorry Sir," said Henry. "We messed up."

"Is there anything we can do to make it up to you?" asked Albert. "Your one of our favorite teachers."

"This conversation is all I needed," smiled Mr. McCauley. "I accept your apology and forgive you. See you all tomorrow."

Math class continued to be unchallenging for Henry. It was hard to make learning fun when there wasn't anything new to learn.

Mrs. Stalworth was Henry's math teacher. She talked in an extremely slow and monotonous manner. She repeated the same things over and over. The boredom of sitting in her class for 50 minutes was excruciating. The combination of repetition and her slow monotonous speech was unbearable for Henry.

It would have been tolerable if he would have been allowed to draw or daydream quietly at his desk. But Mrs. Stalworth didn't tolerate anyone not sitting attentively and trying their best to listen and watch her every slow monotonous move.

During the first week of school, Henry was given detention hall for drawing and not paying attention. He started quietly reading the geometry book as Mrs. Stalworth lectured the class on the first chapter.

"Henry! Why are you not on the correct page?!" shouted Mrs. Stalworth.

"I was just interested to learn about geometry," responded Henry. "I was reading ahead."

"Turn to page 6 now!" said Mrs. Stalworth. "That is another day of detention hall. You need to learn to pay attention!"

Henry made efforts to sit in his seat and at least act like he was watching and listening to his teacher. He found it extremely difficult.

"Henry! Henry! Are you retarded or something?!" Mrs. Stalworth exclaimed.

Henry snapped out of his daydreaming.

"You are making faces like you are retarded. Are you retarded?!" she exclaimed.

"I don't know. My sister use to call me a retard. So, I might be retarded. She has been right before," responded Henry nonchalantly. Most of his classmates laughed at his response.

"Three more days of detention hall! Pay attention so you can learn," said Mrs. Stalworth.

The following week, Henry had his first geometry test in Mrs. Stalworth's class. He finished it within a couple minutes. He sat at his desk for another 20 or 30 minutes in silence. After a few other kids finished the test, he handed in his paper. He didn't want Mrs. Stalworth to know about his mathematical capabilities, and he didn't want to embarrass the other kids in his class.

On Monday, Mrs. Stalworth called each student's name to pick up their test results and all the homework they had handed in. Henry saw the 50% F written on his test before she handed it to him. He quickly flipped through all the homework to see every paper had a 50% F written on it in red ink.

"Fifty-percent? I got everything right. How come I get a 50% on everything?" asked Henry.

"You didn't show your work. You must show your work," said the teacher in her normal slow monotonous speech.

"What work? If I know the answer, then why do I have to write anything else?" asked Henry.

"How do I know that you aren't cheating?" asked Mrs. Stalworth. "You are probably copying the answers from someone else. If you don't do your work, then you can't find the answer."

"I didn't copy from anyone. I got all the answers correct. You never told us that we had to show any work. This isn't fair. If I wanted to cheat, then I'd copy the complete answer if I knew that is what you wanted."

"Now you know," said an unbelieving Mrs. Stalworth. She stared spitefully at Henry.

"This isn't fair. I got all of the answers correct and now I can't get higher than a B this term because there are only two more tests," thought Henry, as he quickly did the math. He knew that 83.3% would be

his best final grade if he continued getting a 100%. He hoped that his teacher would reconsider her logic. He had wanted to make straight A's. She called the next student's name with an obnoxious smile.

Henry sat down with his blood boiling. A few of the other students looked at him in sympathy. Henry frequently helped the other kids when they didn't know how to solve a problem. He liked helping them. They appreciated the way that he could teach them how to do math better than the teacher. His classmates knew that Henry understood how to do math. It was evident to them that Mrs. Stalworth wasn't being fair.

Henry easily managed to make all A's except for the one B that he had in the first term of his geometry class. He took a math proficiency test along with all the other 9th graders. He scored the highest on the test of anyone in his school. The students received their math proficiency results in their math class. Another boy named James asked Henry what he scored. James was pretty good at math himself.

Henry told him his score. James nodded and told Henry his own score. James was also in the top 1 percentile but scored much less than Henry. Henry didn't tell anyone that he purposely didn't answer every question. He didn't know if other kids ever got every answer correct and he didn't want to stand out.

Another math teacher was responsible for an event that was called math field day. The four students that scored the highest on the math proficiency test were required to participate in the county math field day. It was an honor that was mandatory. Henry and James were both told that they needed to report to another classroom after school the following day. They would meet with Mrs. Samuels and the rest of their team to practice for math field day.

The classroom where they met had previously been the room allocated for detention hall.

"Detention hall is in another class today, Henry," said Mr. Barnes.

"I'm here for math field day practice with James," said Henry. Mr. Barnes looked surprised that Henry would be good at math. Henry smiled to himself. Mr. Barnes suspicion was more rewarding to Henry than being selected to attend math field day.

"I must be doing a good job in achieving my goal of not looking or acting like a math prodigy," he thought.

The math field day practice sessions were almost as boring as geometry class. Henry faked his way through it. He made sure he didn't answer too many of the questions. He allowed James and the others to think that they were all as good at math as he was. Faking not being good at math took a lot of effort. Henry really liked math. It was hard for him to not advertise his abilities for a competition.

After a few weeks of practice, Mrs. Samuels picked up all four kids in her car on a Saturday morning. She drove them to the site where the county math field day would be conducted. On the way, she encouraged the students with a motivational speech to concentrate and do well. If they did well, they would get to go on to the state math field day and possibly a national competition.

Hundreds of participants representing every school in the county packed into the gymnasium. Their proud parents sat in the stands to watch their kids perform. Henry had convinced his parents not to come. They had commended him for achieving the honor roll which was published in the Milton newspaper.

"Wow! Great job Henry," said Marsha. "You are doing so much better than you did last year. We are proud of you for making the distinguished honor roll. You are the only one in your class that got straight A's."

Henry didn't show them the letter he received commending him for being selected for math field day. He told them he was participating in an event for kids that liked math. He knew that they would have showed up to watch him if they saw the letter. The letter made it out to be a great honor and privilege. Everyone was excited except for Henry. The other participants enjoyed being part of something where they excelled. The parents proudly watched their children. Surreal smiles were glued to their faces. Henry and Albert called the euphoric out of place smiles boy scout mom faces. They had first seen the bizarre euphoric smiles when they were cub scouts.

"Why are they so happy?" asked Albert.

"I guess because their sons learned how to use a pocketknife and tie knots," said Henry. "They are proud of them."

"Weird," said Albert. "They look like they are on drugs."

Henry looked around at the boy scout mom faces. Even the men had boy scout mom faces.

"If they knew how much their kids get ridiculed at school they wouldn't be smiling," he thought. *"I am glad my parents didn't come."*

Math field day was the last place he wanted to be. Henry felt like he was in a science fiction movie. It was almost as bad as competing in a beauty pageant. Instead of contestants trying to look graceful and sexually attractive to the judges, the other kids tried to outperform everyone else in making calculations in their heads. Everyone wanted a trophy.

Henry looked around at the other kids when questions were asked. When they knew the answers, they had boy scout mom faces too. When they didn't know the answer, they looked dejected. Each question evoked either intense pleasure or pain. They put their full attention into listening to the question and focusing on solving as many problems as they could.

Henry answered the easiest questions but skipped over most of the harder ones even though he knew the answers. He felt bad that he was letting Mrs. Samuels and his three teammates down but the last thing he wanted to do was to go to a state math field day.

His team ended up doing well but not quite good enough to secure a spot at the state competition. Henry performed better than his teammates. He was proud of himself for being one correct answer away from getting a trophy. Mrs. Samuels told everyone how proud she was of them for working hard and doing their best. Everyone including Henry were in a good mood when they were dropped off at their homes. He felt good to have lost but slightly bad for not trying to help his team win. He liked Mrs. Samuels and wished that he had her for his 9th grade geometry class instead of Mrs. Stalworth.

The class watched Mrs. Stalworth drawing on the black board. The chock clashed hard against the board with each angry line being drawn. Even Henry became interested to see what she was up too. Class had just started. She had commenced drawing something on the black board immediately after closing the classroom door. It was clear that she was obsessively angry at something.

After she finished the drawing, she turned around and stared directly at Henry.

"What is this?!" she shouted.

The question didn't confuse Henry, but it was evident that Mrs. Stalworth had something else on her mind. Whatever was on her mind had made her angrier than normal.

"That is an octagon," responded Henry. He watched Mrs. Stalworth intently.

Mrs. Stalworth's face became red with rage. She stuttered as if she was expecting a different answer but didn't know how to ask the question.

Henry recognized that she was looking for another response. He decided to try and help her out. She had piqued his interest.

"If it said stop on it and it was red alongside a road, then it could be a stop sign?" he said questionably.

It was the answer Mrs. Stalworth had been hoping for. She started violently hitting the chalk on the octagon.

"Yes! It is a stop sign! And what are you supposed to do when you come to a stop sign?!" she shouted at Henry.

"It depends," said Henry. He continued watching Mrs. Stalworth.

She started stuttering again and became even more frustrated. Henry decided to elaborate more to find out where she wanted to go with her questioning. It was evident that Mrs. Stalworth needed some help to get to her point.

"If you are in a car then the law says you are supposed to come to a complete stop and look both ways. Then you can proceed when it is safe to do so. If you aren't in a car then you don't have to stop. You can just look and proceed right through it if it is safe to do so. There isn't any reason to stop at a sign if there isn't anything to stop for," said Henry.

"You have to stop! I saw you run a stop sign this morning on your bicycle and you didn't stop! You have to stop at a stop sign!" she exclaimed.

"Are you a policewoman or a geometry teacher?" asked Henry to an unresponsive Mrs. Stalworth.

"If you are a policewoman then go ahead and give me a ticket if I broke the law. I think you are still a geometry teacher. Maybe you should stop wasting our time and start trying to teach us something instead of giving us your interpretation of the law," smiled Henry.

A couple of weeks earlier she had tried to give him detention hall.

"Go ahead and give me as much detention hall as you want. I already have it for the rest of the 9th grade anyway. I have a life sentence," he had replied.

Hector was the only person in the school that had managed that feat, but Henry had been happy to see that Mrs. Stalworth fell for his lie. She didn't bother writing him up for detention hall. Sometimes a good lie helped him to avoid unjustified consequences.

After Henry's question of whether Mrs. Stalworth was a policewoman or a geometry teacher, the entire classroom started laughing uncontrollably. Mrs. Stalworth's face went ghost white. She looked at all the students laughing at her and didn't know what to do next. She opened the door of the classroom and walked into the hallway. The door closed behind her.

Everyone in the class turned to look at Henry with smiles of admiration on their faces. Henry made fists with both of his hands. He slowly and quietly started hitting them on his desk to celebrate his victory. All the other students followed suit to start hitting their fists as hard and loud as they could on their desks. Another student started stomping his feet and shouting which quickly caught on. The entire class were enthusiastically beating their fists on their desks, stomping their feet, and shouting as loud as they could.

Henry enjoyed the moment. It felt good to vent his frustration after a full year of putting up with Mrs. Stalworth. He knew it wouldn't be long for another neighboring teacher to step inside to see what the commotion was all about. When the door opened, everyone looked up to see a dejected Mrs. Stalworth walking slowly back into the classroom. All the kids stopped the commotion. They sat smiling attentively in their seats. Mrs. Stalworth made eye contact with Henry with piercing and angry eyes but had nothing to say. In the hallway, she had concluded that she wasn't a policewoman. Henry had been right. She was supposed to be a geometry teacher.

On the second to last day of school, Mrs. Stalworth read out 5 names of the students that she was recommending for the gifted mathematics program in high school. Once she had read the 5 names, she looked at Henry.

"That is everyone. Nobody else will be recommended for gifted mathematics," she said.

"How about Henry? He is the smartest one in the class," asked James.

"Henry doesn't have the discipline to be in gifted mathematics," replied Mrs. Stalworth. "He is destined for failure."

"That isn't fair! Henry is the smartest in math and he wants to be an engineer! He has to be in gifted!" shouted James angrily.

"It is okay James," said Henry. "I don't want to be in gifted classes. I'm already gifted and so are you."

Henry looked directly at Mrs. Stalworth. She avoided the eye contact. Her feelings were hurt. She had unsuccessfully made a last-ditch attempt to try and hurt Henry's feelings. She ultimately gave him exactly what he wanted. He wanted an easy ride through high school. He only wanted to continue making A's, so he could go to college. Being in a gifted class required more effort to achieve his goals.

Henry never really understood why Mrs. Stalworth didn't like him. He tried to find something that he liked about her, but he had a hard time finding any light in her darkness.

Life was good even if everyone wasn't supportive.

CHAPTER 28

Middle Distance Runner

"Why don't you come out for track?" asked Hector. "It is a lot of fun if you run the half mile or mile. Every day, the coach gives us a route to run but we never run it. We run up behind the school and climb the rocks and mess around."

Henry smiled as he imagined Hector and the other runners disobeying the coach.

"You mean you go to practice to not practice?" laughed Henry.

"We run some," said Hector. "We just have fun doing it. I like the freedom of not being forced to do what someone else wants me to do. You will like it. It is nothing like football or basketball practice."

"I'll think about it," responded Henry.

Henry liked Hector and all the other distance runners that ran track. None of them were bullies, egotistical, lazy, or envious of others. All of them had a quiet confidence. They knew their strengths and were grateful for what they had. They were respectful, honest, hardworking, and happy. Hector might have been the class clown, but he shared all the same traits. Some people misunderstood his disruptive behavior as being attributed to seeking attention. The reality was that he had a level of imagination and creativity well beyond his age. Hector had the confidence, intelligence, and fearlessness to give bullies a taste of their own medicine. He was the epitome of humble. He had perfected the art of dishing out humble pie on anyone that deserved it. He defended weaker people that were wrongfully belittled or oppressed. He was quiet and polite when everyone behaved humanely, but his confidence couldn't keep him silent when injustices happened. None of the distance runners misunderstood Hector.

The running boom of the 1970s was just starting to catch on in Milton. Millions of people across the country had started running to lose weight, improve their health or compete in road races. Like many other Americans, Henry had watched Frank Shorter win gold and silver medals in the 1972 and 1976 Olympic marathons. Bill Rodgers was routinely winning the Boston and New York marathons. The best runners in the world were just as humble as the middle-distance runners that ran track in Milton. Henry admired Frank Shorter and Bill Rodgers. They weren't like a lot of superstar athletes that leveraged their achievements as a license to act like they were superior to everyone else. Running and other track and field events removed any doubt or debate of who was best. There weren't Hail Mary touchdowns, buzzer beater shots, or bad calls from umpires.

"I am going to be a middle-distance runner," thought Henry. *"No more trying to impress football or basketball coaches. The results will speak for themselves."*

Most people hated to run. It made them nauseous. Their lungs felt like they were going to explode. Running could be painful torture. Henry loved running. He felt like he was born to run. Running made him happy. It helped him think clearly. The more he ran, the better he felt.

"Maybe I could be good enough to run cross country and track in high school and that would help me to get into college. I might even be able to get an athletic scholarship," he thought.

The track coach was one of the football coaches. Henry respected Coach Leach. He was the same coach that Henry had overheard asking the head coach about finding him a starting spot on the 9th grade football team.

Henry and Hector were in Coach Leach's English class together. He was one of the few teachers that didn't ever give detention hall. He had even made learning English somewhat fun. He maintained control of the class without anyone getting in trouble. He treated all the students with respect, and he cared equally about every student. He made wise cracks back to Hector that made the whole class laugh. Mr. Leach had been a heavy weight wrestling champion that had been good enough to almost make the US Olympic team. He was a gentle giant that everyone loved.

Middle distance running evidently wasn't his expertise. He focused on coaching the sprinters and the participants in the field events. He did exactly what Hector said he would do with the middle-distance runners. He told them the route that he wanted them to run through Milton.

"I told you so," Hector mouthed to Henry with a smile.

They all took off running in the direction they were told. Everyone followed Hector as he headed off to some rock cliffs located not far from the school. The boys found a good challenging spot to climb up a steep cliff. They threw rocks for a while as they talked and laughed.

After playing around for 30 minutes, they ran back through the woods working up a sweat.

When they got back to the school, they stretched and then headed for the locker room. Henry had a lot more fun in the track practices than he had ever had in football, basketball, or baseball. He enjoyed the freedom of not having a coach around and the comradery with the other runners. He was already beginning to think that it might be better to train, but he generally ran in the evenings after practice anyways.

Track practice continued, the boys' found lots of different places to explore and goof around. One day, Coach Leach disrupted the routine. He had them run sprints because he had read something about the benefits of speed interval training for middle-distance runners. While they were running, they watched Coach Leach walking across the field just as one of the discus throwers was winding up. They watched the discus flying across the field. It took one bounce before hitting Coach Leach in the balls. The middle-distance runners were the first ones to get to him followed by the rest of the track team. They all stood around in disbelief that such a strong giant of a man could be completely disabled on the ground.

"*I guess that's what happens when someone brings a sling shot to fight a giant*," thought Henry.

"You alright Coach?" he asked.

Coach Leach held up an arm towards Henry and the other boys. His mouth quivered in silence like he wanted to stay something but couldn't speak. He managed to wave his arm.

"I think he wants us to give him some space," said Hector.

The boys went back to running their sprints. They watched Coach Leach slowly go to all fours. After a few minutes, he stood up and staggered along as he worked off the pain. All the boys were impressed with his courage. He overcame it all by himself without making a scene.

"No crying or complaining," said Will. "The best way to deal with pain is embrace it and move on. Coach Leach is a real man. He must have balls of steel."

There were only 3 track meets. Most of the other events required qualification to see who the best 3 kids were to compete in the meets. There were lots of sprinters, but only 6 middle-distance runners. They had mutually agreed who would run the mile and the half mile on one of their trips into the woods. Most of the boys liked the idea of not having to compete against each other in practice. They ran track because they enjoyed it.

Henry and Hector both chose to run the mile along with Will.

"Make sure you don't start out to fast," said Hector. "I did that last year. It is embarrassing to have everyone pass you after getting out to a good start."

The gun fired and Henry took off running. The boys from other schools were almost sprinting from the start. He found himself in the back of the pack with Hector and Will. They picked up their pace on the second lap. They encouraged each other as they slowly picked off one runner at a time and then sprinted to all finish behind the middle of the pack.

Henry, Hector, and Will sat together at the back of the bus on the ride home after the meet.

"Our school came in 2nd place," said Henry. "We need to start trying harder so we can help our team win. We aren't contributing if we don't get points."

"A lot of these kids have been running five-kilometer road races," said Will. "It will be hard to get as good as them in two weeks."

"We won't know if we don't try," said Hector.

The following week they still didn't follow the instructions of Coach Leach.

"Let's run the route he told us to," said Hector. "But we will run as hard as we can for half a mile, slow down for a couple of minutes and then repeat the process."

"You mean kind of like running intervals, but we keep running?" asked Henry.

"Exactly," said Hector.

They finished the run in twenty minutes.

"You are back early," said a confused Coach Leach. "Go run some sprints."

For the next twenty minutes they ran sprints with Albert and the other sprinters.

"That felt good," said Will. "I feel like we really did something today."

The next day, Coach Leach gave them a longer route to run. They decided to extend it by a few miles. They ran as hard as they could. The rest of the track team were already taking showers when they finished. They repeated the same routine for the next two days. The day before the second track meet, they went for an easy long run and discussed their strategy.

The gun fired and they positioned themselves in the middle of the pack early. They maintained the pace with the other runners and started their kicks with three hundred yards to go.

They finished sixth, seventh and eighth.

"You got one point Henry," said Hector.

"We got one point," said Henry. "In the championship we are going to get more."

They trained even harder the following week.

"Let's surprise everyone and go out fast," said Henry. "The five guys that beat us always go out fast and finish where they start. Nobody has ever passed us during the race."

"No guts. No glory," said Hector.

"It is going to hurt," said Will.

"Embrace the pain," responded Henry. "Convince yourself that you like it, and you won't be worried about it when it comes. Be just like Coach Leach when he got hit in his balls with a discus."

Henry, Hector, and Will went out hard and maintained a hard fast pace for three laps. They led the field going into the fourth and final lap.

Henry and Hector held off to finish 2nd and 3rd. Will came in 6th.

Coach Leach met them when they walked off the track with a big smile. He bought all three of them a cold Coca-Cola and commended them for their effort.

"We got fifteen points today," said Hector. "That should be enough to help our team win the championship!"

Slim secured 1st place in the shot put. Albert contributed with 32 points in the 100, 200, and relay races. Mike placed 4th in the pole vault. They won the county championship. It felt good to contribute to being on a championship team.

"Are you going to run cross country next year?" asked Hector.

"Yeah, are you?" responded Henry.

"Yes," said Hector. "I think I like running."

"I like it too," said Will. "But I am going to play football. Maybe we can run track together."

Life was good.

CHAPTER 29

The Rise of the New Right

"I'm hungry," said Slim. "Watching Pac-Man eating dots and ghosts makes my stomach growl."

"Me too," replied Albert just as he lost his last Pac-Man life.

"*Wu wo wo wo – boop boop*," went the Pac-Man machine after a ghost caught him.

"I don't know why we waste our quarters playing these arcade games," said Henry. "Let's go get some pizza."

"Me neither," said Albert. "Let's go. I'm done with Pac-Man forever."

"Almost every movie was good today," said Henry. "This is the first time that there wasn't a single movie I didn't enjoy."

"Yeah, 'Caddyshack' and 'Airplane' were both hilarious, and 'The Empire Strikes Back' was even better than 'Star Wars: Episode IV – A New Hope'," smiled Albert.

"Remember when we got caught sneaking into the theatre after the sixth grade?" asked Slim. "We bought a matinee ticket for the first Star Wars movie and then snuck into to see 'Saturday Night Fever' first."

The boys all laughed. They had started going to the movies together when they were in the 5th grade. When they went early, they could buy a cheap matinee movie ticket and then watch every movie in the theater. When they walked out of the theater, a policeman was waiting for them. A cinema employee had figured out they were watching multiple movies and pointed them out to the policeman. He had been watching them for several months.

"That's them!" said the cinema employee. "They have been here all day and watching multiple movies. Arrest them! They only paid for one ticket!"

"Let me see your ticket stubs," asked the policeman.

"If they snuck into the movie, then how come they have ticket stubs for the movie that they just watched?" asked the policeman after all of them produced their evidence without saying a word.

"They must have just got lucky," said the cinema employee. "They have been here for four hours. I know they have been watching multiple movies."

"There isn't any proof of what you are saying," said the policeman. "You need to apologize to these boys."

The muddled cinema employee apologized.

"No problem, Sir," Henry had responded. "You are just trying to do your job."

"We got lucky," laughed Henry. "They caught us coming out of the only movie that we had a ticket."

"We never did get to see 'Smokey and the Bandit'," said Albert. "That was going to be the next movie."

"It sure is nice now that we know everyone that works at the theater," said Slim. "Three dollars and fifty cents to watch as many movies as we want with unlimited free popcorn. We don't even need to sneak in our own snacks anymore."

"It is good to have friends," smiled Albert.

They walked into the Pizza Place. Each of them ordered a glass of water and paid the 10 cents. They found an empty table next to a well-dressed couple in the food court of the mall. The couple were sharing a large pepperoni pizza between just the two of them.

"Five slices left," said Henry. "Hope they leave us at least three of them."

"People like them always buy too much food," said Albert. "There isn't any way they will eat even half of that pizza."

"This is the first time I have ever seen anyone eating pizza with a fork," said Slim.

"People get a college education, good jobs and then they develop an expensive taste," said Henry. "They think they are more civilized than everyone else. They buy too much stuff, but they never quench their desire. If people aren't happy then they won't be happy with more of what they already have."

"They are chasing the American dream," said Albert. "Most people envy them."

"I don't envy anyone that is self-centered and materialistic," said Slim. "They will live shallow lives and won't ever be truly blessed. The richest people are the ones that are content with the least. Happy people don't eat pizza with a fork. Licking my fingers is always the best part."

The boys slowly sipped their water and waited for the couple to start getting up from their table to leave.

"Excuse me Maam," said Henry. "Is it alright if we eat the rest of your pizza or did you want to take it home with you?"

"Sure," responded the lady. She politely picked up the pizza and handed it to Henry with a feint look of disgust at the thought someone would ever consider eating her leftovers.

"Thank you Maam," replied Henry.

"Thank you too Sir," said Albert and Slim to the man. Henry put the pizza down on their table. The couple picked up their shopping bags and walked off to go do some more shopping in the mall.

"Five slices!" smiled Albert. "We did good."

"It's still warm. The perfect temperature!" said Slim as he took a big bite. "I always burn my tongue when we have to buy a pizza."

Slim eyed the two remaining pieces.

"Free pizza tastes good hot or cold," smiled Henry. "Albert and I will split a slice and you can have the other one Slim. You need to keep your healthy figure. High school football practice starts next month."

"Let's listen to what President Carter has to say," said Albert after they all got a free refill of ice water. They sat down on bar stools with several adults that were drinking beer. The cashier turned the volume of the television up as they sipped their ice water. President Carter was addressing the nation about the ongoing energy crisis and eroding faith in the American way of life.

"That was depressing," said Slim. "Who do you want to become the next president? Ronald Reagan or Jimmy Carter?"

"I don't think it really matters," said Henry. "Ronald Reagan is definitely the better actor. He has had a lot of practice. Surely, he can find a better speech writer than what Jimmy Carter just addressed the entire country with. Jimmy Carter doesn't stand a chance."

"Yeah, unemployment is up, crime is up, and Carter can't even get Iran to free the hostages or provide enough gas for everyone's cars," said Albert. "I think Hollywood will win. It will be just like the 'Empire Strikes Back'. Ronald Reagan will be playing the role of Luke Sky Walker."

"I doubt he has a Jedi Master like Yoda," replied Henry.

"It is a different world than when we were kids," said Slim.

"Believe it or not Slim," said Henry. "Most people think that we 15-year-olds are still kids."

It was 1980, Jimmy Carter would have one of the most unsuccessful presidential campaigns in history. Ronald Reagan would humiliate him in debates. Reagan's optimism, humor and reassuring disposition won over the confidence of most Americans. They would affectionately call him 'the Gipper' after a Notre Dame football player named George Gipp of whom Reagan had portrayed in a 1940 film.

The economy was stagnant, the hostage crisis in Iran dominated the news. Liberal college students felt alienated when Carter re-instated registration for the military draft after the Soviet Union invaded Afghanistan. The disaffected liberals would become known as 'Reagan Democrats'. It would be their first time to vote for the Republican candidate.

Ronald Reagan was elected president in a landslide victory. He secured all but five states and the District of Columbia. His acting ability appealed to conservatives of all types with promises of large tax cuts and a smaller government. Once in the office, he followed through with his promises. He reduced government spending and cut taxes for both individuals and corporations. Successful people were healthily rewarded with even more money in their pockets. The administration's vision was that less taxes on the rich would encourage them to buy more goods and invest in businesses which would then trickle down to everyone else. They called it trickle down economics. The reality was that it just made the rich richer. Greedy people never get enough.

The radical counter cultural movement of the 1960s and 1970s had troubled many Americans. They lost confidence in the government and lacked faith in the direction of the country. The Watergate scandal, the Vietnam War and uncertainty in the Middle East added to their mistrust of the government. Inflation, rising crime, and foreign policy turmoil helped win them over to embrace a new conservatism that was giving birth to a new belief system focused on materialism and consumerism. The 1980s would replace hippies with a new demographic label for young white upwardly mobile professionals that would be called yuppies. The yuppies would lead the materialistic rat race to help develop a nation of consumers.

The New Right of populist conservatives would enjoy unprecedented growth. It included evangelical Christians, advocates of a more powerful America abroad, anti-tax crusaders and even liberals that been disenfranchised with higher taxes for social programs that they now considered to be ineffective. They viewed the Democratic Parties efforts to help the poor to no longer represent their newly developed materialistic interests. They wanted to consume more for themselves rather than give donations or help the poor. Just about everyone wanted to keep up with the Jones family.

The fear of communism threatening the freedom of people everywhere would continue growing throughout the American population. Reagan's administration would cut social services budgets and significantly increase military spending. They would fund insurgencies in El Salvador, Nicaragua, Afghanistan, and Grenada to fight against communist governments. Unfortunately, the huge increases in military spending weren't offset enough by the spending cuts. The national debt would accumulate more debt in a few years than it had in the rest of the country's history. A materialistic and aggressive consumer society wasn't an effective means to balance a budget.

Henry and his friends were the first generation to have cable television. MTV's music videos launched the careers of many new iconic artists that were each different in their own way. People would copy the fashion and hairstyles of the artists they saw on television. Michael Jackson would become a megastar. Televised music videos would provide an arena that reshaped sexual identities, challenged societal norms, and renegotiated a new norm where nothing was normal. Gender bending and cross-dressing in the music industry questioned everything. The LGBT community that had been marginalized and unaccepted by society now had a televised platform to express their own views for the first time in history.

The frustration of inner-city black youths would be channeled through rap music and break dancing. Youths of all colors and backgrounds would listen to rap and heavy metal music. The music would capture their sense of malaise with society and feelings of being left out of the upwardly mobile yuppie movement. Pop music would give youths that had once felt unaccepted by society a new hope that being different might one day be accepted.

Popular music moved the masses in multiple directions of rebellion. Cable television became an outlet for popular culture to have an arena for debate. Disenfranchised people expressed their dissatisfaction against the new yuppie ideal that society had created as the new normal. Meanwhile, Ronald Reagan maintained his popularity throughout the 1980s. Just like other presidents before him, he would take a hard-liner stance on drugs. He re declared a war on them. Most adults would support the initiatives to fight the criminals while media outlets and Hollywood propaganda would provide new marketing material promoting drug use and criminality. 1980 would be labeled as the worst year of crime in many cities across the United States. Even suburban and rural areas would see similar levels of crime increase. Rape, murder, robberies, and drug offenses would have unprecedented growth. The Attorney General would make combating violent crime a top priority for Federal leadership.

"Three strikes and you are out!" stated the Gipper to a standing ovation.

The vast majority of the country supported increasing the number of police officers to stop crime in its tracts. Reagan's usage of a colloquialism derived from the national sport of baseball would result in new laws. Locking up people for drug offenses would become the new apple pie. Anyone that had three strikes received a life sentence sitting in prison as opposed to taking a walk to the bench in a baseball game. Many states would pass laws where minor misdemeanor offenses became felony charges. The prison population would rapidly grow from around half a million to almost 2.5 million people over a 20-year period. The minority prison population would grow dis proportionally to the white population. The United States would be the undisputed world leader in locking up the highest percentage of its people behind bars.

Hollywood and cable television would fuel the rebellion. Nancy Reagan combated the crack-cocaine epidemic with her 'Just Say No' campaign. Nancy had good intentions, but the new generation of kids would be just as rebellious as their parents. They mistrusted authority and fell prey to Hollywood, MTV, and peer pressure. Critics of 'Just Say No' would complain that it was too simplistic. It created a stigma that labeled anyone using drugs as bad. Addicts were viewed as outcasts that made a cognizant immoral choice in responding with a yes. Others blamed the violent crime on elevated levels of lead in the blood that mysteriously rewired American brains to be criminals.

Unsurprisingly, new values of prosperity centered on materialism and consumerism started further dividing the countries population into the 'haves' and 'have nots'.

History repeats itself. The people have a hard time remembering. If they learn anything from history it is that they keep forgetting.

CHAPTER 30

Kids Acting Like Themselves

"Sophomores can't use this door," said a senior standing at the main entrance to the high school. Henry and Albert continued walking without losing a step.

"We know. We are Juniors," responded Henry with a lie. He and Albert walked past. Several other sophomores accepted the oppression and tyranny. They turned around to take another door. The seniors were happy with their achievement. They smiled in glee in treating younger students the same way they themselves had been treated.

Sophomores Albert and Henry walked nonchalantly into the school.

"Idiots," said Albert.

The high school was the biggest one in the state with more than 2,500 students. Henry's initial impression of the first day was that it seemed more like what he had expected when he had started junior high school. He had incorrectly assumed that junior high kids would be more mature than they had been in elementary.

The high school kids looked older and for the most part they acted more mature than the kids in junior high school. Other than a few students wasting their own time to try and make sure sophomores didn't use the front door, there wasn't nearly as much bullying and ridiculing going on.

They saw Slim and started walking towards him. A couple senior football players shouted at him.

"Pick up my books and put them in my locker sophomore!" shouted a senior.

"No thanks. Do it yourself," said Slim. He walked straight past them towards Henry and Albert.

They all smiled at each other. The two senior football players walked off to try and find another sophomore to haze and abuse. Slim was bigger and meaner looking than any junior or senior in the school. He didn't accept any mistreatment of himself or anyone else. They gave each other their non-secret fist pump handshake that they had been doing since they were in elementary school.

The boys looked around at the girls. The girls had blossomed into looking like grown-up women. There were a lot more cliques than there had been in junior high school. Some of which were only a handful of kids with a common interest like BMX biking, skateboarding, smoking cigarettes, bow hunting or science. Nobody seemed to really care who they hung out with or that any one clique was better than someone else's. It was cool to like whatever you liked in high school.

"Hi Kyle. Good to see you," said the boys in unison. Kyle walked by without making eye contact or even acknowledging their existence.

"I hope he breaks out of his shell one day," said Henry as he watched Kyle stagger down the hallway.

"All we can do is keep trying to crack the shell," responded Albert.

Owen twisted his way towards the boys with a big smile.

"Hey! How was your Summer!" said Owen.

They greeted Owen. He did their non-secret handshake with each of them. Owen was the only other person that they had entitled to perform their handshake. They all reviewed their class schedule to see what classes they had together and then went their separate ways to the first period class.

The teachers were better equipped than the junior high school teachers. The initial boundary building went much faster without much of a power struggle. Henry quickly saw that nothing really changed in terms of just memorizing and regurgitating information on the tests. High school wasn't going to be any more challenging than junior high school in terms of making A's without needing to make a significant effort.

His chemistry class wasn't much different than biology in junior high except they did experiments with chemicals instead of dissecting frogs. There was a large refrigerator in the class that seemed out of place. The teacher was addicted to Coca-Cola. He used the refrigerator to feed his personal addiction.

"Can we put sodas in your refrigerator and drink them during class?" asked Hector.

"No," said Mr. Parks. "It is my refrigerator and students aren't allowed to have sodas in class."

"I hear what he says, but I see what he does," whispered Hector.

Whenever the teacher left the room, Hector would sneak up to the front of the room and open the refrigerator. He would take out a 2-liter bottle of Coca-Cola and take a big drink. He would sit back down. The teacher would come back in the classroom, seemingly oblivious to what was happening.

Everyone in the class enjoyed Hector's antics and thought it was funny. Henry was happy to see that Hector had acquired an ability to not always say whatever was on his mind. Keeping his mouth shut more often kept him from getting into trouble as frequently as he had in junior high. He was even more elated to see that he hadn't lost his sense of humor. If the teacher had a rule that students weren't allowed to have sodas in his class, then he wasn't sitting a good example by chain drinking Coke in front of his students.

After a couple of weeks of Hector drinking the chemistry teacher's soda, he left the room like he normally did. When Hector opened the refrigerator, it triggered a small explosion. Hector got back in his seat as fast as he could. He didn't get to take his normal big swig of Coke. The teacher walked in with a smile. He didn't say a word.

Henry was impressed that the teacher had figured out someone was drinking from his 2-liter Coke bottle.

"Most people wouldn't ever know," he thought with a smile. It was funny how some teachers were smarter than the students. They found ways to outsmart the troublemakers. They played by the kid's rules instead of pulling out the 'because I said so' card like a lot of adults.

After a couple weeks in high school, Henry recognized that there was also a lot more cooperation between the students to help each other succeed. Students that did their homework were happy to let others copy theirs just before class. Students would hold up their test paper to let other students see their answers. If someone didn't understand how to do something, then they could always ask the others. Henry enjoyed helping other kids understand how to do their schoolwork and pass tests. Everyone enjoyed helping each other. The students worked together to help each other succeed.

He found friends in every class that either enjoyed doing homework or just felt obligated to do what they were told. They would let him copy their homework and he would let them see his test paper when they couldn't remember all the answers. It made school a lot more enjoyable. Some people would call it cheating, but Henry called it co-operation. The goal was that everyone passed and finished high school. He didn't have to waste time doing homework and his friends didn't have to study so much. Cooperation was contagious and it helped bring a strong bond and camaraderie amongst the students.

Henry found chemistry to be the hardest class to understand what he was supposed to memorize. It seemed like math but with letters. He didn't ever understand the logic or the benefit of the subject. Fortunately, he found a friend in his class that enjoyed chemistry and doing the homework. His friend would hand him his test paper whenever the teacher left the room. Henry would copy most of his answers. He decided that it wouldn't be fair to get an A in chemistry since he didn't learn anything. His friend did all the homework and took the tests. Henry earned himself a B while his friend got an A.

Henry was surprised to see so many kids trying out for cross country, but he was happy to find out that all 24 boys and all the girls made the team. Anyone that wanted to be on the team could participate. There weren't any cuts or try outs. All someone had to do was show up and participate. If you were in the top 7 then you ran for varsity and the next 7 ran for the junior varsity team regardless of what grade they were in. Henry liked that there wasn't any favoritism. Running was quantifiable just like mathematics.

Henry and Hector met Frank. Frank had beat them in the 9th grade mile. The three boys soon figured out that they were all still about equal in abilities and better than more than half of the other boys.

There were 3 seniors and 2 juniors that all quickly demonstrated that they were the best runners in the school. All the other runners looked up to them as mentors. They pushed and encouraged everyone to try and improve their own capabilities. Their coach had them do a wide range of different types of training that included long runs, interval training, fartlek's and even an easy day to rest their muscles.

Coach Harry knew a lot more about middle-distance running than Coach Leach had known in the 9th grade. All the boys were somewhat serious to try and improve their running capabilities. Occasionally, Coach Harry would give special lessons like how to run with your eyes always parallel to the ground without any wasted movement or how to keep your feet straight to maximize the distance of every stride. Henry and Hector had a good laugh after the keeping your feet straight lesson. Coach Harry took off running with his feet at an angle like a duck. They had noticed how he ran before and had both been eager to see if he was going to practice what he had just preached.

"Sometimes I get good advice from people that don't practice what they preach," thought Henry. All the boys loved Coach Harry. They all shared a common love for running.

Practices were hard, but Henry enjoyed them. His teammates all encouraged each other to push onwards through the pain. They made each other better runners. They learned to embrace and even enjoy the pain.

"I get butterflies before every race," said Frank. "All I can think about is how much I am going to hurt for the last mile."

"Learn to love the pain," said a senior. "When the gun goes off think about how much pain everyone else is going to have. Accept and embrace it instead of fearing it. Be an optimist and not a pessimist. You have to focus on the prize."

"Think about how you are going to win the race," said another senior. "It is all in the mind. If you think about pain and losing, then you will feel pain and lose. What you resist persists. Reprogram your brain by replacing negative thoughts to positive ones."

They all loved the euphoric feeling they got when they finished a hard practice or race. They consistently did well in cross country meets. As individuals, they didn't excel but as a team they were hard to beat.

Overall, high school got off to a good start. Henry liked it much better than junior high school. He was confident and enjoyed being treated more like an adult.

It didn't take much peer pressure before Henry started drinking. The drinking age was 19 years old, but just about everyone he knew except for Albert and Slim drank beer.

All the boys on the cross-country team drank beer in their spare time. Henry figured it couldn't be that bad since adults were legally allowed to drink. Even Jesus didn't seem to have an issue with alcohol. If he turned water into wine, it certainly had to be alright to drink it.

Catchy slogans in beer commercials that showed a bunch of men working and playing hard and then sitting around a campfire drinking helped persuade him to start. He had never seen Tyrone drink, but he imagined what Tyrone would have said about the beer commercials.

"Don't do it Henry," Tyrone would have said. "If something looks good in a commercial then it is just someone trying to make money from everyone else's misery."

He didn't care much for the taste of the beer, but he liked the euphoric feeling and liquid courage he got when drinking. It was a lot like the feeling he had when he went for a long hard run. Unfortunately, it was a lot easier to get drunk than expending energy running. It was also easier to find other people that wanted to share the feeling. Everyone liked the easy road to get high.

It would take Henry a few years before he would learn the draw-backs of liquid courage. Alcohol made it a lot harder to do the right thing and follow his 8 rules of life of being the man he wanted to be. He was confident in himself to make good choices, but he would learn that alcohol can drive people to make the wrong choices. For Henry, one drink would never be enough and two would always be too many. Liquid courage would cause him a lot of pain. He would learn that everything worthwhile takes hard work and effort.

Life seemed good.

CHAPTER 31

Peace and Destruction at Night

Henry read a lot of books in High School. He checked them out regularly at the school library. He liked reading history books, biographies, and literature classics the most. After reading everything he found of interest in the school library he went to the public library to expand his choices in books. He especially enjoyed books that were banned from the shelves of the school library. A delegation of parents successfully convinced the school to ban *The Catcher in the Rye* which they deemed to be anti-white, obscene, and even a communist plot. Henry wouldn't have read it if it hadn't been for the disgruntled parents that had it banned. He liked the book well enough that he asked the school librarian what other books had been banned so he could read all of them.

Reading in class replaced drawing pictures, daydreaming, or pretending to be interested in the lessons. He didn't like schoolwork, but he loved learning. A lot of girls shared his love for reading. The girls enjoyed emotional evoking books that he didn't find very interesting. When he was required to read specific books as dictated by the board of education, the girls in his classes would happily tell him the story that they read. They were able to succinctly explain the books so well that he easily answered the test questions without ever reading the stories.

"Thanks for telling me about the book Amy," said Henry. "I got a 94% and didn't even read it. You would be a really good teacher."

"Thanks Henry," responded Amy. "I got a 100%. Explaining everything to you helped me. If you wouldn't have asked me so many questions, I wouldn't have gotten a 100%. We helped each other."

The only boys that he knew that liked reading were Hector, Albert and Slim. They read a lot of the same books. They shared their own interpretations of what they learned from reading them. They especially liked talking about banned books that a lot of people wanted to burn. Occasionally they found books that weren't banned that they wondered why other people didn't want to burn. They all agreed that any book that promoted selfishness, social Darwinism and malignant narcissism were a danger to a functioning society. A lot of other people were drawn to the ideals where natural selection and survival of the fittest to the detriment of everyone else was encouraged. It was becoming a new religious world view. Like most other religions, it denigrated and despised all other religions. Despite the offensive nature of the books, the boys agreed that they shouldn't be banned. Banning a book would only result in elevating nonsense to martyrdom status. They chose to be grateful that they had brains to see through ignorance, vapidity, and self-righteousness. During sleepless nights, reading gave Henry something to do when everyone else was sleeping. He questioned everything he read but enjoyed reading opposing views to also question what he thought he knew.

Henry and Hector read *On the Run* by Marty Liquori, *The Complete Book of Running* by Jim Fixx, and every other book they could find about running. He made photocopies or cut out pictures from *Runner's World* magazines of some of his favorite runners. He made an inspirational collage on his bedroom door. The Ethiopian, Abebe Bikila, securing the Gold Medal in the 1960 Olympics running barefoot graced the center of his collage. He pasted a picture of Billy Mills coming out of nowhere to win the 10,000 meters Olympic Gold Medal at the 1964 Tokyo Olympics. Next to Billy Mills was a sketch of Crazy Horse. Both Native Americans were from the Oglala Sioux tribe. He had a picture of a determined young Steve Prefontaine leading the pack in the 5,000 meters at the 1972 Olympics at Munich with the eventual winner Lasse Virén hot on his heels. A black and white photo from the 1920's of the first "Flying Finn", Paavo Nurmi, was pasted just next to his country man, Lasse Virén.

Henry admired the runners in his collage. They all represented hard work, determination, grit, and humility. His collage also had pictures of World War II hero Audie Murphy, the gladiator Spartacus, and Joe Morgan of the Cincinnati Reds. Henry imitated Joe Morgan's elbow flapping when he played baseball to remind himself to keep his elbow up. He attributed his batting success to mimicking his favorite baseball player. Every person in his collage were men that Henry looked up to as role models for something.

Hector, Frank, and Henry would soon be amongst the best runners in the state. They would acquire a lot of ribbons, medals, and trophies but none of them would be super stars at any event. They joked at how they could all run faster than the women's world record in at least one event between 800 and 10,000 meters.

"I think I prefer to run with men," laughed Hector. "I never thought of comparing my times to women. I could win the 800-meters woman's gold medal by 50 meters, or I could lose the men's race by 50 meters."

"We could all train hard enough to beat women in any of the events," said Frank. "Are you going to run on the men's team in college?"

"I don't think so," said Henry. "I am not prepared to devote my life to eating right, training hard and everything else needed to ever make a living out of running. If you aren't in the top five or ten in the world then you don't get paid. How about you?"

"I think I will," said Frank.

"I might do it to," said Hector. "Especially if I get a scholarship."

"I just love to run," said Henry. "I like when we go for a long eight-to-twelve-mile run. We laugh and joke around for the first few miles. After we separate from the coach and the rest of the pack, I like the feeling I get when we push the pace hard. My heartbeat increases. I feel the endorphins bursting through my system. I feel like I am on top of the world and can overcome anything that gets in my way. I like the relaxing feeling I get after a long hard run even more. When I run by myself in the middle of the night, sometimes I lie on my back on my front porch for five or ten minutes feeling the endocannabinoids flooding my body. Nothing feels better than that. I like it even more than the feeling I get when I am drunk. I will keep running just to clear my mind and get high naturally."

"Me too," said Hector. "Running is the best thing anyone can do for long term health. It sparks new growth of blood vessels that nourish the brain. New brain cells make people smarter. It increases the volume of the hippocampus which improves memory and the ability to learn. It decreases the risk of heart attacks and other diseases. It makes people less anxious and happier. Running is good for people. We were made to run."

"You should be a doctor," said Frank.

"I think I will be a doctor one day," said Hector. "Instead of telling everyone to take aspirin or other drugs I can tell them to get off the sofa and go for a run."

"I think the masses would prefer popping pills," laughed Henry. "Running requires effort."

Henry continued to find peace when he went running. As he got older, he increased his mileage. He knew from the books he had read that quality was more important than quantity to improve his times. He preferred long hard runs over quality training that made him better. Intervals and speed training weren't enjoyable. He ran to run instead of running to train. Sitting down for 8 hours in school had never been easy for Henry. Running allowed him to release his energy and it gave him something else to do at night when he couldn't sleep.

He was addicted to the euphoric feeling after a prolonged exertion of a long run. Running calmed his brain down. In school, his mind raced. He tried solving complicated problems where his mind could drive him crazy. He couldn't stop his thoughts that sometimes traveled into a dark abyss of nothingness. Reading and running calmed his thoughts and kept him sane. A good memory and problem-solving abilities were both a blessing and a curse to Henry. Running was both medicine and therapy. It helped slow down his brain and protect him from self-created delusions or societal brainwashing.

When he ran, he concentrated on the sound of his feet hitting the pavement and the beating of his heart. Sometimes he got lost in a complete calmness. He wouldn't remember running the last mile or two. Running was good meditation for Henry.

He liked running late at night best. Traffic, noise, and congestion were replaced with a quiet calm. At busy intersections, he didn't have to stop at red lights or to wait on cars to pass. He could see head lights from far away and people rarely shouted insults or threw beer cans at him at night. The air was fresh without carbon monoxide and other pollutants. Night running was free of distractions and stress. It was just Henry, the moon light, and the road.

People out late at night were generally involved in drinking, partying, or other mischievousness. Henry saw the same cars and people at night. He started watching the routines. Once he knew the routines, there was a certain predictability to what he would see each night. He saw a 1982 black Lincoln Continental with tinted windows just about every night in various places. On several occasions, the black Lincoln sat in a parking lot next to a police car. It became evident that whoever owned the black Lincoln knew all the policemen in town.

"Maybe he is an undercover cop or used to be a cop," thought Henry.

Other times, Henry would see the car in his own neighborhood. Sometimes it stopped in front of houses where Henry knew that drugs were sold. It wasn't unusual that he saw a transaction happening or he had a hunch that the visitors were drug users or addicts. He also knew kids at school that did drugs. He overheard them talking amongst themselves of where they purchased drugs. Everything he saw and heard helped to confirm his assumptions.

It was odd that the black Lincoln associated with both the police and drug dealers. He started carefully following it up streets. It rarely went faster than the speed limit. Henry could keep pace with the Lincoln through the city streets. It slowed down at stop signs and stopped at red lights. It wasn't ever in a hurry. It piqued Henry's curiosity.

The car never stopped anywhere for longer than a few minutes except for a specific bar and when it sat next to a police car. On one occasion, Henry saw the driver reach out a small envelope of his window to the policeman who was parked next to him. The policeman smiled as he took the envelope.

"Maybe he supplies all the drug dealers," thought Henry. *"He must be in cahoots with the police."*

If the policemen wanted to know where the drug dealers were all they had to do was go for a run and watch them.

"Maybe they don't know who buys and sells drugs," thought Henry. *"They use sirens and lights to see what is in the dark instead of being unseen in the dark. I see more than they do."*

Henry wondered whether the man in the black Lincoln might be the same man that had raped Gina. The police hadn't arrested him for raping her. Years before, Albert had told him that Tyrone said he was a drug dealer. If he was paying the police that would explain why they had locked up Tyrone instead of himself. He remembered what the man looked like but hadn't seen him very many times. He couldn't get a good look at him inside of the Lincoln.

"They are taking money and letting him do whatever he wants," thought Henry. He continued running and impressed himself by jumping over some high shrubbery.

A few nights later, Henry saw the police at one of the houses where drugs were sold. They had detained two black men in handcuffs. Henry didn't know their names, but he had seen them before. It wasn't a surprise that the first drug arrest he saw was at the one house where the people selling drugs weren't white.

It was easy to hear cars and see their headlights early enough to turn into an alley, run through someone's yard, or onto the golf course without being seen. Henry decided that it would be best to be invisible as much as possible. He didn't want the man in the black Lincoln or the police to know that he was watching them. If they knew he was watching them then they wouldn't hesitate to find an excuse to lock him up.

His sister Margaret had shown him an article in a popular women's magazine. The article listed the top 10 cities in the country with the highest percentage of gay population. He and Margaret had both been surprised to see that Milton was right in the top 5 with San Francisco, California.

He knew that the owners of several local businesses were gay. His mother's favorite hairstylist was gay as was his partner. One of the baseball pitchers from his high school had thrown a fast-food soda cup full of ice through the windshield of one of the gay business owner's cars. He had thrown it from the back of a pickup truck on the way back from having lunch. Henry didn't understand why anyone would be inspired to target a gay business owner, but he was impressed as much as the other boys that someone could throw an ordinary cup hard enough to go through a windshield. That took skill.

He asked the boy if he had really thrown a Burger King cup through a windshield. He confirmed it was true. He was proud of his own accomplishment.

"Did you get in trouble?" Henry asked.

"They reported it to the school and my parents had to pay for a new windshield," said the boy with a smile.

"That's it?" asked Henry.

"Yep, they said they didn't want to press charges."

"Were your mom and dad mad at you?" he asked.

"Not really," said the boy. "They don't like homosexuals either. They weren't happy that they had to buy a new windshield."

Henry didn't have a gay bone in his body. He was so deeply inside of his heterosexual closet that he wouldn't ever desire to open the door. His heterosexuality didn't stop him from running by a local gay bar. There was more activity at night than other bars. He ran by it more frequently than other places at night in hopes of seeing anything exciting. Most bars were dark with not much happening other than loud music and lots of cars in the parking lot.

The gay bar often had fights. The police visited it more frequently than other bars. One night he saw a man on top of another man in the parking lot. He was beating his fists into the other man's face and chest. A police car slowly crept towards the men on the wrong side of the road. Henry slowed to a walk and moved off into the shadows of a bank. He was close enough to hear the policeman ask a question from his open driver's side window.

"What are you doing?" asked the policeman.

"They're fighting. What do you think they are doing?" Henry whispered to himself. He watched the man turn towards the policeman.

"Beating up on a *faggot*!" shouted the man with snot coming out of his nose.

The policeman nodded his head in satisfaction and then proceeded driving back across to the right side of the road. The snotty nosed man continued beating the other man.

Henry turned around to make sure the policeman was out of sight and nobody else was on the street. He walked quietly up the sidewalk and kicked the man in the face as hard as he could. The man didn't even look up to see it coming.

Henry was impressed with how effective his kick was in snapping back the man's head. The man flipped over to his back. His limp body lay motionless on the pavement. He still had his own snot all over his face and looked to be smiling. The other man had blood all over his face and shirt. He managed to slowly get up. He staggered towards his car as he reached in his pocket for his keys. From the way the man staggered, Henry thought that he felt the effects of the alcohol more than the beat down.

"*He didn't even say thanks,*" thought Henry. "*I don't even think he knows I helped him.*"

Henry turned and started running again. He prayed that the man he kicked in the head would be alright.

"*This town is really messed up. Why would the police not do something to someone who was beating someone to what could be death?*" he thought. "*The only people that get arrested are almost always black. They locked up*

Tyrone for no reason at all. Life would really suck to be a gay black man in Milton."

He picked up his pace and headed towards his home.

Sometimes Henry would meet up somewhere with Hector and Frank and they would go for a long run together. They never ran together in the middle of the night. Hector and Frank preferred sleeping at night. They all enjoyed each other's company when they went for runs during the daylight.

Frank, Hector, and Henry ran by the bar that the black Lincoln frequented on a Saturday afternoon. Two men came out of the bar just as they were passing the entrance. One of them stuck out his leg and laughingly tried to trip Frank.

All the cross-country team were used to people throwing beer cans at them, shouting insults, or trying to open doors and hit them. The worst people were the ones that spit on them. Nothing was worse than being drenched in someone else's snotty spit. Frank easily jumped over the man's outstretched leg. They all continued their run like nothing had happened. After running another 20 or 30 yards, Henry glanced back and got a good look at the man's face. He looked familiar and walked with a limp. He saw the black Lincoln in the parking lot.

"Hank Wilson," thought Henry. *"I hope Tyrone caused your limp when he beat you with a two by four."*

The boys turned the corner. Henry glanced back to watch Hank getting into the driver's side of the black Lincoln.

Several weeks later, Henry was running late in the night when he heard a car approaching. He moved off the road into the camouflage of darkness behind a tree at the side of a house. The black Lincoln drove past. Henry followed it to see where it would go.

After following it for almost half a mile, he thought he wasn't going to be able to keep up. He considered changing his course. The car stopped in front of Mike's house. Henry picked up his speed instead. He ran through the front yards where there were lots of trees to obscure him. He stopped at a spot close enough to see what the man was up to.

Hank Wilson never exited the car. He began to drive away after only stopping for less than a minute. As he drove off, Henry saw that he had stopped by the mailbox.

He ran up the street using his peripheral vision to scan Mike's house to see if there was any movement. The police car wasn't in the driveway and all the windows were dark. Either everybody was sleeping, or they weren't at home.

There was a row of tall pine trees in between Mike's house and their neighbor. Henry turned right into the darkness of the pines. He stopped and listened for any movement or noises. He peeked around the pine trees at Mike's house and still didn't see any lights or movement. He walked to the mailbox and opened it up with his sleeve. Inside he found an envelope without any writing on it that felt like a stack of money.

He stepped back into the darkness of the pine trees and opened the envelope. Inside was a bunch of $100 notes which he estimated to be around $10,000. It was just small enough to fit snugly inside of Henry's running pants just below his waistline without being too noticeable.

He took off running in the opposite direction from where he lived and decided that he'd make every effort to avoid any cars or be seen. He knew that the police chief might get the dogs to track him down. Henry had seen them used to catch people on other occasions. He had seen the scars of people bitten by police dogs. Most of them had been innocent people that had ran in fear of the dogs. The dogs were trained to bite, and the Milton police used them for even low-level non-violent incidents. There wasn't any accountability when the dogs bit the wrong people.

"Most people look for a safe place to hide," thought Henry. *"The best thing to do is put as much distance you can between yourself and the dogs. If you don't go far then why wouldn't you expect to get caught? I can't outrun the dogs, but I can outrun their handlers."*

If the police were going to try and follow him with dogs, he knew they would give up long before they followed his scent for 15 or 20 miles.

He planned a route that would be easy to stay concealed. He made sure that he didn't cross over where he had already run. He jumped over fences and shrubbery to slow down anyone that wanted to follow his odor. Two hours later, he quietly entered his house. He put the money in his shoe box bank. He took a shower and went to bed at 3:23 am in the morning.

Henry didn't like the idea of keeping the money for himself. It didn't feel right to keep something that wasn't his. He decided that he would identify some people that might need some extra money. Christmas was only a few weeks away. His first thought was to put it in their mailboxes. He discarded that idea. He elected to purchase some Christmas cards and stamps to mail the money.

He wore his cotton running gloves and was careful not to leave any fingerprints on the envelopes or paper. He wrote out each address in the same cursive handwriting most unlike his own writing that he had practiced for years. He slanted his writing back to the left like most girls he knew. Hearing about the success of the infamous Unabomber had given him a good education in taking the right actions to not get caught. On the return address, he wrote Santa Claus, 1 Elf Street, North Pole 55555. On each card, he wrote *"Please accept this gift from someone that doesn't need it and may God Bless you"*. He deposited $500 in each of the 20 Christmas cards.

"I wonder if the police would think it looks like a teenage girls cursive?" he thought amusedly.

He drove to a neighboring town and put all 20 cards in a post office box and returned home. On the way home, he reminisced about stealing the money from a mailbox. He didn't have any regrets. It felt good to steal from crooked police and the drug dealer that had raped Gina.

Life was good when redistributing wealth to people that needed it.

CHAPTER 32

Losing Kyle

"Aren't you going to do something?" asked Henry to a teacher standing in the hallway outside of his classroom. They had both just observed another student purposely knock the books and papers out of Kyle's hands. Everything was scattered all over the floor. Other students were moving through the congested hallway as if nothing had happened. Kyle was stooped over collecting all his books and papers off the floor.

"I didn't see anything," said the teacher. He turned and walked back into his classroom. Henry watched him in disbelief and then turned to look at the kid that had victimized Kyle. He looked over his shoulder with a smile of satisfaction.

"Why did you do that?!" shouted Henry.

"Everyone does it," laughed the bully.

Henry bent over to help Kyle pick up his books and papers. He had first met Kyle when he had been in the 3rd grade. Kyle had been awarded the top of the class award as the smartest kid in the class. Henry had successfully found a way to be third in the class. Kyle hadn't ever learned. In grade school, he had been rewarded by his teachers for his conformity and willingness to go along with the system. He was respected by the elementary teachers and perceived as the enemy of the children. Kyle played by the school rules in a never-ending system of trying to be first. The rules in school seemed clear but in life they weren't clear at all. Kyle understood the system, but he didn't have an inkling of how to win at life.

"They wouldn't do that if you didn't carry so many books. Why don't you leave some of them in your locker?" asked Henry.

Kyle gave Henry an angry look. It was clear that Kyle had a good reason to not visit his locker. The lockers were in a dark congested area where kids like Kyle weren't treated very well.

"Aah, maybe Kyle is afraid to go to his locker. The same kid that just knocked his books out of his hands might do the same or even worse things to him when he goes to his locker," thought Henry.

Memories of Kyle being stuffed in his locker in junior high school filled Henry's mind. It had become a game for many kids that became a never-ending thirst. They weren't ever satisfied with the evil they did to Kyle. Stuffing him in his locker became a routine just as common as brushing their teeth or putting on their shoes. Bad behavior was contagious, and most kids didn't care about anybody else's feelings. The teachers in high school bullied kids like Kyle as much as the students.

After picking up the last of Kyle's papers and books, Henry watched him clumsily head down the hallway to class with every book for each of his 8 classes. He was skinny and wore plastic framed black glasses. His long hair on the top of his head was unkempt to the point it was almost an Afro but not quite. Henry thought that he looked like the epitome of a nerd. He looked boringly studious which was a trait that most other students disliked. He didn't have the social skills to even tell Henry thank you for his assistance or advice.

The next day, Henry wasn't surprised to see that Kyle was still carrying the big stack of books. He staggered down the hallway struggling to not drop them. Nor was he surprised to see the same kid that had victimized him the day before coming up from behind Kyle. The bully smiled as he zoned in on his prey. He knocked the books out of his hands again. It was a déjà vu moment with the exception that the teacher hadn't bothered to exit the comforts of his classroom this time.

Henry didn't bother to help Kyle but instead turned around to walk up behind the victimizer. He knocked the single book he was swinging in his left hand all the way down the hall. Both boys watched the book glide down the floor surface narrowly missing numerous students as it glided to a stop.

"What ... did you do that for?! asked the victimizer. He looked at Henry with a confused look as if he couldn't imagine why anyone would victimize a victimizer.

"Everyone else does it!" said Henry.

He turned to look at Kyle picking up his books and then looked back at the boy without saying another word.

The victimizer grunted as if he understood that this was a payback that he had deserved. He turned around to continue his way down the hallway and embarrassingly picked up his book in front of the other onlooking students. It didn't feel good to be a victim. Victimizers felt powerful and in control. Victims were helpless.

Henry had never been able understand or get to really know Kyle, but they both were in the same social studies class.

"Hi, how's it going today?" Henry hopefully asked Kyle, as they entered their classroom. He had never given up on breaking through the barrier Kyle had between himself and the rest of the world.

Kyle ignored Henry with the same lack of acknowledgement he gave everyone else.

"*If only he'd listen,*" thought Henry. "*If he made just a couple of changes in his behavior then he wouldn't be a target of victimization anymore.*"

One day, Henry saw Kyle walking across the parking lot towards their social studies class. He picked up his pace, so he could catch up with him. He hoped this would be the day that Kyle would put down his wall and talk or at least recognize that everybody wasn't an enemy. Just as Henry was almost caught up to him, another boy walking in the opposite direction knocked the books out of Kyle's hands.

This time the victimizer was somebody that Henry knew well and even considered a trusted friend.

"Why did you do that Billy?" asked Henry.

"I don't know …. Everybody does it?" said Billy regretfully.

"Just because everybody else does it doesn't make it right," said Henry.

"Your right Henry," said Billy. "I won't do it anymore."

Billy apologized and helped Henry and Kyle pick up the books.

It was a Friday. Henry liked getting to social studies class early on Fridays because they always had a current event's test. A different student came up with the test questions each week. There was an unwritten code between the students that they shared the questions and answers with their classmates. That way everybody could make a good grade without spending the previous evening watching the news and reading the morning newspaper.

Most of the kids couldn't remember all 10 answers so there were always questions missed. The scores generally ranged from 70 to 100 percent. Henry always got a 100 percent. He didn't view it as cheating as he also had the answers for spelling tests, vocabulary tests and most of the other tests he took in high school. The teachers provided the information and all he had to do was memorize the answers. It was all the same meaningless regurgitation of a small subset of information to Henry. Outside of school, he enjoyed reading the newspaper and keeping up with current events.

Another student quietly read through all the questions and answers that she had prepared for the test outside of the classroom. Henry looked down the hallway and saw Kyle all alone reading through a bunch of notes he had taken.

"*If only, you'd open up and talk to us?*" thought Henry.

"Kyle, do you want to know the answers?" asked Henry.

Kyle looked towards Henry. He shook his head in disgust. It was the first time they made eye contact since elementary school.

The bell rang. All the kids filed into the classroom to take their seats and get ready to regurgitate the answers on the test. After everyone finished, they followed the protocol which had been put in place by the teacher to ensure nobody cheated. They each handed their answers to the student next to them, so everyone graded someone else's paper. Some of the kids corrected the answers to assist their friends in getting better grades.

Just after they finished going through the answers and marking their classmate's papers, Kyle raised his hand. Every head in the class turned towards Kyle. Nobody had heard him speak all year. They were all shocked that he would raise his hand.

"Yes ... Kyle, do you have a question?" asked the teacher, in eager anticipation of hearing his voice and seeing what was going to come out of his mouth.

"This isn't fair! I stayed up last night and watched the local news and NBC News. I got up early this morning and read through every single article in the newspaper. Most of these questions were not on the news or in the paper. Everybody else is cheating and I only got a 60%. It isn't fair!" Kyle said in a loud angry voice.

"Don't you talk to me in that manner!" shouted the teacher. She angrily glared at Kyle.

Henry raised his hand. The teacher nodded to give her permission to open his mouth and say something.

"Maybe Kyle is right. Maybe it would be a good idea if you come up with the questions. That way everyone won't be tempted to cheat," said Henry.

"If anyone is cheating then I will give them an automatic zero! Cheating is not tolerated in my class! Did anyone cheat on this test?!" she exclaimed.

Henry started to raise his hand, but he was at a crossroads. He wanted to stand up for Kyle. Kyle had spoken the truth. He had a right to be angry. Everyone in the class except him were cheaters. Henry wanted to be accountable for whatever he did wrong, but he also wanted to go to college. Getting an F would impact his future. He didn't think it was fair if he would be the only one in the class to get punished. He looked around the class to see if anyone else was going to raise their hand with him.

"If everyone raises their hand," thought Henry. *"Surely the teacher won't give all of us F's."*

All the other kids were looking at their desks except for one boy. Henry could see that the other boy was thinking the same thing as himself. They both motioned like they were going to put up their hands but then they looked at everyone else and chose to chicken out.

"See!" exclaimed the teacher to Kyle. "Nobody is cheating. You just didn't study hard enough!" Henry looked down at his desk. He was ashamed of himself.

"Why didn't I raise my hand," he thought. *"Kyle is right. He is the only kid in the class that wasn't cheating. He should be commended for trying to do the right thing but instead he is being punished. Everyone else in the class is getting rewarded for cheating and the teacher is encouraging our bad behavior."*

The following Monday, Kyle wasn't at school. Henry wondered if he was sick or maybe he was just too angry to come to school. He had felt bad all weekend and been thinking about Kyle a lot. It was Tuesday that Henry learned that Kyle committed suicide by hanging himself in his bedroom closet. It was just after he had finally found the courage to voice his opinion.

Henry was angry at the teacher and partially blamed her for not taking a different angle to resolve the situation. He was even angrier at himself for not raising his hand, following the crowd to be a cheater, and not finding a way to help Kyle before. He had been a coward for being silent. He was complicit in Kyle's death.

There were only six kids and one teacher from Henry's school that went to the funeral. Everyone except for Albert and Slim were from his social studies class. The other boy that almost raised his hand, two girls and the teacher joined them. After the funeral, Henry and the boy from his class were consoling the two girls who were bawling their eyes out. They heard someone blow their horn. They looked up to see their teacher smiling and waving at them as she drove off.

Henry didn't wave back at the teacher. Nobody did. He wondered what would inspire someone to smile and wave after a funeral and why two girls would be so upset about the death of a classmate that they didn't ever even know or seemingly acknowledge. He couldn't understand the teacher's emotions, but he figured the girls must have felt as if they were just as complicit as he was. The only exception was that he was a boy and was supposed to be the one that didn't cry. Inside, he was crushed. Social studies class was meant to promote effective citizenry. He got an A in the class, but he deserved an F. He felt sadness for Kyle and his family. He felt regret that he hadn't been able to do something. Kyle's blood was on his hands.

Inside the church, Henry had seen Kyle's parents surrounded by what seemed to be a supporting and compassionate church family. Kyle's mother had tears streaming down her cheeks. Her husband was consoling her as he struggled to not let his own emotions poor out of his eyes. Kyle's sister wasn't at the funeral. Henry wondered if she was dead too or maybe still a drug addict and a prostitute.

"Why is she smiling?" Henry asked to the other boy.

"I don't know. I was thinking the same thing," he replied. They looked at each other and shook their heads as they watched their teacher drive away.

Life is full of regrets.

CHAPTER 33

The Thrill of Victory

"Watch this," said Henry. He cut in front of the other boys in his gym class. They had all been jumping on a springboard over a gymnastics horse and trying to touch the ceiling. None of them managed to touch the ceiling which was a good 30 feet in the air. Henry had just successfully jumped over the horse and barely scraped his behind on the second of two large mats that were intended to break their fall. He almost landed on his feet like a real gymnast.

He took off running. Everyone watched to see what he had planned. He hit the springboard and started spinning through the air over all the mats. He continued another 10 feet or so straight into a concrete wall. Henry could be a complete idiot sometimes.

His right leg hit the wall first. He immediately felt an intense pain. The other kids came to see if he was okay and complement his stupidity. The gym teacher wrinkled his forehead. He was confused of how Henry could have ended up colliding with the wall in the first place. He hadn't anticipated any of his students could jump so far.

Henry managed to make it through a couple of classes before going to the school nurse. She had him call his father to pick him up and take him to the hospital.

Harold picked him up from school and dropped him off at home. He was working afternoons and didn't want to be late for work. By the time Marsha got home all the natural pain killers had worn off. The same endorphins that he experienced when he was running naturally released themselves from his hypothalamus. Unfortunately, his body didn't generate a never-ending supply. Henry was feeling the pain. Fortunately, Marsha believed him when he told her his leg was broken. She took him to the hospital to get a cast and crutches.

The only thing Henry was happy about in having a broken leg was that he got a free pass to leave each class 5 minutes early. He got to pick a favorite girl in each class to carry his books for him despite not needing any assistance. In Milton, boys didn't carry books for other boys. They each had an excuse to be 5 minutes late for their next class. Every class was reduced to only 40 minutes of boredom. The worst part was that he broke it the day after his 16th birthday. He had taken his written driver's test the same day he turned 16. He had been able to drive a car since he was 12 years old and had been waiting patiently to get his driver's license to be legally allowed to drive. Apparently, it wasn't permitted to take the driver's test with a cast on your leg. He would have to wait a full month before he could receive a driver's license.

As soon as he did get his driver's license, he and Albert started driving to play basketball at different parks around the city. Albert had continued to excel at basketball and a car was the easiest way to get to the best spots to play. Henry didn't follow the doctor's instructions to continue using crutches after he had his cast removed. He did take it easy for a week or so. He didn't run very much or play basketball. He was too excited to get back to normal to continue walking around on crutches.

While he had a broken leg, he did a lot of hopping on his left leg. He hopped to get up and down stairs or across a room when hopping was more efficient than using his crutches. Albert was impressed with Henry's post breaking a leg jumping capability. He was now 5 feet 5 inches tall and could easily dunk a volleyball. He even managed to dunk a basketball with just a little bit of cheating. Henry's right hand was bigger than his left, but he couldn't quite palm a basketball yet. With the aid of some old Stick-Em spray that he still had from pee-wee football, he managed to dunk a basketball for the first time.

The basketball courts in Milton were generally full of people. It was hard to get in a game since there were grown men all wanting to participate. They only picked others to play that had already earned the respect to be entitled to play.

They were the same playgrounds that Henry had watched Harold impress the masses 5 or 10 years before. Now, he and Albert were trying to get on the same courts.

The playground didn't have any tryouts. The court authority was the players that had earned the respect of everyone else. There wasn't any favoritism. If anyone had talent,there was opportunity. Henry and Albert thought it was the best example of a government being ran by the people. Justice was made for the people, made by the people, and answerable only to the people. The players and spectators all sought an eternal justice that was the unchanging law of God. Selfishness and personal interests often reared their ugliness, but the people at the basketball court always pursued the moral high ground.

It didn't take them long to figure out which playgrounds had the best competition and where the competition wasn't as great. During their sophomore year of high school, they played mostly where the competition wasn't the best. They started honing their skills and soon had Slim and a couple of Albert's cousins hitting the playgrounds with them.

Slim played football. He was working towards getting a college football scholarship. All of his football coaches advised him to not play because they didn't want him to get hurt. He played basketball anyways to keep from getting fat and improve his endurance and footwork. Albert's cousins just liked playing ball.

The basketball courts always had a lot of activity in addition to playing ball. Lots of people just came to watch or to be around people when they had nothing else to do. Others came to sell and buy drugs or just look for trouble. It was common to have a game interrupted by the police showing up to arrest someone or a fight breaking out.

Occasionally, they would see Hank Wilson with his black Lincoln. They always watched to see who he associated with. It was normally the boys and men that used or sold drugs. They would make a note of kids that talked to him and would pull them aside when they had an opportunity. They tried to encourage them into taking a different path. They didn't have a lot of success in persuading many of them to not sell or use drugs which disappointed Henry. The pull from the dark side was too strong for many of them to overcome. Especially when they were dirt poor and didn't see a bright future for themselves.

Albert tended to have more persuasion capabilities than Henry. After telling Albert that he had seen his cousin Julius talking to Hank, Albert had words with Julius. He slapped him on the side of the head so hard that he went deaf in one ear for an hour or two.

Julius evidently got the message. Henry never did see him talk to Hank Wilson again, and he didn't ever see Julius during his night runs.

Trash talking and any other measures including cheating and lying about fouls and penalties were common practice on the playground. All the players wanted to win and keep the court, so they could continue playing. They resorted to bullying and lying whenever it helped them secure a win.

Henry enjoyed watching the drama. He was amazed how quickly the games just continued a few seconds after any interruption. People left the court all bloody, in handcuffs, or being dragged off the court by some of the bystanders. Replacement players would quickly be on the court tossing their sweatshirt to the side. The games went on like nothing happened. It was all about basketball and the love of the game.

Henry's team had their own moral code that was different from most of the other players. They never trash talked. They never cussed, and they were always respectful to other teams even when they tried to cheat. All of their aggression was applied to winning games honorably.

When someone from the other team started calling fouls that weren't fouls, they would let one or maybe two slip and then say something like, "Bro, that wasn't a foul. If you want us to start calling everything a foul then we can, but we came to play basketball. Let's stop playing around like children and play ball." In most cases, the crowd would stand firmly behind them as we the people. There was always a general desire to have ultimate truth and fairness on the court. The masses wanted justice.

Henry was always the point guard. He assumed the role of what a coach would typically do. He decided what kind of defense they would run, moved the others around on offense and told them when to slow down, pick it up, or pass more frequently. Albert was always the best player but all of them kept getting better and better.

By their junior year, they only played on the courts where they had the best competition in Milton. They won more than they lost.

"Take that *bitch*!" exclaimed a man. He had dunked over Albert and then pushed him against the fence as he tied the score at 10 to 10.

"Nice dunk," responded Albert. He grabbed the ball and tossed it to Henry who was already headed down the court. Three seconds later Henry dribbled underneath the basket on the other end and flipped the ball up behind his back for an alley-oop dunk by Albert who was trailing him.

Then Henry deflected the in bounds ball to Slim who dunked it over the man that had called Albert a *bitch*.

"Good game," said Slim. He reached his hand out to the man and then turned around to see who was next.

By their senior year in high school, they were the dominant force in Milton and had earned everyone's respect. Henry was amazed of how all the other player's they played against no longer trash talked or even tried to cheat. When they were on the court, it was all about basketball. The other players even started calling fouls when they fouled someone. Double dribbles or too many steps were called by someone on the team that made the mistake. It was their way of playing. Trash talk was contagious until someone put a stop to it. Respect and good manners were just as contagious. The behavior of the most respected players became the normal.

Albert and his cousin Daxter had played for the high school through their junior year, but both stopped playing for the school when they were seniors. They only played in the city playgrounds.

"Why don't you play for the school team anymore?" asked Henry.

"I like the freedom of playing in the park. I don't like it that lots of the better players don't even make the high school team. I didn't get to play as much as I think I should have either," responded Daxter. "A lot of the kids on the team are only on it because their parents donate money to the school."

"Same for me. You only get better playing ball. The best competition is here in the park," said Albert. "At school, it isn't how good you are. It is all about who you know."

During their senior year in high school the fad in shoes was Adidas high tops with white leather and silver stripes. They cost more than most kids in Milton could afford. Henry had found a look alike pair of TRAX shoes at K-MART that only cost 7 dollars.

He bought a pair of the shoes. When he wore them to school several kids commented that he had nice shoes thinking initially they were Adidas. Henry told everyone they were TRAX and made of real *pleather. P*leather was meant to refer to fake leather with the *p* being for plastic. It wasn't long before Albert, Slim, Daxter and a bunch of other kids started buying and proudly wearing 7-dollar TRAX shoes from K-MART. Even a lot of the rich kids started wearing TRAX.

Henry always had a hard time understanding why people liked gold over stainless steel, diamonds over ordinary rocks and leather over pleather. Beauty might be in the eye of the beholder but most of the time the sheep followed the eyes of the people they envied. The people they envied followed other delusional sheep. K-MART unsuccessfully marketed their shoes by asking the question why anyone would want to pay exorbitant prices when they sold shoes with comfort, support and durability of more expensive shoes. Henry thought K-MART had a good point.

"Look, here comes our basketball team," said Daxter, as everyone was sweeping the dust and snow off the court to begin a day of Saturday basketball. They liked to be the first ones at the court to see how many games they could win in a single day. Their record was 11 games in a row. The team that ended up beating them had already lost 2 games against them in the same day. Everyone had known that fatigue instead of talent was the reason they lost.

None of them had ever seen the high school basketball team at the park. Most of them were from the suburbs. They looked out of place wearing their fancy sweats.

"Dressing like that is a good way to get robbed," laughed Daxter.

The high school season was almost over. They had a successful year so far. They had won about 70% of their games with hopes of going to the regional championship and maybe even the state tournament.

All the starters from the high school team and 2 other boys that normally got a lot of minutes walked onto the court. They all greeted each other and started shooting and warming up. All the high school players had on Adidas shoes. Henry and Albert, both caught each other looking at their own K-MART TRAX shoes. They smiled at each other. Their shoes were almost completely worn out, but they had won a lot of basketball games with them. The pleather had lost much of its white paint, and they were each missing a few stripes.

"They will be hard to beat with those Adidas shoes," laughed Henry.

"The shoe doesn't make the player," said Albert. "The player makes the shoe. Let's see what these K-MART shoes are made of. Practice, sweat, effort and desire win games. Shoes are just shoes."

Some other men were also arriving to play.

"Who has the first game?" asked one of the men.

"We were here first, and they have the first game," Albert responded. He pointed towards the high school team.

"How many minutes do we play?" asked one of the boys from the high school team.

"We play to 11 but you have to win by 2. Every basket is 1 point. There aren't any foul shots. Whoever fouls someone has the responsibility to call the foul and anyone can call traveling, double dribble, out of bounds, or anything else. That's the rules. We were here first so it's our court. Since it is our court, you get to have the ball first," explained Henry.

He tossed the ball to Reggie.

"Are we allowed substitutes?" asked Reggie.

"Sure, if you want."

"One on one. Full court press. I got Reggie," Henry said quietly to his teammates. Each of them proceeded to pick their man. They watched the high school team huddle up.

"Are they going to do layup drills or what?" Daxter asked bemusedly.

The high school team looked confident as they lined up to inbound the ball. After all, they were the high school starting basketball team. They were playing other kids from their high school with only two kids that had even been good enough to ever make the school team.

Henry stole the ball on the inbound pass. He took one dribble and tossed it up towards the basket. Daxter grabbed it above the rim and dunked it lightly through the net.

The next inbound was a long pass intercepted by Walter and followed by four quick passes to Slim, Daxter, Henry and lastly Albert for another dunk.

Over the next 1 or 2 minutes, the ball never crossed half court. The score was 5 to nothing.

"Slow it down," said Henry. "No more full court press."

He wanted to give the high school team an opportunity to get the ball across half court. They started running their set plays. Henry and his friends easily switched through picks and moving screens. They didn't let them get off an uncontested shot.

After several trips down the court, the high school team finally managed to make a basket after an uncalled moving screen on Walter. Henry and his team just continued going through the motions casually scoring at will.

With the score at 10 to 3, Henry slowly dribbled the ball down the court. He looked up to see Albert, Slim, Walter, and Daxter standing at the other end as if they were bored with the game. The high school team were in a 2-3 zone defense with their arms held up above their heads just like they had been taught. They had an intense look in their eyes like they were going to give everything they had to make a comeback and win the game.

Henry took a couple dribbles as if he was going to drive from 30 feet. He stopped and took a step back uncontested rainbow jump shot from 28 feet that swished through the net.

Henry and his friends shook hands and told their high school team good game. The dejected high school team picked up their sweats and embarrassingly walked past all the other players that were gathering at the court.

"We got you next," said one of the men, as he and four others walked onto the court. "How come you guys aren't playing for the high school anyway?"

"We just like to ball?" said Daxter. All the boys smiled at each other. They all thought of how much they enjoyed the game and imagined what they could have done against all the other high school teams in the state.

The playground might as well have been Madison Square Garden to Henry and his friends. They played because they loved the game. The thrill of victory was sweet, and they felt the sugary thrill a lot.

"So, let's ball then," said the man.

Life was good.

CHAPTER 34

Flee and Elude

"Look!" shouted Albert. "There is a police car in the water!"

Henry, Albert, and Slim were on their way home from a long day of playing basketball. They had just dropped off Walter and Daxter. It was dark but well-lit from the lights on top of the police car. Henry pulled off to the side of the road. The boys quickly exited the car. Henry opened the trunk to grab a tire iron as Albert and Slim rushed down the hill onto the gulf course.

Officer Carl Lucas had been chasing a speeder and lost control of his car. The boys could only see the top of the police car. It was slowly sinking into the water trap on the 12th hole of the Lakewood Estates golf course.

Albert was the first one to get to the car.

"I can't open the door!" he shouted.

Both Slim and Albert were trying desperately to break the window when Henry made it to the car. One quick smack with the tire iron shattered the driver's side window into small glass pebbles. A quick swipe around the area removed the excess glass as water rapidly swept into the car. It continued sinking into the darkness of the water trap.

Albert managed to unfasten Officer Lucas's seat belt. The three boys pulled him through the window and got him out of the water.

"I never thought this water was so deep," said Henry. The police car sank to just below the surface with the lights still barely visible. "It must be at least eight feet deep."

Officer Carl Lucas wasn't breathing. He was bleeding badly from a gash on his forehead.

Albert took off his wet shirt. Henry used it to apply pressure to the gash on his forehead as Slim started administering chest compressions. Within seconds, another police car and an ambulance arrived on the scene. The paramedics took over.

The boys all gave a sigh of relief when they saw Carl cough out water and start breathing again. They all walked back to the car and left the scene before Officer Lucas was put in the ambulance.

"If I would have known it was Officer Lucas, I don't know if I would have made the effort to save him," said Albert.

"Yeah, that is what I was thinking too," replied Henry. "Anyway, we did the right thing. Regardless of what type of person he is, it wouldn't be right to watch someone drown without trying to help them."

"Agreed," confirmed Slim. "Nobody is perfect. Anyone can one day decide to change their ways."

Albert nodded his head in agreement.

"Should be a good lesson for me to not drive so fast," thought Henry.

Henry had always enjoyed speed. He loved the adrenaline rush. Speed made his heart beat faster and gave him a feeling of warmth and tingling in his limbs.

When he had been younger, it was running that invigorated him. Bicycles brought it to another level. When he was 12, he bought himself a BMX bike which was fun to ride through the woods and going over jumps to see how far and high he could go. But what he enjoyed most was raw speed.

At 14 years of age, Henry purchased a 10 speed Schwinn bicycle. He enjoyed riding it around town. For the first time he had the ability to exceed the speed limit. It was his Schwinn bicycle that his geometry teacher saw him run a stop sign when he had been in the 9th grade. He was one of the few kids that rode their bikes to and from school. Most of the kids either took the bus or their parents dropped them off and picked them up each day. Henry enjoyed the freedom of not being on someone else's timeline. His parents appreciated that they didn't have to be Henry's personal taxi.

The other thing Henry liked about riding a bicycle was that it expanded how far away he could explore. He could ride into the countryside and see towns and roads that he had never seen before. His favorite place to ride was a long arduous trip up a mountain on a 4-lane road. The road looked like an Interstate Highway but wasn't. The speed limit was 55 mph. Bicycles and even hitch hikers were allowed on the road. Henry would make the long trek up the mountain on his Schwinn. He would go across to the other side of the highway and pedal as hard as he could until his pedaling couldn't keep up with the speed.

From then on, he would make himself as aerodynamic as he could and coast in the slow lane. It was almost a 3-minute ride down the mountain. His favorite rides were when he managed to ease over into the fast lane and pass a slower moving car. What he enjoyed most about passing cars was the way the people in the cars looked at him. They acted as if they were in shock, like they had just seen an alien. Nobody expected to be passed by a kid going 60 or 70 miles per hour on a bicycle.

When Henry was 17, he got a used 1977 Buick Regal. It wasn't the muscle car that he would have really liked but he knew that his parents were concerned about his safety. They elected to get something big and not quite so fast to protect him from himself. Henry appreciated that they bought him a car. It was a blessing. Most of his friends didn't have the privilege of having parents that bought them a car. They had to buy their own transportation. Other kids had parents that seemingly enjoyed being taxi drivers.

Sometimes Henry would drive somewhere where he could see in all directions to make sure there weren't any police around so he could drive as fast as he wanted to enjoy the rush of adrenaline.

Around Milton, he had a general rule of thumb. If he saw two police cars within 2 minutes of each other then he would accelerate and drive as fast as he could for a short burst. The odds of seeing a third police car in 3 minutes was close to zero.

One day, he accelerated to 85 mph in a 35-mph zone. He was driving on the main street going through Milton and had just seen a second police car. An angry lady threw her arms into the air and shouted at Henry from her front porch. He looked down at the speedometer. He smiled as the rush of adrenaline overcame his body. He looked up to see an unexpected 3rd police car coming from the opposite direction.

"*Every rule has to have an exception,*" thought Henry.

The last thing that Henry wanted was to have to pay for a speeding ticket. He hadn't had a speeding ticket yet, but he had been with his parents when they had gotten ticketed. He knew that a speeding ticket meant at least 15 minutes of waiting around and ended with a ticket that had to be paid.

He thought of a time when his family was coming home from seeing his grandparents. Harold was driving through a town called Friendly where the speed limit went from 55 mph down to 35 mph. Harold had only slowed down to 45 mph which resulted in him getting a ticket.

Henry found it odd that the name of the town was called Friendly. There was a sign at the entrance on the south side of town when coming from Milton that said, 'Any *Nigger* Seen in this Town after Dark will be Shot'. The sign was a dark contrast to the vanilla pineapple milkshakes sold at the Friendly Ice Cream Parlor.

It was dark when they got pulled over. Henry had been thankful that his family weren't black. It would have really of been an unfriendly experience to get pulled over for speeding and shot in Friendly just for being black. The policeman wasn't overly friendly either. Marsha noticed that there was a lady in a civilian dress sitting in the passenger seat with the policeman as he was writing up the ticket. Henry and Margaret looked back to observe the lady. They saw the policeman lean over and kiss her as he fondled her breasts. The policeman had the light on inside of his car which made it almost like watching a television from the darkness inside of their family car.

It seemed like it took forever to wait on getting the ticket. Marsha wasn't very pleased that a policeman had his girlfriend in the car with him as he showed off his policing skills.

The town only had a few houses and there weren't any traffic lights or stop signs. All they had besides the main highway through town was one single road heading east. Harold commented that it was nothing but a speed trap for the small town to collect money.

Henry also learned from his parents, while sitting in the car, that Friendly was at one time what was called a sundown town. A sundown town was apparently a common northern phenomenon different from the southern one. The South needed black labor. They oppressed and exploited black people but tolerated their presence. In Friendly, they didn't tolerate anyone that wasn't white. They used aggressive policing, racist laws and even vigilante violence to keep black people out. The behavior was apparently deemed acceptable in sundown towns. The entrance sign made Henry think that it might still be a sundown town.

As soon as Henry saw the police car, he maintained his speed at 85 mph. He looked at his rear view mirror to see if the policeman was going to put his siren on and try to catch him.

The siren came on and the policeman slowed down to make a U-turn to pursue Henry.

There wasn't any doubt in Henry's mind that the policeman had put his siren on because of his speeding. He already had a plan and an excuse just in case he would get caught.

Henry was going 85 mph. He knew the distance of each block because he had measured everything in 0.1-mile intervals which he found beneficial for tracking how far he ran every day. The policeman had to come to basically a stop. It would take him a good 10 or 12 seconds to turn around and accelerate to anything more than 85 mph.

Henry was 0.6 miles from Hector's house, and he knew that he had a good hiding spot there. He would be at Hectors 10 seconds before the policeman would catch up to him. Hector's house was one of only a handful of houses that had a driveway that went to a carport in the back yard. A car could be parked on the carport and be perfectly obscured from the road. The first time Henry had visited Hector, he had asked him why they didn't have a driveway like everyone else.

"I don't know. I guess because we always use the back door and that is where the kitchen is. It makes for a short walk to get inside and bring in the groceries," Hector had said, as he shrugged his shoulders. Hector's response made a lot of sense to Henry. But he couldn't help but think how it would also make a good hiding spot if he ever needed one.

Henry slowed to take a left turn and then accelerated again. He thought that his excuse might sound lame to the policeman. His defense was that he didn't know the policeman wanted him to stop since he was going in the other direction. The policeman probably wouldn't be stupid enough to believe him.

"*It's best to just not get caught*," thought Henry.

He took a right on Ridge Road that overlooked the golf course and then turned into Hector's driveway which was the 3rd house on his right.

"*Thank God*," thought Henry, as he saw nobody was home. He pulled all the way forward underneath Hector's carport. He had thought that if someone was home, he would need to drive into Hector's yard to obscure the car. He didn't want to leave tire tracks in his friend's grass.

He heard the siren getting louder. The policeman must have seen him take the right-hand turn onto Ridge Road. He didn't hesitate in making a right turn. He accelerated past Hector's house. Henry barely got a glimpse of the police car as it sped past. He was impressed at how fast the car was.

"*I only had seven or eight seconds to spare*," thought Henry.

He backed out of the driveway and headed back down Ridge Road in the opposite direction. Then, he took the most direct route home and parked the car for a few days.

"*That was really stupid*," he thought. "*Next time, I will just pull over and take the speeding ticket.*"

After Henry got home, he realized that he hadn't been in any trouble with the police since he had been a young kid. He had stolen $10,000 and ambushed a policeman with snowballs without getting caught. It had been almost 10 years since the last time a policeman had threatened himself and Albert after Mike had thrown a snowball at a police car.

A few weeks later, he thought his luck had run out when a police car pulled up behind him and Frank, Joey, and Hector. They were all 17 years old and hadn't been able to wait until they were 19 to be allowed to drink beer. Since they weren't old enough to go into a bar, they found a nice quiet place on the north side of town where they thought they could just sit in the car and quietly drink.

Henry's first thought was to jump out of the car and run, but he decided to stay with his friends. He didn't want to put them in a position where they would have to act like they didn't know who the guy was that jumped out of the car and took off running.

The policeman was overly respectful and nice. He politely had them all get out of the car and hand him their driver's licenses. He held his flashlight and looked at each of their ID's, called their names, and then held the flashlight up to look at their face.

The third name he called was Rob Heiner. Rob was an older neighbor of Joey's but wasn't with them.

Hector, Frank, and Henry all looked at each other.

"That's me. I'm Rob," said Joey.

The policeman didn't seem to notice anything being wrong. He looked at the date of births and saw that only one of the boys was legally old enough to drink. He didn't realize that he wasn't with them.

"*Perception is always the reality*," thought Henry.

"Someone called that there was a suspicious car in the neighborhood. Only one of you is old enough to drink, but I don't really care if you drink or not. I did the same thing when I was your age. Just go find somewhere else to drink where you won't look so suspicious," said the policeman.

"Yes Sir," all the boys said in unison. They each took their licenses back and got back into the car to find another spot. They laughed about Joey being stupid enough to hand a policeman someone else's driver's license and get away with it. All of them agreed, it probably wasn't a good idea but at least it gave them something else to laugh about.

"Well, at least Joey is old enough to drink and drive with his fake ID," laughed Hector.

Henry wondered what would have happened if Albert would have been with them or if they would have been drinking in a car in his neighborhood. He suspected that the policeman might have taken a different action if it wouldn't have been 4 clean cut white kids in the suburbs of Milton. But he did appreciate that the policeman gave them a break.

Life is good when breaks are given.

CHAPTER 35

Rocket Scientist

Henry continued to be unchallenged with the academics in high school. He was grateful for having lots of friends and not many enemies. He enjoyed the camaraderie of playing basketball with his friends and running cross country and track. His team came 2nd in the state in cross country his senior year and only lost by one point. Henry didn't perform very well in the state meet. He crossed the finish line as the 5th man on his high school team. He was disappointed in his performance. All he had to do was pass one more person and his team could have been the State Champions. A couple of the younger runners did exceptionally well.

"I guess that is the spirit of athletics," thought Henry. *"You win some. You lose some. At the end of the day, it doesn't matter. It is just high school. If I would have spent less time drinking, cutting grass, and playing basketball and more time focused on running we would have won. If I would have focused more on running, then I wouldn't have had so much fun."*

On the way home from the state championship, the boys had a good laugh at the time they had stopped at a Pizza Hut on the way home from a meet. It was the only meet where they couldn't get a school bus to transport them. They weren't allowed to have a bus since the meet was in another state.

"We aren't allowed to use a school bus since we have to leave the state," said Coach Harry. "I can take some of you but need someone else to drive. I will give you money for gas."

"I can drive," said Henry. "I will take Frank, Hector and Chad."

"Thanks Henry," said Coach Harry. "I don't understand the rule. It seems riskier to have a student drive than having a school bus driver cross the state line. I know you will drive safely."

They had done well at the meet. They came in first place and were all happy. All four of them had finished in the top ten. They stopped at a Pizza Hut to get something to eat on the 2-hour drive home.

"What would you like to drink?" asked the waitress.

"I'll have a pitcher of Miller Lite," said Hector.

It was meant to be a joke. They were surprised to see her writing on her tablet and then asking each of the others what they wanted to drink.

They were all wearing their high school cross country sweats that clearly indicated they were still in high school. Each of the seventeen-year-old boys ordered a pitcher of Miller Lite just to see if the waitress would serve them.

She brought them the 4 pitchers of beer with frosted glasses while the pizza was being prepared.

"I guess we might as well drink them," said Henry. "She gave them to us. We can use the extra gas money Coach gave me to pay for the beer."

"Wow," said Frank. "I've never had beer from a frosted glass. They are treating us like royalty."

They were sipping their beers when a school bus pulled up outside. The high school cross country team that had come in 4th place started filing into the Pizza Hut. They were surprised to observe the out of state team that had won the meet sitting around smiling and enjoying their beers.

"The coach is going to say something to us," said Frank. "He will probably even tell Coach."

The coach looked at them in disbelief. He shook his head in disappointment and sat down with his team. The boys got a kick out of how the other team kept glancing over at them as they drank their sodas.

Just after the other team ordered, the manager of the Pizza Hut came rushing to the table.

"I need to see some ID's right now!" she exclaimed.

Hector quickly grabbed his pitcher and started chugging it as fast as he could. Henry and the others followed his lead as the manager pulled the almost empty pitchers from their hands.

"You are underage, and I can't charge you for these drinks," she said, as she returned to the kitchen.

"Free beer. That will teach us all a lesson," said Hector.

The coach of the other team shook his head in disgust as several of his runners smiled in amusement.

In track, the same group of boys came in 3rd in the 4x800 meters. Henry and Hector each placed in the 1600 meter and 800-meter race. Frank did better than any of them in winning the 3200-meter race. They all enjoyed running. The camaraderie and fun they had competing was worth far more than any of the trophies they won.

Henry ended up in the top 5% of his graduating class. The school recognized all the kids in the top 5% as something relatively special. It warranted an article in the Milton newspaper with their pictures, future college choices and anything else that the kids wanted to write for the paper.

The only reason Henry had wanted to make good grades was so that he could get into a college of his choosing. He wasn't interested in having his picture in the paper. He hadn't considered how proud his parents would be of his achievement. He was disappointed in himself when Marsha read the comments from all the other kids. Most of them expressed their gratitude to their parents for helping push them to excel in school. Henry just put a short quote that he had read in a book. He had selected the quote because he thought it was stupid. He found the stupidity of it to be funny to read in the paper. In hindsight, he wished he would have shown gratitude to his parents like the other kids did.

"I should have said something to show how grateful I am for my parents," he thought. *"I am fortunate to have them. Thank God I didn't decide to be honest and say something about all the kids that really helped*

me in high school. I could have mentioned the kids that let me copy their homework or my friends in Chemistry and Latin II that let me copy their tests. That probably wouldn't have had a happy ending."

"Sorry Mom," said Henry. "I couldn't have done it with out you and Dad. You taught me the importance of making good grades a long time ago. Most of the other kids couldn't have made good grades if their parents didn't make them study so much. You taught me to not need someone pushing me to excel all the time. That makes you the best parents of all. If I would have written that in the paper it would have made all the other parents feel bad. I didn't want to hurt their feelings. I am grateful to have you as parents."

"Thanks Henry," said Marsha. "We are really proud of you."

"Sometimes the truth doesn't do anything but get you in trouble," he thought. *"Thank God for the fifth amendment. What would I do without the constitutional right to lie by omission?"*

Henry was selected to go to a respected and selective educational program called Boy's State. It was for seniors that had demonstrated leadership capabilities, made good grades, and excelled in legalized extra-curricular activities such as athletics and community service. Henry had a good resume that included being the President of the Baptist Youth Fellowship at his church and taking a community service course at his high school. He enjoyed the community service course because he was permitted to leave school to work at the Red Cross. Instead of sitting in class, he was allowed to move around, socialize, and contribute to society. The Red Cross appreciated his efforts whereas teachers in school expected maximum effort. It was also an easy A that gave him an excuse to not show up for his Latin II class. His teacher allowed him to only come to class when he had a test.

Boy's State was designed to teach them about politics and hopefully inspire them to serve the community as future politicians. It was founded in 1935 to counter the socialism-inspired Young Pioneer Camps.

Slim was selected for Boy's State as well. Henry thought it might look good on his resume, so he decided to accept the invitation even though he didn't have much interest in politics. He was recommended by the Milton Lion's Club. They met regularly in the same community building where half of the town had showed up to participate in the pyramid scheme that had come to town 14 years before. Henry wondered if they weren't the same people who sit the whole scheme up in the first place.

Boy's State wasn't enjoyable. It was a lot like school except that everyone in attendance were white males. It was Henry's first time to spend a full week in the absence of any females or people of other races. It was only upon arrival to Boy's State that Henry understood why Albert hadn't been selected. For whatever reasons, it was clear that being white was a prerequisite for selection. He did learn more about politics. In Henry's opinion, the principal behind politics was to tell a bunch of lies to get the masses to believe in you. Telling people what they wanted to hear gained their support. Creating division and conflict between the voting populations was a necessity to sway the vote to be elected. The masses needed a conflict to pick a side. If there wasn't a conflict, then people wouldn't have anything to vote for. Every world power needed victims to denounce and hate to conceal its own intentions.

Once elected, politicians could do whatever they wanted but they didn't have significant power. The elections created a false perception of reality that brainwashed people into thinking the person that they voted for was looking out for their best interests. The real power was with the people that had control of the money. The money controlled the politicians. The political arena was like watching a fictional movie. It was a reality show of a competition where human beings berated each other with underhanded tactics and arrogantly beat their chests with praise of themselves and their fan base.

"Thank God, other people want to be politicians," thought Henry. *"Someone has to do it."*

After Boy's State, the Lion's Club invited him and his parents to come to the community building so he could express his appreciation for the honor of being selected to go to Boy's State. Henry wanted to make an excuse and not go. His parents told him it wouldn't be right if he didn't go and express his gratitude.

"But what will I tell them? You always told me that if I don't have something nice to say then it is best to say nothing at all. I don't have anything nice to say," Henry said to his parents.

"You'll think of something," said Marsha.

"Maybe I can tell them that I learned that I don't want to be a politician," said Henry. "Governments are just a necessary evil. I'm not very good at being superficial to try and impress the masses to get them to vote for me. I'd love to be a benevolent dictator, but I don't think the people would like my leadership. Maybe I can ask them why they didn't select Albert instead of me. He was more deserving to be invited. I would love to hear their view of why everyone at Boy's State were white."

"You'll think of something nice to say," said Marsha. "Just make up something that will make them feel good about themselves. Be grateful that they selected you. The Lion's Club does a lot to help the community."

When the Lion's Club had Henry go up to the podium to give a speech, they watched Henry give the shortest speech they would ever hear. He thanked them for the opportunity and showed them the T-shirt and the very thick book of state laws he had been given at Boy's State. He returned to his seat by his parents. The Lion's Club looked at him and then to his embarrassed parents. Everyone sat in an awkward and uncomfortable silence.

Henry didn't feel any embarrassment himself. He enjoyed watching the dumbfounded looks on their faces. He felt bad that he humiliated his parents. Fortunately, Marsha quickly took control of the situation. She gave a speech of her own. She inflated their egos and helped them forget all about Henry's short speech. The Lion's Club nodded in satisfaction and pleasure as Marsha told a fictional account of what Henry really wanted to say. Marsha was good at telling people what they wanted to hear. She would have made a much better politician than Henry.

Henry wasn't sure what he wanted to do as a grownup. He thought engineering might be interesting since he liked to solve problems and figure out how things worked. He decided that he wanted to study Aerospace Engineering. It was the most similar degree to being a Rocket Scientist that he could find. The only reason he had a desire to study Rocket Science was that he had frequently heard the phrase that you don't have to be a rocket scientist to do so many different things. He thought that whatever it was, it had to be for smart people. He hoped that he would meet some like minded people that had similar mathematics, memorization, and logic skills as he did.

When Henry had been a junior, he knew a couple seniors that were awarded scholarships to go to a military academy or an ROTC scholarship to a civilian college. He wasn't a valedictorian or a superstar athlete, but he applied and was awarded a scholarship to the US Naval Academy and an Army ROTC scholarship where he could go to any school where he was accepted. He applied for three different universities and eventually decided that he would rather go to school where most of his friends were going. He accepted the Army ROTC scholarship. He ruled out the US Naval Academy when they told him he wouldn't be able to be a pilot due to his non-perfect eyesight. He hoped that he would be able to fly helicopters in the Army. He'd find out later that the Army also required a perfect eyesight to be a pilot. The officers that interviewed him either didn't know the policy or lied to him.

He also chose the Army because he looked up to a lot of Army veterans that he knew. He shared their patriotism and felt compelled to serve his country. The catchy slogans and commercials he had seen on the television probably helped with his decision as well. The commercials gave him an adrenaline rush of being all he could be and doing more than the rest of the world does all day by 9 in the morning. They captured Henry's heart. Getting to see and experience faraway places was right up his alley.

"I wonder what Tyrone would tell me about these Army commercials," thought Henry. *"Probably, just marketing stuff Henry. Don't believe everything you hear."*

Life was good.

CHAPTER 36

Grand Theft

"Smile!" said Marsha. "The three musketeers!"

"Next chapter!" shouted the boys.

Marsha and Slim's mother snapped several photos. Slim stood in the middle with Henry and Albert on his left and right. They had officially graduated from high school. Their arms were around each other proudly wearing their cap and gown.

It felt good to be finished with high school, but they were much more excited about Tyrone getting out of prison. The cake they'd eat tonight would say nothing about graduation. Marsha had made a huge cake that said, "Welcome Home Tyrone! We Missed You!"

Albert's Uncle Daxter Senior oversaw the barbecue. The entire neighborhood sat waiting for Tyrone to show up. Mrs. Thurman insisted on Albert going to his graduation ceremony. She went by herself to pick up Tyrone. He walked out of the state prison for the first time in 10 years and gave a long embrace to his mom.

Tyrone stepped out of the car with the same smile that Henry remembered. Tears of joy freely watered the front yard as everyone hugged and welcomed Tyrone back home. Soon there was nothing but laughter and happiness as everyone celebrated.

"It seems like forever and just yesterday that you left," said Henry.

"Maybe for you Henry. For me, 10 years was a long time," said Tyrone. "It went slow, and I feel like I missed a lot. Things have changed."

The party lasted well after midnight. Everyone slept well that night.

Henry slowed to a trot 1-1/2 miles into a long run. He watched the familiar black Lincoln pull to a stop in front of the post office. Hank Wilson jumped out in a hurry and didn't bother to shut off the engine.

It was 10 o'clock in the morning and broad daylight, but Henry felt something pulling at him to steal the car. He changed his course and took a right towards the post office which was just a short distance up the street.

"*Too risky,*" thought Henry. "*Don't do it. Someone will surely see me.*"

Despite the warning from his conscience, something greater urged Henry onward.

"*Why do I always want to do stupid stuff like this,*" thought Henry. "*I know it is wrong, but I can't stop myself.*"

He pulled his hoody over his head. He scanned the street in front of him and the parking lot to his right. Both were void of any people. He checked his watch and noted the time as 10:02:43. As he reached the back-driver's side door of the black Lincoln, he stopped and bent over as if to tie his shoe. He looked to his left and his rear to again see a street void of people. He slowly bent up to peer over the top of the Lincoln and looked towards the post office. There were 2 people in line in front of Hank Wilson. The man at the post office was doing what he normally did. He was laughing and making jokes. Everyone inside were focused on him. Nobody was looking outside. Hank Wilson smiled in amusement at the man in the post office.

"*I like that post-office guy,*" thought Henry. "*He always has a smile and makes everyone else happy.*"

Henry pulled his sleeves over his hands and opened the door. He put the car in drive being careful not to touch anything with his fingers. He let off the brake and accelerated lightly to 25 mph. He stretched to look at the rear view and side mirrors to make sure nobody came running out of the post office.

He took a right, a left, a right and then left into an alley that was obscured by trees and garages. He knew that Hank Wilson would know his car was missing by now. The longer he spent in the car, the more chances of someone catching him. Time was of the essence. The man at the post office would be calling the police about now if he hadn't already done so. Hank Wilson would be angry at himself for being overconfident and lazy.

Being careful to keep his fingers inside his sweatshirt, he removed the keys and exited the car. He listened for any cars or movement and smiled with the silence. He looked in the back seat and then opened the trunk where he found a single green suitcase that he opened to find two large plastic bags.

Henry cut open one of the bags with a key and saw a white powdery substance that he assumed must be cocaine. He took both bags and emptied most of the contents all over the interior of the car and on the windshield. He poured the rest on the ground around the car before locking the empty bags and the keys in the suitcase in the trunk.

He slid his feet over the prints he had made in the dirt and cocaine. He scanned the area to see if he was satisfied with not having any identifiable tracks. Then he pushed his hands out of his sweatshirt and took off running up the alley. Carefully staying in the grass and shaking off the cocaine that had gotten on his sweatshirt and shoes.

He had an urge to go back to the post office to watch but he knew that was a temptation he needed to resist. It was now 10:07:15. He knew the police would already be looking for the black Lincoln. He turned right on the first street he came too. He picked up his pace to about a 6 minute per mile pace. He headed off in the opposite direction of the post office.

Henry thought about running on top of the flood wall that bordered the river a couple of weeks before. He had imagined that it might be a good place to lose dogs if he was ever being tracked, but he elected to follow the same philosophy he had used in the past. Running on the flood wall would look suspicious. He would put as many miles between himself and the police as fast as he could. He could run at a 6 minute per mile pace for a long time without much effort. He planned a 20-mile run that would go back and forth through the town without ever crossing his path.

He wasn't sure what affect the cocaine would have on the dogs. He smiled at the thought of them sniffing through the cocaine around the car or maybe the empty bags he had locked in the trunk.

"*Do dogs get high or addicted*?" he thought.

As Henry ran, he smiled as he felt the sweetness of revenge. Hank Wilson had raped Gina and been responsible for putting Tyrone in prison along with countless others. It wouldn't bring back Tyrone's last 10 years or take away Gina's emotional trauma, but it felt good to get some payback for them. At least he was out of $10,000 and whatever a couple of big bags of cocaine were worth.

His smile grew at thoughts of Gina. She had graduated college and was now a schoolteacher at Peale Elementary. He had watched her at Tyrone's home coming party. She had overcome her emotional trauma well. She was happy and blessed.

"*Gina will be a good schoolteacher*," he thought.

It would only take Henry about 2 hours to complete the 20 miles. He knew the police wouldn't expect a car thief to go so far. Most car thieves were lazy. As he ran, he revised his plan. He started thinking that if the police were smart enough in trying to track him that they might try to identify specific people that could run like he could. There weren't many people around that could run 20 miles in 2 hours. He hadn't seen a single policeman and decided that being seen might mean getting caught.

After running about 12 miles, Henry stopped running. He started limping like he was hurt. It didn't take long for someone that knew him to stop and ask if he needed a ride.

"Yeah, I twisted my ankle. Can you drop me off at the church? My mom's there and she can give me a ride," said Henry.

"Sure, no problem, Henry. Jump in," said Mrs. Deaner.

Henry got a ride home with someone else he found at the church, and then took off his clothes and carried his sweatshirt and brooks running shoes to the shed. He used some tin snips to cut his shoes in small pieces. He poured some gasoline on the shoes and his sweatshirt in a bucket and burnt them until there was nothing but ashes and a little bit of rubber.

He was glad that the shoes were already almost worn out. He already had a newer pair of running shoes. The brook's outlet was the only place he knew of that had a warranty on their shoes. If you could wear them out in 3 months, then they replaced them free of charge. It had taken him only about 2 months to wear out the other two pairs he had. This was his second pair of free shoes. He had already decided that it wouldn't be right to continue taking their shoes for free. There weren't very many shoes that lasted Henry for 3 months.

After he finished, he put the ashes on the ground and poured some water over it to cool it down. He shoveled it up into a trash bag and threw it in a neighbor's garbage can up the alley.

A few days later, Henry strolled through the mall with Albert, Slim and Tyrone. Albert was going to play basketball at a Junior College in Chicago where his uncle knew the coach. He was excited about the opportunity but even more elated that Tyrone was home from prison. Slim had earned a Division I football scholarship as a top 5-star recruit. They all looked up to see Mike and his father walking towards them.

"Hi Mike. Hi Mr. Rodgers. How are you doing Sir?" Henry said with a friendly smile.

"Great. How are you doing Henry? I read in the paper that you are going into the Army. Well done Son," said the chief of police with a nod. "I am proud of you."

"Thank you, Sir," responded Henry.

Henry smiled. Nobody had any inkling that it had been him that stole the black Lincoln. Nobody would ever know except him and God of course.

"Hey, Tyrone," called Mr. Rodgers after they had walked past him.

"Yes Sir," said Tyrone as he turned around to face the chief of police.

"If you are looking for work, Harry Edwards is hiring at the lumber-yard," said Mr. Rodgers. "If you are interested, I can put in a good word for you."

"Thank you, Sir," responded Tyrone. "I appreciate that, but I've already got plans. I have been studying law for a long time. I am going to become a lawyer just like my father."

Mr. Rodgers nodded satisfactorily.

"Good to hear. That is an honorable profession. I wish you luck," said Mr. Rodgers. "Just so you know, that man that you assaulted was arrested. He's going to be locked up for a long time. It turns out that he was doing a lot of wrong in our town."

Tyrone nodded and continued walking with Albert and Henry.

"Vengeance is with God," said Tyrone.

Henry continued running over the summer. During his night runs, he still heard police sirens. He saw people up to mischievous behaviors but there seemed to be more calmness and peace than the previous few years. He hoped that Milton would continue changing for the better, but he knew that nothing lasts forever. Everything is always either get-ting better or worse.

Life was good.

We don't really know ourselves until we leave where we come from. Do you know what I mean?

BRIAN GODDARD was born in Vienna, West Virginia in 1965. He has a BS Aerospace Engineering, served four years as an officer in the US Army and then worked in the civilian world for more than thirty years prior to becoming an author. He has been blessed to have traveled to all states and more than fifty countries. This is his first novel.

https://www.facebook.com/profile.php?id=100058683353211
https://www.linkedin.com/feed